SHADOW SKYE

BOOK THREE

THE BURNING SWIFT

JOSEPH ELLIOTT

WALKER BOOKS

THE BURNING SWIFT

Text copyright © 2022 by Joseph Elliott
Illustrations copyright © 2022 by Anna and Elena Balbusso

First US edition 2022

Library of Congress Catalog Card Number pending
ISBN 978-1-5362-0749-1

21 22 23 24 25 26 LBM 10 9 8 7 6 5 4 3 2 1

Printed in Melrose Park, IL, USA

This book was typeset in Fairfield LH.
The illustrations were created digitally using mixed media.

Walker Books US
a division of
Candlewick Press
99 Dover Street
Somerville, Massachusetts 02144

www.walkerbooksus.com

FOR TOM, LILS, AND KATE

JAIME

THERE'S SO MUCH BLOOD—TOO MUCH BLOOD. I CAN'T stop it. My hands are sodden, drenched in its warmth, as I press down on where the arrow protrudes from her body. The girl stares up at me, disoriented and confused.

"Agatha, go! Quickly! Find help or she's going to die." Desperation rips my voice.

Agatha takes one more look at her, then stumbles away, shouting for help to anyone who might hear. The girl in my arms starts choking, so I shift her body toward me. From this angle, I have a clear view of the tattoo that stretches from her neck, over her jawline, and onto her cheek. It's some sort of raven or crow, but its neck is at an awkward angle, as if it's been snapped. The tattoo makes it clear she's a deamhan, but she seems different from the others.

I am friend. I help you.

That's what she said, right before the arrow punctured her chest. Why is she here? What does she want from us?

Then there's the other deamhan—the one who shot her. The one who thundered toward us on his giant elk as Agatha and I hurried the girl into the enclave, then roared in frustration when we shut the gate on him. Whatever this girl came here to tell us, he was determined for us not to find out.

"It's okay," I say to the girl. "You're going to be all right." But even as I say it, I know it's not true. She's lost too much blood. With every moment that passes, she slips further away. She tries to say something but can't form the words. Speckles of blood pop from her lips, and she scrunches her eyes in pain.

Beside me, the horse she rode here on keeps stamping its feet as it watches the girl slowly die in my arms. It slipped into the enclave straight after we did, not wanting to leave the girl's side. It towers over me, wild and beautiful. The wind whips its hair around its glossy black head.

There are muffled shouts to my right as a small group emerges from behind the nearest bothan. At the front is Lenox—the Hawk who's been a temporary clan elder since we returned from Norveg—and I also recognize one of Clann-na-Bruthaich's Herbists, a broad lady called Una. Agatha is with them, her cheeks puffing as she struggles to keep pace.

"She's been shot," I say as they draw near, although that much is obvious. "I've been trying to stop the bleeding, but I don't know how."

"We'll take it from here," says Una, replacing my hands with her own and pressing hard on the wound. The girl's head flops to one side, and Una lets out an audible gasp at the sight of the tattoo. "She's a deamhan," she says.

"Yes, but she's not the enemy," I say. "At least, I don't think she is. There's another one outside, though. He's the one who shot her."

"Get to the wall," Lenox says to a couple of Hawks who've joined us. They leave at once. "What makes you think this girl is different?" Lenox asks me.

"She came here to warn us about something. She said she's a friend and that bad men are coming."

"How did she get in here? Did you let her in?" asks Una, her face stiff with scorn. I open my mouth but can't reply. "Did it not cross your mind that it could be a trap?"

"It's not," I say. I don't know how I know it, but I do. "She has something important to tell us. You have to save her."

Una looks at Lenox, who gives an almost imperceptible nod.

"Fine," she says. "We need to get her to the sickboth. Although I fear it may already be too late. . . . Lenox, take her legs. And the two of you," she says to two other members of Clann-na-Bruthaich, "one under each arm. On my count, we lift. Three, two, one."

Without releasing the pressure on the girl's wound, the four of them lift her limp body and carry it across the enclave. Her head lolls, first to one side and then to the other, as she slips in and out of consciousness.

"Out of our way," Una barks at the small crowd that's gathered.

Agatha and I follow them all the way to the sickboth, side-stepping the trail of blood that spatters the grass. Once there, the Herbists refuse to let me and Agatha in, claiming they need space to work, so we're left outside, pressing our ears against the door. The wait is agonizing.

"Is she going to d-die?" Agatha asks me.

"I don't know," I reply. "She's lost a lot of blood."

Blood. Of course. If the Herbists can't save her, maybe there's someone else who can.

I turn away from the sickboth and start sprinting toward the loch.

"Where are you—going?" Agatha shouts after me.

"I'll be back soon," I say.

The loch in Clann-na-Bruthaich's enclave is huge, but I spot the Badhbh right away. He's in the same position he's been in since last night, after we won the battle against the *sgàilean*: sitting cross-legged on a large rock that overlooks the water. I still haven't forgiven him for abandoning us during the fight—for choosing to cower in the nursery instead—but maybe he can redeem himself now.

By the time I reach him, I'm out of breath.

"Excuse me! Hello?" I call, but he continues to stare at the loch as if I haven't spoken.

I climb onto the rock and stand in front of him, blocking his view. He's wearing the same tatty robe he's worn ever since I found him in his small hut off the Scotian coast. The thick gray locks of his hair twist away from his head like tortured snakes.

"We need your help. I mean, I'd like to *request* your help." I correct myself, remembering how particular he can be. "There's a girl. She's lost a lot of blood, and I think she's going to die. Can you help her?" He still doesn't meet my eyes. "Look at me, dammit!" I draw the sword that hangs at my hip. It still has a faint red glow from the magic the Badhbh instilled in it—magic that grew

4

stronger when I fed it my blood during the battle against the *sgàilean*. Seeing it again sends a secret thrill through my body. The Badhbh's eyes flick to the blade, betraying mild curiosity at the fact that it's still glowing.

"Are you threatening me?" he asks, his rich voice seeping into my bones.

"No, I . . ." I don't know why I drew my sword. I just wanted to get his attention. "She's only a girl," I say. "She's young. Please."

"Your emotional bribery is wasted on me. Leave, unless you wish to be forced."

"She said we're in danger, that someone bad is coming. That means all our lives are at risk, including yours."

That gets his attention.

"Who's coming?"

"I don't know. She didn't say. That's why you need to save her."

"What makes you think I could help even if I wanted to?"

"Because you're the Badhbh! Blood magic is what you do, isn't it? She's bleeding to death. . . . There must be something you can do."

He's wasting so much time.

"You want another lesson in blood magic, do you?" His eyes are intense, boring straight though my own. Before I can utter a response, he stands up and lowers himself off the rock. "Take me to her, then."

I slip my sword back into its scabbard and jump down from the rock, stumbling in my haste to lead the Badhbh back to the sickboth. "It's this way," I say.

The Badhbh doesn't exactly hurry, but he moves with a bit

more speed than his accustomed stroll, which is the best I can hope for.

Agatha sees us approaching. "Is he going to help?" she asks. "Are you going to—h-help?"

"Move," says the Badhbh.

Agatha steps aside, and he swings open the sickboth door. Inside is a frenzy of shouting and repressed panic. Six Herbists surround one of the beds, their bodies crammed together, hiding the girl from view. Most of the other patients are sitting up, craning their necks to see what's happening. The arrow that tore through the girl lies in two bloody pieces on the floor. The Badhbh strides straight over to her.

"What's he doing here?" Una asks, adding, "Jaime, Agatha, out," when she notices we've crept in as well.

"You're not going to save her," says the Badhbh.

"Not with you breathing down our necks we're not."

I take a few steps closer to the bed, peering between the Herbists' backs. The girl's eyes are closed, and her face is ashen. The Badhbh picks up a short blade from the side of the bed, then reaches out and grabs my wrist.

"What are you doing?" I ask. I try to pull away, but his grip is firm.

"Do you want to save her or not?" he says.

"Yes, but . . ."

"I've told you before: blood magic cannot occur without blood."

Without another word, he pries my fingers apart and slices the blade across my palm.

"Wh—?" My knees buckle as the blood spills out, and a scream catches in my throat.

The Herbist nearest to us turns his head. "What on earth . . . ?" he says.

The Badhbh pushes him aside and makes a similar incision across the girl's hand, which hangs lifeless at the side of the bed. He then forces me onto my knees and presses our two palms together.

"Don't stop what you're doing," the Badhbh says to the Herbists, who are all staring at him openmouthed. "This will help, but she needs you as well. You," he says to one of them, "bind these two together."

The Herbist wraps a length of cloth around our hands and fastens it with a tight knot. Above me, the Badhbh mutters a string of indecipherable words. A harsh burning sensation rushes from my shoulder to my fingertips. I clench my teeth and squeeze the girl's cold hand in my own. I'm starting to feel dizzy. I focus on her face, willing it to show some sign of life. The Badhbh's muttering gets louder, and then he tuts and shoves the blade he's still holding into my free hand.

"Cut me," he says.

"What?"

"Do it now." He holds his palm toward me, his eyes ablaze. Something tells me I need to obey.

With trembling fingers, I trace the blade across his leathery skin.

"Deeper!" he says.

I press the blade in harder. A thick sweat breaks out over my forehead.

"Enough."

I drop the blade, and it clatters to the floor as another wave of dizziness spills over me. The Badhbh slaps the Herbists away and places his cut hand over the girl's chest wound, repeating the same words over and over. He bares his teeth and his nostrils flare. Everyone in the room holds a collective breath. The searing pain in my own hand grows more intense as if every part of who I am is being sucked out of me. I scrunch up my face and grab a fistful of blanket. Just when I think I can't take any more, the Badhbh stops talking and the pain trickles away.

"Her eyes," Agatha says. "She's o-opening her—eyes."

It's true: the girl's eyes flutter open, and she takes a deep, life-affirming breath.

The Badhbh removes his hand from the girl's body and wipes it on the side of the bed. "You can take that off now," he says, indicating the cloth that binds me to the girl.

Una helps me remove it, unable to hide her disbelief at what she's just witnessed. I expect there to be a messy gash across my palm, but when the cloth drops away, the wound has already healed. All that remains is a crooked line, tender to touch.

I stand up, feeling every drop of blood that pounds through my body. Traces of the Badhbh's magic are still inside me, which is both terrifying and exhilarating.

I turn to the Badhbh. "What happens now?" I ask.

The Badhbh looks at me as if the answer is obvious. "Now we find out what it is she has to say."

AGATHA

LENOX SAYS I'M NOT ALLOWED TO VISIT THE DEAMHAN girl because she needs to rest, but it was me who saw her first. Also I saved her from the deamhan man on the big white deer. That means I'm allowed to visit her, so I'm going to do it. It is a little bit sneaky to do that but only a little bit. I want to talk to her and say hello to be kind. I'm good at being kind.

It was the Badhbh man who saved her with the blood magic. I saw him do it and I couldn't even believe it. It is good she didn't die. I already know why she came here. She said it to Maistreas Eilionoir and Kenrick when they asked her the questions, and now everyone is talking about it. People are saying that King Edmund is coming to get us with a big army. He is the Ingland king. He has the biggest army ever and he wants to kill us dead. That is why I want to speak to the deamhan girl. First I want to say hello and be kind, and then I want to know more about the Ingland king as well.

The big animal horse is outside the sickboth. It is the girl's one she rode here on. I have never seen a real horse before. It is black and shiny all over and it has white hair that is long and pretty.

"Hello, horse," I say to it. It does not reply because I didn't say it in my head. It will hurt my brain if I do that and I am fed up of all the headaches. I want to touch the pretty hair so I put out my hand. The horse shakes its head a little bit and then lets me stroke it. I think it is a friendly one.

I do lots of strokes on the horse hair and some pats on its head and then I go inside the sickboth. There are lots of people in the beds. They are the ones that got hurt by the shadow things when we had to fight them. Most of them are sleeping because it is nearly nighttime.

"Agatha, what are you doing in here?" asks Una. She is an Herbist from Clann-na-Bruthaich.

"I came to see the—the deamhan girl," I say.

Una shakes her head. "She needs rest. I made that very clear to Eilionoir and Kenrick."

"She had lots already," I say. She rested half of yesterday and all of today. That is a lot of rest.

"Yes, but she still needs more."

"I will only say hello quickly," I say. "I f-found her so that's what's—fair." I do a pretty smile and say, "Pleeeease," a very long one.

Una does a scrunched-up face which I think will mean that she will say no, but then she says, "Okay, but don't stay long. And don't exhaust her."

"I won't," I say.

She let me because she likes me. When we had to fight the shadow things, Una was in the nursery with me, helping the children. She had a sword and she killed a shadow thing. She is very brave.

She shows me where the deamhan girl is and then goes to check on the other people. The girl has her eyes a bit closed, but when she sees me she opens them more.

"Hello," I say to her. "I'm—A-Agatha."

"Hello," she says. "I Sigrid." Oh yes, she said that was her name when she was on the horse. I forgot it and now I remember it.

"Are you poorly?" I ask her.

"Hurt," she says, "but alive. You open gate. You help. Thank you."

She's right: it was me who had the plan to open the gate and also I helped Jaime carry her into the enclave. "You're welcome," I say. "I'm g-good at—helping. You are in Clann-na-Bruthaich's enclave now. It is not m-my enclave because I am Clann-a-Tuath but we are staying here because the—the nasty Raasay people are in our—enclave and they won't leave even though we asked them nicely."

She looks at me confused. I think I said too many words. "Would you like to be my—friend?" I say. I say it slow so it is easier for her to understand. Also I take her hand and pat it two times.

"Yes, friend," she says, and she smiles.

"You are a deamhan," I say.

"Deamhan your name for us, yes."

I point at her face. "I l-like your—tattoo," I say.

"Thank you," she says. "Raven." A raven is a type of bird. I know that. "Sorry my speak bad."

She means her talking. She speaks our language strange because she doesn't know how to do it properly. That's okay though.

"Would you like me to—stroke your hair?" I ask her. It is a nice thing to do sometimes.

"No," she says. She doesn't want that.

I think of something else nice to say. "Would you like to meet Milkwort?"

She is confused face again because she does not know who Milkwort is. I take him out of my pocket and put him on her bed. He runs up her legs to her tummy to say hello.

"He is a vole," I tell her.

"Vole," she says. "In Norveg language we say *snoti*."

I laugh at that a lot. It is very funny because of snotty nose. "Shall I call you Snotty?" I ask to Milkwort and I say it in my head as well so he can hear me. He does not think it is funny and he ignores me. Sigrid is stroking him and he likes that.

I have done lots of being nice now, so I can ask about the Ingland king. "Is it t-true the Ingland king is coming with an—army?"

"Yes," she says. It is a bit hard for her to speak and her voice is breaths. "Ingland king coming. Big, big army. Konge Grímr coming too."

No, that's not right. Konge Grímr is dead.

"Konge Grímr is d-dead," I say. "The sh-shadow things got him in the—the mountain room."

"Not dead. Shadows not kill him. He in Ingland. He come here."

This is even more bad and the worst. Konge Grímr is the most horrible man ever. He made the Nice Queen Nathara be killed and he wanted to kill me and Jaime as well.

"Why is he in—in Ingland?" I ask. "Why is he c-coming—here?"

"Revenge," says Sigrid. "He want to kill all Skye people who escape mountain—most of all the boy who bring shadows and girl who make bats rip his eyes."

That's me. I'm the girl and Jaime is the boy. But he is wrong because I didn't make the bats do that. All I said to them was to put out the fires so the shadow things could come in and help us. They did the ripping out his eyes by themselves. My stomach is sick on the insides. I do not want Konge Grímr to get me.

"I am the g-girl," I say.

Sigrid's eyes go wide surprise. "He say you speak to animals."

"Yes," I say, although I don't want to talk about that. People always ask me and it is more boring to speak about it now. Sigrid does a yawn and looks sleepy tired. "Do you want to sleep now?" I ask her.

"Yes. Tired."

I stroke her arm a little bit. "You are a g-good—friend to help us," I say, then I pick up Milkwort and I wave goodbye. She is a nice one Sigrid but what she said is bad bad bad. I have to find Jaime and tell him what I found out.

I open the sickboth door and there is a surprise there. It is a man. The outside is dark so I nearly bumped into him. It is the

Badhbh man. He looks at me not happy and he does not move out of the way.

"E-excuse me," I say, which is being polite.

He doesn't say anything and also he still doesn't move. He does not like me I think. It is because I took his sword when the shadow things came, which made him cross. I was being the hero and he was being the coward so I am the right one.

"Agatha," he says. "The girl who speaks to animals."

"Y-yes," I say.

We have not talked much before. He looks at me for a long time and I do not like it.

"I h-had to take your sword," I say. "I—needed it to get the sh-shadow things."

He doesn't say anything else. He is an old face and a tangle beard. I step to the side to get past him. Still he doesn't move so I have to squeeze. Why is he doing that staring? It is rude to stare and he is rude.

I walk away from him. I look back lots of times and he is still outside the sickboth and watching me go. When I get to the bothan where Jaime sleeps, I do not go in the door. I walk around to the back and then look out from behind the wall. Now I can see the Badhbh man and he cannot see me. It is called spying and it is clever. It is how you know more things.

The Badhbh man is far away now and small, but I am a good Hawk so I can see him. He goes to Sigrid's animal horse and puts his hand on its neck. I think maybe he is going to take the horse away but he doesn't. He walks back to the sickboth door and looks around him. Then he opens the door and goes inside.

He is not sick. Why did he go in there? He is being sneaky about something.

I am finished doing the spying now so I go inside the bothan. The lanterns are still lit and people are awake talking. Jaime is at the other end sitting on one of the beds. Aileen is there and so is Crayton and Maistreas Eilionoir. I smile my biggest smile when I see Crayton. I wave at him and he waves back. He is one of the bull people. I like the bull people. Also I think one of them is my father. It was Maistreas Eilionoir who made me think that when she told me my father was not from our clan. She wouldn't tell me anything else about him though and I am not allowed to ask. If he's not from our clan then he must be one of the bull people. Maybe one day I will meet him and I cannot wait.

Maistreas Eilionoir does her hand flappy which is saying "Come here" to me. I was going to come anyway. She didn't need to do that flapping.

"Agatha, good timing," says Maistreas Eilionoir when I am close. "I was planning on finding you afterward, but as it is, I can speak to you all at once." She pats her hand on the bed and Jaime moves up so there is more space for me to sit. "As I'm sure you will have heard, there is an army marching north from Ingland, intent on our destruction. At least, that is what the deamhan girl claims, and I am inclined to believe her. Both Kenrick and I have questioned her extensively, and I can fathom no reason for her to lie; all she has prompted us to do is increase our guard and prepare for battle, neither of which would be to our enemy's advantage.

"The army is the biggest that has ever been known. The girl

overheard the kings boasting that it may contain as many as a hundred thousand men . . ." Everyone is quiet when Maistreas Eilionoir says that. It is so many soldiers coming. She makes a small cough sound in her throat and keeps talking. "Not only that, but the girl says they'll be armed with powerful weapons and accompanied by *dark creatures*, whatever that might mean." Aileen holds on to Jaime's hand. His mouth is open wide. "Needless to say, the situation is . . . desperate," says Maistreas Eilionoir, "and we need all the help we can get. Our sole aim right now is to bring together as many allies as we can — to forge an army of our own."

"Have you spoken to the other Skye clans?" Jaime asks. "They'll help us, won't they?"

"We've sent messengers, yes, imploring them to march here with the utmost haste. Apparently, the king of Ingland is intent on killing every living Scotian, so they are in as much danger as we are. If the clans agree, they should arrive in the next couple of days, but even with their support, we are likely to be outnumbered fifty to one."

That is not good. The army is too big.

"What about the Bó Riders?" Jaime asks Cray. "Will they come? They'd be safer here, behind the enclave walls."

"I can certainly ask," says Crayton. "It makes sense to me. I'll go back tomorrow at first light."

"Your support is received with gratitude," says Maistreas Eilionoir. She holds Crayton's fists and squeezes them tight. "The more of us there are, the greater our chances of survival."

"We should ask the R-Raasay people to come—too," I say.

They all look at me when I say it.

"They're not our allies, Agatha; they're our enemy," says Aileen.

"Not all of them are—enemies," I say. "Hector and Edme are nice ones."

Hector and Edme are Lileas's parents. They are Raasay people but they are kind because they helped me and Aileen when we were locked in the prison bothan. It still makes me sad when I remember Lileas because she was my friend and the nasty deamhan Knútr killed her.

"I can go to them and a-ask them for help to be our—allies," I say. "I know how to get there. We were n-nice and told them about the shadow things, so maybe they will—like us now."

"Hmm . . ." says Maistreas Eilionoir, which is a thinking noise. "Perhaps you're right. We share a greater mutual enemy, so may need to lay our differences aside."

"But they locked me and Agatha up," says Aileen. "We nearly died! Not to mention the fact that they're responsible for the deamhain invading us in the first place."

"Aileen, keep your voice down," says Maistreas Eilionoir. "That sort of talk will only spread panic, which is the last thing we need right now."

Aileen shuts her mouth. The people close to us turn their heads away. They are only pretending not to listen. Everyone knows about the deamhan girl and the army and they want to know more. I think again about what Sigrid told me, that Konge Grímr is still alive. I cannot even believe it.

"That won't be necessary," Maistreas Eilionoir says to a question Jaime asked. "Perhaps it would be best for them to go alone. What do you think, Agatha?"

I forgot to do good listening so I don't know what to answer. I look at Aileen and she looks big surprised so I do a big surprised face too. I think that is the right one.

"Let me discuss it with Kenrick and the others," says Maistreas Eilionoir. She stands up to leave.

"What about K-Konge Grímr?" I say.

"What about him?" asks Maistreas Eilionoir.

"He is c-coming too and he wants to get me and—Jaime."

"What?" says Jaime.

"I thought he was dead?" says Aileen.

"Where did you hear that?" Maistreas Eilionoir asks me.

I don't want to say it because I wasn't supposed to speak to Sigrid but I did. Maistreas Eilionoir is cross. I think she knows I spoke to her.

"Yes," Maistreas Eilionoir says in a whisper voice. "According to the girl, the Norwegian king survived the attack in the mountain and has traveled to Ingland seeking vengeance."

Jaime stands up. "He can't be . . . ?" He is breathing fast.

"Jaime, look at me," says Maistreas Eilionoir. "He may be coming, but know this: our entire clan and all of our allies will do everything in their power to protect you. Both you and Agatha. We won't let him get his hands on you. You have my word."

"But how can you promise that?" says Jaime. "How can we ever win? Even with all of the Skye clans *and* the Raasay islanders *and* the Bó Riders, there still won't be enough of us."

Maistreas Eilionoir scrunches her mouth into a small crinkle. "We'll find a way," she says.

Jaime bites on his knuckle and shakes his head. Aileen and Crayton don't say anything either. They do not think we can do it, but we can. We are Clann-a-Tuath and we are the best one.

I am not afraid.

JAIME

"SOUNDS LIKE YOU UPSET THE WRONG GUY," SAYS CRAY. He's sitting opposite me, gulping down the remains of his morning meal. Mine lies on the table in front of me, untouched. It's still early, the first rays of light barely tickling the clouds.

"I guess so," I say.

"Must make you feel pretty special, though, that he's sending a whole army just for you?"

"Not really. . . . The army's mainly King Edmund's, and he's sending it to eradicate *all* Scotians, so it's coming for you as much as it's coming for me." There's some comfort in that, I suppose — that we're all equally doomed. I barely slept last night, plagued with thoughts of what's coming.

"I guess that makes me special too." Cray does that annoying side smile of his and nudges my leg under the table.

"We all know how great you think you are; you don't need to remind me," I say, knocking his knee back in return.

"And don't let anyone tell you otherwise!" He spins his empty bowl on the table, and we both watch as it whirls around before slowing to a halt. "You haven't told me what happened with the *sgàilean* yet," he says. "Aileen said something about you summoning a load of them and then destroying them by yourself?"

The sword suddenly feels heavy where it hangs at my hip. What he's saying is true, but it's hard to remember it clearly. "I'm not sure what happened. The sword sort of . . . took over. It must have been something to do with the Badhbh's enchantment. It started glowing brighter, and then, when I raised it in the air, all the *sgàilean* came flocking."

"But the Badhbh enchanted all of our weapons—why were the *sgàilean* suddenly drawn to yours?"

I shrug. I don't tell him that I was cut during the battle and fed my blood to the sword, making it stronger. Nor do I admit that the sword still glows even though everyone else's weapons returned to normal once the last *sgàil* was destroyed. I haven't mentioned either of those facts to anyone, not even Aileen. I'm not sure why I'm keeping it a secret, but I am.

"Well, I'm impressed," says Cray. "We wouldn't have won that fight without you."

"I learned from the best," I say, inwardly beaming at the compliment.

"You absolutely did. Right, I'd better go." He swings his legs over the bench and slaps the table with the palm of his hand. "I'll never get used to these," he says. It still amazes me that until coming here, he'd never eaten at a table. He stands up and stretches his arms as wide as they'll go while unleashing a loud yawn. He finishes it with a quick shake of his head.

Hopefully—if the rest of the Bó Riders agree to come here—it shouldn't be too long before I see him again, but the thought of him leaving still gives me a small jolt of panic. Last night, it occurred to me that the nightmares I'd been having about wildwolves and the deamhain have stopped since being back with Cray.

"I'll ride with you to the kyle," I say.

"You don't have to do that. It'll mean a long walk back for you."

"I know, but I want to. And the walk will do me good. It's been a crazy few days; I could do with some time to clear my head."

"You can't bear to see me go, can you?"

"That's not it at all. I just want to make sure you actually leave—you've been hanging around for ages. What's the polite way of telling someone they've overstayed their welcome?"

Cray laughs, and the sound makes me smile.

"Come on, then, let's go find that hairy beast of mine."

"I need to put on some extra layers before we go—I'll meet you at the Lower Gate."

"Sounds like a plan."

I leave my meal uneaten and make my way across the enclave. Before long, I find myself walking past the bothan where the Badhbh's been staying. As I pass, I trace my finger over the cut on my hand. The scar is jagged and ugly but doesn't hurt. If anything, it pulses with life. With magic. What happened in the sickboth keeps racing through my mind—the surge that rushed through me while my hand was bound to the girl's. It's the same feeling I had when I fed my blood to the sword, and my body itches to feel it again.

I shake my head. Magic is not *dùth*. It's forbidden for a reason. And yet . . .

I retrace my steps until I'm standing outside the Badhbh's door. I peer over my shoulder to check that no one's watching, even though I'm not doing anything wrong. I knock on the door, tentatively at first and then a little harder. It shudders open, and the Badhbh's face fills the gap.

"I was wondering when you'd show up," he says.

I don't ask how he knew that I would. He opens the door wider to let me through. Inside it's dark and cold; he hasn't bothered to light a fire or open any windows. The only source of light is from a lantern in one corner, which burns with a weak flame. It's a small building, designed for one. It was probably built for one of Clann-na-Bruthaich's elders, but since the attack by the deamhain, Kenrick is the only elder they have left.

A weathered bag lies on the bed, containing the few possessions the Badhbh brought with him, which he still hasn't unpacked. I stand in the middle of the room, not knowing what to say. I stretch my fingers wide, feeling the tightness of the scar.

"Well?" says the Badhbh. "Do you plan to speak, or is it your intention to stand there in silence all day?"

"I . . . I want to know more," I say in a hurry. "About what happened the other day. About blood magic."

"Why?" The Badhbh's lips drift into a crooked line.

I shrug. I can't bring myself to tell him the truth: that the magic made me feel more alive than I have in months.

"I was under the impression that magery is forbidden on this island," he says.

"It is." I lower my eyes to the floor. It's covered in dust and splinters of straw.

"So am I correct in thinking you would be punished for even discussing it?"

My nod is so slight it's barely there.

"There is strength in dissent," says the Badhbh, "so that's as good a place to start as any. I should warn you, though: blood magic is a wild and unpredictable art. If you choose this path, there may be no turning back from it."

"I don't want to know how to do it; I just . . . I just want to learn about it."

"That's how it starts." The Badhbh crosses the small room, his movements measured and precise. He examines a nail sticking out from the edge of the bed, then presses his finger into it until it pierces the skin. He holds the finger in front of his face, watching as a red bead of blood blooms from the cut. "The blood that runs through your veins contains the very essence of life; it powers your entire body, and where there is power, there is potential. That is the fundamental principle of blood magic: to harness the power within blood and redirect it. It's as simple as that."

"That doesn't sound very simple to me."

A droplet of blood falls from his finger onto the floor, where it soaks into the hardened mud.

"*Sahcarà om rioht liuf,*" says the Badhbh. The words feel heavy and intense.

I wait, half-expecting the ground to shake or something to spring forth from where the blood landed, but nothing happens.

"What do those words mean?" I ask.

"It's the First Incantation. A simple enchantment that requests the blood to do your bidding."

"So why did nothing happen?"

"It's not enough to merely say words. You need to channel your will at the same time, to focus on what it is you want the blood to do. Try it."

I balk and step away from him, from what he's asking me to do. "No. I don't want to."

The Badhbh shrugs, a lazy motion. "Of course, it takes many years of dedication and training to hone your skills; you can't expect to become a blood mage overnight."

"I don't want to become a blood mage," I say again.

"Is that so?"

"Yes. How many times do I have to tell you?"

He looks as if he doesn't believe me, or he disapproves, or both.

"Why did you make me cut your hand?" I ask, with more hostility than I intended.

"To help the girl, of course."

"But why did you make *me* do it? Why didn't you just do it yourself?"

The edge of the Badhbh's mouth twitches, but it's definitely not a smile.

"Blood magic is stronger when the sacrifice is made by someone else," he says. "Stronger still when it comes from a place of darkness. That is why it had to be you."

My heart thuds against my ribs. "I don't know what you're talking about."

"Oh, I think you do. You're desperate to purge yourself of the darkness inside of you, but it can be your greatest strength. If you draw upon it—upon the pain and anger you feel—it can unleash immense power."

It's not the first time he's spoken about a darkness inside of me. The last time, we were on the mainland, sitting on opposite sides of a campfire. Back then, I denied it. Right now, I say nothing. I was wrong to come here.

"I should leave."

"We saved the girl's life, don't forget," says the Badhbh. "In the right hands, great power can achieve remarkable things."

"But it can also lead to death and destruction. You proved that yourself when you created the *sgàilean*."

The Badhbh doesn't reply. He doesn't even blink. He's shown time and again how selfish he can be: making the *sgàilean* even though he knew what they were capable of; abandoning Nathara when she was only a child; protecting himself during the battle against the shadows rather than helping the children who were in the room with him . . . Was he always this cruel, or have years of blood magic gnarled his insides? I turn away from him. My hand hovers above the door latch.

"There's an army coming," says the Badhbh, "and if your clan is to defeat it, you'll need magic more than ever."

I shake my head and glance back. "The elders won't allow it. It was different with the *sgàilean*—they were created by magic, so we didn't have a choice."

The Badhbh strides toward me with uncharacteristic speed. My whole body tenses, thinking he may be about to strike me. Instead, he reaches out and unsheathes my sword in one swift motion. He holds it upright, examining it. The magic glows duller with every day that passes. I don't know why that bothers me as much as it does.

"The magic within this sword saved your life and your clan," the Badhbh says. "You'd be wise not to forget that." He strikes the blade with the back of his hand, causing it to emit a dull twang. "What did you do to it?"

"Nothing," I say.

The Badhbh raises his unruly eyebrows. "Only someone with a propensity for magic could keep the blade alight this long. Merely offering it blood would not have been enough."

I swallow, and it feels as though I'm gulping mud. "Are you going to tell Maistreas Eilionoir?"

The Badhbh slides the blade back into my scabbard.

"No," he says. "For now, all this will be our little secret. Isn't that what you want?"

JAIME

I STUMBLE OUT OF THE BADHBH'S ROOM AND RACE TO MY own bothan. What was I thinking, approaching him like that? I push all thoughts of him and blood magic from my mind as I shove on an extra pair of socks and sling a cloak over my shoulders. I'm not like him and I never will be.

By the time I reach the Lower Gate, Cray is already there, waiting for me on Bras, his mighty bull.

"You took your time," he says with a grin.

"Sorry," I say without looking him in the eye.

He pulls me up behind him, and even though it's as uncomfortable as ever, some of the tension flows out of me. Maybe that's why I wanted to accompany Cray—for one last bull ride.

The Moths on guard winch open the gate, revealing the wide expanse of the Isle of Skye on the other side of the enclave wall. We pass under the archway, and the island explodes around us: vast plains, thick with prickly heather and wild gorse, fringed with dark forests of towering evergreens.

I scan the trees for any signs of the deamhan who attacked Sigrid. Last time I was out here, he was charging toward us on his giant elk with murder in his eyes. The Scavengers followed his tracks and came to the conclusion that he'd returned to Ingland. The Hawks haven't seen him since either, but there's still a chance he could be out there somewhere. . . .

As we move away from the enclave, something catches my eye in a nearby forest: a shape, slipping between the trees.

"Did you see that?" I ask Cray.

"See what?"

"I'm not sure. A figure, maybe, in the forest over there. I don't think anyone's supposed to be out right now."

"I didn't see anything. We can go and take a look, though, if you want?"

I shake my head. "No, it's fine. It was probably just a deer."

Bras breaks into a gallop, and the enclave soon fades away behind us. I keep my eyes on the trees until they're no longer in view.

We ride in silence, past puddles tinged with frost and sparse autumnal trees grasping in vain at their last remaining leaves. A biting wind—made even colder by the speed of the bull—nips at my ears. It feels like winter is creeping in even sooner this year. I risk taking a hand off Cray's waist to pull my hood tighter over my head. As I do, Bras lurches into a small ditch, and I nearly lose my balance. I squeeze my legs into the bull's sides and grab hold of Cray. Knowing Bras, he probably did it on purpose, the cheeky beast.

Holding on so tightly makes my new scar tingle. Some of

Sigrid's blood is inside me now, just like my blood is inside her. It makes me think: so much hatred in this world is based on what blood runs through our veins, but if my blood could save Sigrid — someone from a land hundreds of miles away — surely that means we're all the same, really? I don't know. . . .

When we arrive at the kyle — the channel of water that separates Skye from mainland Scotia — Cray dismounts, and I flop down next to him. Bras wanders across to the shore and sniffs at the water, anticipating how cold it's going to be. The last time Cray and I crossed here, we were nearly pulled under by sucker eels. The memory makes me shiver. Cray shows no signs of being nervous. I suppose he should be safe as long as he stays on Bras's back.

"This is where I ditch you, then," says Cray, giving me a light punch on my arm. "Try and stay out of trouble until I get back, okay?"

"You are coming back, aren't you?" I say.

"Of course I am."

"But how can you be sure? It's been ages since you were last at the cove — what if imitators attacked while you were gone? Or what if your tribe doesn't agree to come back here? They may think they stand a better chance of defending themselves where they are, or in the time it takes you to reach them, the southern army could arrive in Scotia and cut you off, or—"

"Jaime, breathe." Cray puts his hand behind my neck and draws our foreheads together until they're touching. "Just breathe." I lift my hand to the back of his head. His hair is soft and warm. I slow my breathing to match his, and then we share three deep breaths.

"Everything's going to be okay," he says, releasing his grip on me.

I lower my hand and take a small step backward, looking up at him. He smiles at me, and I don't know why, but I lean in and I kiss him. At first he's surprised, but then he kisses me back, and in that moment, nothing else matters and everything feels right.

The realization of what I'm doing—of who I'm kissing—rushes in, and I break away, shaking my head.

"I'm sorry," I say.

"Don't be," he replies.

"I don't know why I did that."

"It's fine." He steps forward and reaches his hand out to comfort me, but I push it away.

"Don't touch me," I say.

"Jaime . . ."

"You should go."

"It's not—"

"I don't want to talk about it. I shouldn't have done that. It was a mistake. Please, just go." I stare at the hard earth beneath our feet. Withered grass creeps through the dry cracks.

"Tell me what you're thinking. We should talk about this."

"No. We shouldn't. Not now, not ever."

"Jaime, please . . ."

I look up at him. "I mean it. We shouldn't be doing this. We shouldn't even be friends. This . . . Whatever this is, it's not right."

Cray holds my gaze a few moments longer, then sighs and turns away.

I do the same, spinning around and marching up the bankside.

Part of me is desperate for Cray to come after me—to tell me

I'm wrong and that everything is going to be okay—but when I glance back, he's already mounted Bras and the two of them are wading out into the water.

STUPID. SO STUPID. I *KISSED* HIM. WHY THE HELL DID I do that? It's disgusting.

It's wrong.

I keep walking, storming through bracken and stumbling over rocks, my face tight with scorn and self-loathing.

If my clan knew what I'd done . . . It's not *dùth*. They can't ever find out. Yes, I've done other things they would disapprove of, but those were all justified by the circumstances. What happened with Cray definitely wasn't. I spit and spit again, and then scrub my mouth with the back of my sleeve until it's raw, but nothing gets rid of the filthy feeling inside me. I can't speak to Cray again. I won't. This is all his fault.

There's a small pond on my right. I tear through the reeds that protect its bank and drop to my knees, scooping up handfuls of muddy water and sloshing them into my mouth. The water smells of bile and tastes even worse, but I don't stop. I scoop, rinse, spit, scoop, rinse, spit, over and over again in some sort of manic ritual.

It's not enough. I grab a clump of reeds in each hand and thrust my whole head under the water. An icy cold envelops me, shutting down my senses. When my lungs plead for air, I ignore them and shove my head deeper.

Ever since the battle in the mountain, I've been longing to feel *something*, but not this. Not this pain. I can't stand it. Yet it's always been there: the knowledge that I desired something I was never allowed to want, an evil hidden deep within me. I've spent my whole life trying to suppress it, but now it's refusing to be ignored.

I tear my head out of the water and collapse backward onto the bank, heaving in ugly lungfuls of frozen air. My face is so cold it burns. I squeeze away my tears and look at the sky. Small flakes of dust drift down all around me. Not dust, snow.

I close my eyes and imagine the flecks landing all over my body, slowly burying me, one flake at a time.

THE WALK BACK TO CLANN-NA-BRUTHAICH'S ENCLAVE IS a slow torture. I'm soaking wet and can't stop shivering from the cold. As reluctant as I am to return, I know that if I don't, I'll soon freeze to death.

Halfway back, a high-pitched hum drags me out of my thoughts. I scan the bleak horizon but can't make out the source of the noise. It seems close—really close, as if it's coming from my body. I look down.

The sound is emanating from my sword.

I unsheathe it and hold it in front of me. Snowflakes melt on its blade like fading souls. The humming is faint but persistent, like a dull ache. The deep red glow has almost completely faded; it won't be long before all its power is gone and it returns to nothing more than a drab piece of metal. The hum pierces me, as if the sword is pleading not to let that happen.

The Badhbh's words drift through my head: *There's an army coming, and if your clan is to defeat it, you'll need magic more than ever.* Maybe he was right. Maybe there *is* something I can do for my clan.

I bring the tip of my finger to the end of the blade and jab it in. I feel a sharp rush, a release. My finger stings, but I barely notice. Perhaps I even like it. A thin dribble of blood trickles down the length of my finger. I smear it over one side of the blade and then the other.

At first, the sword doesn't respond, but then the blood starts to disappear as it's sucked into the metal. The humming stops, and the sword glows brighter, as if the magic has been slightly revived. I squeeze the hilt tighter, taking strength from its power. With the sword in my hand, everything is a little easier. It helps me be the person I want to be—someone worthy of my clan. I keep hold of it until Clann-na-Bruthaich's enclave comes into view, then slide it away before the Hawks on the wall see its glow.

Once I'm inside, all I want to do is find a fire to dry myself and then crawl into bed and sleep, but as soon as I pass through the gate, Aileen spots me and calls my name.

I lower my head and quicken my pace, pretending not to hear her, but she comes running up and stops me with a light touch on my arm.

"Jaime, I was calling you," she says. "Is Agatha with you?"

"No," I reply, a little too curt. "Why would she be?"

"I don't know, but she's missing. I'm worried something's happened to her. We were supposed to meet with Maistreas Eilionoir at first light this morning to discuss the Raasay islanders, but she never showed up and no one can find her."

"You know what Agatha's like," I say. "She probably got some foolish plan in her head and wandered off." I wave my hand and start walking away.

Aileen follows me, jogging to keep up. "Jaime . . ."

"What?" I glance up at her without slowing my pace.

There's hurt in her eyes, which she blinks away. "You're wet," she says. "What happened?"

"I don't want to talk about it."

"Did something happen with Cray?"

My heart misses a beat.

I kissed him. I kissed him. I kissed him. What do I do, Aileen? Tell me what to do to feel normal again. I'll do anything. Please.

"No, nothing happened," I say.

"Was it hard, saying goodbye?"

"Why would it be hard?"

"Because you're friends," she says. "And everything's pretty terrifying right now, so who knows when you might see each other again?"

"It was fine," I say. I spin the metal bracelet on my wrist in frantic circles. I haven't taken it off since the day Aileen gave it to me.

"Will you miss him?"

"What are you doing?" I snap.

"Nothing. I was just . . . I was only asking."

"Well, don't. Leave me alone."

I march away, abandoning her to the angry wisps of snow. I just need sleep, to cover myself in a blanket and hide from the world.

On my way to the bothan, I pass an abandoned well. The stones have collapsed on one side, and ivy crawls over its remains like a sly beast. On the ground next to it there's a small scrap of something dark. I don't know what makes me pick it up, but I do. It's a piece of material, damp from the snow. I hold it up in front of me and recognize it immediately. It's Agatha's hood, and by the looks of the tear marks, it's been ripped off her cloak with aggressive force.

A sinking feeling fills my stomach.

Aileen was right to be worried. I think something bad has happened to Agatha.

Sigrid

I'M FEELIN BETTER THAN WHAT I WAS, THAT'S FOR HEK sure. Swear Øden, yesterday I felt like I was bein drowned by a thousand fires, but now I'm much more chirpin. I've even been outta my bed for a few tromps, just testin my legs still work proper.

Evryone's been comin in wantin to know evrythin about Konge Grímr and King Edmund and the Inglish army what's comin. I tell them what I can—the pipbits I overheard when I was chained to Konge Grímr—but there isn't much more to say. Then a man came in to take the broken piece of chain off my wrist. He was bulkin, with a blazin-orange beard, and he burnt the chain right off. Donal, his name was. I had to keep hek still when he was doin it so he didn't set my whole arm into flames. It sure is brimmin to have it gone. Means I'm not reminded of that grotweasel king evry two blinks.

My other hand itches, though, like a badger what's got fleas. There's a scar there that makes the skin tight. The old lady Maistreas Eilionoir told me they had to cut across my hand to save me, after I got shot with the arrow. I don't remember much about what happened. One moment I was sittin up on Eydis, feelin *ríkka* as hell at havin made it all the way here; the next I'm fallin and bleedin and the whole world's gone pigsick. As I was bein dragged through the gate, I snatched a peep of Bolverk, chasin us on his bulk elk. Course it was him what fired the arrow. That skittin harskrat. I dunno how he survived the fall after Eydis pushed him off the cliff. It was a hek long way down, but I was foolin not to check. I couldn't see proply cuz of how much the sky was spewin, but I shoulda made sure all the same. And I shoulda sent his elk runnin, so he didn't have no animal to chase me on too. There are lots of things I shoulda done.

"How are you feeling?" ses Una. She works in this healin house. She's been changin my dressins and bringin me food and water whenever I need it. Yesterday, fever stomped through my body like a speedin hog, so Una fed me like I was a babkin. I gotta thank her proper for that.

"I good," I say. "I go outside?" My foreign-tongue speakin hasn't got no better.

Evry time she comes over, I ask if I can go outside, cuz I'm gettin bug jitters not havin no fresh air all the days long. Una usually ses I'm not well enough, and maybe later, but this time she ses, "Okay, I think you're ready. Let's get you dressed."

I can't scramble outta the sweaty blankets quick enough. My clothes have been waitin patient by the side of my bed. I start pullin on my old tunic.

"Easy, slow down," Una ses.

She helps me lift the tunic over my head. It's been washed,

but there's still a pink smear over the front and back where my blood spilled. The hole where the arrow cut through isn't there no more, though. Someone musta stitched it up after washin it. They sure are yipper, these Skye people. Granpa Halvor would like them.

Thinkin of him makes my heart crack. He's such a long ways from here, and doesn't know nothin about where I am or why. He'll be worryin about me with evry sun what passes. I wish I could let him know I was doin all right—that I was helpin people, doin somethin he'd be proud of—but there isn't no way to tell him that.

Outside is bright and the wind is hek blades, but I don't mind that none. The air tastes of sweet grass and of the tasty chew what's bein cooked not too faraways. I suck in three deep breaths. It's brimmin bein outside again.

A horse whinnies like it's tryin to get my attention. Eydis! She's standin not two spits away, like she's been waitin for me this whole time. I run to her and wrap my arms around her neck. She's the most hek *ríkka* horse in the whole world. Not only did she get me all the way from King Edmund's skittin palace to Skye, but she saved me more than once on the way.

She nods her fat kog, so I rub the white stripe that runs down her nose like I know she wants. Her loller slips outta her mouth, and she gives my face a thick, soggin lick.

"Eydis, you great slobberin beast!" I say to her, and I hug her again.

"Looks like she's happy to see you," ses Una.

"She happy. I happy," I say in the foreign tongue.

Someone comes runnin over to us. I recognize him straight-aways. It's the boy who caught me when I fell off Eydis, the one what brought me into the enclave. He doesn't look too smirks.

"Hello," he ses with a little wave. His hand's got a scar along it the same as what mine has. When he sees me gawpin, he covers it with his sleeve.

"Hello," I say back.

"Good to see you're feeling better," he ses.

"Yes," I say.

He's holdin three rotten carrots, which he offers to Eydis. She crunches them up quickspit and nuzzles her head into the boy's side. Looks like they've been makin friends while I've been healin.

"I'm Jaime," he ses. He tries to smile, but he's not foolin no one.

"Sigrid," I say, in case he's forgotten.

"We were about to go for a walk," ses Una. "Would you like to join us?"

Jaime shakes his head. "I can't. Actually, I wanted to ask you something, Sigrid. About Agatha. She came to visit you last night, didn't she?"

Jaime speaks fast, so I have to concentrate hard to follow what he ses. "Agatha come," I tell him. "We talk. She show me vole and we talk."

"Did she say anything to you about leaving the enclave? Or going away anywhere?"

I shake my head no.

"What's all this about?" asks Una.

"She's missing," ses Jaime. "No one's seen her since this morning. A group of us are heading out to search the forests nearby."

"Too danger," I say. "Bolverk." They shouldn't be goin out doin that.

Jaime and Una both look at me, their foreheads frownin.

"What's Bolverk?" Jaime asks.

"Bad man," I say. "Arrow. Danger."

"Oh, the deamhan who shot you?" ses Jaime. "He's gone; our Scavengers followed his elk's footprints back to the mainland."

"Danger," I say again.

"I'll be okay," ses Jaime, though this time his voice hesitates a speck. His hand wraps around the handle of the sword what's swingin by his side.

"I go too," I say. Agatha helped me, so if she's in trouble I wanna help her in return.

Una laughs, though it doesn't sound like she's findin anythin funny. "You're not well enough to walk that far," she ses.

"We go on Eydis," I say, puttin my hand on the saddle to show I mean it. "Better for Jaime on horse. Safer."

Una opens her mouth but doesn't say nothin. Course, just cuz it's *safer* on Eydis doesn't mean it's safe. I was ridin her when I got shot, more's poor to me. But it'll be even less safe for Jaime to be walkin if Bolverk's still out there. Bolverk's a sneakin weaselsnake and no mistakin, so there's evry chance he's still lurkin nearby. At least if we're on Eydis, it'll be faster to get away.

"Actually, that'd be good," ses Jaime. "We'll be able to cover more ground on a horse. Although I've never ridden one before—are they easy to ride?"

"Yes, easy," I say. I stick my foot in one of the stirrups and reach for the far side of the saddle. Eydis moves her head low and bends her front knees to make it easier for me to climb on, but my arms haven't got no strength in them.

"Here," ses Una, liftin me up from behind and plonkin me on Eydis's back. She's bulk and strong so it's easy for her. "If you insist on going, I don't suppose I'll be able to convince you otherwise." She helps Jaime up behind me. He's a flapmess of limbs as he tries to get his balance, and he hek near falls off the other side. I can't stop myself from smilin. I shouldn't laugh, really. When I first rode Eydis, I wasn't no good at balancin neither.

Una waves us off, tellin me I gotta ride slow and that I should come back soon. I tell her I will. I don't wanna make her fiery, since she's been so nice to me and all.

The sky is fish-eye gray. Looks like it's been snowin from the white smudges what are splattered over some of the buildins. There isn't no snow on the ground, though. It musta melted, cuz the grass is wet and muddy. Jaime shows me the way to the gate. There's already a group of twelve or so people there when we arrive, who gawp at us when we turn up on Eydis.

"Sigrid's going to help," Jaime ses, introducin me to a man called Lenox who has eyebrows so thick it's like two slugs are livin on his face.

"Very well," Lenox ses. "The plan is to spread out so we can cover more ground."

"We'll head to the woods northwest of here," ses Jaime, "in case she decided to go to our old enclave."

"Fine," ses Lenox. "But don't venture too far. And stay away from the Raasay islanders; you know they're not to be trusted."

Jaime nods. The gate opens and the people start goin off in

diffrunt directions. I look out to the spot where I fell off Eydis. There isn't no sign of anythin happenin, but the memory is blazed deep in my mind. Bolverk must've been over there when he fired it, just past that high patch of brambles. My body twitches without me wantin it to. *Come on, there isn't no time to be gettin no quivers.* I give Eydis a whistle and she trots through the gate. Jaime leans forward and points into the distance, to a dark patch of trees.

"That way," he ses.

I tug on the reins gentle to get Eydis in the right direction, then whistle again. Eydis's ears jig back and forth as she sets off at a trot. I'm sure it's not as slow as what Una would want, but Eydis prefers goin fast, and so do I. After all that time with no exercise, I gotta let her stretch her legs a bit. Jaime doesn't say nothin as we're trompin, like he's lost deep in his own thinkin.

"Thank you," I say after a few slogs of silence. "For help me."

"You're welcome," he ses. There's a long pause, then he ses, "So you came all the way from Ingland?"

"Yes."

"What's it like there?"

I think back to King Edmund's palace with its sneerin people scoffin their faceholes all the day long, and then the journey north through Ingland with its rottens givin me and Eydis the dirty eye as we passed. Not forgettin that skittin kerl who tied me up and tried to cook me for her and her sickweasel brother to eat. "Here is better," I say.

He asks me if I saw any terror beasts while I was goin through Scotia—wildwolves or killin shadows or creatures called imitators what can change their skin to look like anythin they want. I tell him I didn't see none of those things.

The clouds above us curl and groan like maybe they're gunna spew.

"You have scar same as me," I say, openin my hand.

"Yes," he ses, "I do." He explains how a man called the Badhbh cut us both and joined our bleedin hams to stop me from dyin. Sounds cracked to me, but I sure am glad he did what he did. The Badhbh gave me some of his own blood as well, Jaime ses. Now he mentions it, I remember seein the matchin scar on the Badhbh's palm. It means all three of us are connected—their blood is a part of me now.

The Badhbh came to visit me the same night Agatha did. He didn't tell me his name, but from Jaime's describin, that must be who it was. He had a scraggin beard and an even more scraggin face, and he asked hek loads of questions about King Edmund and Konge Grímr. There was somethin about him what made me feel a bit twistgut, but I spose he can't be that bad, since he saved my life and all. Right before he left, the Badhbh said, "My daughter was about your age the last time I saw her. You remind me of her." I asked what happened to her, but he wouldn't tell me no more about it. I ask Jaime if he knows.

"Only what he told me," ses Jaime. "Which is that the old Scotian king took her away in order to force the Badhbh to make the killing shadows. Then the great plague came and she died before he could save her."

"Oh," I say. Praps that's why the Badhbh looked so sad.

When we reach the trees, Eydis slows to a walk. There's

brambles and crackin branches aplenty beneath her hooves. Other than that, it's quiet in the forest, like someone sucked out all the sound.

"Agatha!" Jaime calls. I shout it too, even though it sounds too loud. We take turns, shoutin evry few clops. Birds launch themselves from the trees, spooked by our yellin.

A little whiles later, both our voices are croaks from shoutin so much. There's still no sign of Agatha. Somethin moves on our right.

"Did you see that?" Jaime asks me.

"Yes," I say.

I click my tongue, and Eydis turns around. She stops when she sees the creature peer out from behind a tree. A stag. A big one with towerin antlers and burnt-red fur.

"Thistle-River?" Jaime ses, as if he's askin the stag a question. "I need to get down," he ses to me. "Wait here." He swings his leg over, his knee knockin into my back as he goes. "Sorry," he murmurs, and he jumps to the ground.

He creeps toward the stag with his hams in the air. The stag watches him, frozen to the spot, its gawpers wide.

"Are you Thistle-River?" Jaime asks the stag. "You remember me? I'm a friend of Agatha's. She's missing. We're looking for her. I don't suppose . . . I know you can't understand me, but . . ."

He's real close to the stag now, and he holds out his hand. The stag shuffles forward a crumb and sniffs it, then pokes it with its tongue. Afterward, it bows its head as if recognizin him from the smell and the taste. Jaime bows his head too, then the stag bounds away, turnin its kog toward us evry few blinks as it goes.

"I think he wants us to follow," ses Jaime. "If it's the stag I think it is, then he's a friend of Agatha's — she helped save him and his herd. Maybe he knows where she went." He takes off after the animal, and I follow on Eydis. I've never heard of anyone bein friends with a stag before, but then I've never of heard of anyone who can talk to animals neither.

It's hard goin, weavin in between the trees. The deer's white rump pops in and out of the gaps in fronta me. Spiny leaves whip at my hair, but I don't slow for nothin; if the deer knows where Agatha is, we can't lose its trail.

Jaime is ahead, so he sees the body first. It's part hidden under bracken and moldin leaves. The deer is on the other side of it, stretchin its neck to make sure we see what it's come here to show us. The person's hand sticks out at a strange angle, its fingers pale.

I jump off of Eydis fast as a snake. I know straightaways that the person is dead. And one look at the ink on his face tells me exactly who it is.

Bolverk.

JAIME

UP CLOSE, I RECOGNIZE THE DEAMHAN IMMEDIATELY. He's the one who dragged our elder chief through the enclave on the morning the deamhain first attacked. He was in charge when all this horror began. He's also the man who shot Sigrid with an arrow. I should feel grateful that he's dead.

It's not obvious what happened to him. There are no wounds and there's no blood. Perhaps he was poisoned. His mouth hangs loose, as if in a silent scream. Could Agatha have had something to do with this? Surely not. More questions, and I'm still no closer to discovering what happened to her.

Now I'm torn. Should I return to the enclave to tell them about the deamhan, or do we carry on riding north in search of Agatha? The deamhan stares up at me with empty eyes. We have to keep looking for her. Whatever happened here, it was something terrible, which makes me even more determined to find her as soon as we can.

We continue north, shouting her name as we go. There's

certainly a chance that she's on her way to our former enclave; she traveled there once before, and only yesterday she was talking about asking the Raasay islanders for their support. What I'm less sure of is how Agatha could have left Clann-na-Bruthaich's enclave without anyone noticing. There's also the torn hood from her cloak, which no one is able to explain. Something about all this just doesn't add up.

As we travel farther north, I tell Sigrid about the Raasay islanders and how they betrayed us to her king. I don't say that it happened on my wedding day, nor do I mention the girl I was made to marry. My heart grows heavy at the thought of Lileas. I picture her the first time I saw her, dressed in her orange wedding robe, so timid and young. She turned out to be as brave as she was kind, even though I only knew her a few days. A stab of grief shudders through me. I flick my head up to the sky. Its stark grayness pounds my eyes. If only things were different. . . . Lileas and I may have been mismatched, but we could have lived a happy life together; I truly believe that. A content one, at least. My clan approved of her—that's the most important thing. It would never be like that with someone like Cray. Two men should never be together. The elders are very clear about that.

As soon as I think of Cray, I'm flooded once again with sickening feelings of guilt and rage. Why do my thoughts always lead back to him? I need him out of my head, gone forever.

"You are okay?" Sigrid asks from in front of me. She must have felt my body tense.

"I'm fine," I say, although that's far from the truth. I grab the hilt of my sword and use the power within it to steady myself. The blade starts to hum again, piercing through the clop of Eydis's hooves. I've given it my blood a couple of times now, but it's never enough to keep the magic from fading. Why am I never enough?

I slide the blade out a fraction, keeping my eyes on the back of Sigrid's head in case she turns around. My fingers creep over the cross-guard until I feel the warm metal at the base of the blade. I press my fingers into the sharp edge until my skin splits and the droplets trickle down. The cruel release comes once again, rushing through my body as the sword grows warmer and brighter. Stronger. I drop it back into the scabbard and stick my fingers in my mouth to suck away the pain.

I half-wonder if the sword is taking more from me than my blood, but I push that notion aside. I need the sword; it's helping me bury all the wrong thoughts and sick feelings that refuse to go away. It makes me strong.

❧

WE CATCH OUR FIRST GLIMPSE OF THE ENCLAVE JUST before sunset. Sigrid jiggles Eydis's reins, and the horse comes to a stop. *My clan's* enclave. The sight of it makes me long for the time when I felt safe within its walls. Although, if I'm completely honest with myself, I was never truly happy there. There was always a part of me that felt like I didn't belong—that I wasn't the person my clan wanted me to be.

"What we do now?" Sigrid asks me.

It's a good question. We haven't seen any traces of Agatha the whole way here, and it's unlikely she could have walked this far in one day. Lenox made it clear that we shouldn't approach the Raasay islanders, so the sensible thing to do would be to make our way back before it gets too dark. Only, now that we're here, with the enclave in sight, I'm thinking Agatha's idea might have been a good one. Perhaps we *should* be asking the Raasay islanders for their support. And perhaps *I'm* the one who should be asking them. Lileas was from Raasay, after all, and although our marriage turned out to be nothing more than a ploy to deceive us, maybe I can remind them that a union between our people is possible—for real this time.

"We should at least ask if Agatha is inside," I say. "And we can tell them about the army at the same time. We'll make them speak to us out here."

I have no intention of going inside. Not only would it be insanely dangerous, but I might run into Lileas's parents. I couldn't face them, not after what happened to her.

Sigrid agrees with the plan, so we ride a little farther before leaving Eydis to graze and continuing on foot. As we creep closer, the Hawks—or whatever the people of Raasay call their lookouts—appear along the top of the wall. If Raasay's long-range weapons are as impressive as we've been led to believe, they could probably take us out from here if they wanted to. The inside of my mouth feels brittle and dry.

"Wait a minute," I say to Sigrid.

She stops and watches as I veer toward a spindly rowan tree. I snap off one of its low-hanging branches and strip it, leaving the bright red berries exposed. I raise it above my head and swing it back and forth—a sign that our intentions are peaceful. I don't know if they have the same custom on Raasay, but hopefully they'll understand what it means. The wind is strong, so I have to use both hands to prevent the branch from blowing to one side. Each time the branch passes my face, it gives off a heavy waft of sweet earth.

Sigrid marches on with confidence. I'm about to tell her to hold back, but then remember that the people of Raasay once formed a pact with the deamhain, so her presence might make them more inclined to speak with us.

The chimes around the enclave wall ring out in a mess of confused clangs, warning of our approach. Once we get within calling distance, I tilt up my head and swallow. All of the launchers on the wall are aimed at my face. Balancing the branch on one shoulder, I grab the handle of my sword with my opposite hand, allowing its power to trickle through my fingertips.

"My name is Jaime-Iasgair of Clann-a-Tuath," I shout, although my tongue feels thick. "I was married to Lileas, daughter of Raasay, and I respectfully request that your clan chiefs come out to speak with me. We're here in peace. You have my word."

To emphasize my point, I let go of the sword handle and raise the rowan branch above my head again. As I do so, a metal bolt shoots toward us, demolishing the branch and raining splinters over our cowering bodies.

"That not nice," says Sigrid.

I sling the remainder of the branch onto the damp grass as the Southern Gate creaks open.

"You may enter," a voice booms from the wall.

"We don't want to enter," I call back. "We wish to meet with your chiefs out here, on neutral ground."

Another bolt shoots past us, skimming Sigrid's arm. She gasps but holds her stance.

"You are in no position to negotiate," calls the voice. "You come in or you can go back to where you came from."

"What do you think?" I ask Sigrid.

"We go in," she says.

"We go in," I reply.

As we approach the gate, I keep my eyes on the launchers, which follow our every move. One overenthusiastic guard, and we'll both be dead. I hold on to the handle of my sword once again.

"Leave your weapons on the ground outside," says the voice from above.

Ò cac. Of course they're not going to let me take a sword in. But I need it. I can't leave it behind. My chest cramps at the thought of being without it, but the only other option is to be pierced through the heart with a metal bolt. . . .

Sigrid isn't carrying any weapons, so she marches on without looking back. I unbuckle the strap at my waist and let the sheath drop to the ground. The next few steps are hard, as if the sword is pining for me, forbidding me to abandon it. I bite the inside of my cheek and force myself to keep going.

Once I've caught up with Sigrid, the two of us walk through the gate, into my former home. The moment we're inside, someone releases the lever, and with a deep boom, the gate slams shut behind us.

AGATHA

I HAVE TO ESCAPE, I HAVE TO ESCAPE, I HAVE TO ESCAPE.

I'm waiting for a good moment to run away, but it is hard with my hands tied up and being on the animal. He tricked me and he lied. It was so mean of him to do it and I hate him. Now I am a long way from my Skye island and my clan.

I do not want to be here on the mainland. It is where the bad things happen. There are wildwolves here that might eat me, and other animals too. Also the army is coming and maybe they will see us and maybe they will kill us. Everything that happened is bad and I do not know how I can escape and run away.

I am on the big white deer animal. Its name is an elk. It is the one that the deamhan with the scar had, but now he is dead. The Badhbh man killed him. The Badhbh man said to me if I try to escape he will do the same to me. He is such a mean bad horrible man and he tricked me and he lied. I hate him.

He is also on the white elk. He is sitting in front of me and it is him who is taking me away. I don't know where we are going. I asked him lots of times but he won't say it.

I keep thinking how it happened. It is the only thing I can do while we ride bumpy all day. The Badhbh man said that the deers were in trouble and needed my help. I wanted to help them because Thistle-River is my friend and all of them are my friends. The Badhbh man showed me a new way to get out of the enclave which is through a well. It is a secret way and I didn't know it. The well was small which made it hard and my cloak got caught on the top and nearly strangled my neck. I followed the Badhbh man all the way through the tunnel and when we came out, we were in a forest and outside the enclave. It is clever to have a long tunnel.

"Where are the—deers?" I asked him. Then I turned around and it was a big surprise. The white elk animal was there and so was the scar deamhan man and so was Catriona.

Catriona gave me a horrible smile. She is my worst one. I hate her. She does not like me because I found out her bad secret which was Kenrick locked in her floor. She tried to kill him so she could be the Clann-na-Bruthaich leader. When her clan found out they sent her away which is called banished. I did not know why she was with the scar deamhan.

"That's the wrong girl," said the scar deamhan.

"No, it's not," said the Badhbh man. "The plan has changed."

The scar deamhan looked from Catriona to the Badhbh man.

"We had a deal," he said. His face was an angry one. "Sigrid in exchange for both your lives."

"I am taking this girl and I am taking your elk," said the Badhbh man.

The scar deamhan pulled out his ax. Catriona took a step away. "What did you say?" said the scar deamhan.

"The information you provided has been very useful, but your assistance is no longer required," said the Badhbh man.

The scar deamhan lifted his ax but the Badhbh man was quicker. He held his hand toward the scar deamhan and twisted his wrist. There was a crack which was the scar deamhan's neck and then he fell to the ground and was dead. I could not even believe it.

"You killed him," said Catriona.

"I did," said the Badhbh man. "Now help me get her on the elk."

"What about me?" she asked.

"You can stay here. I will tell the Inglish king of your involvement. Perhaps he will be merciful."

"But—"

"Think carefully before saying anything further," said the Badhbh man.

Catriona looked very cross but didn't say anything else.

That's when they tried to put me on the elk. I didn't want to do it and I screamed and kicked and said "No, I don't want to" but then Catriona got very close to my ear and said in a whisper voice, "Do you want this man to kill you like he killed that deamhan?" Her breath was very horrible like dead worms.

"N-no," I said. I did not want to be dead.

"Then stop kicking and do as he says."

I had to do it, so I got on the elk. They tied up my hands, then we left Catriona in the forest and rode to the water which is how you get to Scotia. I was hoping and hoping and saying please in my head that one of the Hawks or the Scavengers would see us and say stop, but no one saw us and no one did the rescue. We crossed the water on the elk's back and my feet got very wet. Now we are in Scotia and my toes are cold.

It is very high on the elk. Even higher than Duilleag and Bras who are Mór's and Crayton's bulls. I do not like it so high up. It makes me feel like I might fall off. Its antlers are thick and wide ones that stick out to the side. The Badhbh man told me if I tried talking to the elk I would regret it. I did it anyway because I can do it in my head and the Badhbh man didn't even know. I thought the elk could help me hurt the Badhbh man with its big antlers and then take me back to my Skye island but the elk told me no. It said whoever holds its reins is its master and it will only listen to them. That is a stupid way to be. I told that to the elk which made it even more grumpy and cross. It wouldn't speak to me again after that.

When it is nearly dark, the Badhbh man stops the elk and tells me to get down.

"W-why?" I say.

"Because I told you to," he says. He has to look over his shoulder to talk to me.

The ground is a far way below. "I don't know—how to get down," I say.

The Badhbh man sighs then lifts one of his legs over the elk and drops to the ground. He raises his hand to help pull me down. I look at the reins. Maybe I can grab them quick.

"Don't even think about it," says the Badhbh man.

He saw me looking. I take his hand and fall down off the elk. It hurts all the way to my knees. The ground is wet leaves and sticky mud. I am sore all over my body with aches.

"W-why are we stopped?" I ask.

"To eat and to sleep. You want to do both those things, I presume?"

I nod my head a big one. I am very hungry. The Badhbh man opens a bag which is tied around the elk's neck. He takes out some food and passes it to me. It is a hard piece of meat. I do not take it.

"What is it?" I ask him.

"Meat," he says.

"I know it's—meat." I'm not stupid. "What—animal meat?" I remember when the Stewer gave me deer meat and I ate it because I didn't know. I was sick afterward when I found out.

"I don't know," says the Badhbh. "Just eat it."

I shake my head no and I am frowning.

"Fine. Go hungry, then," he says.

He takes a bite out of the meat and looks at me while he chews it.

"It's rude to s-stare," I say to him. He doesn't reply so I say it again. "I said it's rude to stare. Also it is r-rude not to answer when someone is—talking to you."

"I suppose that makes me doubly rude, then," says the Badhbh man.

It does and he is right about that.

"Where are we g-going?" I ask again.

"The less you know the better," he says.

"But I want to—know it," I say.

"You want to help your clan, don't you?"

"Yes," I say.

"Then do exactly as I say."

I am confused now. "Are we h-helping my clan?" I ask.

"Yes," he says.

"How?"

"You don't need to know that yet."

He's wrong. I do need to know it. I want to help my clan but what if he is lying? I do a growl noise. He doesn't look at me so I do an even louder one. He still doesn't look at me.

"Why were you with C-Catriona?" I ask.

The Badhbh man chews his food very slowly and then swallows it. "I discovered her lurking in the woods outside the enclave and let her believe we were working together. She showed me the secret entrance through the well so I could get you out without the guards noticing. I never had any intention of allowing her to accompany us, though; her plans do not coincide with my own."

"She is a b-bad—one and—nasty," I say.

The Badhbh man takes another bite of food and doesn't reply. Somewhere I don't know where, an animal makes a bark noise. I hope it is not a wildwolf come to eat me.

"The rope is h-hurting my—wrists," I say.

The Badhbh man sucks in his cheeks. "If I take it off, will you try to escape?"

"Yes," I say.

"Then I cannot do it."

Oh. I should have said a lie one.

When he has finished eating all the meat, the Badhbh man searches in the bag again and pulls out another rope.

"I'm going to tie you to a tree so you can sleep," he says. "I sincerely advise you to comply."

I do not know those words *sincerely* and *comply*. What I do know is that I don't want to be tied to a tree. If the wildwolves come in the night, I won't be able to run away.

He takes a step toward me and goes to grab my hands, so I kick him hard between his legs. It is a very painful place to be kicked if you are a man. That is why I did it. It is a bit naughty and also clever.

The Badhbh man shouts out angry and pain. I go quick to the elk and hold on to its reins and say to it, *I have your reins now so you have to help me*. It does not reply. It is still mad that I called it stupid I think. It will not help me and it is too high to get on its back on my own so I leave it and I run. It is hard because of my hands tied together and running isn't my best one. My breath is fast and my chest is hurting puffs.

I keep running faster fast as I can. The ground is thick with plants that want to trip me. I cannot hear the Badhbh man. I think he is still hurt and cannot chase me. I keep running fast so fast. My chest is pain and my legs are aches but I do not care because I did it. I escaped. I got away.

I stop.

The Badhbh man is in front of me. I did not get away.

How did he get there? Unless I ran in the circle. It was hard to know which way.

He holds up his arm toward me the same way he did to the scar deamhan when he killed him.

He's going to kill me. He's going to kill me and I will be dead.

I turn in the different direction and run again but something is wrong in my body. It is hot in my insides and I am slowing down because my legs aren't working properly. My head is hot and my hands and my tongue. He is turning me into fire, I know it.

I fall onto the ground. My whole body is burning like a stick and there is crackles in my ear. Then the hot is gone. The Badhbh man's boots come closer toward me. When he is next to me, he stops. His dirty boots are close to my nose. He bends down and then his face is next to my face.

"I suggest you don't try that again," he says.

JAIME

INSIDE THE ENCLAVE, THE FIRST THING I NOTICE IS THE scorched earth. For as far as I can see, the ground is black and lifeless, and several of the nearest bothans bear marks of destruction: hollow doorways, stone walls streaked with tentacles of ash, thatch rooves eaten away to nothing. What happened here?

"Jaime-Iasgair?"

A woman runs up to me and squeezes the top of my arm. I recognize her immediately and my heart starts to thump.

"Edme," I say. I met this woman briefly on the morning I was forced to marry her daughter, but this is the first time we've spoken. I don't know what to say. There's nothing I *can* say.

"Why have you brought a deamhan here?" she says, eyeing Sigrid with mistrust.

"She's a friend," I say. "She's not like the others."

Edme gives a half-nod but remains wary. "I heard what happened to Lileas," she says. I can hear her daughter's name catch in the back of her throat. "I want you to know that I don't blame you in the slightest. It was them. The deamhain. We never . . . We should never have trusted them." She aims these last words at Sigrid, who shrugs and nods as if she agrees.

"I'm so sorry," I say, which doesn't feel like nearly enough. "I tried, but . . . I let her down."

Edme wipes her eyes with a single finger. "Enough of that talk. You can't spend your whole life lost in blame. I'm trying to follow that same advice myself."

I sigh, releasing a little of the tightness in my chest. "We're looking for a girl from our clan called Agatha. Is she here?"

"She was," says Edme. "About a week ago. But she escaped with the girl she was with, and they haven't been seen since."

It's hardly a surprise, but the disappointment still hits me hard.

"Edme," calls a voice as several people come down from the wall. "Stand away from the prisoners."

"We're not prisoners," I say, trying my best to sound assertive.

Beside me, Sigrid angles her body as if readying for a fight.

"He's right," says Edme, giving those approaching a steely gaze. "This is my son-in-law, and none of you will lay a finger on him."

"Don't be ridiculous," says a woman with a mop of acorn-colored hair. "We need to take him for interrogation."

Edme grabs hold of my wrist. "You're not taking him any-where. He's the only family Hector and I have left. Our daughter was murdered. *Murdered.* Or have you forgotten that? Whatever Jaime's come here to say, he deserves to be treated with respect."

No one knows how to react to that. Edme looks at me.

"Take me to your chiefs," I say. Agatha may not be here, but I can still carry out her plan.

Edme leads us across the burned-out enclave, and no one tries to stop her. Gradually, the signs of fire lessen and the tufty grass returns. We approach the Gathering, which is teeming with people eating in small groups. Several heads turn toward us and conversations trickle away.

Edme stops in front of one of the tables and says, "I believe you've already met our clan chiefs, Balgair MacSween and Conall MacLeod."

It's them. The two men responsible for the attack on our enclave and everything that's happened since. A seething rage prickles my skin, which builds until it's pumping through my entire body.

They stop chewing at precisely the same moment as recognition dawns on them. Balgair's grip tightens on his knife. He is the broader of the two, with a rugged beard and scabby cheeks. Conall is slightly older, with a saggy neck and stooped shoulders. His nose is crooked and swollen, as if recently broken.

"What is the meaning of this?" asks Conall, looking from me to Sigrid and then back again.

"You remember Jaime-Iasgair?" says Edme. "You used him in the same way you used my daughter."

"Edme. We've spoken about this." Balgair's voice is tight and controlled. His eyes flick to the people around us, who are all looking in our direction, waiting to see how the chiefs will react. "Why are you here, Jaime-Iasgair?" He spits out my name as if it is a morsel of meat gristle.

A silence rips through the Gathering. The entire clan of Raasay is staring at me. I reach for the comfort of my sword before remembering it's no longer there.

"People are coming," I say. "From the mainland. An army. Thousands of them, and they're going to kill us. You too." I don't sound very convincing. Even I wouldn't believe me.

Conall starts to laugh, which soon breaks into a hacking cough. Balgair says nothing. He stares at me as if he wants to break every bone in my body.

"What pathetic ploy is this?" Conall asks. "What are your elders planning? To lure us out of the enclave and murder us on open ground so they can reclaim this place for themselves?"

"No," I say, but the word is caught by the wind and snatched away.

"How very brave of them to send a boy to do their dirty work," Conall continues. "They could have come up with a more convincing lie, though."

"Army is true," says Sigrid, banging her hand on the table.

"And who are you?" asks Balgair, looking at her properly for the first time.

"Sigrid," she replies. "I meet Ingland king. He bad man. He want to kill all people here."

Balgair's laugh is an ugly bark. "Everyone on the mainland is dead," he says. "Your story is preposterous."

"I know it sounds that way," I say, "but I promise you it's true."

"We didn't believe the two girls at first either," says Edme. "The ones who warned us about the shadows. That also sounded like a ridiculous story, but they ended up saving our lives."

"Stay out of this," says Balgair.

"She's right," I say, grateful for Edme's support. "We saved your clan once before; is it so hard to believe we may be trying to do it again?"

"One of those girls broke my nose," says Conall. His hand drifts toward his battered face and hovers just below his nostrils. "And they set our enclave on fire as they made their escape. I'd hardly call that the actions of an ally."

It's not your *enclave,* I want to scream.

"It's actually quite clever," says Balgair. "Warn us about a real threat to gain our trust, then make up a pretend threat to slaughter us."

"That's not what's happening here. Please—"

"Take them away and lock them up," says Conall. "Although you'll have to be creative about where, since those girls burned down our prisonboth."

"No, please. Wait—" My hands are forced behind my back, and someone grabs hold of my shoulders.

"Let him go."

I didn't see Sigrid pick up the knife, but she now has it firmly pressed into Conall's neck. Her face is fierce, but the hand holding the knife remains steady.

"Let him go," she says again.

Balgair nods, and the two men restraining me release their grip.

"Don't do anything rash," says Balgair, holding his palms toward Sigrid as if she's some sort of wild animal.

Conall's eyes look like they are about to burst out of his head.

A thick vein in his neck pulses under the pressure of the blade.

"It is not the girl who is being rash," says Edme. "It is you. None of us were consulted on the deal you made with the deamhain. Because of you, my daughter is dead. My only child." Tears stream down her cheeks. "And I'm not the only one questioning your decisions. We're all living here, pretending to be content, but the truth is we're riddled with the same guilt. This ground is soaked with blood, and it stains our souls."

Sigrid looks at me from behind Conall, urging me to talk. I take strength from Edme's words; not only does she not blame me for what happened to Lileas, but she's standing up for me against her clan.

"What Edme says is true," I say. "This is not your home. You stole it from us in the most cowardly way, and as a result you will never be happy here."

"Were you happy here?" Balgair asks me.

"What do you mean?"

"When you and your clan lived in this enclave, were you happy?"

I shake my head a little, confused as to what point he's making. "Of course we were."

"You were happy even though you stole this land from us first, *in the most cowardly way*?"

"What are you talking about?"

"I see they don't teach you the true history of your people. Allow me to educate you. My people lived on this island long before yours did, boy. When your ancestors—and the ancestors of all the other Skye clans—traveled across from the mainland, they decided they didn't want to share this island with people who had differing views from their own. They disapproved of the gods we worshipped, of the values we held, and the traditions we practiced. So they pushed my people away. They bullied and they burned and they murdered until my people had no choice but to flee to Raasay. So you see, it is not as simple as this enclave belonging to you, for who truly ever owns the land we walk across?"

That can't be true. Can it? There are hints in some of the old *òrain* that our ancestors used to fight, but none of them mention the Raasay people ever living on Skye. I look at the faces of everyone around me, and I see it: their longing for this land, the truth that this island was once theirs.

But why would the elders keep that from us? To prevent us from feeling guilty? Do other people in my clan know? I shake my head, trying to make sense of it all. It was so much easier to believe that the people of Raasay were the enemy—that they were in the wrong and that's all there was to it—but life is rarely as simple as it seems.

"If what you claim is true, then yes, you're right," I say, my voice faint. "My people have wronged yours, and you have wronged mine, but we now face a much bigger danger. The army that's coming . . . if we don't help each other, we're all going to die. All of us." The people at the back of the crowd are craning their necks. I need them to hear this.

Before I lose my nerve, I step onto an empty bench, which

wobbles under my weight. I find my balance and then move from the bench to a table. No one tries to stop me. "I have traveled the length of this island, and it is *big*," I say, trying to suppress the tremor in my voice. "There is enough room on this land for all of us. More than enough. My ancestors may have driven you from it, but my clan will welcome you back." It seems so obvious now that I'm saying it out loud. I don't know if the elders will agree with what I'm about to offer, but I'll convince them somehow. It's the only way. "Help us and—if by some miracle we survive the battle to come—you can live wherever you choose, however you like. I know my promise may not be worth much to you, but it's all I have to offer."

I stand up a little straighter. "An army is on its way from Ingland. We thought the mainland was uninhabited too, but it's not. The plague in Scotia was created by King Edmund, and he is very much alive. Not only that, but he's joined forces with Konge Grímr and the deamhain from across the seas, and between them they are determined to kill every man, woman, and child living on this island. We know this because of the girl here, Sigrid. She escaped from Konge Grímr and risked her life to warn us, the same way she is risking her life to warn you all now."

Sigrid lifts her head a fraction and adjusts her grip on the knife. Long trails of sweat drip down Conall's face.

"I have stood face-to-face with Konge Grímr," I continue, "and he cannot be reasoned with. He's merciless, and his deamhain are the most ruthless warriors you will ever encounter. If you don't form an alliance with us, they will destroy you and everyone you hold dear. You cannot defeat them alone.

"I know an alliance between us may seem unobtainable, but it wasn't so long ago, on the day I was married to Lileas, that the majority of us believed it was possible. There was hope that day, and we can find that hope again. I trust Edme, and I know many of you were as horrified as she was when you discovered what your chiefs allowed to happen here. This is how you redeem yourselves, how you live without the guilt I know you're feeling. This isn't about who's right and who's wrong, it's about survival in the face of total annihilation; if we don't fight together, everyone you know and love will be gone. . . ."

I'm out of breath. I don't know what I'm expecting to happen next, but I suddenly feel foolish standing on the table, exposed to the wind.

From within the crowd, a voice shouts, "I swear my allegiance to Clann-a-Tuath. I will fight by their side, for my people and theirs."

Everyone turns to see who spoke, revealing Hector, Lileas's father, standing resolute and proud. He nods in my direction.

"I swear my allegiance to Clann-a-Tuath," Edme shouts from beside me. "I will fight by their side, for my people and theirs."

"I swear my allegiance to Clann-a-Tuath," calls someone else, and one by one, the shout is echoed around the Gathering.

Sigrid steps away from Conall and lowers the knife. "Your people say yes to help us," she says. "Now you say yes too."

Conall pulls himself to his feet, wiping at a smudge of blood on his neck. His jaw is tight as he scans the faces of his clan.

"You have made yourselves very clear," he says to the crowd. "And Balgair and I would not be honorable leaders if we did not respect your consensus." He looks up at me, still standing on the table. "If you can prove that this army you speak of is real, then the people of Raasay will lend you their support."

Agatha

IT HAS BEEN A LOT OF DAYS NOW ON THIS STUPID ELK traveling and I do not want to do it anymore. I am still not escaped. I want to go home. I want to be on my Skye island where my clan is. I am so tired in my legs and my bottom and my bones. I have to keep my eyes open wide because if I close them I will fall asleep and then I will drop off the elk and be hurt a lot. We only sleep for a short time in the nights. The Badhbh man ties me to a tree and it is not comfortable and twigs poke me. I don't like it when he does that.

The only good thing is Milkwort is with me. I talk to him when I am tired and when I am bored. I had the plan that Milkwort could chew through the rope to make me free, but the rope was too thick and made his teeth sore. I did not want his teeth to be hurt so I said it's okay and thank you for trying, Milkwort.

The places we go past are different to when I was in Scotia before. Sometimes there are lots of bothans next to each other and people too. The Badhbh man makes the elk stay away from the people but I spot them because I am a Hawk. I am good at seeing things. People means we are not in Scotia anymore. I think we are in Ingland.

I am hungry all the time but I won't eat the meat that the Badhbh man gives me. He says I am a "bloody obstinate child." I don't know what that means but it is not true. He says I need to eat something so he gives me some bread and some plants he finds. It is never enough and my tummy is always rumbles.

Now there is an enclave in front of us and the Badhbh man does not move away from this one. He makes the elk go straight toward it. It gets bigger and bigger. Actually it is not an enclave because it doesn't have a wall and it is much more huger. When we reach it, I cannot even believe what I see. There are bothans everywhere that are tall and squashed together and so many people. More than a hundred or more than a thousand. It is a horrible smell like inside a fish. A dead one. Also it smells like feet when they are poorly. The ground is stones and the people walk on them. I don't know where they're going. They wear strange clothes that are different colors and sometimes dirty. One man has an animal like a small horse. It has lots of pans on its back. Two children run past and splash the mud. A group of men are drinking. They crash their mugs together and it makes a clink sound. The people look at me and the Badhbh man. One lady grabs the girl next to her and covers her eyes with her cloak. The elk makes loud clicking noises when it walks on the stones. We are going slower now because of all the people.

"Remember what I told you," the Badhbh man says to me. "Keep your mouth shut and don't speak to anyone."

I don't want to speak to anyone anyway.

We keep going farther and there is even more people who are all shouting. They talk the same words we do but they sound strange when they say them. There are lots of big carts in two lines and each cart has something different in it like blankets in bright colors or spoons or red apples and green ones or big gray prawns covered in flies. The men are shouting for the other men and women to come and look at what's in their carts. There is too much noise. I try to put my hands over my ears but it is hard because my hands are tied together. I can see what's in their carts. They don't need to shout it.

We walk past a cart full of long orange and purple vegetables. The elk puts its mouth on them. The Badhbh man pulls on the reins to make the elk's mouth move away but the elk already ate some. The vegetables go into its mouth and it chomps. It even eats the green bits at the end.

"Hey," shouts the man next to the cart. "You'd better be able to pay for those."

"We're just passing through," the Badhbh man tells him.

"I don't give a rat's arse where you're passing," says the man. "You owe me three pennings." He steps beside us and puts his hand on the elk's saddle. His face is red. He only has beard above his lip which makes him look very funny and also silly.

"I don't have any money," says the Badhbh man. He keeps looking straight ahead. "Let go of the saddle."

"Not until you pay me," says the red-face man.

The Badhbh man looks down and then kicks the man hard on his nose. It makes a smack sound. The man says, "Aaah!" with the pain and falls to his knees. There is blood in his mouth.

"Stop them!" he shouts. "Stop the thieves."

The Badhbh man kicks the elk hard lots of times until it lifts up its front legs. My bottom slips and I am going to fall off. I have to hold on so tight. My teeth go crunch together. The elk's legs wave in the air and it makes loud barking sounds. The men and the women are afraid the legs will kick them so they push each other out of the way. The elk starts to run. It can go faster now because the people move. The red-face man still shouts but no one stops us. The elk is too fast.

We turn and turn and turn again. The ways we go are thin because the tall bothans are too close together. It makes it dark as well. We are far away from the carts now and the smell is even worse. I hold my breath for a long time so I do not have to smell it. When I suck in my next breath, it makes a loud noise. The Badhbh man looks at me to know why I am making the noise. He does not ask me and I do not tell him.

There is a tower peeping over the top of the tall bothans. Sometimes I can see it and sometimes I can't because the ways are so twisty. It is gone again and then we go around a corner and it is in front of us. I do my mouth open when I see it. It is bigger even than the Dunnottar Castle and that was very huge big. There are lots of big flags that go flappy in the wind. They all have the same picture on them which is an animal one like a cat.

"We have arrived," the Badhbh man says to me in a quiet voice. "Remember: don't say a word."

There are lots of men who are all wearing clothes with the same cat picture on. I think they are the Ingland soldiers. When they see us, they pull out their swords and point them at us and the elk.

"Stop where you are," one of them shouts. He has a gray stubble face and fat lips. "That elk belongs to the king. Where did you find it?"

The Badhbh man pulls the reins and the elk stops. "I seek an audience with Their Royal Majesties King Edmund and Konge Grímr," he says. "I have something valuable they will want to see."

"Your accent—where are you from?"

"I will speak only with the kings," says the Badhbh man.

"Raise your hands where we can see them," says the same one soldier. The Badhbh man lets go of the reins and puts his hands in the air. "And the girl."

That's me who is the girl. I put my hands up as high as I can. It is not very high because of the tied up. I want them to know that I am not mean like the Badhbh man is. I do a pretty smile at them with all of my teeth.

"What's wrong with her face?" says a different soldier. He is a younger one and staring.

"Nothing's wrong with my—face," I say. "I am very b-beautiful—actually."

"You can't just march up here and demand to see the king," says the first soldier with the stubble face.

"Yes, I can," says the Badhbh man.

"Look, I'm the one with the sword here, buddy, and I'm telling you that you can't."

"I can because I already did. My very doing so is proof against your assertion. Go to your king and tell him that I have valuable intelligence on the clans of Skye and the rest of his Scotian enemies. I come with the *teanga-bèist* girl as my prisoner, who I will give to him as a peace offering in exchange for my life."

What? He is going to give me to the Inglish king!

"No!" I shout. "You cannot do that!"

The Badhbh man's head snaps back to look at me. "Be quiet," he says. "Trust me."

"You shouldn't let him in," I say to the Inglish soldiers. "He is a b-bad man and he will make your b-blood turn to fire in your—veins," I say.

The Badhbh man's face is very cross now. I don't even care.

"Will he, now?" says the stubble soldier.

"The girl is a fool; she knows not what she says."

I am not a fool. He is wrong to say that.

The soldiers talk to each other. They do it quiet so we cannot hear what they are saying. Then the one who speaks the most says to us, "Wait here." He opens the long doors and goes inside the building.

The other Inglish soldiers stay in front of us pointing their swords. It is boring to wait. I put my arms down because they ache but one of the soldiers says "Hey!" and wiggles his sword at me which is to mean put my arms back up again. I do it and I am cross.

I watch the flags on the poles. They make clacking sounds where the wind whooshes them. An animal runs past us that is a rat. One of the soldiers moves his sword quick and hits the rat in two pieces. The other soldiers laugh and tell him it was a good one. He wipes his sword on the bottom of his trousers. Inside my pocket Milkwort moves around in circles. He did not see what happened but I think he heard. I tell him to stay where he is and to keep quiet.

After a long time, the doors open and the stubble soldier comes back out. He talks to the other ones in a quiet voice.

"The king has agreed to see you," he says to us. "Dismount and follow me."

The Badhbh man slides off the elk first and then I do it, with a wobble. The stubble soldier doesn't take us through the tall doors. We go under an arch and around the side of the big wall. The other soldiers come too and they still have their swords pointing at us. Someone takes the elk a different way. I do not say goodbye to it because it is a grumpy elk and not my friend.

There is a man standing next to a small door. He has the most strange clothes that are blowy and purple. He is a thin man and his skin is droopy.

"Welcome," he says when we are nearer. His voice is soft and high like a girl voice. "My name is Aldric. I am an adviser to the king. I hope these men have shown you the courtesy you deserve."

Aldric holds out his skinny hand. The Badhbh man takes it and shakes it. At the same time, Aldric pulls something quick from his pocket and snaps it on the Badhbh man's wrist. It is a bracelet. The Badhbh man looks at it and is angry. He lifts his other hand but the stubble soldier grabs it and puts on another bracelet. The soldier next to me puts bracelets on my wrists too. They click over the top so he can put them on without untying my hands. They are

77

made of glass and are heavy. Inside there is a black liquid that is sloshing. Something sharp from the bracelets goes into my wrists with a sting.

"Ow!" I say. "It hurts. Take them—off."

The black liquid goes into my arms and inside my blood veins. I can see it under my skin. I do not want it to be inside me. I try to get the bracelets off but it is too hard to do it. I bite at them with my teeth.

"I wouldn't do that if I was you," says the soldier who put them on.

I am angry in my insides. I want to hit the soldier very hard but he has a sword and will stab me if I do that. He should not have put those bracelets on me. I did not want him to do it and it was mean. The Badhbh man is scrunching his fingers like he is trying to make the soldiers' blood turn to fire or snap their necks but nothing happens.

"What is the meaning of this?" says the Badhbh man. "I'm here to help you. I brought the girl."

"I'm afraid His Majesty is mistrustful of all Scotians," says Aldric. He nods to the soldiers and they move us through the small door.

We go down lots of steps which are dark and cobwebs. It is hard to see anything and I nearly fall.

"Where are we g-going?" I say. No one answers me so I say it again and again. Still no one answers so I shout it very loud.

Then I stop because I see the bones. We are at the bottom of the steps and there are fire torches on the walls. It is a big room and a long one. There are bars from the floor to the ceiling on both sides. Behind some of the bars are skeleton bones. They were prisoner people I think and now they are dead.

The soldiers take us to the end of the room. There is a loud clunk sound which is some of the bars opening to be a door. The soldiers make the Badhbh man go through and then push me in too. It is a prison cage we are in. I turn around to get out but the door is already shut and locked.

"I will inform the king of your arrival," says the droopy man who is called Aldric. "I'm sure he will be . . . overjoyed."

He moves away from the bars and the soldiers leave with him. Their footsteps are loud when they go and their armor is clanky sound. I turn to the Badhbh man and I am my biggest scowls ever.

"This is y-your—fault," I say. "Why did you b-bring me here? It was a—a bad plan and you are—"

"I told you not to speak," says the Badhbh man. "By revealing what I am capable of, you may have doomed us both."

"I don't care!" I shout, and I kick the bars. "I hate you and I don't care!"

"Well, you should care, because *these* change everything." He means the bracelets on his wrists. "Don't you see? My plan was to end this war before it began, but now . . ."

What does he mean "end this war"?

"You said you were going to h-help King—Edmund! You were going to g-g-give me to him."

"I said that to get close to him. You should have trusted me; I would have stopped King Edmund and put an end to everything."

"I don't believe you! You're a liar and—"

79

"Shh." The Badhbh man holds up one hand to make me stop talking. "We are not alone."

I look to where he's pointing at the corner of the prison room. Something is moving in the shadows. An animal. A big one. It is locked in the same cage with us and I think we woke it up.

It sniffs the air and growls. I take two steps back and my shoulders press against the bars.

The animal's claws make click sounds on the floor stones. It growls again and then steps out of the shadow.

My tummy feels all horrible when I see it.

It has sharp sharp teeth and bright eyes staring. One of its eyes is yellow and the other is blue. Its tongue falls out of its mouth and drips with hot mouth spit.

It is the worst of all the animals.

It is a wildwolf.

Sigrid

UNA TAKES OFF THE BANDAGE AND INSPECTS MY WOUND.
It's rough and a speck gristly, but other than that, it looks pretty
chirpin. It doesn't hurt neither. Una applies some sorta balm what
makes my skin tingle, then tells me I can put my clothes back on.

"I don't know what that man did to you, but you sure are healing fast," she ses. "Despite the fact that you rode *all the way* to the
north and back again."

She's isn't gunna let me forget that anytime soon. I don't think
she's really skapped, though, specially cuz it looks like Jaime and
I might of convinced the Raasay people to help. I came back two
days ago, bringing some of their people with me so they could
talk with the Skye leaders. Jaime hasn't returned yet. The Raasay
chiefs made him stay in their enclave in case it turned out he
was lyin. I didn't feel too sparkin about leavin him there, but
he reckoned it'd be okay. He also said it was important I let his
clan know that we didn't find Agatha, so they'd keep searchin
for her.

"Ahh, Sigrid, I hoped I'd find you here." Lenox walks over to my bed, his sluggy eyebrows jiggin. "I trust you're healing well?"

"Remarkably well," ses Una, answerin for me.

"Then I would like to borrow you, if I may. The last of the Skye clans has just arrived, and the leaders of all three would very much like to talk to you."

"Okay," I say. "I go."

I follow Lenox out of the sickboth to another buildin not faraways. There are all sortsa people inside from all the diffrunt clans. Lenox introduces them and then ses he's gotta go but that he's sure I'm in safe hands.

Soon as he's gone, the people start with their questionin. I give them answer after answer, but they keep on askin more. They pick at my brain like scabby crows, tryin to find any crumb of information that might help in some way. I start gettin tired and wonder how much longer I've gotta do this for.

"Tell us again about the dark creatures the king mentioned," ses a gray-haired man. He's from Clann-a-Cheò I think. Or was it Clann-an-Iar? Usually I wouldn't have no problems rememberin somethin like that, but my brain's turned to cabbagemush from all the talkin. I already told him evrythin I know about the "dark creatures," which is basically nothin. King Edmund kept his loller still on that one.

Before I can reply, someone else asks, "Did they give any indication of time? Of when they'd be leaving? Or how long they thought it would take to get here?" The new woman speakin is from Clann-a-Duslaich, the Clan of Dust. She's short and her hair's in tight curls. Her hams are so dry there's cracks runnin all over them, formin deep red sores. She scratches them with her thumbs while she talks.

"No, King Edmund say—" But then I'm interrupted again. The more people that're talkin, the harder it is to work out the meanin of their words. I close my gawpers for a speck. All this foreign-tongue talkin is givin me headrot.

"Did the kings mention whether they would be accompanying the army themselves?" asks an elder woman from Clann-a-Cheò.

I hadn't thought on that. I doubt King Edmund's gunna come. He's convinced a Scotian is gunna kill him, after all—cuz of some stupid dream he had hek years ago. That's the whole reason he's sendin the army, cuz he reckons if he kills all Scotians, he won't never die. He's definitely cracked, thinkin that. "King Edmund very old. Maybe he no come. Konge Grímr like fight. I think he come."

"Perhaps if he does—"

The chimes from the wall outside start ringin loud, cuttin her off.

"The Fourth," someone ses.

Evryone starts shoutin and pushin toward the door.

"It can't be the army already, can it?" ses the woman with the skittin hands. She picks at one of her crustin knuckles without even realizin she's doin it.

"If they left soon after the girl, there's no reason why it couldn't be," ses the Clann-a-Cheò elder.

"But we're not ready. We need more time."

Their cries and fears follow them out the door, and I'm left alone in the room. I take a deep breath, then go out after them.

Outside it's a clutterflap of panic. Evryone's runnin and rushin this way and that. From the snatches of words flyin past me, I learn there's war boats approachin from the north. The word *deamhain* splits the air. It's wreckers, come from Norveg. Konge Grímr must've changed his plan and sent word for them to come straight here. This is all happenin too quick.

There are so many people from diffrunt clans that no one knows who's in charge. Evryone's just yellin and runnin and not doin anythin what'd actually help.

I gotta see the boats for myself. I sprint to the wall. The steps leadin up to it are bulk stone ones what make my thighs ache. I haven't never been up on the wall before. The view from the top is towerin, and I gotta steady my knees to stop the wind blowin me straight back off again. That wouldn't end pretty, that's for hek sure.

The people on the wall are more organized than the ones runnin batcrazy down in the enclave, cuz Kenrick and Maistreas Eilionoir are up here, tellin evryone what they've gotta do. There's people from all five of the diffrunt Skye clans by my reckonin, all workin together to prepare for what's comin. Some are linin up big contraptions for firin arrows, some are lookin through spyglasses at the boats, and others are rushin in with more stones and arrows and weapons. Someone starts a fire with a whoosh and uses a branch to pass the flames between the loaded arrows. The harsk smell of burnin oil wafts through the air. The chimes are still clangin thunders. It's even louder up here, and the insides of my ears are threatenin to burst.

I push my way through the people to get a view of the water. There's a hefty distance between the enclave and the sea, so it's hard to see much, but the boat is definitely a wrecker one. There's only one of them, though, meanin a couple of hundred wreckers at most. With all the new people what have arrived here and the protection of the wall, the Skye people should be able to defend themselves against them easy. Havin said that, Granpa Halvor always told me that Konge Grímr's wreckers were the sneakiest and most ruthless in the world, and even a small group could do a hek lot of damage.

"They've reached the shore," ses a girl with a spyglass. "A couple of them are disembarking. Three. No, four. Definitely deamhain. And they're . . . It's strange, they're . . ."

I don't need no spyglass to see it. The four wreckers what are walkin toward the enclave have their arms out wide and their fingers spread. A sign of peace, similar to what me and Jaime did when we approached the Raasay enclave.

"It's a trap. It has to be," someone ses.

"Let's not be too hasty," ses Kenrick.

"Yes, let them come," ses Maistreas Eilionoir. "But keep the launchers aimed."

The wind pummels us from the west. The fire on the arrows sloshes around like a drunkard's tankard as the four wreckers walk closer. I can see them proper now. It doesn't look like they've got weapons. There's two men and two women. The man in front has gotta be the one in charge. His hair is dark and lank, threaded with a couple of scraggin braids. He's slim, his cheeks hollow, but he stands tall and proud. I can't see none of his ink clearly from up here. When he's about twenty paces from the enclave, he stops and the other three do the same.

"Greetings," he ses in the foreign tongue, so evryone on the wall can understand. "We come in peace. We may look like your enemy, but I assure you we are not. We are here to help."

"Who are you?" Maistreas Eilionoir shouts back at him.

"I've been known by many names over the years," he ses with a gentle smile, "but you can call me Mal-Rakki."

Mal-Rakki! It can't be. Can it?

"No shoot!" I say. "No shoot." I push my way past the yelpin bodies to the nearest arrow launcher and give it a shove, but the woman holdin it grips it tight and doesn't let it move.

"Sigrid, do you know this man?" Maistreas Eilionoir asks me.

Evryone on the wall falls silent, their faces full of questions.

I look down at the man below. He's starin curious at me. Truth is, I don't know him from anyone. He could be part of some new bloodsplash plan Konge Grímr and King Edmund choked up after I left. But if he really is Mal-Rakki . . .

I think back to all the things Granpa Halvor taught me about him, wonderin if there's some way I can know for sure. Most of what Granpa used to say was just about how great he was, how he was gunna return from the ice caves and set us all free one day. He certainly don't look how I imagined he would.

"Mal-Rakki?" I ask him. It's the only words I can get outta my yapper.

"Yes," he ses in our language. He musta spotted my raven ink and realized I'm from Norveg too.

"Is it really you?"

"It's really me," he ses.

I stare into his eyes for a long moment and I know it. I know it's true. Cuz of the calm etched in his face or the hope in his peepers or somethin, I dunno.

Tears are fillin up my eyes. I've been waitin for Mal-Rakki my whole life, and now he's in front of me, not five spits away. I don't know if the tears are happy ones or sad, though, cuz now he's here, it seems bugdumb that I've been waitin for him so long. He's just a man, after all. What can one man do? I wipe away the tears with my sleeve, pressin so hard it roughs my cheeks.

"Why you here?" I ask, changin back to the foreign tongue so the Skye people don't think we're chattin secrets.

"I've come to offer my support." He's talkin to evryone now. More people have come up onto the wall, and evryone's stretchin their necks, tryin to get a look at him. "I understand you face an imminent attack, led by the Inglish and Norvegian kings. We are here to lend our strength to your cause, for we share a mutual enemy: Konge Grímr. My brother."

His words are followed by a harsk silence, until Maistreas Eilionoir breaks it by sayin, "Don't move, any of you," to Mal-Rakki and his companions. She turns to the people aimin the launchers. "Keep your arrows pointed at them, and if they move, shoot them." Then she takes me by my wrist and leads me away from the edge. She leans in close. Her breath is smoky and smells of shrewnuts.

"What do you know of this man?" she asks me.

"He Mal-Rakki," I say, which is a foolin answer, but I'm findin it hard to think of words right now.

"I know he's Mal-Rakki," ses Maistreas Eilionoir. "That's about the only thing I do know about him. What else?"

"He Norveg king's brother. Kind man. He think Konge Grímr bad. King not like and want Mal-Rakki dead." I dig into the ground with my heel. It's hek skap not bein able to speak their language better. "Mal-Rakki run far to caves ice in north. Other people go too. They rebel army and live in caves too."

"Have you ever seen this Mal-Rakki before?" Maistreas Eilionoir's chin is covered in lots of tiny hairs, though it's not really the time to be noticin somethin like that.

"No," I say, followed by, "It him."

"How can you be so certain?"

I can't explain it. It's the sparks of hope what've crept into my stogg. That's how I know.

"It him."

⋙

MAISTREAS EILIONOIR AND KENRICK AGREE TO LET MAL-Rakki into the enclave, but only him, and people frisk him as soon as he steps inside to check he's not hidin no weapons.

"You must forgive our precautions," ses Maistreas Eilionoir as she leads him across the enclave. Kenrick follows and so do I. They want me with them to confirm whether parts of his story are true or not. The crowds we pass stare at us with wonderin gawpers.

"There's no need to apologize," ses Mal-Rakki. He speaks the foreign tongue good. "You are right to be wary; I have heard of the abuse you recently suffered at the hands of my brother. The way he uses people as slaves is one of the many things we disagree upon."

We enter a small buildin what's made of stone like all the buildins here. It's got thick straw for its roofin and a fire inside makin it creamy warm. We sit on log stools in a small circle—just me, Maistreas Eilionoir, Kenrick, and Mal-Rakki. *The* Mal-Rakki.

I know I shouldn't stare, but I can't help it. He's got a face of angles, with a long nose and a sharp chin. His ink is brimmin and hek beautiful, clearly done by some master *tatovmaðr*, not like mine. There's a leatherback turtle underneath his left eye, pointin right for determination, and a rock ptarmigan nestin under his chin what means dignity. His cheeks are scattered with saxifrage flowers and curlin waves, dragon spears and mountain pines. Curved around the outsides of his eyes are two matchin otters, meanin compassion. I haven't never seen no one with otter ink before.

The dark blue and red of his ink makes his eyes shine even brighter. They're pale gray and as piercin as a fox's. Maybe that's why they call him Mal-Rakki. *The White Fox.* He catches me starin, and I whip my head away. The room is too hot and I'm wearin too many clothes. Sweat is startin to gather at the base of my back and across my chest.

"Why don't you start from the beginning and tell us exactly why you're here," ses Kenrick.

Mal-Rakki begins to talk. He talks for a long time: about how he challenged his brother Konge Grímr and was then forced into hidin to save his life, and about the rebel army what joined him in the ice caves and how they've been waitin for their moment all these years. When they heard about the shadows comin and all the slaves bein freed, they knew the time for action had arrived.

"Norveg has been returned to the people," ses Mal-Rakki. "In the time since Konge Grímr has left, my supporters and I have inspired a civil uprising. We have taken control and plan to use that power to establish a new, fairer society. We can only do this if Konge Grímr does not return. He is the last obstacle to be overcome. The revolution we've set in motion has, for the large part, been welcomed—we have control of the hollow mountain and many people have risen to support us. But that was only possible on account of Konge Grímr's absence. If he and those loyal to him return, the tides may turn; his subjects are scared of him, and frightened people do foolish things."

"So you wish to join our allied forces?" asks Kenrick.

"I do," ses Mal-Rakki. "It will be much easier to defeat him with your support, which is precisely why I came. Consider it the start of a new allegiance between our nations—one based on trust and respect. I understand you have a powerful weapon—a legion of shadows that can be unleashed upon him."

There is a sniff of a silence, which Maistreas Eilionoir fills. "The *sgàilean*—the shadows to which you refer—are no more," she ses. "They turned against us and had to be destroyed."

Mal-Rakki doesn't do a very good job of hidin his disappointment. "That is . . . unfortunate," he ses.

"Indeed," ses Maistreas Eilionoir. "But we are forming a new army of allies, for which your support would be greatly appreciated. How many soldiers have you brought with you?"

"Sixty."

Maistreas Eilionoir scoffs like a pig burpin. "That's not very many."

"The majority of my supporters had to remain in Norveg to

maintain the peace. The country is in a fragile state. Sixty warriors is all we could spare, but I assure you they will fight with the
strength of five hundred."

"You are aware we are vastly outnumbered?" ses Kenrick.
"Sigrid here claims there is a hundred thousand–strong army
marching toward us."

"That is a daunting prospect, to say the least," ses Mal-Rakki,
"but I have been fighting impossible odds my whole life."

"Your optimism is honorable, if misguided," ses Maistreas
Eilionoir.

"Is there no one else on the island who will rally behind you?"
Mal-Rakki asks.

"All of our allies have already been approached," ses Kenrick.
"There is no one else."

"Unless . . ." I say.

All three of them turn to me so quick I wonder if I've said the
wrong word.

"Unless what?" asks Maistreas Eilionoir.

It's probly hek foolin, but I gotta say it. "People in north
Ingland no like King Edmund. Maybe they help." Jaime managed
to convince the Raasay people, even though they're sposed to be
this clan's enemies. Maybe someone could do the same with the
people in the north.

Maistreas Eilionoir chews on her lip. "You spoke to these people?" she asks me. "You know this to be true?"

"Yes," I say.

"Then we should approach them at once," ses Mal-Rakki. "If
there's even the slightest hope."

"But . . . problem," I say. "The people . . ."

"What problem?" Maistreas Eilionoir ses. "What about them?"

I think about the kerl who tied me up, who tried to slice me with her knife and had her skittin pot in the corner, bubblin with water.

"They eat people," I say.

AGATHA

THE WILDWOLF IN THE PRISON CAGE BARKS SO LOUD I think it will explode my head. Then it runs at me. I press my whole body into the bars. I am trapped and there is nowhere to go. It jumps to bite my face and I scream and close my eyes. There is a tumble noise. I open my eyes and the wildwolf is on the floor. It tries to get me again but something stops it. I look at the Badhbh man. I think maybe it is him doing the stopping but he is in the corner doing nothing. The wildwolf turns to him and tries to get him next, but it can't do that either.

There is a chain. That's why the wildwolf can't get us. The chain is around its neck and connected to the wall. As long as we stay on this side of the prison cage the wildwolf cannot eat us. That is a big phew.

It is barking more now because it is angry, I think. It shakes its head and bits of its spit go in the air. It is very smelly like nasty things and wee and it is dirty with mud. I hate the barking so loud in my ears.

"Be quiet!" I say, and I say it in my head so it can hear me.

It stops barking then and looks at me. *You are the screaming girl,* it says.

It knows me. It's one of the wildwolves from Scotia that was in the fight with the bull people. I screamed in their heads to make them run away. This one must have ran all the way to here. That is a long way. I don't know why it did running so far.

Please stop barking, I say. It answers me by barking more and it pulls against its chain so hard I think it will snap or break. Its yellow eye and its blue one are wide and hungry. I ask it again three times to stop the barking but it won't listen to me. I cover my ears and close my eyes and wait for the horrible to be over.

It hates me the worst because of the screaming. That was a long time ago and it should forgive me. It thinks it is my fault that it's here in the prison cage but it is wrong. I didn't say for it to come to Ingland, did I? It should have run the other way and then it would not be here. That would have been more clever.

After a long time of barking, the wildwolf growls and then falls down on the floor and goes to sleep. All the barking and pulling on the chain made it tired, I think. It is better for my ears now the noise is stopped.

"It spoke to you, didn't it?" says the Badhbh man.

"I'm not t-talking to you," I say. My head hurts and I am too tired.

"If we're to get out of here alive, we have to work together," he says.

"No," I say. "You are a mean, bad man and I—h-hate you." I scratch underneath the bracelets with my teeth. It is bad itchy and hurts where the needles go into my skin. There are still black lines inside my arm from the liquid.

"Come here and I'll take that rope off, at least," says the Badhbh man.

I don't want his help but I do want the rope to be off. I hold out my hands and do a pout. He can come to me.

He stands up and walks to where I am.

"If I untie you, you're not going to do anything foolish, are you?" he says.

"I'm not stupid," I say. "I'm very—clever. You are the stupid one for c-coming here."

"Perhaps," he says. "That will be revealed in due course. If I can get the king to trust me, there may still be a way to stop him."

He pulls at the knots around my wrists until the rope comes free. I do not tell him thank you. I put one hand over the pocket where Milkwort is to let him know he's safe. He wants to come out but I tell him it is too dangerous because of the wildwolf. It might smell him and wake up and eat him.

Now that my hands are free, I try to pull the sharp bracelet needles out.

"Be careful with that," says the Badhbh man.

"Take them—off," I tell him.

"I can't," he says. "Not without a key."

"What are they? Why is there the—black?"

"It's a chemical they've fed into our bloodstream. I've never seen anything like it. It's altered the connection between me and my blood, blocking my abilities."

"But I can't d-do the blood magic. They should not have put them on me."

"Perhaps the liquid stops all forms of magic, so they thought it would block the connection you have with animals. But it hasn't, has it?"

"Crayton says t-talking to—animals isn't magic. It's *communication*." That is a long word. Crayton taught it to me. I like saying it because it's clever.

"So you did speak with the wolf?"

I turn away from him and cross my arms. I'm not telling.

"You hopeless girl," says the Badhbh man. That is not friendly or nice. Also, I am not hopeless so it is a lie. "If you can speak to the wolf, you can convince it to help us when the soldiers return."

"It won't—help us," I say. "It h-hates me and it wants to eat us. That is all it said."

"I'm going to wake it so you can try again." The Badhbh man stands up.

"No," I say.

"This is important."

"My head hurts," I say. "It—it makes my h-head hurt when I do it. I don't—want to do it again. The wildwolf doesn't want to speak to me and it w-won't—let me."

The Badhbh man pulls at the hairs on his eyebrow. They are long ones and curly and yuck.

"What if I could help with that?" he says. What does he mean help with that? "If I could teach you how to make it easier to talk to the wolf, would you do it then?"

"It is not a wolf, it is a w-wildwolf," I say. He keeps saying it wrong.

He does a slow blink. "Okay, the wildwolf. If I teach you how to strengthen your skills, would you try again?"

I think about it for a long time. "Yes," I say. It is a lie answer. I am not going to talk to the wildwolf again, but I do want the Badhbh man to teach me what he knows. That is why I said the lie. Sometimes only a small lie is an okay one. Also the Badhbh man lied to me when he took me away so it is my turn to lie now and that is fair. "Yes," I say again, and I nod.

"Good," says the Badhbh man. "As you may be aware, I used to work for King Balfour, the last Scotian king. I was his physician for many years and consumed every book I could lay my hands on, including ancient texts on magery and other forms of the occult. The king had them sent from throughout the kingdom and beyond, but mentions of *teangannan-bèist* such as yourself were scarce. The general consensus was that they were a myth, nothing more than a legend."

I yawn. He is doing so much talking which is not teaching and is boring.

"I'm sorry, am I boring you?" he asks me.

"Yes," I say. I'm glad he knows it.

He does a humph sound like the ones Maistreas Eilionoir does.

"Well, let me cut to the point, then," he says. "There was only one book I remember that appeared to have any sort of credibility on the subject. It was written by a follower of Tòmas, who was the first Bó Rider."

"I know who—Tòmas is," I say. Crayton's mother, Murdina,

told me about him. He lived a long time ago and was the first person to talk to the bulls and ride them. I turn my head toward the Badhbh man to listen to him better. I like hearing about the bull people. Maybe the Badhbh man knows which one is my father. I am not supposed to think about that but maybe I will ask him.

"The author of the work described Tòmas's methods for talking to animals. Apparently, some animals are stubborn, and that makes them harder to speak to, but Tòmas developed a technique that could make any animal pay attention. He used the same method to communicate with large groups and much bigger animals as well."

"How?" I ask to him. "H-how did he do it?"

"According to the book, you need to calm your mind, picture your inner voice like an arrow, and then send that arrow fast into the head of whatever animal you are attempting to communicate with."

"What do you mean an—an arrow?" I ask. I do not understand it.

The Badhbh man opens his mouth to tell me, but a noise stops him. It is the feet of people coming.

"We've run out of time; the soldiers are returning," says the Badhbh man. He stamps on one of the wildwolf's paws, then steps back so the wildwolf cannot get him. The wildwolf yelps and jumps up with angry teeth. "Quick, try it now," says the Badhbh man. "Turn your thoughts into an arrow and tell the wolf that we will unchain it if it helps us escape."

"It's not a w-wolf," I say again. "It's a wildwolf."

The Badhbh man scrunches up his crinkle hands like he is cross. He cannot be cross with me because what I said is right.

"Just tell it," he says. He shouts it loud because the wildwolf is barking again.

"No," I say. I cannot do it because he didn't explain it properly and I do not know what he means the arrows.

"You stupid girl," he says.

"I am not st-stupid," I say. The angry inside me is bursting hot. I kick the Badhbh man as hard as I can. He falls down and is holding his leg where I kicked it. "I told you before that I am not stupid. You should have listened to me when I s-said it."

The soldiers are back. There are four of them. They rattle their swords against the metal bars of the cage and say, "Hey, what's all this noise?"

The noise is the wildwolf barking and me shouting and the Badhbh man saying "Ow" because I kicked him.

One of the soldiers has lots of keys which jangle. It is the same soldier from before with the gray stubble face and fat lips. He opens the door. The other three soldiers step into the prison cage and point their swords at us again. The wildwolf snaps its big mouth but they stay away so it cannot reach.

"King Edmund wishes to see you," says the soldier with the keys. "Come quietly and you will not be harmed."

Going to see King Edmund is better than being stuck in the cage with the wildwolf so I do it what he says. I stay close to the bars so the wildwolf cannot bite me. It stares at me mean with its different-colored eyes. I do not speak to it and I stick out my tongue.

The soldiers take me and the Badhbh man away from all the cages and up some steps. They are different steps from before.

When we are at the top, there is a door and we go through it. Then we are in a new place. The first room is stone walls and cold but then we go down long corridors that are pretty and nice. Some of the doors we go past are open and I look inside. We are walking too quickly to do a long look but I see chairs and women in puffy clothes, and big hanging material and people pictures on the walls. The ceilings are high ones and some of them are painted gold and red and patterns.

I ask the soldier where we are. He doesn't answer me so I ask him lots more times and then he tells me "Be quiet" and that we are in King Edmund's home and it is called a palace. I've never heard of that before. A palace is even bigger than a castle and nicer.

I ask the soldier if I can have something to eat because I am hungry but he says no. I ask him why not and he says there is no time. He is wrong because I can eat and walk at the same time. I tell him that but he still doesn't give me any food.

We go up some steps and then we are in a corridor that has soft on the floor. It is red and squishy under my feet. At the end of the corridor are two big doors. We go through them. Now we are in a big room with a high ceiling and a huge fire. There are people in the room. Some of them are Inglish soldiers and some of them are deamhain.

One of them is Konge Grímr.

My heart goes very fast when I see him. He looks different and horrible. He is standing on the other side of the room talking to some of his warrior people. He still has long animal cloaks around him and his antler crown. It is his eyes that are different, because he doesn't have any. It is what the bats did to him in the mountain room. Where his eyes should be is red and scars.

A young boy is next to him. His face is freckles and scared. He stares at me for a long time. Everyone else in the room goes quiet when they see us.

Konge Grímr puts his hand on the boy's head and squeezes it. The boy stands on his toes and whispers something in Konge Grímr's ear. He looks at me when he says it. Konge Grímr smiles a nasty one.

"Agatha," he says. His voice is loud in the room. "Welcome to your execution."

Sigrid

TRUTH BEIN TOLD, I'M BRIMMIN TO BE AWAY FROM THE enclave again. The people are nice and they treated me good, but it's a ram riot there now. Too many people, too many clans, too much panic, too much to do.

The old woman, Maistreas Eilionoir, and the other Skye clan leaders agreed it was plum thinkin to ask the northern Inglish for help. The only way to get there quick, though, is by horse, and the only horse in the enclave was Eydis. Sure as the moon, I wasn't gunna let no one else take her. So here I am, back in Scotia with Eydis, same as we were before. Sept this time Mal-Rakki's ridin with us.

I think the Skye people were glad to be rid of him. There was a hek lot of talk about whether he should be trusted. Maistreas Eilionoir believed he was who he said he was, but some of the other leaders didn't. Sendin him to Ingland pleased evryone, includin Mal-Rakki. They had to send someone with me, cuz there's no way I'm convincin anyone with my cowcrap foreign tongue, and it'd be risky sendin someone from Skye, cuz Scotia and Ingland have been enemies since forever. Mal-Rakki's thinkin was that, given his experience inspirin rebellions, he was probly the best person to try and persuade the northerners to help. He's gunna need their help and all, since the Skye people don't have their killin shadows no more.

Before we left, Mal-Rakki took me to his longboat to grab a loada scram to take with us. We're gunna give it to the northerners as a peace offerin, since they're all so desperate for food. It was my idea, which Mal-Rakki said was a great one. Maybe it'll keep them from eatin us instead. . . .

The rebels on the boat helped us pack it all up. It was *ríkka* meetin them. Whatever Mal-Rakki asked, they were chirpin to do straightaways, like they didn't doubt one speck of anythin he did or said. Not like Konge Grímr's wreckers, who follow his orders outta duty and fear.

When we were ready to leave, the rebels put their hands on my head one at a time and wished me high fortunes for the journey. Then they said their goodbyes to Mal-Rakki, and evry single one of them looked at him the same way: like they believe he can do anythin.

Mal-Rakki's sittin in fronta me now. We've been takin turns ridin in front, and I'm fine with that. Even from behind, I'm the one leadin the way; the map I saw in King Edmund's palace is still in my head, clear as ice. We're headin to Caerlisle, which is the nearest northern town. I was frettin that two of us would be too much weight for Eydis, but she doesn't seem to mind none. I think she's happy to be outta the enclave again too. We're ridin fast, just the way she likes it. Una wouldn't be too smirks, but she isn't here to frown, and my wound has healed up good. The speed is makin streams rush outta my eyes. Scotia whips pasts us in a mudblur haze.

It's hard gettin my head around evrythin that's happened. First findin Bolverk dead in the trees, then Mal-Rakki turnin up, and now returnin to the place where someone tried to eat me. But that kerl was rotten and desperate. She said it herself: she didn't wanna do it, but she didn't have no food nor no hopes of gettin any. She blamed all that on King Edmund. That's what gave me the thinkin. If the rest of the northern Inglish hate their king as much as she did, maybe they'll consider helpin. We've gotta try. This isn't just about helpin the Skye people no more. Now Mal-Rakki's here, stoppin Konge Grímr could change the whole world.

After hek slogs, we stop for somethin to eat and to give Eydis a rest. I'm sweatin rivers from all the ridin. Mal-Rakki reaches into one of the saddlebags and pulls out some chew for us both. The meat is hard and tasteless, but the carrot bread's a bit more scrammin. Eydis stays nearby, munchin on the grass.

"Was it cold, livin in the ice caves?" I ask while I'm chewin. It's a bugdumb question. Course it was cold. I got a million and one questions I wanna ask him, so why the sky was that the first one what came out? At least we can speak in our own language now it's just the two of us. That makes talkin a hek lot easier.

"Not as cold as you might think," ses Mal-Rakki. "We built homes deep within the caves that were well insulated. It was damp and dark, but we found peace there."

He doesn't talk like what I thought he would. His voice is low and he speaks slow, like he's thinkin on evry word. He moves the same way: slow and thoughtful. In my head, he was always louder, bolder, stronger. I'm not sayin I'm disappointed; he's just diffrunt is all.

"What will happen when you go back to Norveg?" I ask. "If you kill Konge Grímr. Are you gunna be king?"

"No," ses Mal-Rakki. "But if the majority of the people want me to lead, I will put a new system in place—one where leaders are elected by everyone, not granted power on account of their birth."

"But the monarchy's the will of Øden," I say, shocked at the thought of him challengin that. "It's always been that way."

"So says the king. . . . You seem like a clever girl, Sigrid; in fact, I know you are because you survived the journey from Ingland to Skye with nothing but your own initiative. So it shouldn't come as much of a surprise to you to learn that people lie. Adults lie, particularly those in power."

"I know they do," I say. "They lie to get what they want, to keep what they have, and to make people do the things they don't wanna do themselves. That's what my granpa Halvor ses."

"Your granpa sounds like a wise man. Unfortunately, it's the same with the monarchy. You said it's the will of Øden, but who is it that preaches that 'truth'? The king, and those in his favor—including the religious leaders who benefit from him being in power. And they'll all spin that lie, and stretch it to justify any actions they choose, for as long as it's in their interests to do so."

"But too many people believe the lies already. How you gunna change the minds of the whole country?"

"By telling people the truth. I'm not denouncing the will of Øden. If it was Øden's will for my brother to be king, why can't it also be his will for me to expose my brother's corruption and supplant him? Konge Grímr is powerful but not loved. The people have accepted his rule because they don't believe there is an alternative. I plan to offer them one."

I wanna believe that'll work, I really do, but . . . "There's a hek lot of people who don't like you, you know. Plenty what don't trust you neither."

"I know," ses Mal-Rakki. "My brother has done an exceptional job of spreading lies about me—threading mistrust deep into all sectors of society in case I should ever reappear and challenge his authority. Which is why I'll never be able to make any meaningful change while he's still alive; his influence is too far-reaching and the fear of him too great. I don't believe in unnecessary violence, but in this instance, ending his life is the only way. Only once Konge Grímr is gone will I be able to expose his lies and offer a positive alternative—for everyone, especially those who have less."

I nod. Evrythin he ses makes hek sense. It's what Granpa Halvor always promised he would come back and do. It's what we always wanted—someone who cared about us rottens and gave us more of a chance in this harsk world. Yet I'm strugglin to get proper lightnin splashes inside of me. I don't know why. Maybe it's cuz, lookin at Mal-Rakki now, I'm not convinced that he can do it.

No, I've gotta trust him and believe in him too. Cuz if there isn't no hope, what's the point of even tryin?

Soon as we've swallowed our chew and Eydis has had a chance to breathe for two blinks, we're back up and ridin. Me and Mal-Rakki can't hear each other too good over Eydis's cloppin hoofs, so we tromp on without talkin. I'm in front again, and evry now and then I lean forward and whisper yipper words to Eydis, tellin her what a *ríkka* horse she is. The best one ever. She doesn't slow down once, that's how brimmin she is.

Jaime told me about all the killer animals what live in Scotia, so I'm not that surprised when I see the blood. It's smeared in a line through the grass in fronta us, like somethin's been dragged across the path. I jostle Eydis to a stop. She sniffs at the blood and shakes her kog. What's strange, now we're lookin, is that the blood suddenly stops a few spits from where we are, like whatever was bein dragged just disappeared into nothin.

"It'll be a wild sheep or a goat, killed by a wolf," ses Mal-Rakki.

"So where's the body?" I say.

As if to answer, somethin cries out in pain, but the sound is too close, like the creature's right next to us. Eydis whinnies and stomps her feet. I pat her neck until she calms, then slip off her back. Mal-Rakki gets down too.

The cry comes again. It's an earsplittin, weepin sound. I follow it to the end of the blood trail, but somethin's not right. The green of the grass is shiftin slightly in a not-real sorta way.

"What the—?" ses Mal-Rakki, lookin down at the writhin, cryin form that's sometimes grass, sometimes earth, and some-times hot flashes of cracklin red.

"An *imitator*," I say, usin the foreign-tongue word Jaime taught me.

"What's an imitator?"

I don't get too close cuz Jaime warned me how dangerous they are. This one is hurt real bad. There's a cut down its calf, bleedin out like a gutted fish. It's the only part not changin color.

"We should help it," I say.

"I'm not sure that's a good idea."

I'm not sure neither, but I'm already back at Eydis's side, rummagin through the saddlebags for somethin to stop the bleedin. Una gave us plenty of supplies before we left—bandages and ropes and stinkin pastes for who knows what. I grab it all and bundle it toward where the imitator is lyin.

"Sigrid, wait," ses Mal-Rakki, followin close behind me. "Are you sure you want to use all our supplies on an animal?"

"It's not an animal," I say.

"What do you mean?"

"It's a person what's been changed somehow," I say, recountin what Jaime told me. "It's been merged with part of a jellysquid, meanin it can change the colors of its skin, but at one point it was a human, just like us." Another person trashed and twisted by King Edmund's skapfiend ways.

I approach the imitator real slow and then kneel next to it, watchin out for any sudden movements. I can see it clearer now. It's starin at me fierce. Its eyes haven't got no white parts, and there's no color in them neither; they're just big, bulgin black. Its fingers are spread through the grass, shimmerin as they match its texture. It's the fingers I've gotta watch out for—that's where their poison is, which is strong enough to send me straight to the High Halls.

The cut on its leg looks deep. It needs stitchin, and the imitator's not gunna like that one speck.

"I help," I say in the foreign tongue, not knowin what language it understands or even if it understands any language at all. "I friend."

It doesn't react none, just keeps on starin with its skinned-goat stare. I show it the piece of rope in my hand and then, slow as a swamp, creep my fingers toward its leg. It lets me tie the rope below its knee, which stops the worst of the bleedin, then I pour salt water over the cut to clean it. The imitator quivers some but doesn't move away.

Now comes the hard part. I thread the needle and hold it up for the imitator to see, so the sharp doesn't give it no surprises. I haven't never had to mend someone like this before, but I read how to do it in one of Granpa Halvor's books. And I know how to fix up torn clothes, which isn't too diffrunt. How hard can it be?

I pinch the two halves of the cut together and then shove the needle into the flesh. The imitator's mouth opens wide, and it lets out a twistgut howl. Its toothless gums flash purple and black. At its sides, its fingers start twitchin. Swear Øden it's definitely thinkin of strikin me. Praps I should ask Mal-Rakki to hold down its arms, although I gotta feelin that'll make it even more fiery.

"It's okay," I say, tryin to sound reassurin.

As I pull the thread out through the other side, the imitator jerks its leg away and makes a swipe at my face. *Jarg!* I pull back just in time. Mal-Rakki goes to draw his sword, but I tell him no. I raise my hands to show the imitator I don't mean no harm. Its chest is goin up and down, up and down. The needle and thread are still hangin from its leg.

"Yes, hurt. Pain," I say. "But I help you. If no help, you bleed, you die."

The imitator's head moves very slowly. Maybe it's just my imaginin or maybe it was a nod. I reach for the needle and start sewin up the wound again. This time it lets me, though its leg shakes with the pain, and it's growlin rotten. Evry time I dig the needle in, hot ripples of burnt orange shimmer over its body. They twist and spread, their edges turnin dark red and bruise purple before meltin away again. It's kinda beautiful seein it. Mal-Rakki hovers just behind me, his hand still on the hilt of his sword.

When I'm finished, I lean back to take a look at my work. Truth bein told, it's a bit of a wreckmess. The stitches are clunky and uneven, and drips of blood dribble through the gaps, but it'll hold. I smother the whole wound in balm and wrap it tight. The imitator has been silent for a while, starin up at the sky. I was worried it might of died from losin all that blood, but as soon as I finish with the bandage, it scrambles to its feet. It looks at what I've done, then looks at me. It takes half a creepin step toward me, its fingers flexin, its back hunched, like its gunna thank me by pumpin my body full of poison. Mal-Rakki lifts his sword out a flick, warnin the imitator not to try nothin foolin. The imitator flashes us its gums again, then turns and limps away, soon dissolvin into the land.

I let out a hek bulkin breath.

Mal-Rakki's hand is on my shoulder. "Well done," he ses. "That was the right thing to do, even if it didn't appreciate it. The world would be a whole lot better if there were more people like you in it."

I'm brimmin when he ses that.

I need to wash my hands, what are sticky and red, but that can wait. Right now, all I wanna do is get away from here. The rush I felt while helpin the imitator has gone, leavin me nothin but sapped. I don't trust that imitator as far as I can spit. There isn't nothin stoppin it from sneakin back around and attackin us from behind. I don't regret helpin it, but somethin tells me I was lucky to get through it alive.

Eydis walks over to us; she's as keen to keep movin as I am. I pull myself onto her back and Mal-Rakki does the same. The land around us looks colder now and more harsk. A dark cloud passes overhead, threatenin to spew.

"Let's get the skit outta here," I say.

Eydis whinnies and clops off as the first flecks of rain start pricklin my face.

JAIME

WHEN I ARRIVE AT CLANN-NA-BRUTHAICH'S ENCLAVE, IT'S
filled with more people than I have ever seen. It's been four days
since I left, and it looks like a lot has changed in that time.

An escort of Raasay islanders brought me back in one of
their small fishing boats; while I wasn't exactly thrilled to be at
sea, I was grateful not to have to walk the whole way. Maistreas
Eilionoir came to meet me at the Lower Gate and is now leading
me through the throng of bodies.

"Who are all these people?" I ask her. To my right, a large group
practices sword strokes in perfect unison, and under a shelter on
my left, a team of Wasps is hammering at something with intense
concentration. A big-armed woman sweeps past us rolling a boulder.

"They're the other Skye clans," Maistreas Eilionoir replies.
"Almost two thousand people altogether, as well as sixty deamhain
rebels and several hundred of the bull-riding tribe."

"The Bó Riders are here?" My stomach flips.

"Yes. They arrived a short while ago. They're setting up their tents outside the western wall. Our allies have grown substantially. Still not nearly enough to face a force of a hundred thousand, but better than we had a few days ago. And now it seems like the Raasay islanders will be joining us as well—I understand we have you to thank for that?" There's a hint of a smile on her lips.

I tilt my head and shrug a little. "Did you say there are deamhain here as well?"

"They arrived from Norveg yesterday, led by Konge Grímr's brother. It appears they oppose their king and are using this as an opportunity to dethrone him. Whatever their reasoning, I welcome their support."

"How are we going to feed everyone?" I ask.

Maistreas Eilionoir guffaws—a rare sight. "Of all the questions, that is the one you deem most important?" she asks.

I shrug again. Food has been scarce since we returned from the hollow mountain.

"Your concerns are unnecessary. Clann-a-Duslaich and Clann-a-Cheò were able to bring extensive provisions with them, so we should have enough to last us the next few weeks. If we survive that long."

If we survive that long . . . The chances still seem slim, even with the Raasay islanders' support.

"Has Agatha returned?" I ask.

"No," says Maistreas Eilionoir, her mouth a brittle twig.

My heart sinks. I thought she would've shown up by now. "What's being done to find her?"

"After the initial search came to nothing, Clann-na-Bruthaich's best tracker was sent farther afield to keep looking."

"That's it?" I say. "Agatha's been gone for days and all you've sent to find her is *one person?*"

"Jaime, calm down. I'm as worried about her as you are, but there's only so much we can do, especially given the additional defenses we're all scrambling to complete. Agatha is smart and resourceful. She can look after herself."

She's right, but it doesn't make it any easier to accept. There's an army approaching, after all, and Agatha's out there somewhere, alone.

Maistreas Eilionoir pushes open the door to her bothan, and I follow her inside. Three makeshift beds have been crammed into the small room — it looks like even Maistreas Eilionoir has to share. There are no chairs in the room, so I perch on the edge of one of the mattresses. The straw inside pokes my thighs.

"Tell me about your time in the north," says Maistreas Eilionoir. "Do you believe the Raasay islanders can be trusted?"

"Yes," I say, "I do." I tell her about the appeal I made and how they rallied together in support of me. "The chiefs of Raasay wouldn't let me leave until they'd corroborated my story by sending some of their people here, but I didn't feel like a prisoner. I stayed with Lileas's parents, who treated me well."

In truth, Hector and Edme could not have been kinder. They introduced me to other members of their clan and taught me more about their beliefs and customs. At night, Hector fed me hearty stews and warm breads, and Edme told me stories about Lileas. I smiled as I listened, noticing how rekindling memories of their daughter helped ease their grief.

"They're not bad people," I tell Maistreas Eilionoir. "At least the ones I met weren't. I think they genuinely want to help."

"Good. Good," says Maistreas Eilionoir, deep in thought.

This morning, when I was told that I could leave, the first thing I did was rush through the Southern Gate to retrieve my sword. Luckily, it was where I'd left it, half-buried among the damp grass. Fastening it onto my belt was like reattaching a lost limb. I never want to be without it again.

"The rest of the Raasay islanders are going to join us here soon," I say. "Once they've finished gathering their weapons and supplies."

"Yes, that was what we agreed when we were negotiating with them. Let's hope we can make this work, otherwise—"

There's a knock at the door, and a young boy enters. His blond hair hangs around his face in wild tangles.

"Hello, Maistreas Eilionoir," he says, trying to catch his breath. His eyes dart around the room. "Kenrick asked me to give you a message."

"Well?" says Maistreas Eilionoir. "What is it, Owen?"

"It's the Bó Riders," he says, then he smiles a little, as if he's about to say a rude word. "They're . . . *singing*."

"What?" says Maistreas Eilionoir. "Not on my island, they're not." She pushes past me and marches out of the bothan in the direction of the Lower Gate.

Owen wipes his nose on his sleeve, then shoots out as well. I follow, letting the door slam shut behind me.

"What are you going to say to them?" I ask when I catch up with Maistreas Eilionoir.

"I'm going to tell them to stop, of course," she replies without slowing her pace or looking in my direction.

"But it's different in their tribe," I say, remembering how the Bó Riders sang when I was with them in Scotia.

"Singing is not *dùth*, as you well know," she says. "When they're on our island, they obey our rules."

"But it's not *our* island."

Maistreas Eilionoir stops and turns her head toward me like a scorned owl. "What could you possibly mean by that?"

"The Raasay chiefs told me their people used to live here and the Skye clans forced them to leave. It's true, isn't it?"

Maistreas Eilionoir's eyes narrow ever so slightly. She sniffs. "Our ancestors acted in the best way they saw fit to uphold the values of our clans, just as I am doing now."

"But how can we hope to cooperate if we won't even—"

Maistreas Eilionoir holds up one of her hands, warning me not to say anything more. "If I want your opinion, I shall ask for it," she says.

She leaves me standing there, a burning heat flushing my cheeks. I sprint to the western wall and climb the stone steps two at a time. At the top, I nearly run straight into Donal, who's placing the last few stones on a new hearth.

"Jaime, lad!" he says, his smile big and genuine. He stands up and runs his fingers through his bright red beard. "What a nice surprise."

"Hi, Donal," I say, squeezing the fist he offers me. His other hand is still bandaged from the battle with the *sgàilean*, when he caught a sword in midair to prevent it from colliding with my face. He saved my life, and I'm never going to forget it. "Great to see you up and about."

"You know me: I'm like the bird with nine lives, I just keep getting back up again." He gives one of his high-pitched chuckles, which are so at odds with his imposing stature. "Besides, if there's a job that needs doing, you can't keep me away. I hear I've got you to thank for my being alive."

"You could say that," I say, blushing a little. "We both kind of helped each other."

"That we did, lad. That we did." His good hand swings around and pats my shoulder, the gesture filled with clumsy affection. "So, what brings you up here in such a hurry?"

"Can you see the Bó Riders' camp from here?"

"Sure can." He leads me to a spot a little farther along the wall. We both peer over and hear the singing at once. It drifts toward us from the conical tents below. It's so strange to hear it. No one has sung on Skye for as long as any of us have been alive.

"Oh. That's not going to go down well," Donal says.

I spot Murdina and Mór—Cray's mother and sister—putting up one of the final tents, along with Finn, their healer. All of the Riders work as they sing, preparing food and sharpening their spears. Some sing high and others low, their voices blending in perfect unity. The words are in the old language, so I don't know what they're saying, but I find myself nodding to the rhythm, subtly enough that Donal won't notice. The tribe's bulls and cows roam without a care and lounge on the spongy turf.

Maistreas Eilionoir appears—as I knew she would—storming around the outside of the wall from the direction of the Lower Gate. Donal and I watch in silence as she approaches the Bó Riders, gesturing wildly. Murdina walks up to her. We're too far away to hear what either of them says, but not long after, Murdina calls to her people, and the singing comes to an abrupt end. Satisfied, Maistreas Eilionoir nods, then leaves in the same direction she came from.

"It's a pity, really," says Donal. "It wasn't doing any harm."

I turn my head toward him. "Do you really think that?" I ask. I've never heard anyone question something un*dúth* before.

Donal raps his knuckles on the hard stone wall. "It sounded quite nice to me. . . ." he says. "The problem with tradition is that it can be dangerously stubborn. But what do I know? I am but a mere worker Wasp."

Below us, the Bó Riders continue their tasks in silence. At the far end of the camp, one of the tents opens and Cray steps out. He rubs his hands over his face and makes his way to the communal fire. My body breaks out in hot sweat. I feel itchy all over.

"You all right, lad?" Donal asks me. "You've gone pale."

"What? Yes, I'm fine."

He knocks my chin with his fist. "If it's the Inglish army you're worried about, that's perfectly normal, you know?"

"It's not that." I glance at the Bó Riders again. At Cray.

"Whatever it is, you can always talk to me about it."

His kindness is unbearable. And he's wrong; I could never tell him the truth.

"I have to go," I say. I turn and slump down the stone steps before he can question me further.

When I reach the bottom, a small group of children rushes past me, chasing one another. Their laughter rings through the enclave like an evil taunt. What if Cray told someone about what

I did? What if my clan finds out? It was easier to forget about him while I was with the Raasay islanders, but now that I'm back and he's so close . . .

The sword at my waist starts to hum, the sound louder than ever. When I picked it back up this morning, its glow was almost nonexistent, so I gave it some of my blood right away. Now it already wants more. I can't keep on doing this forever. I need to speak to the Badhbh, ask if there's another way to keep the sword strong.

I half-walk, half-jog to his bothan, but when I get there, the door is ajar and the windows are open. I enter without knocking, already knowing what I'm going to find: the bothan is empty and the Badhbh is gone.

He's abandoned us. That *diachdaidh* coward! I bet he's run into hiding, like he always does. I wonder how long it's been since he left. His things were packed the last time I came here—was he already planning on leaving? I should have known as soon as I saw the bag. First Agatha, and now the Badhbh. I don't suppose . . . Could her disappearance have something to do with him?

The humming from my sword grows more insistent. With the Badhbh gone, my weapon contains the only magic left in the enclave, and I'm the only person who can prevent it from fading. There's a tightness in my chest that I try my best to ignore. I owe it to my people to keep the sword strong.

I draw the blade, which lights up the room with its soft pink glow. Feeding it blood is no longer enough. To make it truly powerful, I'm going to have to invoke new magic; that much is clear to me now. It may be the only way to protect my clan.

Before I change my mind, I slice the top of my thumb—a deeper cut than I've done before—and hold it against the flat edge of the blade. I take a breath.

"*Sahcarà om rioht liuf,*" I say, remembering the First Incantation as if the words are still in the air from when the Badhbh last spoke them. At the same time, I will the blood to increase the sword's strength—pouring all that I am into the command, as the Badhbh instructed. I give the blade more than my blood; I feed it all of my shame and self-loathing and regret.

The sword is hungry, sucking more and more of me into its depths. The rush is addictive and intense, and it's hard to tear my thumb away.

Afterward, I feel light-headed and sick, but the incantation worked: the blade glows fiercer than it has since the battle with the *sgàilean*. It fizzes with new power. I slip the sword back into its scabbard and rip off a piece of bed cloth to wrap around my thumb. Then I creep out of the bothan, shaking away the niggling voice that reminds me what the Badhbh once warned: that blood magic is the darkest of all magics—and the most likely to corrupt.

Agatha

THE SOLDIERS WHO BROUGHT US HERE MAKE ME STAND in the middle of the room. More soldiers come in with something heavy made of wood. It has wheels that squeak. They put it next to me and the Badhbh man and it is tall up to the ceiling. A rope hangs from the top piece of wood. At the end of the rope is a circle loop. I don't know what it's for that circle loop or why they brought it here.

"You're making a big mistake," says the Badhbh man. "Where is the king? I demand to speak with King Edmund."

The doors open again and someone says in a loud voice, "Pray silence for His Royal Majesty King Edmund and Her Royal Modesty Lady Beatrice."

Everyone is quiet and more soldiers come in. This time they are carrying a big chair made of wood. A very grumpy man is sitting on it. He's wearing armor all over his body. It makes creak noises when his legs swing. Only his hands and face are not armor. He is very old that man. I know it because of the wrinkles. The soldiers in the room stand up straight when they see him. I don't do that because why should I?

A lady comes into the room as well. She is the only Ingland lady here. Her clothes are green and I like them because they are pretty. Next to her is a very funny thing which is a pig. It is a big one and a fat one. It walks next to the lady and makes an oink sound. The lady looks at me quick and then looks away.

The soldiers carry the old man to the corner of the room away from us. The chair is a special one because the sides are big cats with pointy ears. They are not real cats. They were made with wood. It must be nice to sit on that special chair. The soldiers put it down and stand around it. The ones in front kneel down so the old man can see. Then the soldiers pull out their swords and point them at me and the Badhbh man.

"Two Scotians in my palace . . ." says the old man. His voice is scrapes and horrible. He said "*my* palace" which means he is King Edmund. I am clever to think of that. "I never thought I would see the day when I would allow your type through my doors. You're lucky to still be alive, of course; my orders are to have all Scotians killed on sight. The only reason you are still breathing is out of respect for my new friend here." He points to Konge Grímr. "He wished to be present for your execution, girl. And I thought, perhaps I would like to witness it myself. So here we are. Wine!"

A man comes up to him with a big gold cup and a jug. He pours red liquid from the jug into the cup. The man drinks some of it, then nods and gives the cup to the Ingland king. King Edmund raises the gold cup into the air.

"A toast: to the first Scotian killing of many. To new friend-ships and the eradication of old enemies."

The Ingland king raises the cup to his mouth but before he can drink the Badhbh man shouts, "I am not your enemy." King Edmund lowers the cup. "I brought the girl to you as proof," says the Badhbh man. "Do what you want with her, but spare my life. I can tell you exactly where the Skye clans live, all about their defenses and—"

"No!" I shout at the Badhbh man. "You shouldn't—tell them those things. You're a—a b-bad man." I am all hot inside. I try to kick him with my foot but the soldiers pull me back.

"Silence, both of you," says King Edmund. "As grateful as I am for the girl, I am afraid you are too dangerous to let live—espe-cially if you are as powerful as the girl claims. I don't trust any Scotian, so the country of your birth has already condemned you."

"Perhaps we should not be so hasty." It is Konge Grímr who says that. King Edmund does not look happy. "Any power he has is being blocked by the restraints, just as you claimed it would be, so where is the harm in keeping him alive a little longer to gain what use we can out of him?"

There is a chain that connects Konge Grímr to the boy next to him. I didn't see that chain before.

"As long as he is alive, he is a threat," says King Edmund. "All Scotians are a threat. I don't know how you and your people are still alive," he says to me and the Badhbh man. "My sol-diers went to the farthest reaches of Scotia and reported back that everyone was dead. Wherever you were hiding, however you deceived them, I am about to rectify that error: your people will be extinguished. And you are about to be the first of them to die."

He waves his hand at the soldiers next to us, and one of them does a winding lever which makes the rope loop go down. When it is lower, he holds the rope in his hands.

"Which first, Your Majesty?" he asks to the king.

"It bothers me not," says King Edmund. He takes a big gulp from his gold cup and then licks his lips. His tongue is long and wet.

I have to do something. I am trying to think of a clever plan to run away and escape but it is too hard because the soldiers are holding me and the swords are pointing.

"Do the man first," says the Ingland lady in the pretty clothes.

King Edmund looks surprised when she says it. "Lady Beatrice," he says without looking at her. "I did not expect you to have an opinion on the matter."

"He is the more dangerous of the two. I do not feel comfortable in his presence, Your Majesty," says the woman who must be Lady Beatrice.

"Very well," says King Edmund, and he waves his hand again. He's always doing that waving.

"No, no!" says the Badhbh man. He pulls at the bracelets hard and shouts loud because of the hurt. A soldier pulls the Badhbh man's arms behind his back so he can't try to take off the bracelets anymore. Then the one with the rope stands in front of us. He smells yuck like bad armpits. He puts the rope loop over the Badhbh man's head. Oh. It is a rope for killing. I saw the elders do that to a goat once. It was not nice to watch it. They pulled the goat up into the tree by its neck, and its legs went kicking. It died that goat. It was before I knew how to do talking to animals but I know it was scared because I saw it. Now the Badhbh man is going to be killed with the rope and then I am going to be killed too.

"Wait," says the Badhbh man. "Please. I'll do anything. I could be valuable to you. I'll help you defeat the Skye clans."

It makes me want to hit him and hurt him so much when he says that.

The smelly-armpit soldier does not listen to him or stop. He does the rope tight around the Badhbh man's neck and then winds the lever again. The rope goes up and the Badhbh man goes up with it. His neck strains long and there is veins. Bulging ones. The smelly soldier winds higher and more. The Badhbh is standing on his tippy-toes now.

What's that? There is a sound on the other side of the room like an animal coughing. It is a person. Everyone looks at him. The soldier stops doing the winding. It is one of the people next to King Edmund doing the coughing. He does the sound again and again, and his face goes red and purple. His hands grab at his neck. He cannot breathe. He falls onto the ground on his knees, then on his side. His mouth is foam around it and his eyes are red. He is dying. I don't know why.

"Impossible," says King Edmund. His eyes are wide scared ones like the goat I remembered. He looks at the dying man and then at the gold cup in his hand. He throws the cup on the floor. The liquid does a dark red puddle. Oh. The dying man is the one who drank some of the King Edmund's drink. The king puts his hands to his throat. "I have been betrayed," he says. His breathing is choky whistles. "How have you done this?" he asks the Badhbh man.

The Badhbh man is still standing on his toes. "Wasn't . . .
me. . . ." he says in a strangle way.

People start shouting. Lots of the soldiers run to help King
Edmund. He starts to cough. Someone turns the man on the floor
onto his back. He isn't moving. Konge Grímr shakes the boy with
the chain. "What's happening? Tell me what's happening!" he says.

"The king has been poisoned!" shouts the soldier next to King
Edmund. "There are traitors in our midst!" The soldiers in the
room are panic. Some of them turn their swords toward the deamhain. My heart is going bump bump bump with all the thumping.

Konge Grímr shouts something loud in his language. He
shouts it to the other deamhain in the room. I do not know what
the words mean but when he says it, all the bad happens. The
deamhain move at the same time. They grab at the Inglish soldiers
and push them and hit them. The Inglish soldiers try to stop them
but the deamhain are too fast and too good at the fighting. They
take the Inglish soldiers' swords. The deamhain by the doors shut
them and lock them so no one can leave. Then there is killing
and nasty. Oh oh. I do not like it and I scream very loud. It is all
around me and horrible. I don't know what to do. The soldiers that
were holding me are gone but there is nowhere for me to run or
hide. Everywhere is dying people and fighting trouble.

King Edmund falls from his chair with a big crash. His wrinkle
face is purple and his eyes are big bulges. He crawls toward me
and the Badhbh man like a snake going through the grass. His
armor makes more clank sounds.

The Badhbh man spins on his toes next to me. His hands pull
at the rope on his neck. I don't want to help him because he is so

mean, but I have to do it because I am kind. I go to the lever that the smelly-armpit soldier used and try to turn it. It is stuck. I can't do it. Maybe it is locked.

A soldier sees what I am doing and runs toward me but a deamhain woman cuts him with a sword before he gets to me. He falls to the ground and is dead.

King Edmund is still crawling like the snake toward us. He is slower now and there is foam out of his mouth. He raises his hand up toward the Badhbh man.

"Howww . . . ?" he says in a croak sound. He thinks it was the Badhbh man who made the poison drink.

Lady Beatrice steps through the fighting people. The fat pig follows her. She kneels down next to King Edmund and lifts his head.

"My wife," King Edmund says to her.

"Before you die, there's something important I need you to know," she says. She leans in close and says in a whisper voice, "It was me."

Sigrid

IT'S THE MOST SCRAGGIN PLACE I'VE EVER SEEN, AND sure as muck I've seen plenty of harsk places since leavin my own rotten shack back in Norveg. It only took a couple of days to find it. From my rememberin of King Edmund's map, Caerlisle is the biggest town in the north of Ingland, which is why I thought of goin there. It sure is a bulkin place. Maybe it was nice a thousand moons ago, but evrythin's crumblin and broken now. Most of the buildins haven't got no rooves, and plenty are fallen down or over-taken by plants and vines. Looks like there used to be neat paths made of stones, but now giant tree roots burst outta them, knockin the stones in all directions. Praps we were wrong comin here. It doesn't look like no one lives here no more.

Somethin clatters to our left. Eydis stops walkin. Her whole body tenses beneath us.

"It's just a rat," I say, spottin it scurryin along the top of one of the buildins. It's not *just a rat*, though; it's the most bulkin rat I ever saw. Here's hopin there isn't too many of them rattlin around this muckdump.

Eydis carries on walkin.

"What should we do?" I ask Mal-Rakki. "There's no one here."

"I wouldn't be so sure. . . ." he replies.

No sooner has he said it, someone walks out in front of us. She's a long way up the broken path and just stands there, not movin. Eydis slows right down. Mal-Rakki's hand hovers over the handle of his sword. There's a dagger in my boot, but I don't pull it out just yet.

As we get closer, we see the person is a kidlin, a speck younger than what I am. She's holdin a stick carved to a point and there's a blowpipe and some darts hangin at her waist. Her face is grim as hell and she don't look none too friendly. Two lines of mud run from her eyes to her chin like thick tears.

I open my mouth to speak to her, but the blink I do, she bolts. I click for Eydis to chase after her. It could be a trap, but what choice have we got? We haven't got time for bein cautious. We need these people's help and we need it now—the two kings' army could already be marchin.

We turn a corner in time to see the girl disappearin left at the end of the next path, but when we get to that junction, she's nowhere in sight.

"I've got a bad feeling about this," ses Mal-Rakki, drawin his sword.

"Me too," I admit. "Praps we should turn back?"

There's a speedin *fwoosh!* followed by the sound of splittin wood. That little *kvillótt* threw her skittin stick at us. Mighty good job Mal-Rakki saw it comin quick enough to smash it midair before it could jab us rancid.

I jump down off of Eydis.

"I'm goin after her," I say.

"I'll circle around in case she tries to escape," Mal-Rakki replies.

We're a team now, me and Mal-Rakki. The sound of Eydis's hooves fades away, only to be replaced by the harsk huffs of my own breathin.

I spot the girl scramblin off the roof where she threw the stick. She sees me comin and tries to run, but I'm faster than what she is and soon catch up with her. I dive and tackle her to the ground. She lets out a gruff humph as her chin scrapes the ground. She's tryin to get her hams on the darts at her waist, but I'm not lettin none of that nasty happen. I spin her onto her back and pin both of her arms to the ground. She spits at me but misses. I bare my nashers and then knee her in the stomach. It's not a thumpin one, just hard enough to make sure she knows she doesn't wanna mess with me. A couple of tears trickle outta her eyes. She's lookin hek battered and a little scared. Good.

"Where people?" I ask her. "I want speak leader. Where?"

"Sable," she ses to me. "Sable."

"What's *Sable*?" That word wasn't in Granpa's foreign-tongue book.

The girl struggles under my grip. I give her stogg another bunt with my knee in case she's started to forget who's in charge here.

"Sable's our leader," she ses. "I'll take you to her."

"Good. Yes. Good."

A high-pitched squeak interrupts our yappin. It's another of those bulk rats, sniffin around a few spits from where we are. When the girl sees it, her eyes go gapin, like she's more scared of the rat than she is of me.

"Get off!" she ses.

The rat creeps closer, its piercin red eyes bulgin outta its face like two blisterberries. Its front teeth hang over its mouth, yellow as sourmilk.

"I'm serious," ses the girl. "We gotta get away! If it bites us, we're dead."

I pull her up, keepin hold of her arms and twistin them behind her back. The rat runs at us, bolder than what I thought it'd be, but the girl kicks it as soon as it's near. I'm too busy gawpin at the rat to notice the girl's scraggin foot as it swings all the way back, slammin its heel into my shin.

I yell and let go of her arms. She scarpers quickspit around the nearest buildin.

"*Skítr,*" I swear. "Filthy little weasel."

I chase her around the corner and see her runnin bangsmack into Eydis and Mal-Rakki. She hasn't got a flea's chance in a thunderstorm of escapin now. Mal-Rakki leaps off of Eydis and blocks her way.

"I think it's time you started behaving," he ses.

THE GIRL LEADS US TO A BUILDIN SHE CALLS THE Warehouse. It's not tall like the king's palace, but it's hek bulkin all the same. And skittin, of course, like evrythin else in this cracked town. She ses this is where we'll find Sable and that she's the one we wanna talk to. We haven't seen no one else while we've been trompin, even though we've passed hek loads of buildins. When I ask the girl how many people still live here, she replies by sayin "Lots," but Øden only knows what the skit that's sposed to mean.

Mal-Rakki is walkin with the girl. He's not exactly holdin her hostage, but his sword is drawn so the girl knows she shouldn't have no foolish ideas about tryin to escape. I'm back ridin Eydis. Mal-Rakki said that'd be best in case I've gotta make a swift exit, though I'm not plannin on fleein without him.

We enter the Warehouse through the space where the doors used to hang. It's just a shattered gap now, a whale's mouth suckin us into its belly.

Inside it's dark. It smells of pig farts and picked scabs. Water drips through holes in the ceilin, makin splashes what echo all around us.

"Well, this is a chirpin place," I say.

Mal-Rakki doesn't say nothin in reply, cuz he's already spotted the woman at the other end of room. She's sittin on a big chair what hek near swallows her up. Her elbows rest on the chair's puffed-up sides.

"You shouldn't have come here," she ses. Her voice is low and weary, as if she's tired of life and evryone in it. The sound of it fills the room and echoes from wall to wall.

Mal-Rakki clears his throat. I'm fine for him to do the talkin. Like he said, he's used to rallyin folk in support of him, and he speaks the foreign tongue a hek lot better than I do.

"My name is Mal-Rakki," he ses to the woman, "and this is Sigrid." He makes a show of puttin his sword back into its sheath.

"The girl here is not a prisoner. You're free to go, child." The girl looks at him like she doesn't quite believe it's true, then scampers away, outta the Warehouse. It's just us and the woman now. Mal-Rakki carries on creepin slugs toward her. Eydis follows, one hoof at a time.

"That's close enough," ses the woman. She's got the same mud tears down her face as what the girl had. Her hair is tied up, but a few scraggin strands stick out here and there. Her clothes are old and ripped. She isn't neither young nor old. Just gaunt.

"You're Sable?" asks Mal-Rakki. "The leader of this town?"

"My name's Sable, yes. As for whether I'm a leader . . . I suppose I'm as close as you'll find in these parts." The chair she's sittin on is bulgin with some sorta stuffin and is covered in a dirty pink material. It probly looked nice at one time, but now its grimed, and bits of fluff are stickin out in all directions. Sable turns her attention to me. "Nice horse. I've not seen one of them in a long time." She licks her lips. "Such things are . . . extremely valuable around here."

"You no touch her," I say, showin all of my teeth.

"Believe me, if I was gonna take her, I would've done so already. You were lucky to make it this far. There are plenty of people here who would've snatched her from beneath you without you even having the chance to gasp."

I'm startin to get jitters now. Somethin doesn't feel right. Maybe we should leave while we still can.

"How many people live here?" asks Mal-Rakki.

"You're from Norveg," ses Sable, ignorin his question. I guess she knows from the ink on our faces. "You're a long way from home."

"We are," ses Mal-Rakki. "We need your help. And I believe we may be able to help you in return."

"You can't help us," Sable ses. "I know about the army and I know you Norvegians are a part of it. We've got nothing here, so whatever you were sent for, you can forget it. King Edmund has taken enough from us already."

"We not sent by him," I say. "We hate King Edmund. And Norveg king."

Sable lifts an eyebrow but doesn't say nothin.

At that moment, one of the bulk skittin rats scuttles outta the darkness and races toward us. Without hardly a blink, Sable pulls out a blowpipe from somewhere in the folds of her clothes and shoots a dart at it. It strikes the rat right behind its ear. With a shrieksqueak, the rat slows to a crawl and then flops onto its side. Its nashers bite down on nothin for a few slow sniffs, and then it's still. The dart remains in its head, stickin up at the ceilin.

Sable stands and walks across to the rat. Me and Mal-Rakki watch her without speakin. She plucks the dart from the rat's head. It makes a squelch noise as it comes out. Then she picks up the rat by its tail and holds the dart for us to see.

"Tragic, really," she ses. "Killed by its own venom . . ."

"What do you mean?" asks Mal-Rakki.

"It's what we use on the tips of our darts: venom from the rats. If you've not encountered death-rats before, you should count yourself lucky."

"Why?" I ask.

"They're the reason this town is so cursed. One of the reasons, anyway." Sable drifts back to her battered chair and lowers herself into it. She tosses the death-rat onto the floor in fronta her, where it lands with a splat. "They devoured our crops, raided our homes, killed our babies. I suggest you never let one close enough to bite you."

"I didn't know rats could be venomous," ses Mal-Rakki.

"We have His Royal Heartless to thank for that."

"King Edmund?"

"They came from Scotia, from the rats he infected with the plague. The disease King Edmund sent killed off the Scotians but not the rats. With each generation they grew larger, and the sickness inside them turned into a deadly poison. When food became scarce, they ventured south and became *our* plague. They have their uses, though." She spins the dart between her fingers, then nudges the dead rat with her boot. "This one must've come up from the sewers below. . . . Evil critters."

"Why else this town so bad?" I ask. She told us the rats were only one of the reasons.

Sable sniffs, then wipes her snouter with her fist. "You said you could help us," she ses to Mal-Rakki, ignorin me completely.

"Yes," ses Mal-Rakki. He tells her about King Edmund and Konge Grímr's plan, although it seems like she knows most of that already. Then he explains how he's taken over Norveg and made an alliance with the Skye clans, and that they're lookin for more people to join their resistance. She's surprised to hear there's people alive in Scotia.

"But we're not a threat to either of the kings," she says. "Why would we risk our lives helping you?"

"Because King Edmund is a tyrant," ses Mal-Rakki. "And over-throwing him is the right thing to do."

Sable laughs, a hollow sound. "It's a lot harder to do the 'right thing' when you don't know where your next meal is coming from. Survival is all that matters now. Survival at whatever the cost."

"It doesn't have to be that way. This is your chance to reclaim your lives. Your king abandoned you, sentenced you to a life of squalor. It's time to oppose him for all the wrongs he's done."

"You've got no idea about the wrongs he's done us," ses Sable. She doesn't exactly shout it, but there's smokin fire in her words.

"Then stand up to him. Show him that you are willing to fight. Not just to survive, but for what's right; for a better future for your children."

Sable sucks in her cheeks, makin her look more skeleton than human. "I wish I could, believe me. But . . . it's not as simple as that."

"Why not?" asks Mal-Rakki. "What happened here, Sable?"

She doesn't answer. I'm not sure what I make of this woman. Maybe cuz she reminds me too much of the rotten kerl who tried boilin me last time I was in these parts. Although, bein fair, even though there's hunger in her eyes, it's not aimed in our direction. And it's true what she said, that she coulda shot a dart in both our necks with two puffs from her pipe the moment we walked in, and that woulda been the end of us. So she can't be that bad.

"We bring food," I say, thinkin maybe it's time I started tryin to help convince her.

"Yes," ses Mal-Rakki, like he forgot about that part. He unloads the sacks from Eydis's side and lays them on the ground. Sable stays in her chair, but her peepers keep flickin to the sacks. "We brought as much as we could carry, but there's plenty more we'd be willing to offer in exchange for your support. If we were allies, both the Clans of Skye and the Free Nation of Norveg would do everything in their power to help you establish a better life for yourselves. You could even relocate to Scotia, should you wish — away from the oppression of the death-rats."

"I appreciate you bringing food," ses Sable. "But the people of this town have lost too much already. They've got no desire to go to war. And they have no real reason to trust you."

"Perhaps I could speak to them myself?" ses Mal-Rakki. "Help convince them?"

"What makes you think they're not already listening? In a place like this, you're always being watched. . . ."

Takin their cue from her, people start revealin themselves from all the nooks and holes of the Warehouse, where they've been hidin. There's maybe thirty people, all holdin pointy sticks like what the girl had, and all of them women. They've got the same two mud lines runnin down from their eyes, crackin their faces.

"Where the skit are all the men?" I ask Mal-Rakki. It's like in the king's palace, sept the other way around, cuz down there it was only men and no women.

Mal-Rakki's wonderin the same thing and asks it to Sable.

"This town has a dark past," she ses. "The men who once lived here . . . They were—"

Fhwiss! Her sentence is interrupted by the sound of a flyin dart. I don't know who fired it or where it went. I'm scannin the whole room, but there isn't no one lookin guilty. The women are all glancin around them too, like they're expectin somethin bad's about to happen.

Mal-Rakki's hand reaches toward Eydis to steady himself. His face is pale. Stickin outta the side of his neck is the dart. The veins next to it pulse and twinge.

"Sigrid . . ." he mutters, then he collapses bangsmack onto the ground.

Agatha

ALL OF THE INGLISH SOLDIERS IN THE ROOM ARE DEAD. Some of the deamhain are dead too. King Edmund is not moving. His face is frozen purple crying. I think he is dead as well.

I am not dead. I am alive. I run to the doors to escape, but a deamhan grabs me on my arm before I get there.

"Not so fast," she says. She has a big ferret tattoo across her face. It starts at one ear and goes over her nose all the way to the other ear. It is dark blue with red hair and a red eye. She holds me tight so I cannot move.

One of the other deamhain cuts the rope above the Badhbh man's head. He falls onto his knees and does loud breathing. The deamhan pulls him to his feet and ties his hands behind his back.

Lady Beatrice is next to King Edmund's body. She stands up. There are spots of blood on her clothes. All around, the deamhain are holding the Inglish soldiers' swords. The boy with the chain brings Konge Grímr forward. He tells him where to step over the bodies. Konge Grímr is smiling.

"Lady Beatrice," he says when he is near her.

"Konge Grímr," she replies.

"What do we do with you, I wonder?" Konge Grímr moves his head around and the antlers on his crown go swish. I stare at the place where his eyes are not.

"I very much suggest you let me live," says Lady Beatrice. "You will have a difficult time explaining what occurred here without me."

"Who poisoned the king?" Konge Grímr asks her.

"I do not know," she says.

She's lying. It was her. I heard her say it.

"I will spare your life, but only if you cooperate with me entirely," says Konge Grímr. "You must corroborate my story that King Edmund was murdered by the Scotian mage and that this whole massacre was his doing."

"I can agree to that," says Lady Beatrice. "But in return, you will support my claim as queen of Ingland and suppress any who oppose me."

Konge Grímr does a deep laugh. "And why would I do that?"

"Because if you don't, you risk losing everything," says Lady Beatrice. "King Edmund is heirless, so the battle for the throne will be messy and unpredictable. Why risk having a new king who may be . . . less accommodating than I?"

"You've seen what my warriors are capable of," says Konge Grímr. "They were weaponless yet managed to disarm and defeat a room full of the king's best soldiers. We could storm this palace and take it for our own."

"And then what?" Lady Beatrice asks. "The people wouldn't follow you, and neither would the army."

"But they'll follow you? A woman? I've seen how women are treated in this country."

"I have more allies than you might suppose."

Konge Grímr is quiet and he is thinking. "Okay," he says. "But the attack on Scotia must still proceed as planned. That is nonnegotiable."

Lady Beatrice sucks in her cheeks and then looks at me and the Badhbh man. "You can have the army, but I get the prisoners."

"What do you care for them?"

"I don't know how they achieved it, but I believe they are responsible for my husband's death. He always claimed he would be killed by a Scotian, as you know. I want to see them slowly rot."

"No," says Konge Grímr. "The girl must be executed. Her crimes against me are too great."

"That may be so, but she is still young. I will not allow my first act as queen to be the murder of a child. Trust me, she will be placed in our darkest cell and will never again see the light of day."

Konge Grímr does a sniff like he's trying to smell where I am. "Fine, you can have the girl, but I want the mage."

Lady Beatrice stares at him and does not blink.

"Deal."

Konge Grímr finds her hand and shakes it.

"To our new alliance," he says.

"May it be prosperous for us both," says Lady Beatrice.

~

I AM BACK IN THE PRISON CAGE. THE BRACELETS ON MY wrists sting the worst ever. I scratch around the needles but it only makes the itches worse. The Badhbh man is not here. They didn't bring him back with me and I don't know where he is.

The wildwolf growled when the deamhan pushed me in but it doesn't bark anymore. I am careful not to walk too close to where it is. I need a clever plan to escape but I cannot think of one. I am too hungry, that is why. All I can think of is the hungry. A woman came and threw some bits in but it was hard bread and vegetable skin peels. That is not nice food. I ate it anyway but it was not enough. I shout for more food and I say please lots of times but no one comes.

This is the one, two, third prison room I have been in. First it was the one in the mountain in Norveg, then the bothan in our enclave that the Raasay people put me in, and now this one the third one. Why are people always putting me in the prison rooms? I am a nice person. Don't they know that?

I know what will cheer me up and it is Milkwort. I didn't want the Badhbh man to see him, but now that he's gone, Milkwort can come out of my pocket. I feed him some of the vegetable skin peels that I saved. He likes them and is happy. Even yuck vegetable peel is nice when you are a vole.

Me and Milkwort play a game. It doesn't have a name, the game. We made it up. It is a fun one. How it works is I put Milkwort on the ground next to me and close my eyes. Milkwort has to try and reach my head without me feeling him. If I know where he is, I am the winner. We play it six times. I am the winner two times and Milkwort is the winner four times. He is very good at that game.

The wildwolf watches us from where it sits in the shadows. Sometimes its lips twitch to show its teeth and it licks them. It is hungry I think, like me.

I won't let you eat me, I say to it.

The wildwolf starts barking at me then because it doesn't want me talking in its head. Milkwort doesn't like the noisy so he runs back into my pocket. The Badhbh man said my talking to animals can be more powerful if I make my mind be calm and do the thoughts like arrows. I don't know what he means when he said that but I try it. I think of the shape of an arrow in my head when I speak.

We can help each other, I say.

The wildwolf is still barking and my head starts to hurt. I don't think I did it right. I do a big breath to make inside my head more calm and try again.

Stop barking, I say. This time I imagine the arrow hitting the wildwolf fast. The wildwolf stops barking and starts growling instead. Maybe the arrow worked a little bit that time.

Do you want to escape? I say. That makes the growling stop. It does want to escape. It says one thing to me and that is *How?* I tell it that I do not know how, but if it helps me, then I will help it. Two brains are better than one, after all. That's what Maistreas Eilionoir says.

It thinks for a long time. Its nose is twitching.

There is a stone, it tells me. *It is loose.*

What stone? I ask. *Where?*

It bashes its head into the wall. One of the stones wibbles. It *is* loose! The wildwolf says it has hit it lots of times but it can't get it out. It thinks maybe I can do it with my fingers in the cracks.

Come closer, the wildwolf says.

I don't know. I want to look at the stone closer, but maybe the wildwolf is doing the trick on me.

I'll come, I say. *But you stand over there.* I point to the faraway side.

The wildwolf moves away like I say, but it could still jump to where the stone is and get me. I have to be brave. I take small steps forward. The wildwolf watches me with its different-color eyes. My heart is beating hard thumps. I bend down onto my knees and poke the stone. It is a good loose one. If I scrape out the sandy bits then maybe it will come out.

There is a growling behind me. I turn quick. The wildwolf walked around while I wasn't looking and now I am trapped. Its lips go up to show its teeth. It bends its legs like it's going to pounce.

Don't you dare! I say. The wildwolf snaps its jaws twice. *If you hurt me, you will never be free.*

It stops and has a think. It doesn't pounce but it doesn't move away either.

I carry on doing the scraping with my fingers. I look back at the wildwolf lots of times to make sure it doesn't come any closer. Then the stone wiggles more and I pull it out. I did it! It is dark through the hole and hard to see what's there.

We need to make the hole bigger, I say to the wildwolf.

As I turn around, the wildwolf runs at me. *No!* I put my hands in front of my face. There is a crash and a crack noise. The wildwolf's head hits into the stones around the gap. It does it again. Oh. It is not getting me, it is helping.

We work together. The wildwolf does the banging and I do the scraping. Milkwort helps too by being the lookout because we are making a lot of noise. Soon the hole is big enough for me to climb through but the wildwolf leaps in first. The chain around its neck pulls tight. The wildwolf barks lots of angry ones. It comes back into the prison cage and stands in front of the hole. I ask it to move please so I can go through. It shows all of its teeth and tells me no. It thinks I won't come back. I promise that I will.

The vole, it says.

What does it mean, the vole?

Leave the vole, it says.

Leave Milkwort? I can't do that. It is too dangerous and Milkwort is my friend. The wildwolf snaps its jaws and tells me that is the only way it will let me past.

I don't know. I ask Milkwort what he thinks. He says he will stay.

Okay, I will be quick, I say to him. He is a very brave vole.

The wildwolf says if I do not come back or if Milkwort tries to run away, it will eat him. It is horrible that wildwolf. I say good-bye to Milkwort and promise I will come back soon. The wildwolf moves out of my way and I climb through the hole.

On the other side of the wall there is another wall. That is not good. There's a gap in between the walls that is a tunnel. I have to walk sideways along it. Cobwebs stick on my face and I do not like it. Also it is dusty and my nose does sneezes.

The first way I go, there is a door but it is locked. That is the dead end. I go the other way and it is drip dripping and smells of pond. I go past lots of prison cages that are similar to my one. I can see into them because of the tiny holes in the walls. I think this tunnel is for doing spying on prisoners. It is a clever spy tunnel.

I turn a corner and then I am going a different way. There are strange animal noises in this part. Some sound like barking and others are shrieking and clicking and strange. The prison rooms here are different because they have walls all the way around them. There are still holes for spying, though. The first rooms have lots of wildwolves inside. They are running around and barking. The next rooms have cages in and the wildwolves are locked up, but they are not wildwolves anymore. They have been changed. Some have eyes that are too big or too many legs and some have long teeth and fat bodies and horns growing out of their heads. I cannot look at them for a long time because they are not right and it makes my tummy sick.

Someone is talking. They are in the next room. I walk to it and look through the spy holes. The room is a circle shape and the walls are black bricks. When I see the people I do a gasp. Konge Grímr is in the room and so is the Badhbh man. There are other deamhain there too. One of them looks at the wall where I am. I think she heard the gasp I did. It is the deamhan woman who grabbed me when I tried to run away. She has the ferret tattoo on her face. I hold my breath so I don't make one tiny sound. The ferret woman looks back at Konge Grímr.

"We have an understanding, correct?" Konge Grímr says.

"Yes," says the Badhbh man. He is on his knees and there are cuts and bruises on his face. His eyes are sad ones.

"Louder," says Konge Grímr.

"Yes," the Badhbh man says again.

"Good, then let us begin."

"Are you sure this is a good idea, Your Supremacy?" says the deamhan with the ferret face. Her hair is dark color with braids and beads. I wonder if my hair would be pretty with beads and braids in it.

"Hold your tongue, Erika," says Konge Grímr.

"Forgive me, Your Supremacy," says the deamhan who is called Erika. "I was merely going to suggest you try it on me first, in case something goes wrong."

"No," says Konge Grímr. "His power is not limitless. The more he makes, the weaker they will be. I want it to be the most powerful the world has ever known and obey only me. For that, there must only be one, and it must be mine. The Badhbh and I have been talking a great deal and we understand each other. He wants to live, whatever the cost. He has no loyalties, only fear. He is also aware that should he betray me, many years of the most brutal torture await him. Isn't that right?" The Badhbh man looks at the floor and doesn't say anything. "But if he does everything I ask, I will set him free. A simple arrangement." Konge Grímr nods at two of the deamhain, who pull the Badhbh man onto his feet. Then Konge Grímr holds out his arms. "Let us begin," he says.

The Badhbh man does a deep breath and then tells the deamhain to hold the king's wrists tight and not let go. I don't know why he said to do that. The Ingland boy moves away. He can't go far because of the chain. One of the other deamhain picks up a bucket and pours water on the fires. All of them do sizzles and go out, except for the one in front of Konge Grímr. There is a shadow on the wall now. Konge Grímr's shadow. Spike antlers come out of its head.

"These need to be removed before I can proceed any further," says the Badhbh man. He holds up the bracelets on his wrists.

"Do it," says Konge Grímr to the deamhain.

Erika the ferret face deamhan says something in her language. Konge Grímr shouts at her. She bows her head and points her sword at the back of the Badhbh man's neck.

"One wrong move and you'll regret it," she says.

I look at her mouth when she speaks. It is not nice to have dark blue ink covering her lips and her tongue.

Another deamhan walks to the Badhbh man and takes off his bracelets. He has a special key that does it. I need that key for mine. As soon as the bracelets are off, the black in the Badhbh man's veins goes away. He moves his fingers slowly and looks at Konge Grímr. Two more deamhain draw their swords and point them at him.

The Badhbh man is sweaty on his head. He looks at the swords, then swallows and says some words. I do not know those words because they are old-language ones I think. When he says them, Konge Grímr's shadow grows big and bigger, all the way to the ceiling.

"For the next part, I require a blade," says the Badhbh man. He points to one of the deamhain's swords. "May I?"

"No, you may not," says the deamhan.

"I have explained how this works," says the Badhbh man.

"Give it to him," says Konge Grímr.

The deamhan hands it over but he is not happy. Erika ferret face presses her sword closer into the back of the Badhbh man's neck. He does a shudder in his shoulders.

"This may hurt," the Badhbh man says to Konge Grímr.

"Good," says Konge Grímr. "Then I'll know it's working."

The Badhbh man holds the sword tighter. He is staring at it hard and breathing loud. More sweat is going down his face. He looks at Konge Grímr and then I know it. He is going to kill him! This is his chance. He was telling the truth when he said he had a plan, and this is the plan now.

Do it, I think. *Do it!* I hold my breath in my mouth and push my hands into the wall. The Badhbh man does one more step closer to Konge Grímr and raises his sword. *Yes, do it now!*

But then the Badhbh man's hands wobble and he lowers the sword. He squeezes his eyes and then makes a small cut on the back of Konge Grímr's leg. That is not stopping him! I kick the wall with my foot. That was his chance and he didn't do it. He is a coward for not killing him.

Konge Grímr's blood runs down onto the big shadow.

"We also need Inglish blood, do we not?" says Konge Grímr. "To prevent it from attacking my new army."

The Badhbh man does a small nod.

"Use the boy," says Konge Grímr.

"What?" says the boy. "No, please."

A deamhan drags him over.

"Don't you want to help protect your people?" Konge Grímr

asks him. The boy nods. He looks like he is going to cry. "Then give the man your hand."

The boy holds out his hand and the Badhbh man cuts the tops of his fingers with the sword. He makes the boy press his hand onto Konge Grímr's shadow. The shadow grows again.

The Badhbh man says more strange words and then he slices the sword fast across the floor by Konge Grímr's heels.

There is a sound like horrible whispers that gets louder and louder. Konge Grímr's shadow rips away from his body and goes in fast circles around the room. The antlers on its head make horrible shapes on all the walls.

It is a *sgàil*, and now it is free.

Sigrid

MAL-RAKKI'S BODY IS SLUMPED ON THE GROUND. I CAN'T leave him there, but I can't stay where I am neither.

"Run!" Sable shouts. "Get out of here."

Eydis already knows we gotta leave and makes for the way out, but before we get there, people come fallin through the holes in the ceilin on long ropes, yellin high-pitched cries. They're all women too, but they haven't got mud tears like Sable and the others; their mud goes horizontal across their eyes in one long smear.

Evrythin goes batcrazy as the two groups start fightin each other. *Fwiss! Fwoosh! Hwush!* Darts fly past me faster than I can see. Eydis is takin me one way then another, but there's always someone in our path, and their pointed sticks are lookin to stab us.

A woman swings down from the roof right next to me, and before I've got two blinks to react, she kicks me in my side and I tumble off of Eydis's back. My left foot gets tangled in the stirrup, so when Eydis bolts, she drags me with her. The ground scrapes my back and bashes my head. I kick and wrench my foot, tryin to get it out. Eydis rears up as three of the smeared-face women snatch hold of her reins. My foot slips free and I roll to one side, reaching for my dagger, but it's no longer there. It musta fallen outta my boot when I was bein dragged. What the skit do I do now? Swear to the high sky, if those women hurt Eydis . . .

Some filthy kerl comes runnin at me, her sharpened stick pointin. I get to my feet and prepare my stance, like what Granpa Halvor taught me. As the woman strikes, I twist outta the way and kick her in her chest, hard as a storm. She coughs and falls backward. That's her dealt with, but more women are comin. I don't wanna leave Eydis, nor Mal-Rakki neither, but if I don't get outta here quickspit, I'm gunna be caught as well, and then there won't be no hope for any of us. I grab the woman's stick and sprint to the side of the Warehouse. The wall is split, and one thump with my shoulder is enough to crack the wood and let me through. Then I'm outside and I'm runnin, fast as I can, I don't know where to.

Inside the Warehouse, the fight continues. Above the yells and the stompin, a horse whinnies in fear.

I'm sorry, Eydis . . . I'm sorry.

~

FROM WHERE I'M HIDIN UNDERNEATH AN UPTURNED cart, I watch as the women flee from the Warehouse. The ones who ambushed us lead Eydis away, with Mal-Rakki's body slumped over her saddle. The women walk speedy, pointin their sticks in all directions to make sure no one follows. Rot them all to hell for what they did. I wanna run at them and grab Eydis right outta their skittin hams, but I gotta be smarter than that.

First, I gotta follow them and see where they go. I wait until there's no chance of them seein me, then squirm out my hidin hole. I've still got the stick I picked up. Its sharp end glistens with somethin tacky. Venom.

"If you're thinking of trying to rescue them, I'd think again."

I spin around and Sable is there, like she knew where I was hidin and has been waitin for me to crawl out. I point the venom stick at her throat. She doesn't flinch none.

"You bad," I say. "You tell women attack." I'm so fiery I'm snortin gales.

"No," she ses, "that's not what happened. There are many different factions here, and I'm nothing but a mediator between them. It's not my job to keep them in check. The women who took your friend and your horse probably thought you were allies to King Edmund, the same as I did. It doesn't help that he's a man, of course, 'cos we're all mistrustful of them. There's been a truce between the factions for years, but there's nothing like the arrival of food to incite a new skirmish."

Food. She'd better mean the sacks we brought and not Eydis and Mal-Rakki.

"Where they take them?"

"I don't know, and I'm telling you now: you need to forget about them and leave. They're already dead."

"No," I say. I won't believe it. I lower the venom stick. "You wrong. I find them and I save them."

She shakes her head and watches me leave.

Stupid skittin grotweasel doesn't know nothin about nothin. And all that yappin has given the thieves the chance to get away.

Lucky for me, Eydis is still callin out hek brays, which gives me somethin to follow. She's a good girl; she knows I'll be lookin for her.

I sneak from corner to corner, keepin my gawpers wide for anyone who might be spyin, or any of those creepin death-rats, cuz I don't wanna be runnin into none of those neither.

The place they take Eydis and Mal-Rakki is a few slogs from the Warehouse. It's another bulkin buildin, only this one's got a proper roof over the top and better walls without cracks. I stand on my toes to peer in one of the windows. It's hard to see proper cuz there's sheets hangin on ropes what stretch from one side of the room to the other and back again. Mal-Rakki's slumped in one corner on a bunch of blankets, his arms and legs tied. His eyes are open, starin straight forward, and he isn't movin none. No, wait—his chest is driftin in and out a speck. He's still alive. I gotta get him outta there, but how in a thousand winters am I gunna do that?

I follow Eydis's whinnies and peer around the corner of the buildin. She's tied to a large tree, guarded by three women. The tree hasn't got no leaves, and its spiky branches prick the sky. The women all have venom sticks and hard faces. Isn't no gettin past them. Another two women are settin the hearth to light a fire and a third is sharpenin a knife on a special rock. It sparks evry time she draws it back. Eydis watches the knife on uneasy feet. She's right to be frettin: these rotfiends are plannin on eatin her. No way am I gunna let that happen. I need a distraction. Somethin big. There's only one thing I know for certain these people are scared of, but it might be the most hek foolin idea I've ever had.

I creep back to the Warehouse and slip inside. There isn't no one there no more. After killin the death-rat, Sable said they come from the sewers below. If there's a way for them to come up, then there's gotta be a way for me to get down. All I gotta do is find the rats and make them follow me somehow. Then I can lead them to the women, where they'll cause enough of a distraction for me to free Mal-Rakki and Eydis. That's the plan, anyways.

I cross over to where the rat came from and bash the floor with my stick, listenin for somewhere hollow soundin. Then I find it: in one corner, the floor is so moldy and rankdamp it's completely fallen through. When I jab it with the stick, the wood breaks away, revealin a dark space below. I drop a stone through the hole. A sniff later, there's a splash from below. So there's water down there. It sounded like the drop was quite far. Too far to jump without the risk of smashin my legs, that's for hek sure.

Lucky for me, the women who swung in and caused all the clutterflap left too quick to take their ropes with them. There's one a few spits from me, curled up like an adder's skin. I tie one end to the tufty pink chair, cuz it's the heaviest thing I can find, and drop the other end down the hole. Once the rope is secure, I wrap my legs around it and lower myself over the edge. It's tricky goin with the stick in one hand and not bein able to see nothin neither. The stench is so harsk it makes my eyes leak. I keep goin down, but then the chair above me shifts, joltin the rope. My legs unravel and I slip. The rope burns my hands. I don't know how far I've still got below me, but I can't hold on no more. I let go of the rope and fall.

Water splashes as I hit the ground, and pain jolts through my legs. Somethin sharp jabs my forearm. I'm all right, though; the drop wasn't far and I landed on my feet. Nothin's broken. Though I'm feelin hek woozy all in a sudden. I look down at my arm, and from the light shinin in from above, I can just about make out the rip in my sleeve. There's a scratch on my skin, tricklin blood. *Jarg!* I musta cut myself with the stick when I fell, and now the venom from its tip is causin havoc. A numbness creeps through my arm before seepin into the rest of my body. My eyes freeze wide open, so I see evrythin as I crash down into the water.

I can't move no part of my body. Not even my eyeflaps for blinkin. Lucky the water isn't deep and I landed on my side, otherwise I'd drown and no mistakin. The water stinks rotten as hell, like dog muck and sick breath.

I don't know how long I lie there before I hear them, but straightaways I know exactly what's comin. The sound is distant at first, nothin more than a soft scurryin, but it soon comes closer, turnin into a jumbled hellroar, full of desperate scratchin and evil squeaks. They can smell me, I reckon, and there isn't nothin I can do about it.

The death-rats are comin.

JAIME

THE RAASAY ISLANDERS' LONG-RANGE WEAPONS ARE EVEN more impressive than we'd been led to believe. They brought them here yesterday on three large boats, then gave us a demonstration of their power, which left us all standing in awe. Their launchers can fling metal spikes several hundred yards, they have catapults strong enough to hurl the mightiest boulders, and their enhanced crossbows can fire arrows more than three times the distance of ours.

The plan is to position them along the coastline between Skye and the mainland, using the channel as a protective moat; the water is our best line of defense. While the army is figuring out how to cross it, the Raasay islanders will rain carnage on them, which should hopefully cause enough destruction to force a retreat.

The leaders of the Skye clans were so impressed with the weapons, they want to make more, but the Raasay islanders refuse to reveal their secrets. They won't let anyone close to the weapons and insist they're the only ones allowed to fire them. It's ridiculous. How are we supposed to cooperate if they won't even trust us? Instead, they've agreed to make more themselves, and we've been tasked with supplying them with the materials.

The dispute about the weapons was the first of many. The Raasay islanders also wanted to put out offerings to the Forgotten Gods (which was never going to be allowed), they expected separate accommodation for each of their small family units, and it nearly came to blows when they were told they would only be served two meals a day as opposed to their accustomed three. The air has changed since their arrival; it crackles with the threat of an approaching storm.

"Little tighter, lad," says Donal.

I increase my grip on the log that Donal is currently sawing. He grinds the saw in a mesmerizing rhythm, releasing peaty dust into the air. I hold my breath so I don't breathe it in.

We've been sawing logs at the Wasps' creation site all afternoon. When Donal asked if I wanted to help him out today, I jumped at the opportunity. I'm glad for the distraction, and it's good to feel like I'm contributing. My role is to hold the logs while Donal does the hard work, but he insists what I'm doing is just as important. He frequently stops to tell me what a good job I'm doing and what a great team we make. He's right, I suppose; we've been working fast and focused, and now have an impressive mountain of logs to show for it.

"Hi, stranger," says a voice behind me.

Donal stops sawing, and I release my grip on the log. As I turn, I come face-to-face with the wet nose of a Highland bull.

A tongue whips out and licks me across my mouth. I cry out, trip over my own legs, and topple backward, smacking my backside on the ground.

From on top of her bull, Mór laughs so hard she snorts. "Got you good!" she says. The sound of the sawing must have masked their approach. I pick myself up and brush off some of the dirt. Mór's bull, Duilleag, lets out a deep moo.

"What are you doing here?" I ask. I risk a quick glance to check that Cray isn't about to join her.

"You could at least pretend you're pleased to see me."

"I am," I say. "Sorry. Hi. This is Donal. Donal, this is Mór." I like Mór and we've been through a lot together, but not knowing what Cray's told her about me is making me feel on edge.

Donal stands up and puts out his hand to hold her fist. "Nice to meet you," he says.

Mór doesn't know what she's supposed to do, so slaps his palm with her own.

"Same to you," she says. "Nice place you have here."

"It's temporary, but it's a home," says Donal, taking the opportunity to stretch his back.

"I've come for the wood," says Mór. "Duilleag and I volunteered to take it to the Raasay islanders."

"Great. Shall I load you up, then?" asks Donal.

"Please. Fill the sidebags as full as they'll go—Duilleag is even stronger than he looks." She gives her bull an affectionate pat.

Donal and I start transferring the logs into the two bags that hang at Duilleag's sides.

"We thought you would've come to see us by now," Mór says

to me, sweeping her hand through her cropped blond hair.

"Sorry, I've been busy. . . ." I give a weak gesture to the pile of logs.

"The whole tribe's here. Murdina, Hendry, Cray . . . Everyone's been asking after you."

I focus on what I'm doing and don't meet her eyes.

"There was some debate at first over whether coming here was the best move," she continues, "but Cray convinced us. You know what he's like; he basically kept arguing until everyone agreed. You should join us for evening meal."

I glance over at Donal, who turns aside, discovering a sudden need to examine the log in his hands. From the way I'm blushing, he probably thinks I'm attracted to Mór. How much simpler that would be.

"Maybe," I say.

"Well, don't sound *too* enthusiastic about it. . . . Right, that's probably as many as we can squeeze in for now. I'll be back for more soon."

Without saying goodbye, she spins Duilleag around, and the bull gallops through the enclave in the direction of the Lower Gate.

"She was fun," says Donal once she's gone.

"Yes," I say, picking up another log for him to saw.

"And the boy she spoke about—Cray. He's the one I met in the sickboth after you returned from the mainland, right?"

"That's right," I say, although my throat appears to have turned into bark.

"He seemed nice too."

My heart is really pounding now. I don't say anything else in case my voice gives me away.

Donal looks at me, his eyes slightly narrowed as if trying to figure me out. "It gets easier, you know," he says after a while.

"What does?"

"Life." He gives me a sympathetic smile while using the blunt edge of the saw to scratch the back of his neck. "But only if you let it."

I DON'T JOIN THE BÓ RIDERS FOR EVENING MEAL. I NEVER had any intention of joining them. I told Cray I didn't want to see him again and I meant it.

I hold out my bowl, and the Stewer fills it right to the brim with a thick, steaming liquid. Thanks to the abundance of food brought by the other Skye clans, evening meal has become most people's favorite time of the day. Tonight's stew gives off sharp wafts of pungent fish mixed with wild garlic and fresh rosemary.

The tables are crammed. Each of the clans has already laid claim to certain seats, meaning no one really mixes. Every mealtime, I scan the tables, hoping I might spot Agatha sitting on one of the long benches, smiling, but I'm always disappointed. It's been over a week now since she disappeared. Despite all the people, the enclave feels empty without her.

From what I can gather, the Badhbh fled around the same time as Agatha did, but no one saw him leave either. It feels like too much of a coincidence to me. I spoke to Maistreas Eilionoir, and she agreed to send someone to the Badhbh's hut in Scotia in search of them both. I don't trust the Badhbh in the slightest, so it's certainly possible he took Agatha, but what I can't figure out is why.

I slide onto one of the benches beside Aileen. The hulking arm of the man next to me digs into my side.

"Hi," I say to Aileen.

"Hi," she replies. "You okay?"

"Yes," I say. "You?"

"Fine," she says.

That's how most of our conversations have been recently—brief and full of half lies. I scoop a large spoonful of stew into my mouth. It scalds my tongue, making my eyes sting. I quickly swallow, and it leaves a hot lump in my throat.

"Mind if I join you two?" says Donal, followed by an "Excuse me, ladies" as he squeezes in between two women on the bench opposite us. "I hope Jaime's been telling you what an expert log-chopper he makes."

"Not exactly," says Aileen. "He hasn't told me much about anything recently."

I ignore her jibe.

"Well, he should, because he's great," says Donal, pointing his spoon at me. "How's your day been, Aileen?"

"It's been strange, to be honest." She peers over her shoulder to check no one's listening. "The Raasay islanders let us take one of their boats out again but insisted on two of their people joining us. We were successful in terms of the haul—the fish were practically jumping into our laps"—she lowers her voice to a whisper—"but I never feel that comfortable on their boats. The Raasay people kept commenting on everything we did, as if we were fools and they knew better."

"There's a strange atmosphere, I agree, but it's complicated," I say. "Did you know they used to live on this island?"

Donal shakes his head and looks surprised, but Aileen nods. "I heard that," she says, "but wasn't sure if it was true."

"They were here first," I say, "but our ancestors forced them to leave. All of the hostility between our clans stems from our ancestors deciding that the Raasay islanders' beliefs are wrong, and they therefore have no right to live on this island."

"What did you just say?" asks a voice from behind me. I turn to find a large man looming over me.

I gape at him. He reeks of the sea. "Pardon?" I say.

"You just said our beliefs are wrong and we have no right to live on this island."

"No, I didn't. . . . I—"

"Don't tell me I'm lying; I heard you with my own ears."

"That's not what he meant," says Donal, getting to his feet.

"Stay out of this," says the man, jabbing his finger at Donal before turning back to me. "You're the boy who came to our enclave. I watched as you stood in front of everyone and promised we could set up a new life for ourselves here, but now I overhear you saying the exact opposite. Do you take us for fools?"

Everyone at our table has fallen silent. Other Raasay islanders drift closer to see what's happening.

"That's not—I wasn't—" I try to explain, but the Raasay man is no longer listening.

"This boy is a liar," he proclaims to everyone around him, "which means his clan is using us."

"That's not true," says Aileen.

"It's been obvious ever since we arrived: you don't respect us any more than your ancestors did, and I'm sick of it."

I'm starting to panic, so I instinctively reach for my sword to calm myself down. The man sees what I'm doing and his eyes narrow, thinking I'm about to draw my weapon. He yanks me from the bench by the top of my shirt.

"No, I wasn't—" I say.

"Let him go," says Donal, leaping over the table and seizing the man's arm.

The Raasay man flings me to the floor and squares up to Donal. "You want a fight, big guy?" he asks.

Donal raises his hands in peace. "That's not going to solve anything. This is all just a misunderstanding—"

"Yeah," shouts someone from my table, "but it wasn't a misunderstanding when his chiefs let the deamhain into our enclave to massacre us."

Donal turns to see who spoke, which is when the Raasay man swings the first punch. It collides with Donal's jaw, sending him sprawling back onto the table. Bowls and mugs scatter, spilling their contents. More people start to shout and then the table next to ours is upturned. I watch from the ground, wide-eyed, as more people throw themselves into the fray. Donal disappears among the throng of bodies. He only has one hand to defend himself with—if his injured one gets knocked, it could reopen the wound. Every now and then, his face appears between flailing arms and twisting bodies as he tries to pull people apart and put an end to the fight.

Then something changes. Donal's eyes open wide, and a flash of pain cracks across his face. He's sliding, falling to the ground. No one else has noticed—no one's seen what's happened. I get up and run at the group, pushing people aside, desperate to get through.

"Stop!" I scream. "You have to stop. He's hurt!"

My frantic yells pierce the crowd, and it drifts apart, revealing Donal, slumped forward with his head on his chest.

I skid onto my knees by his side. "Donal. What happened?"

He lifts his head, and his face is pale, awash with sweat.

"I think he got me, lad," he says.

He leans back to reveal the knife in his stomach. Blood blossoms out of it in widening circles.

"Why is no one doing anything?" I shout at the silent crowd. "Someone help him!"

A man rushes forward and examines the wound. "I'm an Herbist," he says. "I'll do what I can." He removes the knife, then barks some orders, causing a small group to dash in the direction of the sickboth.

"You're going to be okay," I say to Donal as I lower his head onto the grass. "You're the bird with nine lives, remember?"

He grits his teeth as he tries to smile. "I think maybe I used them all up this time," he says.

I pick up one of his mighty hands and hold it in my own.

"Stay with me," I say. "Stay with me."

This is all too familiar. Last time, it was Sigrid's hand I was holding, our wrists bound as my blood brought her back to life. But the Badhbh was there then. Now he's gone, and I don't know how to do it. I'm not strong enough—

I have to try.

I let go of Donal's hand and pick up the bloodied knife by his side. I steady the blade over my palm, ready to slice open my scar, but before I have the chance, Donal reaches up and grabs my wrist. His head gives the slightest shake.

"I can save you," I say, almost choking on the words in my desperation for them to be true. "I watched the Badhbh. I know how to do it."

"No," says Donal, his voice growing weaker.

"But you're not allowed to die. I won't let you." Hot tears sting my eyes.

"You're a good lad," he whispers. His eyelids slowly close and then drift apart again. "Just be yourself, you hear me? Yourself is enough."

He lets go of my wrist, and his hand falls to the ground. A glaze mists his eyes. I look to the Herbist, but I already know what he is going to say.

He shakes his head. "There was nothing I could do."

I lean back on my hands and roar at the sky.

Agatha

I GO INTO THE TUNNEL LOTS OF TIMES BECAUSE I AM digging a hole. It is at the far-away end where the ground is softer. I have to use my hands and it makes my nails dirty black with the mud. I don't know where the hole will go but hopefully it will make me be escaped.

The wildwolf in my prison cage makes me leave Milkwort behind when I go. I always come back so the wildwolf should trust me now. It is a girl wildwolf and her name is Gray. I chose that name for her. She did not want to have a name but I said she had to have one. Otherwise what would I call her? I asked her if she wanted to be called Hairy or Sharp-Teeth or Wolfy and she said no and no and no. They are all good names for a wildwolf. In the end I decided that Gray is best because that is the color of her fur. Some of her fur is white but Gray-and-White is too long to be a good name. Gray does the listening when I'm in the tunnel in case someone comes.

I haven't seen the Badhbh man or Konge Grímr again. Maybe they left to go to Skye already. Konge Grímr has the giant shadow thing as well now and that is the worst. I have to stop him. That is why I have to escape quick and dig faster.

Sometimes when I am in the tunnel, I talk to the other wild-wolves. I go to where their prison rooms are and speak to them from the other side of the wall. They are very loud and crazy because when they smell me they want to eat me. It is hard to make them listen. I practice making my mind calm and doing my words like arrows fast into their heads. I am getting better at it. Sometimes all the wildwolves hear me at the same time, but the only thing they say is that they do not want to be locked up and let us out.

I tried to talk to the broken wildwolves too—the ones with the horns and legs and eyes where they shouldn't have them— but they didn't reply. All I heard was hisses and nasty. I don't think they can talk those ones. When I told Gray about them she did lots of growls and was angry, but it's not my fault. She is growly a lot and I mean it.

Gray is barking. That means someone's coming. I do a quick run and climb through the wall. There are footsteps I can hear. I put the stones back in the hole as fast as I can, so the person won't know I got out. It looks a bit wiggledy so Gray stands in front of it to hide it. When I turn around, the person there is a big surprise. It is the Lady Beatrice and her big fat pig.

"Hello, Agatha," she says.

I do not say hello back. She told Konge Grímr that she wants me to rot in this prison cage so she is not a nice one.

Gray barks at the pig but then she gets bored and stops. The pig shoves its nose through the bars. I move back so it doesn't get me.

"It's okay; he's only saying hello," says Lady Beatrice. "This is Prin."

I give Prin a stroke on his nose and he oinks. He is a funny pig.

"I'm sorry it has taken me this long to visit you. Things have been . . . difficult since my husband's demise."

I do not know what is a *demise* but I nod my head to agree.

"How are you?" she asks me. I don't know why she is pretending to be nice.

"I don't like it in here," I say.

Lady Beatrice nods. Then there is something strange, which is tears go down her face.

"Why are you—crying?" I ask to her. I am the one who is locked up in the prison cage.

She wipes her cheeks. "The girl—Sigrid—did she make it to Skye? Did she find you?"

How does she know Sigrid? "Yes," I say, but then I think maybe I shouldn't have said it.

"There is hope," Lady Beatrice says next. She looks far away when she says it.

"You killed—King Edmund," I say.

Her eyes go wider when she hears me say that. I think she will tell me it is not true but she says, "Yes. I did."

"Why?" I ask.

She opens her mouth and then closes it again. "It's complicated," she says. "Lots of reasons. So many reasons. You being one of them."

"Me?"

"Yes, you."

"What about m-me?"

"He was about to have you killed, and I didn't want that to happen."

I don't know what to say to that.

"He was wrong," I say.

"About what?" says Lady Beatrice.

"About it being a p-person from—Scotia who—killed him. He was wrong, because it was y-you."

Lady Beatrice nods her head and passes something through the bars. It is wrapped in thick paper. "I brought you this," she says.

I unwrap it and it is food! There is meat and not-stale bread and an apple and softcake. I am so happy to have the food! But maybe it is a trick. . . . Maybe Lady Beatrice is trying to poison me like she poisoned her husband.

"It's safe, I promise you," says Lady Beatrice.

She rips off a small piece of softcake and puts it in her mouth. That means there isn't poison. I pick up the rest of the softcake and take a big bite. It is the best one I ever ate. My mouth is full and there is crumbs.

Gray starts barking. She can smell the meat and wants it. Lady Beatrice looks around worried that someone might come. I throw the piece of meat to Gray to make her quiet. She gobbles it up and doesn't even say thank you. I didn't want to eat that meat anyway. It could be deer meat or goat meat or bird meat or a different animal meat. I don't want to eat any of those animals anymore. I will be like Milkwort and only eat vegetables and bread and cake.

"W-why are you being kind and giving me food?" I ask to Lady Beatrice.

She looks at me and bites her lip.

"Because . . . King Edmund wasn't wrong. He *was* killed by a Scotian, but he spent his life not realizing there was one right by his side." She swallows and moves her hair so it is away from her face. "I am from Scotia, Agatha. Just like you."

It's not possible. She can't be from Scotia. She is an Ingland lady.

"You c-can't be," I say. I am a whole head of confuse.

"I almost forgot, I brought this." She reaches into her clothes and takes out a key. I stand up excited.

"Is that the k-key to open the door?" I ask.

"I'm afraid not. No one seems to know what happened to the cell keys after King Edmund died. My guess is that they were taken by Aldric—the king's adviser—but he's denying it. He doesn't trust me, and I don't trust him. . . . I did find this one, though, which will open the restraints on your wrists."

"Oh, that is good. Yes—do that . . . please."

I hold my arms through the bars and Lady Beatrice uses the key to clunk off the bracelets. The needle coming out of my wrist is the best feeling ever. The black in my blood veins goes away and is gone. I scratch hard on where the bracelets were because of the itching. It is so good to have them off. Maybe Lady Beatrice is a nice one after all.

"Konge Grímr has left," she says. "He has taken the Badhbh and King Edmund's army and is now marching full speed toward Scotia. I've spent the past few days trying to find a way to recall them, but my efforts have come to nothing. I've sent word to my allies in the north of Ingland, but they are no match for what's heading their way."

"But you are the q-queen now," I say. "The army has to do what—you say."

"I hoped they would, but that's not the case. When I told Konge Grímr he could have the army, I thought there'd be a way for me to regain control of it later. But the military is a force unto itself." Prin the pig starts sniffling Lady Beatrice's hand. She scratches behind his ears while she talks. "Many people in this city don't respect women the way they should, Agatha. Perhaps you've noticed that?"

I nod my head to say yes.

"I've spent the past fifteen years trying to change that, secretly creating allies both in the palace and throughout the country, silently laying the foundations to one day succeed the king and change this country for the better. But your arrival forced me to put the final stages of my plan into action before everything was in place. My supporters welcomed my announcement as queen, but there are still those who challenge my claim to the throne— including the leaders of the military." She holds on to one of the prison cage bars and squeezes it. "They don't believe a woman has what it takes to rule a country, so swore themselves to Konge Grímr, thinking they're carrying out King Edmund's dying wish by going ahead with the invasion. It's a disaster. The only way to ensure I remained queen was to let them leave, but I fear the price I paid was too high. . . .

"I'm rambling." She shakes her head a little bit. "Sorry, I can tell I'm confusing you. Perhaps I need to start from the beginning."

Yes, she is confusing me. She uses too many long words. "You said you were from—Scotia," I say.

"That's right, Agatha. Not just Scotia, I'm from Skye. I'm Clann-a-Tuath, just like you. We're from the same clan. We're family."

"But h-how?" That can't be a true one. "If you're from Skye then w-why are you—here?"

Lady Beatrice does a deep breath. "It was a long time ago. . . . You've heard of King Edmund's plague, I presume? The one that killed nearly everyone in Scotia?"

"Yes," I say. Everyone knows about that.

"For many years no one from Ingland went near the country. Rumors of walking corpses and killer shadows kept everyone at bay. But about twenty years ago, King Edmund's paranoia grew worse. He was no longer convinced his plague was a success, so he sent troops north of the border to check. After crossing into Scotia, the soldiers split up across the country. The expedition that went to the Western Isles was led by a man named Garrick. He was an honorable man—and a handsome one—and what he found . . . was me.

"It's so strange to be saying this. I've kept this secret my whole life . . . but I know I can trust you, Agatha."

I nod. She can trust me. I nod a very lot. I want to know more.

"I was only young at the time, barely eighteen. Garrick was a couple of years older. I was a Seal, and the day we met, I'd traveled to the south of the island with some of the other Seals to trade vegetables with Clann-na-Bruthaich. The others left to organize the trade, leaving me to keep watch over the boat. I was staring at the mainland when I saw fire flickering on the shoreline. I thought I'd spotted the first sign of Scotians since before the plague and couldn't resist finding out more. I should have waited for the other Seals to return, but I was reckless and impatient. If there was a discovery to be made, I wanted to be the one to make it. I snuck away in the boat and rowed myself to the mainland.

"As soon as I reached the shore, I knew I'd made a terrible mistake. The men were drunk and definitely not Scotian. I tried to sneak away, but one of them spotted me, and then the whole troop set upon me. They dragged me from my boat and started bullying answers out of me—who I was and where I'd come from. They were prodding me and touching me and leering in all kinds of horrible ways. Then Garrick showed up and told his men to let me go. The soldiers refused. They said I was nothing but filthy Scotian scum and they could do what they wanted with me. Garrick disagreed, and they started to argue. Seizing my opportunity, I drew one of the soldier's swords, but then things spiraled out of control. Luckily, Garrick chose to fight on my side, against his own men. Before long, we were the only ones left alive.

"I wouldn't say we fell in love straight away, but our lives were immediately bound by the trauma we'd experienced. We were also both curious to find out how the other lived—it was the first time anyone from our countries had met in over twenty years, after all. Over the next five days, I stayed on the mainland and the connection between us grew ever stronger. When he told me he had to return to Ingland before King Edmund sent more soldiers in search of him, I knew I had to go too. There was no other option for me.

Don't misunderstand me—I loved my clan with all my heart, and I still do—but I wanted to see more of the world, and this was my opportunity to do that. Also, I wanted to be with Garrick."

Lady Beatrice does a little pause and looks around her. I shuffle closer to say keep talking. She swallows and then says, "Garrick agreed to keep the existence of the Skye clans a secret. He told King Edmund there was no one living on the Western Isles and that his men had been set upon by wild animals. The king trusted Garrick and believed the lies. He was finally convinced no Scotians were left alive and never sent anyone back there.

"At first I hated life in the palace. I found it claustrophobic and loud, and they treat women like we're inferior beings. To make matters worse, I couldn't speak in public for years in case someone recognized my accent. Garrick had to teach me how to talk like an Inglish woman and how to behave like one too. I missed Skye terribly and thought about returning many times, but by this point I was in love. Garrick and I married—a tradition that is still allowed here—and he was the kindest husband. We laughed every day. The morning I discovered I was pregnant was the happiest of my life."

She smiles, but it is a sad one.

"Why are you s-sad?" I ask.

Lady Beatrice looks up at the ceiling "This is all too much. It's bringing everything back." She does a breath, then looks at me again. "King Edmund found out about the baby and wanted it for himself. He'd had several wives over the years, but none of them had borne him a child. He decided the answer was to marry a woman who was already pregnant and pretend the child was his own. The woman he chose was me. He had Garrick imprisoned and then forced me to marry him, threatening to torture Garrick if I disobeyed. What could I do? I was trapped. My only solace was the child growing inside of me. Not long after, I gave birth to the most beautiful baby in the world."

There is so much in the story she has told me. My head is full of it.

"What h-happened to the baby?" I ask.

"She grew up to be one of the strongest and most courageous girls I have ever met," says the Lady Beatrice.

"Oh," I say. "Does she live here too?"

"She's standing right in front of me."

I look behind me. There isn't anyone standing in front of her. Only me.

Oh. Oh. I am the baby. I am the girl. I am standing in front of her.

"It's—me?" I say.

"It is," says the Lady Beatrice. There are tears on her cheeks again. "You are my daughter, Agatha. I am your mother."

Sigrid

THE SKAP CRITTERS ARE ALL AROUND ME, FILLIN UP THE sewer with their deathly squeaks. I'm still lyin in the wet, still can't move no part of me to get away. The death-rats' noses are sniffin, and their big berry eyes catch what little light there is down here. They're tryin to work out whether I'm a threat or whether they can eat me easy. I'm sure not a threat right now, with the venom from that skittin stick freezin me solid.

The death-rats were the reason I came down here, but I wasn't plannin on my body bein locked solid when they arrived. They creep a few steps closer, movin as one. Their squealin is really batterin my ears now. I answer their shrieks with ones of my own. At least my voice is still workin. I scream and hiss, which makes them jolt back a speck, but it won't hold them off for long.

Come on, body, move. Move! Or you're gunna be rat chew and no mistakin.

The fingers on my left hand twitch, or was that just my imaginin? No, they're movin. They curl around the stick what's still in my palm. The death-rats sneak forward again, their nashers twitchin. I've got just enough movement in my hand now to jerk the stick a little. I do it in the direction of the nearest death-rats. The arm's still full of numb, so the swings are weak and erratic. A couple of rats scutter back, but the rest hold their ground, starin fire at me. I jolt again and again, willin my body back to life with all my might. A little more feelin returns to my arm—enough for me to swing the stick behind my back and above my head, threatenin the rats I can't see not to come closer. The venom is tricklin outta my face now too. I can blink and twist my neck, but my feet and my other arm are still stuck deep.

The rope's danglin where I left it. I heave myself toward it usin my one good arm, stoppin evry two blinks to swing the stick wild at any death-rats what get too close.

There's enough strength in me now to creak up onto my knees. My legs are comin back to life, though they're full of cramps and tingles. The arm I stabbed still hangs limp by my side. I'm gunna have to climb the rope with only one hand, and there isn't no way I can do that while still holdin the stick, meanin I gotta ditch my only weapon.

With one last swipe to keep them back, I throw the stick at the nearest rats and pull myself off the ground. My good arm burns; I gotta be quick. I wrap my flailin legs around the rope and heave myself a little higher. The rats are squeakin thunder, hek skapped that their chew's escapin. They dash to the sides of the sewer and start crawlin up its walls, hopin to get to the top before I do. Lucky for me, the sides are steep, so they keep slidin back down.

I smash my teeth tight and ignore the pain, usin my knees to grip the rope and my hand to pull me up, one sniff at a time. I'm sweatin rivers from the strainin. The death-rats are climbin on top of each other in one big squirmin tangle. I try not to think about what'll happen if they reach the top first.

A painstakin heave later, I'm almost there. A couple of rats are already waitin, their noses pokin over the edge. I bash one with my fist and elbow another outta my way as I hurl myself through the hole. I haven't got no time to catch my breath. I get up and I run.

Or at least that's what I try to do; runnin isn't easy with my body still shakin and my bad arm flappin loose. I stumble more than once as my legs learn how to work again. I'm breathin so hard it's like a whole storm's puffin out of my yapper. The death-rats sprawl outta the hole after me. I haven't got no choice but to keep goin.

My thumpin footsteps echo around the cracked walls of the Warehouse. The buildin's exactly how I left it, only now I got a mad swarm of death-rats chasin me. In a cowcrap sorta way, that was kinda what I was hopin for.

Outside, the day is bright. I don't look back, just carry on runnin. Rememberin's easy for me, so I know which way to go. Left, right, left again, round the corner, past the tumblin wall. I risk a quick glance behind me, just to check. The death-rats are gainin.

I trip, not seein the cracked stone in fronta me until it's too late. I fall to the ground, grazin my knees. The rats sense their chance and come at me even faster. I get back up, scoldin my legs for bein so weak, and keep goin. I haven't got no time to brush away the dirt. I haven't got no time for nothin.

The slog to the buildin where Eydis and Mal-Rakki are feels like it takes forever, but at last it comes into view. Now comes the hardest part, where evrythin could go to hell and back.

Mighty Øden, be my guide. May it be your will.

It's been a long while since I prayed, but sure as mud I need some prayin now.

Between my own huffs and the death-rats' scutters, we're makin a hek lot of noise, so it's not surprisin that the women see us comin. The first to spot us shout out an alarm, then evryone rushes out of the buildin and climbs onto the roof. They must be thinkin it'll be easier to defend themselves up there. They're yellin curses and firin darts, but they're firin them at the rats, not me. It makes the death-rats hek fiery, and as I dash around the side of the buildin, they storm up the walls, onto the roof. I slip through the door. No one tries to stop me. I can't see what's happenin above, but it sounds like hek clutterflappin; just the distraction I need.

Mal-Rakki's alone, in the same corner he was in before. He's got a rag in his mouth what's stoppin him speakin, but he makes muffled sounds and nods his kog, which means the venom musta worn off. I run over and pull the rag outta his mouth.

"Sigrid," he ses.

"Still me," I reply, tuggin off the ropes what tie his hams and ankles.

"We need to get out of here," he ses next, like that might not of been my plan all along.

"I know," I say. "But first we gotta get Eydis. Let's go."

Mal-Rakki is still wobblin from the venom. He musta had

more in him than me, cuz my legs are almost back to normal now, and even the arm what got cut has started comin back to life. I put Mal-Rakki's hand on my shoulder and help him take his first steps across the room, then out the buildin and around the back to where Eydis was. The women and the rats are still wagin wars on the roof.

A thousand horns to Øden, Eydis is alive, tied to the tree, just as before. I wanna run to her, but I gotta be slow for Mal-Rakki's sake. When we're near, I wrap my arms around Eydis's neck and nuzzle in my head. It's only a quick hug, cuz that's all we've got time for.

"I was always gunna come back for you," I say to her. "You knew that, right?"

I untie the ropes quickspit and pull myself onto her back. As soon as Mal-Rakki's up too, Eydis bursts into a gallop, as eager to get away from this muckdump as we are. We leave the death-rats and the women still fightin, without them even knowin we've escaped.

Eydis stomps over the crumblin paths, sendin hek quakes through my teeth. We turn around one corner, then another. It's a diffrunt way from when we arrived, so I'm mainly guessin, but I think this is—

A woman steps out in front of us and holds up her hand. It's Sable. We're goin so fast we nearly crash straight into her. Eydis shudders to a halt. More women appear all around us on the broken rooftops. *In a place like this, you are always being watched. . . .*

"I'm impressed," Sable ses to me. "Let's talk some more, shall we?"

NOTHIN HERE IS QUITE WHAT IT SEEMS; THAT'S WHAT I'M discoverin. We're in a new buildin now, one what looked skittin from the outside, same as the others, but inside it's chirpin and warm. There are six beds down one side, made spick with patterned coverins. We sit down on mismatchin stools made outta scraps of wood and metal and decorated with engravins. A few women mill about the room. There's probly more watchin us from somewhere we don't know about — that seems to be their way here.

"You no eat us?" I ask once more, just to be sure.

Sable scoffs. "No, that doesn't happen here. Although there are pockets in bleaker parts of the north where people've been driven to such lows." She shakes off the scraggin overcoat she's been wearin and replaces it with a much nicer-lookin one. "We're fine with people believing the situation's the same here; we've worked hard to create an appearance of squalor. That's why we always meet newcomers in the Warehouse: to convince them we've got nothing worth taking. To an extent, it's not an illusion—we're a humble community, but we survive fine enough. Making the town look bleak and abandoned is an extra layer of protection."

"Protection against what?" asks Mal-Rakki.

Someone hands us each a cup of water. I glug mine down quickspit. I didn't realize I was so parched. Another woman gives me a piece of cloth to dry my hair and clothes, which are still damp from the sewer. I'm not smellin too perky neither.

"The question you should be asking is, protection against *who*?" ses Sable.

"King Edmund . . ." I answer.

Sable nods. "He's done more than just ignore the north. More than unleashing the rats that ended up devastating our livestock and our land. He's the main reason we're reluctant to help you. We challenged him once before, and it didn't end well."

"You're talking about your men?" ses Mal-Rakki. "What did King Edmund do to them?"

"You already know," Sable ses, gesturin around her at the room full of women.

"He kill them," I say. I can tell by the look on her face. That skittin sneaksnake. "Why?"

"When the rats first came, we asked for his help," ses Sable. "He refused, so we stopped supplying goods to the capital. Never defy a king—that's what we learned—especially one with an army. I suggest you pass that advice on to your allies. King Edmund crushed our rebellion by storming this town and killing every single one of our men. Fathers, brothers, grandfathers, teenagers . . . There hasn't been a grown man here for over six years." Her eyes flick toward Mal-Rakki. "Until you arrived."

"Surely that should make you more resolved to join our fight," ses Mal-Rakki. "Don't you want to avenge your fallen kin?"

Sable lets out a sapped sigh. "We thought that's what we wanted at first, but we never truly believed justice was possible. Our whole lives we've been told we're weak just because we're women. That's the way it's always been. It's the reason King Edmund let us live—because in his eyes we're *only* women. But we've grown strong. We've taught ourselves to be self-sufficient, how to use weapons, how to fight. It was only ever meant as a means of defense, though, in case the king's army returned. Our young boys are growing up, and we've always feared that King Edmund would come back for them one day. The idea of taking the fight to him . . . None of us would've ever considered it. Perhaps until today."

She looks at me, and I'm thinkin, *What the skap did I do?*

"That stunt you pulled with the death-rats, Sigrid . . . " she ses. "Well, you showed us just how much one person can achieve when she sets her mind to it. One girl, no less. Perhaps it's time we stopped cowering away, hoping everything's gonna turn out all right in the end."

"So you help us?" I ask.

Sable looks to one side and sucks in a bulkin breath, like she's strugglin between what her heart wants to do and what's gunna keep her safe.

The door to the buildin flies open, and a sweaty woman runs in. She doesn't bother closin the door. A harsk wind follows her.

"News from the south," she ses, like the words can't fall outta her yapper quick enough. "King Edmund's dead. She's done it: Lady Beatrice is queen."

What? That's *ríkka* news. The best!

Sable's mouth drops open. "No. Really? She always promised us she would, but I never thought it'd be possible."

"Lady Beatrice stop army!" I say. If she's queen now and King Edmund is dead, maybe there isn't gunna be no fightin after all.

The messenger woman shakes her head. "The army rebelled against her and is following Konge Grímr. They're already on the march."

Sable stands up, knockin over her stool, what clatters to the ground. "Call an emergency meeting of the faction leaders," she ses. "Change is coming, and I sure as hell wanna be a part of it. Spread the word for everyone to get prepared."

"Prepared for what?" asks the woman.

Sable's face is hard and fierce.

"For battle."

JAIME

"ONE OF OUR CLAN MEMBERS IS DEAD," SAYS MAISTREAS
Eilionoir, her voice sharp.

A light snow blows around her like a swarm of white flies.
Donal's body lies by her feet, uncovered, for everyone to see. His
clothes are stained with dark red circles. I want to look away, but
I can't stop staring. I've washed my hands so many times, but the
feel of his blood still clings to them, making them brittle and tight.
Aileen squeezes my arm. There are thousands of people here—
everyone from the Skye clans, as well as the Bó Riders and the
Raasay islanders. Everyone came.

"His name was Donal," Maistreas Eilionoir continues, "and
he was one of the most skilled and humble Wasps our clan has
ever known." She pauses to swipe her wispy hair across her forehead. "The man who committed this vile crime has been handed
over to the chiefs of Raasay. They wanted me to emphasize that
they in no way condone his behavior—he has been imprisoned
and will receive a just punishment in due course. As for the rest

of you: this is not the first disagreement to break out between us, but — if this alliance is to survive — it must be the last. That is all."

She signals to the grave diggers, who pick up their spades as the crowd starts to disperse. That's it? That's all she's going to say? It's not enough; Donal deserves more. I push my way forward with no real idea of what I'm about to do.

"Jaime, where are you going?" Aileen calls.

I reach the front and step onto the wooden block that Maistreas Eilionoir was just standing on.

"Wait," I say, but no one reacts. "Stop! I need you to listen." The people closest turn around, and it creates a ripple effect until everyone is facing me. Maistreas Eilionoir watches me with curiosity. I can do this. I spoke out once before; I can do it again. I reach for the handle of my sword. The slightest touch is enough for its power to simmer through me. "Donal was my friend," I say. "He was a great, kind man and . . ."

"We can't hear you," shouts someone from the back.

I suck in a lungful of frozen air. "Donal was a great man," I say again, louder this time. "His death can't be for nothing. I won't accept that. I can't. He . . . well, he died defending me. It was just a stupid misunderstanding. We're so . . ." I'm grasping for words, the right ones lost in the haze of my mind. There's a sea of faces staring at me, pitying me, expecting me to fail. I was wrong to think I could do this.

Then I see Cray, standing in the middle of the crowd. Despite what happened the last time we were together, he smiles at me. It's only a small smile, but it's enough. I raise my head and address the crowd once again. "We're all so desperate to find one another's faults," I say. "Why is that? Yes, we may have different opinions and beliefs, but when it comes down to it, it's the same blood that runs through our veins. We're all human; we're all the same. And right now, all we have is each other.

"There's an army marching toward us *at this very moment*, and the only way we can defeat it is if we stand together. What's the point of fighting for this world if it's one full of hatred and judgment? I mean, if some people want to sing, why can't we just let them?" Maistreas Eilionoir's eyes bore into me. I shift my body to avoid her stare. "That's what Donal believed, and it's what I believe too. It doesn't cause anyone suffering or pain, so who's to say if it's right or wrong? Why can't we just let each other live how we want to live and be who we want to be?"

Tears spring to my eyes, and—for the first time in my life—I'm not afraid to let them fall. I almost laugh as their wetness streaks my cheeks. "Look at me. I'm crying, and I don't care. In my clan, crying is not *dùth*—it's a sign of weakness—but right now it is my strength. I want you to see my pain. It's the pain of someone hurting because we're all too damn stubborn to get along.

"Donal is gone, yes, and nothing is going to bring him back, but we can honor his memory by learning from his death: that intolerance and mistrust are not the way forward. We have to find a way to accept our differences and treat each other with respect. Otherwise we'll never truly be united. I . . . ." I sigh and lower my head. "That's all I have to say."

I step down from the wooden block and wipe the tears from my cheeks. My hands are trembling. Snowflakes land on my cloak and sink away into nothing. I half-expect Maistreas Eilionoir to pull me aside and reprimand me, but she says nothing. As I make my way back through the throng of bodies, more and more people start patting me on the back.

"That was some speech," says Aileen once I reach her.

I shrug. "I don't know. . . ."

Aileen puts her arm around my shoulders and pulls me into her. "I'm so sorry, Jaime. I know he was your friend."

He was more than my friend. He was one of the few people who truly liked me just for being me.

We watch in silence as the grave diggers set to work. Once the hole is deep enough, Donal's body is lowered into it. It's not him anymore. It's a cold husk, devoid of everything that made him great. How can someone be so present one moment, then so entirely gone the next?

Maistreas Eilionoir throws the first handful of soil into the grave.

"Caidil gu bràth," she says. *Sleep forever with peace.*

Other clan members do the same, and then the Raasay islanders and Bó Riders follow suit. I'm sure they usually bury their dead in a different way, but right now they're choosing to respect our tradition. It's a start.

I'm one of the last to scatter soil. The snow has melted into the ground, making the earth mushy and cold. When I go to throw the soil, it clings to my fingers. I wipe my hand on the leg of my trousers.

"Goodbye, Donal," I say under my breath. *"Caidil gu bràth."*

AILEEN AND I WALK TOWARD OUR BOTHAN IN SILENCE. On the way, night crashes down on us with brutal swiftness. It's stopped snowing but is still bitterly cold. The sword at my hip gives off a probing hum, but I ignore it. Donal stopped me from using blood magic for a reason; I'd be disrespecting him if I cut myself now.

All I want to do is hide in my bed and shut out the world, but I know deep down that's not what's best for me.

"Which way to the meeting tree?" I ask Aileen.

"Over there." She points. "Why?"

"Let's take a detour."

I let her lead me, because my sense of direction is essentially nonexistent, and the meeting tree soon comes into view—what's left of it, anyway, after I set it on fire when the *sgàilean* were first unleashed. By accident. Not that that stops the stab of guilt I feel whenever I see it. It's mangled and charred, a pathetic remnant of its former grandeur.

"So, do you want to tell me what we're doing here?" Aileen asks.

"We're going to climb it," I say.

Aileen's face scrunches in confusion. To prove I'm serious, I put one foot on the trunk and reach for the lowest branch. The branch snaps, showering us in slushy snow. I shake it out of my hair and give Aileen a sheepish look, then try another branch, testing it first this time. It takes my weight, and I haul myself up. I keep climbing, higher and higher, navigating the fractured branches as they moan and creak. A fine sooty grime comes away with every hold so that by the time I reach the top, my whole body is covered in black.

Aileen follows me up and plonks herself onto the branch next to me with an exaggerated sigh.

"Please tell me there was a good reason I just covered myself in this crap," she says, reaching across to wipe her hand over my face.

"Hey!" I say, twisting my body away from her, but she doesn't let off her assault. "Seriously, stop it, I'm going to fall!"

"I'll stop once my hands are clean!" she says, laughing.

I laugh too, batting her away with one hand while keeping a firm hold on the tree with the other.

Then I stop. So does Aileen. After all that's happened today, laughing doesn't feel in any way appropriate. The silence that follows is mountainous.

"I'm sorry for how I've been with you recently," I say, my voice faint.

"No need to apologize. We've all been through a lot."

"That doesn't make it right."

Aileen looks at me, waiting for me to say more. I continue staring straight ahead.

"Are you okay, Jaime?" she asks me.

My instinct is to lie, to tell her yes like I usually do, but I can't keep on lying forever.

"Not really. . . ." I say. Tears prickle my eyes. Aileen's already seen me cry once today, so I don't suppose it matters if she sees it again. The sobs come, violent and strong.

"Jaime . . . Hey, hey. It's okay, Jaime. It's okay."

She wraps her arm around me in an awkward side hug, and I weep into her shoulder.

"What happened to Donal wasn't your fault," she says. "There's nothing you could have done."

"I know. . . . I know. . . ." I sit back up and rub the tears away with my filthy hands. "It's not just that."

"Then what? I know there's something. Talk to me, Jaime."

My shallow breaths are sucked away by the darkness. I spin the bracelet Aileen gave me around my wrist and remember Donal's final words: *Just be yourself. Yourself is enough.*

"Something happened," I say. Aileen leans in closer to catch my strangled words. "I did something, I . . ."

"Jaime, you're shaking."

"I don't know how to . . . I can't . . ."

"It's all right, Jaime. Whatever it is, we'll—"

"I kissed Cray."

A vicious breeze curls through the branches.

"Oh. Okay . . . Why?"

"Because I wanted to. I don't know. Because I like him. Because I think he likes me too."

"But Jaime, that's not . . ."

"*Dùth.* I know. You think I don't know that? But I just gave a whole speech on how we need to accept each other's differences, right? What if this is the same thing? My whole life I've been made to feel like there's something wrong with me for ever being weak or scared or having these other . . . feelings. But . . . what if I'm not wrong? What if it's the elders who are wrong?"

I'm crying again, but this time the tears are silent and defiant. "In Cray's tribe they don't care who he's attracted to; they just want him to be happy. Surely that's more important? Isn't that what we all deserve?"

I stop to catch my breath. My whole body is tense as I wait for Aileen's reply. I can sense her staring at me, weighing everything I've said.

"I always knew you were brave," she says, "but I never knew quite how much until now."

I turn to look at her, and there are tears in her eyes.

"So you don't . . . mind?"

"Jaime, you're my best friend. Of course I don't mind. All I want is for you to be happy. You deserve that more than anyone." She grabs hold of my shoulder and squeezes it tight, looking me straight in the eye. "We're probably going to be dead soon anyway, so we've got to take what joy we can from this world before we go, right?"

I give her a weak smile, which doesn't come close to expressing how grateful I am to have her in my life.

I told the truth and the world didn't end.

"What about the elders and the rest of the clan?" I say.

"What about them?"

I pick at the branch we're sitting on; its bark strips away in tacky scabs. "Well, I doubt they're going to be as understanding as you. . . ."

"The world is constantly changing, Jaime, and it's up to us to steer that change in the right direction. Show them how positive your love is, and I'm sure they'll eventually come around. And if they don't . . . well, that's their issue, not yours."

She's right. She's always right. "So what should I do now?"

"About what?"

"About Cray."

"Whatever you want to do. Just follow your heart."

I squeeze my bottom lip between my fingers. "I may have told him I never wanted to see him again. . . ."

"That does sound like the sort of stupid thing you'd say."

"Thanks."

"Just tell him you didn't mean it and that you're sorry you're such an inconsiderate craphole."

I give her a gentle shove, and she retaliates by pushing me back much harder—so hard that I almost fall out of the tree.

"Whoa!" I yell, scrabbling for a tighter hold.

"It's all right, I've got you," says Aileen, pulling me back up. She winks at me, and I smile. A genuine one this time. "I'll always be here for you, Jaime. You know that, right?"

"I know. Thank you. You're the best."

"It's true," Aileen says. "I am."

AGATHA

I AM MOUTH OPEN SURPRISE AND I CANNOT SAY ONE thing. She said she was my mother.

"Please forgive me," says Lady Beatrice, who is also the queen and who is also my mother. Unless she is lying. She's lying, she's lying, she's a liar.

"F-forgive you for—what?" I ask.

"For sending you away. I had to. It was the hardest decision I've ever made, but it wasn't safe for you here in Ingland."

"W-why?"

"Because of how you were born," says Lady Beatrice. She puts her hands on the bars between us. "You are different, Agatha; surely you are aware of that?"

"Because I'm so brave?" I say.

"No, not that. . . ." says Lady Beatrice. She closes her mouth tight. "If the king had found out about your . . . condition, he would have had you killed. I believed Skye was the only place you'd be safe, so I sent you away with my most trusted aide, with

instructions to hand you over to Maistreas Eilionoir. I wrote a let-
ter begging Maistreas Eilionoir to take you in.

"Why didn't you come back to Skye too?"

"I wanted to more than anything in the world—please believe
me when I say that—but it wasn't possible. If I'd run away, the
king would have hunted me down and discovered there were still
clans living on Skye."

Hmm. Maybe she is not lying. She said "Maistreas Eilionoir,"
which is what made me think it. Otherwise how would she know
her? I need to test Lady Beatrice to be sure.

"What food do we eat on the l-longest night?" I ask. I am so
clever to think of that question.

The Lady Beatrice is confused, but then she smiles. "You mean
the winter solstice? I'd forgotten we used to celebrate that. . . . It
may have changed in the years I've been gone, but it always used
to be octopus stew."

"Yes!" I say. "That is what we eat. It is octopus stew!"

She knew the answer so she is my birth mother. It is true. And
the kind soldier Garrick is my father. I cannot even believe it!

I smile my biggest smile. I have not done that smiling since
they put me in this prison cage. Lady Beatrice my mother smiles
too and puts her arms through the bars. I hug her tight. It is hard
to do it because of the bars but it is still the best one. Prin the pig
does some happy oinks. He wants to join in with the hug.

"When can I meet—Garrick my f-father?" I ask. I am so happy
to meet him.

Lady Beatrice pulls away from me and shakes her head sad.
"I'm afraid your father is no longer with us."

"What do you—mean?" I ask to her.

"King Edmund had him executed."

"Oh." That means dead. I only just knew him and now I will never meet him.

"I'm so sorry, Agatha," says Lady Beatrice. "After sending you away as a baby, I told King Edmund that you'd died in childbirth. He was furious and took Garrick's life to punish me. He truly was an evil man."

"You should have k-killed him—sooner," I say.

"I thought about it many times, especially in the early days. But keeping him alive was the best way I knew to protect my clan. To protect you. The king viewed me as weak and submissive, but I had more sway over him than he realized. More than once, I managed to convince him that he didn't need to send more men into Scotia 'just to check.' If I'd killed him sooner, who knows who would have succeeded him. King Edmund's hatred for Scotians poisoned people's minds throughout the palace, so I couldn't risk the unpredictability of a new king. But know this: I was always thinking of you, Agatha—every single day since I was forced to send you away. I promise you that."

She puts her arms through the bars again and squeezes my hand. I squeeze her hand back and rub it on my cheek.

"Well, isn't this a quaint family reunion," says a voice in the shadow.

A man steps forward. It is Aldric, King Edmund's adviser man, the one with the droopy skin. In his hand is a dagger.

Lady Beatrice steps away from my prison cage.

"Your Modesty," Aldric says to her.

"It's Your *Majesty* now," says Lady Beatrice.

"You will never be *my* queen," says Aldric. He spits at her feet. "And as soon as the lords hear the truth about you, you won't be anyone's queen, you filthy Scotian scum."

This is not good.

"How dare you speak to me like that," says Lady Beatrice.

"I will speak to you how I like. You are a traitor to the crown, and I'm going to make sure everyone knows it. Now stand back."

He waves his dagger and kicks at Prin to make him move. The pig does more oinking and runs away. Then Aldric takes out a big lot of keys from his pocket. Lady Beatrice was right — he does have the prison keys. "I am going to open this cell, and you are going to enter it. Stand away from the door." It is me he says that last part to. I don't want him to hurt the Lady Beatrice so I do what he says. In my head I am thinking, *The keys the keys, he has the keys.* And then I have the plan. I ask Milkwort if he thinks it is a good one.

Milkwort pokes his head out from my pocket. He sees the keys and tells me yes, he can get them. I say it is dangerous because maybe Aldric will hurt him with the dagger, but he tells me he doesn't mind dangerous. I like when he says that because that is what I say sometimes. I take him out careful so Aldric doesn't see.

When Aldric opens the door, I put Milkwort on the floor. Milkwort runs through the bars and up Aldric's leg. Aldric doesn't know he is there. It is like Milkwort is playing the game we made up, the one where he has to run to my head without me feeling where he is. Milkwort is so good at it.

Aldric makes Lady Beatrice go into the prison room with me

and shuts the door. Milkwort runs down his arm and then Aldric shouts and drops the keys. Milkwort bit him on his fingers. He is such a clever vole to do that.

I am quick and reach through the bars. I grab the keys and throw them into the corner of the prison cage.

"You little pest!" Aldric shouts at me. He opens the door and swings the dagger, but it doesn't get us. I step back and so does Lady Beatrice. "Stay over there, both of you."

Milkwort runs back to me and into my pocket. Aldric comes in to get the keys but when he reaches the corner, what he finds is Gray the wildwolf. He didn't know she was there because of the shadows. Gray snaps her mouth on Aldric's leg.

Aldric screams and drops his dagger. It spins away and he cannot reach it. I tell Gray to stop. Aldric is a bad man but I do not want him to be dead. I say stop again but Gray won't listen to me. I cover my ears so I cannot hear the crunching.

"Come with me," says Lady Beatrice as she takes the keys.

She holds my hand and leads me out of the prison cage. Soon Aldric is not shouting anymore. Lady Beatrice takes me past the other cages and down a corridor way. This is where the rooms with the other wildwolves are. I hear them bark as we go past. Lady Beatrice takes a fire torch from the wall so we can see. She opens a door and we go inside. It is the round room with the black bricks where the Badhbh man made the shadow thing. It smells horrible like yucky seaweed.

"Are you okay?" she asks me.

"Yes," I say. I am okay.

She lets out a big breath. "Well, I think that proved just how dangerous the truth can be. . . . You must promise never to tell anyone what I told you. Can you promise me that?" I nod my head a big one. "Good girl. Okay, stay here. This is probably the safest place to hide while I figure out our next move."

"No," I say. Now that I am out of the prison cage, I need to leave. "I have to go b-back to Skye. I have to—help my—clan."

"That's the last place you should be going."

"I have to," I say again.

"Agatha, you can't. Everything I've done—poisoning King Edmund, my trade with Konge Grímr—it's all been to protect you; if you leave now, it will have been for nothing."

"Not if I s-stop Konge Grímr," I say. "You saved me so now I can save our—clan."

"How can you possibly do that? The army is too big."

"I can do a lot! I am brave and I have c-clever plans and I can—stop them all."

"But you're just a—" Lady Beatrice puts her hand over her mouth. "Forgive me. Perhaps I have been in the south for too long. . . . You're right; you are brave and clever, but Konge Grímr is a dangerous man, and he now has thousands of soldiers at his disposal."

"I stopped him before, when we were in N-Norveg. I will stop him again," I say.

"Skye is hundreds of miles away, Agatha. How would you even get back there?"

The wildwolves are still barking and it echoes in the tunnel. That is what gives me the plan.

"I will ride on a wildwolf," I say.

"What do you mean?" Lady Beatrice asks me.

"I promised the wildwolf in the prison cage that I would s-set her free. She wants to go back to Scotia and—and she knows how to g-get there. Also she can run—fast. She can take me with her."

"Agatha, that wildwolf will *eat* you. You saw what it did to Aldric."

I did see it and it was not very nice. "I will tell her—not to eat me," I say.

Lady Beatrice moves the fire torch so she can look at me more better. "So it's true . . . you can communicate with animals?"

"Yes," I say.

"Incredible. How?"

"I just think the thoughts in my—head," I say. "And some-times they s-say things back to me." I do not tell her that Gray is a growly one and doesn't like me very much.

"Even if you *can* talk to it, and even if it does agree to help, it's far too dangerous. . . . I've only just found you; I can't bear the thought of losing you again so soon."

"I'm going," I say, "and you can't—s-stop me."

I walk out of the room away from her. Lady Beatrice comes after me. I know that because I hear her feet.

"Agatha, wait!"

She touches my arm and I turn around. She looks at me for a long time.

"You really are determined to go, aren't you?"

I nod my head yes, a big one. "I can h-help," I say. "You have to—trust me."

She scrunches her lips. Her eyes are shiny. "Okay," she says.

"If you really think you can make a difference, I'm not going to stand in your way. But only if you can assure me that the wildwolf will do what you say."

We go back to the room with the prison cages. Gray is pulling on her chain to get out. She twists and makes snarl noise and the chain is clanging. Aldric's arm is in the corner sticking out. The rest of him is in the shadows and I don't want to know it. When Gray sees us, she barks. Why is she always doing that barking? It is so annoying to me.

Stop barking, I say to her in my head. *I have come to make you free.* She stops doing the barks.

Yes, free, she says.

I say I will unchain her if she takes me back to Scotia. She tells me no. She says she already helped me make the hole in the wall and I promised I'd set her free if she did that. That's true, I did promise that.

"What's it saying?" Lady Beatrice asks me.

I can't unchain you unless you take me, I say. *Please. I need to help my family.*

She growls a lot and is not happy. She walks around and is thinking. Then she stops and says okay she will take me to Skye. That is the good news. But only if I set the other wildwolves free as well, because they are *her* family.

But there are so many of them, I say. *What if they hurt me or get me with their claws?*

Gray says she will stop them if they try. She is the leader so they will listen to her.

It is more dangerous and I do not know. If I ask Lady Beatrice I think she will tell me no, so I do not ask her. I am thinking something else. Maybe if I make the wildwolves free they can help me stop Konge Grímr. I don't know if they will do it, but I can try. I tell Gray yes, I will set them free.

She barks once and grins with lots of teeth.

"Did it agree?" asks Lady Beatrice.

"Yes," I say. "She will take me back to Skye." I step into the prison cage.

"Wait," says Lady Beatrice. "I'll do it."

The keys are still in the corner where I threw them. It is the same corner where Aldric is dead. Lady Beatrice walks past the wildwolf slowly and then bends down and picks up the keys. Her hands are shaking.

The chain is around Gray's neck so Lady Beatrice has to go close to the wildwolf's mouth to unlock it. I nod at her to keep going. She reaches out her hand. Gray sniffs it and her lips are twitching.

Don't you bite her, I say.

Gray chomps her teeth and doesn't reply. Lady Beatrice does one more step forward and tries the different keys in the lock. She keeps looking at Gray the whole time. She is very brave my mother, just like me.

After lots of tries, the right key clicks and the chain falls off. Right away, Gray runs past us and out of the prison cage.

"Where is it going?" says Lady Beatrice.

We follow Gray and look. She runs down the same corridor I

was in with Lady Beatrice and howls. The other wildwolves howl back. It is so loud with all the howls and echoes.

"Someone's going to hear!" says Lady Beatrice.

Gray comes back to where we are and runs at me fast. She stops when her face is close to mine. She is nearly as tall as I am. She looks into my eyes and does not blink.

Set them free, she says.

SIGRID

WE'RE HEK SLOGS INTO SCOTIA NOW, FARAWAYS FROM Caerlisle, and there are so many northern women marchin with us—hundreds of them! The news that Lady Beatrice is queen was enough to inspire nearly all of the factions to join us. Sable told us how Lady Beatrice has been feedin them information for years, tryin to recruit them for a revolution she's been plannin. She's a shrewd clucker, that Lady Beatrice. It took a couple of days for evryone to get organized, but now we're goin, we're makin good pace. Here's hopin we make it to Skye before the army does.

There's a spatterin of stone shacks where we've stopped for the night, but it doesn't look like no one's lived here for a long time. First thing we do is check there's no one lurkin and that there isn't no death-rats scramblin about neither. I've seen enough of them to last me a thousand forevers.

While the women are settin up their shelters, I take off Eydis's saddle and clean the clutterumble outta her hooves. She thanks me with hek nuzzlin, what nearly knocks me off my feet.

"Easy, Eydis," I say, laughin. "You tryin to bruise my kog or what?"

She snorts outta her nose, which is her way of laughin. I scratch the white stripe on her head, and she tries to lick my hand with her slimy loller. I feel bad that I haven't got nothin nice to feed her, specially since she's been so brimmin at takin us all the way to Ingland and back. I call to Mal-Rakki that I'm gunna go search for somethin she can eat what isn't just grass.

"You comin with me, Eydis?"

She doesn't reply—obviously, cuz she's a horse—but she plods along next to me. I'm thinkin since people used to live here, they musta planted some kinda fruit trees or vegetables or somethin. There isn't nothin nearby, so I wander a bit farther, skirtin around the northern women's camp. Although they're on our side now, some of the women still give me the queazyflips.

After a few tromps searchin, I find an old plum tree. I'm both chirpin to see it and a bit snufflin, cuz it reminds me of the one outside Granpa Halvor's shack back home. He grows the most hek *ríkka* plums in the whole of Norveg. Golden juicers, there isn't nothin sweeter. I can't help from wonderin if I'll ever eat one again.

Then I remember the stone—the one from the plum Granpa Halvor gave me right before I was stolen away. I kept it the whole journey across the sea and all the whiles I was ridin up to Skye, but with evrythin that's happened since, I'd completely forgotten about it. My hand dives into the pocket where I used to keep it in. The pocket's a large empty space. Nothin—the stone's gone. No, wait, what's that buried in the corner?

I pull out the crinkled stone and press it to my lips. It's the closest I've felt to Granpa in a long time. A tear trickles outta my eye. One is enough. I wipe it away and turn my attention back to the plum tree. There's still a few fruits left, witherin up on the highest branches. Eydis lifts her head toward them, but they're too high for her to reach.

"Don't you worry, girl, I'll get them for you."

It's an easy climb, and soon I'm pluckin the plums and droppin them down for Eydis to gobble. They're shriveled and a bit rotten, seein as how it's so late in the season, but Eydis don't seem to mind none. She scoffs them up from where they've landed. I climb back down, and she rubs her head on my arm.

"Come on, then, we'd best get back," I say. "It's gettin dark."

The sky is bright purple; I haven't never seen a sunset like it. The clouds tumble across it like rips of flamin mauve. Even after all the grim what's happened, it's important to still notice when things are beautiful. That's what I think, anyways.

Sable said Mal-Rakki and I should take one of the shacks and wouldn't hear nothin of our protestin, so that's where we're gunna sleep. There's just about enough room for Eydis to come in too. Mal-Rakki's lit a fire inside, and the whole place is hek crispin. I sit close to the fire and hold my hands out toward it. The heat makes my fingers tingle.

"How are you doing?" Mal-Rakki asks, sittin down next to me.

"Good," I say.

He places a hand on my shoulder and gives me an intense stare.

"I've been thinking again about what you did back in Caerlisle," he ses. "With the death-rats. It was so incredibly brave; a risky strategy but a brilliant one. Not to mention the fact that it also helped convince Sable and the other women to join us."

"I couldn't just leave you there. Nor Eydis neither."

Mal-Rakki is smilin suns. "You'd make an excellent addition to the rebel army, you know, should you ever want to join us."

My heart is brimmin. Sometimes I forget exactly who it is I'm with, cuz he's just a man, same as any other. But he's not just a man. He's Mal-Rakki. *The* Mal-Rakki. And he just invited *me* to join his army. If someone told me three moons ago that I'd be travelin through Scotia on a horse with Mal-Rakki, savin his life and bein asked to join the rebels, I'd of said they were either cracked or lyin. But here I am, and that's what's happenin. Funny how life carries you away on its tide and takes you to the most unexpected places.

"How many rebels are there?" I ask, surprised I haven't thought to ask that question sooner.

"More than I ever hoped for, although the past few winters have been particularly harsh. There are close to four hundred of us left. I brought sixty with me, and the rest are holding the peace back in Norveg."

"You were gone a long time. Didn't you get bored of waitin in the ice caves all those years?"

"Not at all. We filled the days with hunting and combat training. I also spent a lot of time on my own just *being*, either sitting in silence or going for long walks, surrounding myself with nature. I found great serenity in those moments, through focusing on the present rather than dwelling on troubles from the past or the uncertainty of the future."

"Sounds like you miss it. You don't regret leavin, do you?"

"Of course not. In some ways I do miss that life, but I couldn't stay there forever with the knowledge of what my brother was doing."

"So you always planned on comin back and kickin him out?"

Mal-Rakki laughs. "In a manner of speaking, yes. We were just waiting for the right opportunity. We frequently spent the long nights discussing the formation of an ideal society—freed from the constraints of power-hungry rulers—and always dreamed that one day we would put that system into place."

"Do you think it's gunna work?" I shuffle back from the fire. It's gettin too hot, and the smoke's makin my eyes ache.

"The road ahead is precarious and unpredictable, but yes, I have every faith that we will succeed. Our time has come, and our time is now."

There's a glimmer of somethin stirrin in my stogg that feels a lot like hope.

"Why'd you do it, though?" I ask. "You musta had a nice life livin rich before you stood up to the king, defendin us rottens. Why'd you leave all that behind?"

"Because it was the right thing to do," he ses, like it's the most obvious answer in the world. "My brother's rule has been fueled by hatred, but hate is not the answer. I have faith that virtue will always conquer evil in the end. It has to. Otherwise what's the point of living?"

In all the days since breakin free from Konge Grímr, I haven't never once dreamt about what my future might look like, but hearin Mal-Rakki talkin now, anythin seems possible. I was wrong to ever doubt him. He's evrythin I ever hoped he would be and more. He may not be as loud or as brash as the leader I was imaginin, but he talks more sense than anyone I've ever met. We've gotta win this fight, cuz if he becomes the leader of Norveg, evrythin changes.

With Konge Grímr defeated, I could even return to Norveg. . . . Granpa Halvor won't believe the half of it when I turn up and tell him evrywhere I've been. I reach into my pocket and give the plum stone a squeeze.

"The people will follow you, I know it," I say, sittin up and starin straight at him. "We've been waitin our whole lives for you."

"I won't let you down," ses Mal-Rakki.

"And I'll help too, if I ever leave this skap country. I'll help convince them."

"I'd be honored to have your support."

Course, if I go back, I'll have to see Mamma. Truth bein told, I don't never wanna see her again—not after what she did to me—but I spose I'll have to at some point. . . .

"What are you thinking about?" Mal-Rakki asks.

"Nothin," I say.

"So why's your face wrinkled up like a moldy pea?"

Curse my face for bein so open. "I was . . . thinkin about my mother."

"You miss her?"

"No." My frown is so deep it's devourin my eyes.

Mal-Rakki doesn't ask nothin more about her, but the silence is gratin, so I tell him how she sold me to Konge Grímr for nothin more than a few pennies, what she then used to drown herself in slosh.

Mal-Rakki nods while I talk, like he understands some of my pain.

"Betrayal is always worse when it's by someone close to you," he ses. "But do not underestimate the redemptive power of forgiveness. Not for her, but for you. I'm not saying she deserves your forgiveness, nor telling you that you should give it to her, but harboring resentment sours our insides. If you can find a way to release the pain, you will feel lighter for it."

I don't know about that. Although thinkin about it now, I spose if she'd never of done what she did, I never would of met Mal-Rakki, and I wouldn't of been able to warn the Skye people about the kings' plans neither. So there are some goods what have come outta it. All the same, I'm not plannin on forgivin her anytime soon, that's for hek sure.

"Can you hear that?" Mal-Rakki asks me.

"Hear what?" I say. All I'm hearin is the crackle of the fire.

Mal-Rakki jumps up quickspit and pours water over the flames. Now all I'm hearin is the hiss and crunch as he stomps on the ashes.

"What is it?" I ask.

He puts his finger over his lips and beckons me to the door. It's dark as sin outside, though there's a hek lot of stars, which make the sky look sparkin.

"You hear it too?" ses Sable, joggin toward us from her camp.

Other women come out of their shelters and stand with their ears to the wind.

Mal-Rakki nods, and we follow Sable into the night. The air is sharp with ice spikes, what steal the heat straight outta my body.

A few paces from the shack, I hear the sound Mal-Rakki was talkin about: a repeated thump, thump, thump, thump. It's a long ways away, gentle but persistent. I haven't got no ideas what it could be. From what the Skye people told me, there isn't sposed to be no one livin in these parts. Unless . . .

We trek up a slope to get a better view of the valley below us. A gasp slips outta my yapper as soon as I see them. Mal-Rakki pulls me down. I knew it would be big, but still . . . seein it now makes my guts turn to weevils.

Row upon row of flickerin shapes, marchin through the night—a sprawlin mass what swallows the hillside like a monstrous shadow. It's endless, spreadin far and wide in all directions. Even from this distance, the sound of their footsteps pulses through me. The shine from a thousand torches lights their way.

It's the two kings' army.

JAÍME

AS SOON AS I'VE GULPED DOWN MORNING MEAL, I CROSS
the enclave to the Lower Gate. I force myself to sprint so I'm less
likely to change my mind. It's already taken me two days to muster
up enough courage to do what I'm about to do. The Moth standing
guard is a Clann-na-Bruthaich woman I've not met before, who
has a shock of bright auburn hair. Her piercing blue eyes narrow
as I approach.

"Can I help you?" she asks.

"I need to leave," I say. "Please."

"Why?" she asks. She shakes her face into the breeze to clear
the loose strands of hair from her cheeks.

"I need to see the Bó Riders."

"Why?" she asks again.

"I have a message for them. . . . For Mór." I'm terrible at lying.
I'm sure the Moth can tell. "She was working with us the other day."

Us. Me and Donal . . . Donal's face as he fell, his body trapped
in the throng. The knife, the knife, the knife—

"No one's allowed out without Kenrick's or Eilionoir's authorization, as I'm sure you well know. Since Agatha's disappearance, they're stricter on that than ever."

"Please . . ." I say. "It's important."

She makes a clicking noise with her tongue. "You're Jaime, right?"

"Yes," I say, not sure whether admitting that is more or less likely to convince her.

She nods a couple of times and then approaches the mechanism that opens the gate. She hauls off its metal binding and begins to wind the wooden lever. The gate creaks open.

"Just this once," she says. "And only because we owe you."

"Thank you." I flash her a soft smile, which she doesn't reciprocate.

"Don't be long."

I push myself through the slim gap and then I'm out, on the other side of the enclave wall. The grass is crisp beneath my feet, still recovering from last night's frost. It's so strange to think that the first time I stepped foot outside an enclave was only a few months ago. So much has changed since then. So much change is still to come. I glance in the direction of the kyle, half-expecting to see King Edmund's army charging toward us, but the land is still. A large flock of tiny birds sweeps through the sky, changing direction every few moments in graceful swirls. On a morning as peaceful as this, it's almost hard to imagine the horrors that are coming.

I have the sword. The sword is my strength. The sword will protect us.

The Bó Riders' camp is a short walk around the western side of the enclave. I hear them before I see them: the sound of their singing floats on the wind. No one has come to tell them to stop, so it looks as if they're allowed to do that now.

Before long, their conical tents come into view, arranged in two wide semicircles. The massive herd of Highland cows and bulls is spread around them, lounging in the heather. Their tails whip at invisible flies. Two mighty fires burn in front of the tents, and several of the Bó Riders sit close to them, eating. As I approach, a couple of people stand up. One of them is Finn, the young Herbist—or *healer*, as they call him—who nursed Agatha back to health after the battle with the wildwolves. He folds his muscly arms and gives me a big smile.

"Jaime! Good to see you. How have you been?" He walks over to me and puts a warm hand on the back of my neck. He then pulls me forward until our foreheads touch, and we breathe together in the Bó Riders' accustomed greeting.

"I'm okay," I say afterward.

"Have you eaten? Join us!" He gestures toward the blankets around the fire. A few other Riders beckon me over, shuffling to create some space.

"I actually came to see—"

"Look who's finally decided to pay us a visit," says Mór as she glides out of one of the tents. The flap falls behind her with a heavy slap. "Good morning, perky." She also touches her forehead to mine. "Have you come for breakfast?" That's what they call morning meal.

"Um . . . no. I've already eaten, thanks. Is . . . uh, is Cray around?"

"Oh, and there I was thinking you missed my witty company," says Mór. Despite the impassive look on her face, I'm fairly sure she's joking.

"He's already left, I'm afraid," says Finn.

"Left? Left for where?"

"I thought you two weren't talking?" says Mór.

How does she know that? What's Cray told her?

"Your leader came and spoke to us at first light," says Finn.

"The bossy little one," says Mór.

Finn nudges her with his elbow.

"Maistreas Eilionoir," I say. "What did she want?"

"She was looking for someone to cross over to the mainland and scout for the enemy," says Finn. "To find out how far away they are. Of course Cray was the first to volunteer. He left with Bras almost right away."

My heart collapses. What if someone spots him? They must have scouts of their own. Imitators, trained soldiers, who knows what else . . .

"When did he leave?" I ask. First light wasn't that long ago. "I want to go with him."

"I suppose you might be able to catch him before he crosses the channel," says Mór. An almost imperceptible smile tickles her lips. She exchanges a look with Finn.

"I'll take you," Finn says. "Gailleann is faster than Duilleag."

"No, he's not," replies Mór.

"He is and you know it."

"Prove it, then. I'll race you."

"You're on."

They both whistle at the same time, and their bulls come charging from opposite sides of the camp. Duilleag—Mór's bull— arrives first. She leaps onto his back without him breaking stride.

"Looks like you're taking Jaime!" Mór calls out behind her.

Finn lets out a competitive "Ha!" Gailleann has to stop in order for me to mount him, which increases Mór's lead.

"Hold on tight," says Finn once we're both up. "This is going to be wild."

He's not wrong.

I've ridden Highland bulls plenty of times before, but never as fast as we're riding now. The world is spinning past us at such speed that it's nothing but a messy smudge. I increase my grip around Finn's waist, convinced I'm about to fly off at any moment. The sound of Gailleann's galloping pounds my ears. I close my eyes, thinking that might help, but it gives me a rush of nausea. Eyes open is bad, but eyes closed is even worse. My teeth crunch against one another, and my spine feels as if it's about to crack. Mór and Duilleag are a speeding blur in the distance.

"You all right back there?" Finn shouts.

"Just about," I call back.

He laughs; he's enjoying this. He leans forward a little farther. My arms are wrapped so tight around him, I'm forced to move forward too. His clothes smell sweet with a bitter edge, like apples dipped in mud.

The gap between us and Mór begins to decrease. Turf flies up around us as Duilleag's mighty hooves smash the ground. The kyle appears in the distance, but there's still no sign of Cray. Duilleag and Mór dip out of sight, down a slope that leads to the channel. We reach the ridge in time to see them come to a rambling halt at the edge of the water. The shoreline is dotted with Raasay islanders, still hard at work crafting new weapons. A few glance in our direction, but most ignore us, engrossed in their task.

"Told you Duilleag was faster," says Mór once we've trotted the last few paces over to her.

"You had a head start," says Finn. "And Gailleann had to carry two of us."

"Excuses, excuses . . ."

"No sign of Cray, though," says Finn.

I'm not really listening to them. "Is that him?" I ask, pointing at a dark shape in the channel, bobbing on the waves about fifty paces away. "Cray! Cray!" I shout until my voice goes hoarse. The person in the water doesn't turn around.

Finn puts two fingers in his mouth and whistles. I shove my hands over my ears, it's so loud. Several of the Raasay islanders look over their shoulders in surprise, and so does Cray. I imagine him squinting, trying to work out who's calling him and why. He turns Bras around, and they make their way back, emerging from the water at a slow plod. If Cray is surprised to see me, he doesn't show it.

"What's wrong?" Cray asks.

"Nothing," says Finn.

"So why are you here?"

There's a silence, which both Mór and Finn are expecting me to fill. My tongue feels fat in my mouth.

"Jaime wants to go with you," says Mór.

"Does he?" says Cray. He's staring at me, his eyebrows raised in either surprise or disdain.

"I do," I say, the words soft yet loaded. We're in almost the exact place we were when I pushed him away and told him we couldn't be friends.

"Fine," says Cray. "Take your boots off. Your feet are going to get wet."

I slip down from Gailleann's back and wince as the impact of hitting the ground reverberates up my legs.

"We'll leave you to it, then," says Mór.

"Race you back," says Finn, already encouraging Gailleann to start moving.

"We raced already. Duilleag won, remember?"

"Thought we'd try a fairer one . . . unless you're scared you'll lose this time?"

"Never," says Mór.

"Then let's do this. *Siùd!*"

The two bulls stampede away, the sound of Mór's and Finn's taunts slowly fading into nothing.

Cray watches me take off my boots and socks and roll up my trousers. I can't think of anything to say. My heart is beating fast but not in a bad way.

"So you wanted to come with me, did you?"

Now that I'm with him, I'm more certain than ever that this is what I want. I nod, still finding it difficult to speak actual words.

"You'd better come up, then," he says, reaching out his hand. I let him swing me onto Bras's back. "At least we don't have to worry about sucker eels this time."

He's right, and I do feel safer wading out into the water on a giant bull rather than swimming across on my own. That's not to say we couldn't still be attacked by deathfins or killer rays, though. . . . I slide my arms around Cray's torso. The warmth of it brings tears to my eyes.

As Bras trundles forward, the water bites my toes and then creeps up my shins. It burns with a searing cold until my legs turn numb. Although it's tormenting me now, this water is going to be our protection; as long as we can prevent the army from crossing this channel, we'll be safe.

Bras swims with confidence, his hair floating around him like the roots of a wandering fern. Memories of the sucker eels come slithering back. I jerk my legs out of the water and — although it makes it harder to balance — sit cross-legged on Bras's back. Cray peers around to see what I'm doing but doesn't comment. Neither of us speaks until we're halfway across, at which point I finally find the words I've been struggling to say.

"I'm sorry. About what I said the other day. I was . . . confused. About everything. I still am."

The cool sea air tugs at my cloak. I pull it around me a little tighter.

"You don't need to apologize," says Cray. "I can't imagine how hard it must have been for you, growing up being told something like that is wrong."

I swallow. It feels lumpy. "You're my friend, and I like spending time with you. That's all I know."

"That's good enough for me." He glances over his shoulder and smiles. My head collapses into his back, and I smile too.

WHEN WE REACH THE OTHER SIDE OF THE KYLE, BRAS sprints for a few hundred paces to shake off the water, then we stop to make a quick fire. Once we're dry, Cray puts out the flames and we continue on our way.

I find myself looking for signs of Agatha. There's a chance she came this way, especially if she was taken by force. The tracker who was sent to the Badhbh's hut hasn't returned yet, so I don't know what he found, if anything at all. As I scan the horizon for any sign of movement, the enormity of the risk we're taking begins to sink in. Cray assures me that we'll see the army long before they see us—and that Bras can move much quicker than they can—but I'm not convinced.

"What if they have more imitators, sent ahead to spy us out?" The fingerprint-shaped scars on my neck start to itch.

"We've taken them on before; we can do it again," says Cray, although he uses the opportunity to slide out his spear from the loop beneath our knees.

My own weapon grows heavy by my side. The moment I think about it, it starts humming, sharp and persistent. I wonder if Cray can hear it too. It's begging me to make it stronger for whatever we're about to face. I've resisted giving it more blood since Donal's death, but now, with the army so close, I'm not sure I can deny it anymore. I need the sword's protection, and for that, I need it to be strong.

I ask Cray if we can stop, pretending I need to relieve myself, then slink behind the biggest tree I can find. The blade has lost some of its brightness again, despite the incantation I spoke the last time I cut myself. It's no surprise, really—I'm not a real blood mage. I'll have to try again.

I roll up my sleeve and cut across my upper arm, high enough that it'll be hidden by my clothes. Something feels wrong about what I'm doing: hiding behind a tree, keeping secrets from Cray, making myself bleed . . . but I do it all the same.

A stream of blood drips down into the crease of my elbow. The sword is hot in my hand and buzzes with greed. I place the blade over the cut and smudge the two together. As the sword draws in my blood, I mutter the incantation, trying to pour sadness and rage into the words, but I find it hard to channel my grief. Perhaps there was something in the air in the Badhbh's bothan that made it easier, or maybe it's because being with Cray makes some of the darkness inside me drift away.

To compensate, I let the sword suck more blood from me than usual. It takes and it takes, making me feel light-headed. Eventually, I tear the sword away and return it to its scabbard, then rip off the bottom of my shirt to use as a bandage. Once I've tied the bandage tight, I pull down my sleeve and step out from behind the tree. The fallen branches crunch beneath my feet as I make my way back to Cray.

"Everything okay?" he asks.

"Never better," I reply, but as soon as I've spoken, my head empties of all thought. I lose my balance, and I collapse onto the ground.

⬤

WHEN I COME BACK AROUND, I'M DISORIENTED AND confused. Cray says I went unconscious but not for long. He asks more than once what it was that made me faint, but I tell him I don't know and insist I'm well enough to carry on.

My head is throbbing, and my arm feels cold. Again, I'm swamped with fears that the blade is taking too much from me. The sacrifice was worth it, though; the sword now feels powerful again, and its strength is my strength. I'm doing this for my clan, for our future. I won't let anyone take this weapon from me, which means no one must know about it. Not even Cray.

We ride hard the rest of the day, through tremulous grasses and over swollen hills, the ground toughened by the frosty weather. By the time the sun starts to set, my body is a mess of aches and pains.

Cray pulls Bras to a halt and looks over his shoulder at me. "It'll be dark soon, and we're too far inland to turn back now. The good news is the army isn't as close as we'd feared. I suggest we set up camp here and then continue our search at first light."

I'd guessed that was going to be his plan. Spending the night on the mainland fills me with about as much joy as jumping off a cliff, but we haven't got much choice. For someone who's had as many negative experiences in Scotia as I have, I sure find myself spending a lot of time here. Not only that, but spending the night alone with Cray now makes me feel . . . I don't know.

Cray dismounts with an acrobatic half-twist. I roll my eyes at his blatant showing off, making sure he notices my disapproval. He grins, then holds up his hand to help me. I swing my leg over and drop to the ground. Once down, I keep hold of Cray's hand for a beat longer than I need to. He looks at me, then at our connected hands. Still, neither of us lets go. He smiles, and there is so much warmth in his look, I swear I've never felt happier.

Something behind me distracts him, and the moment breaks. His face changes in a flicker from content to concern, and he drops my hand.

"*Ò mo chreach!*" he says.

"What? What is it?" I ask, spinning around.

"It's them," he says. "The army. In the distance, over there." He smears the palms of his hands down his cheeks. "We're about to be in a whole lot of trouble."

Agatha

"WHAT DO YOU MEAN WE HAVE TO LET ALL THE WILDWOLVES free?" says Lady Beatrice. She looks at me like I am a crazy girl. "We can't. That's one step too far."

"We h-have to," I say. "Otherwise Gray won't take me back to Skye."

"Who's Gray?"

"The—wildwolf. That's the name I gave her."

"You *named* the wildwolf? They're not pets, Agatha."

"I know they're not p-pets."

Gray is walking backward and forward in front of us.

"If we let the other wildwolves out, what's to stop them from attacking us?" says Lady Beatrice.

"Gray says they—won't. I've been speaking to them through the walls so they know me already. I'm going to ask them to help me stop Konge Grímr."

Lady Beatrice shakes her head but goes into the corridor. I go too and so does Gray. Lady Beatrice stops next to the first room with barking inside. The wildwolves are jumping loud and scratching on the other side of the door. I speak to them in my head and tell them it's me, the girl from the tunnel. I tell them I will only let them out if they do not hurt us. They are moving excited so it is hard to hear properly what they are saying. I ask them again and they say, *Yes, yes, let us out, let us out.* They talk in fast words.

"Okay, o-open the—door," I say to Lady Beatrice.

"Think carefully about this, Agatha. I can't hear what they're saying, so only you can make this decision. Please be sure."

I do not know if I trust the wildwolves. It could be a trick or a nasty plan but I have to do it. I nod to Lady Beatrice.

"I hope you're right," she says. She finds the key and opens the door.

The wildwolves burst through and knock Lady Beatrice back. There are six of them and they are on top of each other in a rush to get through the door faster. When they see me and the Lady Beatrice they turn to us and are going to pounce.

Don't eat us, I say. I try to say it in all of their heads, but the arrows don't come out right. The wildwolves come closer. Gray runs in front of us and barks. The other wildwolves growl and then stop and turn away. Phew, they did not eat us. Gray was not lying when she said they would listen to her.

We go to the other rooms and Lady Beatrice opens the doors. Gray stops the other wildwolves from coming near us too. When they are all free, I try to count them but there is too many and they are moving. I think there is sixty or one hundred or even more than that.

"Can you tell them to be quiet?" says Lady Beatrice. "Someone is going to hear and come looking."

I tell them to stop barking but they don't do it. I do a big breath to be calm and try doing the arrows into their heads. *Be quiet or people will come and you will not be free* is what I say. Most of them stop barking after that. I think it worked. Lady Beatrice opens her mouth and then smiles.

"There are other wildwolves," I say. "In c-cages. But some-one—did something to them. They wouldn't t-talk to me and they don't look right anymore."

"Those are the victims of King Edmund's . . . experimenta-tions," says Lady Beatrice. "He had an unhealthy fascination with *meldery*—using dark arts to forge animals together in an attempt to create new beasts to use as weapons. I'm afraid Konge Grímr may have taken some with him."

That is another reason I have to stop him.

"Can we set the broken ones free?" I ask.

"If you can't speak to them, it's not safe," says Lady Beatrice. "But I'll help them if I can, once you've gone. Right now, you need to leave. Follow me."

We go far to the other end of the corridor. There is a tunnel there that is smaller. The wildwolves follow us doing lots of yap-ping and snaps. Voices shout from the big room where the prison cages are.

"Someone's discovered you've escaped," says Lady Beatrice. "Quick—go now—down this passage. It'll lead you to a door. It'll be bolted but unlocked. It's the way they use to bring in prisoners without anyone knowing."

More shouting. People are coming into the corridor.

"This isn't how I wanted to say goodbye," says Lady Beatrice. She hugs me a quick tight one. I squeeze her too. "I love you, Agatha, my beautiful, brave daughter. You're everything I ever dreamed you would be and more. We'll see each other again one day; I hope that with all my heart."

What she said makes my insides fluttery.

"Goodbye, Lady Beatrice my—m-mother," I say, and then I have to go. I run down the passage. All the wildwolves come too. It is dark and gets darker and I do not have the fire torch. I put my hands out and feel only wildwolves. They sniff me and growl and want to eat me still.

If you eat me you will not escape, I tell the closest ones. They remember it and do not bite me yet. I follow where they go. They can see better in the dark than me.

The wildwolves stop. I nearly trip over them stopping. They are at the end where the door is. I push through their smelly hair and bodies to feel the door. They are growling at me a lot when I do that. The only light is a line on the ground which is a crack under the door. It helps me know where the door is.

The shouting men voices are coming closer. I look back and see fire from their torches. They are soldiers with swords and they are in the tunnel. I have to be quick so quick.

I feel all over and find the bolt. It is cold like frozen. I pull it hard with my strength and then it clunks across with a pinch on my hand. I haven't got time to say the ouch.

"We know you're down here. Give yourself up!" shouts one of the men. I am not going to do that. Their running feet are close now.

"What the bloody—" says one of the soldiers.

They have seen the wildwolves. Some of the wildwolves turn around and bark. The soldiers hold out their swords. The blades are shining yellow and orange because of the fire from their torches.

I pull on the handle and the door opens with lots of dust. Wind from outside blows the dust into my face and I choke coughs. It is nighttime and dark. The only light is from the moon and the stars. The wildwolves rush past me and out through the door. Behind me there is sword sounds and angry barks but I do not want to know it. I step through the doorway and the outside squeezes my face. It is cold but also nice air to breathe it.

Climb on, says a voice in my head. It is Gray. She says I am being too slow.

It is easier getting on her back than climbing on a bull because she is smaller. I lie down and hold on to her fur. All of the wildwolves run from the palace. They go past the dark buildings and through the mud and away. Gray howls at the sky and then we run away too.

THE SUN COMES UP TO MAKE THE DAY AND IT IS PRETTY pinks and yellow. Then the clouds come in and it is a more dull color. At least it is not raining. Gray's body is warm so it keeps me warm. The wildwolves move very fast. Sometimes one of them barks and then all the other ones bark too. When Gray lifts her head, I have to hold on even tighter. Her bark is a loud one.

We are a long way from the palace now. There are no buildings here, only grass and trees and no people. We did it! I am escaped and going back to my Skye island. It makes me so happy inside my bones.

While we are riding, I tell Gray about Konge Grímr and ask if she and the other wildwolves will help me stop him. She tells me no. She doesn't want to go near people because they hurt her and put her in prison. I ask her again and practice the arrows to try and make her listen more. I say that Konge Grímr and the army are the bad ones so if she helps us defeat them then no one will put her in prisons anymore. She still tells me no. She says when people are together they are too nasty and too strong. She is right about that sometimes.

In the middle part of the day, we pass a bothan with smoke coming out of the top. In a field next to it there are lots of cows. The wildwolves move along the fence until they find a way to get underneath and then they chase after the cows and get one. I am sad for the cow, but also the wildwolves have to eat, don't they?

I get down from Gray in case she wants to eat too. She tells me she does not need food because I gave her some last night. I think she means Aldric. I did not give him to her. He did that by himself.

Gray might not want food, but I do. I am very hungry for some. I won't eat dead cow though yuck. Maybe there is some food in the bothan. I walk toward it. The grass is wet and swishes. When I am close, I stand on my toes and look in the window. There is no one there in that room. Something has a nice smell that is herbs and smoky. The door is unlocked so I go inside. It is warm from the hearth where some food is cooking. I have to be quiet like a tiny mouse. I cannot take the hot food because my hands will burn but I find some bread and a vegetable and something yellow and hard. I pick up the yellow one and bite it. It is delicious taste like cheese and cream. I have one more bite and then I put it with the vegetable and the bread and wrap it in a cloth.

It is bad to take things when someone doesn't give them to you. Maybe I should say hello to the person who lives here and ask if I can have the food please, but also they might say no. Then I wouldn't have any food. So I do not say hello and I take the food.

I open the door to leave but oh—There is a woman standing there. She is a big woman. Her face is red and she has lots of potatoes in her arms. The potatoes are dirty.

"What the devil?" she says. She drops the potatoes.

"You dropped your potatoes," I say.

"What are you doing in my house?" she says. She sees the cloth in my hands.

"The w-wildwolves are e-eating your—cow," I say.

The woman turns her head to the field and hears the barking. She picks up a long, sharp farming tool and runs to the field. I go as well, but I stay away from where the woman is. There is a mess in the field that is not a cow anymore because the wildwolves ate it all. The wildwolves aren't there. They are gone and so is Gray. Now what do I do?

The woman sees the cow mess and makes a cry noise. Then she comes running at me with the tool above her head. She thinks it was me who killed the cow but it wasn't. All I did is eat the cheese. I look for somewhere to hide or run.

There is a bark noise behind me. Gray! I am big happy phew to see her. I climb on her back. It is even more hard to hold on with the food as well. Gray runs away fast.

"Th-thank you for the f-food," I shout to the woman.

She shakes her tool in the air and gets smaller and smaller behind us.

I say thank you to Gray for not running away and leaving me. She does a huff sound and tells me I should stay away from people because people are bad.

I am a person and I am not bad, I say.

She does not answer me when I say that.

WHEN IT IS NEARLY NIGHTTIME WE STOP IN A CAVE. WE are with the other wildwolves again now because we catched up with them. The cave is for sleeping in because the wildwolves are tired from running all day. I am tired too. I eat some of the food I took and give some bread to Milkwort. He doesn't like the wildwolves so he stays in my pocket and doesn't come out. That is a good idea because the wildwolves might want to eat him even though he is a small one.

I'm going to make a fire. I know how to do it. I make a circle in the ground with my heel and fill it with dry leaves. Then I go and find small twigs for the first part and bigger branches for on top.

When I come back into the cave, a big group of wildwolves is watching me. Maybe now is a good time to talk to them about Konge Grímr. Gray told me they would not help, but if I explain then maybe they will say yes.

I put down the branches and do a deep breath to make my head clear like I practiced. Then I think of the words like arrows going into all of their heads at the same time.

There is a bad man in Scotia, I say. The arrows work. They hear me! I tell them about Konge Grímr and ask if they will help me stop him.

The wildwolves bark and their voices are in my head.

Stop talking.

We won't help people.

We need to run far away.

I'm going to eat you.

Eat me? Which one said that? There are too many of them and too many voices. One of them runs at me and pushes me hard with its head. I fall over and land on the branches. It hurts in my side a lot. The wildwolf is a big one. It stands over me and its drool goes on my face. It snaps its mouth crunching. *Go away!* I say. But it's not listening and I can't be calm in my head or do the arrow. It is going to eat me. That is why Lady Beatrice said it was too dangerous. The other wildwolves come around like they want to eat me too.

The big wildwolf opens its mouth. Its teeth are pointy and yellow.

Another wildwolf jumps over my head, straight into the one on top of me. It is Gray. She smashes into the big one and they go tumbling on the ground. Then they leap back up and fight with lots of snaps and biting. It is harder for Gray because she is smaller, but also she is more clever and ducks out of the way. She does a fast circle and then scratches the big wildwolf with her claws and bites its ear. Then she pins it to the ground and stands on its head. The other one does a whimper noise. Gray lets it go and it walks away.

All the other wildwolves are looking at me and at Gray. She barks at them because she is cross. I am cross too.

I am not your enemy, I say to them all. I say it with the fastest arrows I can do. *And I am not your food. I made you free. I am nice! Konge Grímr and the Inglish army are the bad people. They are the ones who locked you up and hurt you and they will do it again because they are mean and they don't care. That is why you should help me. If we stop them, everything will be better. You can be free and the people will not hurt you anymore.*

My head is banging sore now because I spoke too much.

To be left alone, says Gray. *That is what we want.*

So help me! I say.

Gray says she will think about it. That is better than saying no. I tell the other wildwolves sorry for being in their head because I know they don't like it. And I say to Gray thank you for stopping the other wildwolf. That one is at the back of the cave, licking its leg. I don't think it will get me again.

I pick up the twigs and branches. I am a bit shaky but I still have to make the fire. The leaves are dry which is good. I use the flint from my belt to do the sparks. It is only a bit hard for my fingers to do it. The flames are small and I am worried they will go away. I blow on them to give them some air. That is a clever thing to do. The fire spreads and catches onto the twigs. They crackle and burn smell. Now it is a bigger fire. I get more branches from outside the cave and add them to the top so it will burn for a long time. It is a good fire now and I'm so clever to make it. It is nice and hot. I sit next to it and let the warm make me happy like toast.

Gray watched me make the fire from far away. She does not like it. I tell her it is safe and she should come closer to be warm like me. She doesn't reply. I lie down and close my eyes because

I am tired and my head is aches. The next time I open my eyes, Gray is next to me and next to the fire. She is asleep. She is happy like toast now too.

I add some more sticks. The flames make shadows on the walls. They make me think of Konge Grímr's shadow with its spiky antler head and horrible hands that want to rip everyone apart. I watch those shadows for a long time until I fall back to sleep.

JAIME

"WE NEED TO GET CLOSER," SAYS CRAY. HE'S TALKING
about the army; it might be the worst idea I've ever heard.

"Closer? Why on earth would we want to get closer? We need
to get away from here as fast as we possibly can!"

I pull at the skin of my neck, feeling the rough creases of the
scars. The army is a swarming mass of black specks on the far
horizon, like an infinite blanket of death. It devours the landscape
as it marches. Flags flutter on tall poles—dark silhouettes against
the dense pink sky. I feel sick. This is real. The army is real, and
it's coming straight for us.

"We might discover something that could help us win the battle," says Cray.

"Or we could get captured and killed. We came here to find
out how far away they are, and now that we know, we need to
go back to pass that information on. They're only a day or two's
march from Skye—we have to warn the clans."

"Just a little closer," says Cray. He jumps on Bras's back.

Damn him for being so stubborn.

"I have no idea why I like you," I say.

"Oh, so you like me, do you?" Cray grins.

Even now, in the face of unimaginable terrors, my cheeks burst with heat. I say nothing as he pulls me up behind him, then Bras begins a wary trot in the direction of the enemy.

We stick to the trees and give the army a wide berth. Once we're nearer, Bras stops and Cray takes out a spyglass. I try to gauge his reaction as he looks through it, but he doesn't give anything away. He lowers his hands, licks the inside of his cheek, and then hands me the spyglass. I pause, unsure if I want to see, then raise the spyglass to my eye.

A gasp sticks in my throat. I knew the army was big, but nothing could have prepared me for the reality of it. The sprawl extends for as far as I can see to both the north and the south: thousands upon thousands of Inglish soldiers armed with lances and swords and shields; hundreds of horses wearing spiked battle armor; hordes of deamhan warriors covered in their distinctive tattoos. And then there's the cages, with whatever they have trapped inside them; all I can make out is the occasional flash of teeth and huge spiked limbs that stick through the bars like giant crabs' legs.

I grab hold of Cray's arm for support. "There's no way . . ." I say. "We don't stand a chance."

"It doesn't look good, but we still have the channel, remember? They won't all be able to cross the water at the same time, and it doesn't look like they've got any boats."

I nod, but I'm not really listening. I wrap my fingers around the handle of my sword, which emits a low hum as I absorb some of its strength.

The soldiers stop to make camp for the night and start erecting an uncountable number of tents. I'm still trying to process it all when I see him. The Badhbh. He's talking to a group of men who are lighting a fire.

That *diachdaidh* traitor! I knew he was a coward, but I never would've guessed he'd run to the enemy.

"The Badhbh's with them," I say.

"You're kidding! What's he doing there? Have they captured him?"

"It doesn't look like it. He's chatting with some of the soldiers as if he knows them. I think he's *helping* them. What the hell!"

"Okay, I think we've learned enough—and none of it good. We should head back to Skye."

"Wait." I can't believe I'm about to suggest this. "I think we should get closer. I need to speak to him—to the Badhbh."

It's Cray's turn to look incredulous. "That really isn't sensible."

"He disappeared the same time Agatha did. He knows what happened to her, I'm sure of it. I have to ask him. If there's a chance she's here, we have to rescue her."

What I don't mention is that I also have a sudden, desperate need to ask the Badhbh why the magic in my sword keeps fading and how I can prevent it from happening. If I'm completely honest, maybe that's the main reason I want to speak to him and I'm just using Agatha as an excuse. . . . No. I shake my head and push that thought away.

Cray stares at me, specks of starlight glinting in his eyes.

"Wow," he eventually says. "You never fail to surprise me. No matter how reckless my plans are, you always manage to surpass them."

I smile, and so does Cray, though there's tension in us both.

"Thanks. . . . If that was intended as a compliment?"

"I'm fine for you to consider it one." Cray taps his chin with his fingers. "One problem, though . . . I mean, we have an infinite number of problems right now, but the first one that springs to mind: if the Badhbh is working for the Inglish, won't he kill us the moment he sees us, with that"—Cray makes a clicking noise with his tongue and twists his hand—"neck-snapping trick of his?"

"I don't think so," I say. "From the little I know about him, senseless killing isn't his style. All he cares about is himself. As long as we don't threaten him, I think he'll talk to us. Besides, he and I have a . . . connection of sorts."

Cray puffs out his cheeks. "As long as you're convinced."

"So you'll help me get to him?" I bury my hands inside my cloak to try and stop them from shaking.

"Sure. Like you say, if Agatha's in trouble, the least we can do is try."

"Thanks." I shift my weight from one foot to the other. "So . . . um . . . how do we do this?"

Cray laughs. "All ambition and no strategy, eh?"

I give a sheepish shrug.

"Well, first of all, we should wait until it's darker," Cray says. "We'll keep track of the Badhbh to find out which tent he's staying in, then creep in when everyone else is asleep."

Hearing the plan out loud makes it sound even riskier than

I'd first thought. Somewhere in the distance, a bird shrieks. Cray takes the spyglass from me and commences his vigil.

We take turns watching the camp. As darkness descends, the majority of the soldiers retire for the night, but two remain positioned outside the Badhbh's tent and show no signs of leaving.

"What do we do about them?" I ask.

"We need a distraction," Cray replies. "New plan: we send Bras charging into the camp, and in the chaos that follows, we sneak in."

"Won't that put Bras in danger?"

"He's big enough to look after himself, aren't you, scruff-face?" Cray ruffles the hair on the top of the bull's head.

I hold on to the hilt of my sword. "Okay, if you're sure," I say.

Cray takes off the sidebags and hides them in the dense bracken. He gives Bras a quick hug, wrapping his arms around the bull's mighty neck. "Speed true, my friend," he says. He whistles and pats Bras on his rear end, and Bras responds by galloping off in the direction of the camp. Cray watches his progress through the spyglass. Without it, all I can see is the occasional shifting black lump. An outburst of clatters and shouts in the distance informs me that Bras has met his target.

Without looking at me, Cray grabs my shoulder and gives it a squeeze. "Let's go!"

He pockets the spyglass and rushes out into the night. I follow close behind him, the long wet grass flicking droplets into my face as we run. The swishing of our footsteps is uncomfortably loud, as is the sound of my anxious breathing.

As we draw nearer to the camp, the area Bras stampeded

through becomes immediately obvious. Tents have been pulled down, and people are darting around trying to figure out what happened. The closer we get, the more the tents blur into one another—so much so that I become disoriented and have no idea which one contains the Badhbh. I follow Cray, trusting he still knows where we're going.

When we're no more than a few hundred yards from the encampment, Cray slows his pace and stoops. I copy him, crawling along beside him. He stops outside a tent, which I presume is the Badhbh's. The soldiers have gone, like Cray predicted. My body is so tense, it feels like it might crack. After a quick glance around us, Cray unbuttons the entrance to the tent and steps inside. I shake off my fear and follow him in.

The moment we enter, the darkness inside the tent swallows us whole. There's no fire, no lantern, nothing.

"Cray?" I say.

"I'm here." His hand touches my arm.

"Well, well," says a voice in front of us. "This is quite the surprise."

My whole body freezes. No one moves. No one speaks.

My fingers hover over the handle of my sword. We need to be able to see. . . . I don't have much choice.

I ease the sword out of its scabbard, and it fills the room with its eerie red light. Cray's face is tinged with surprise at the sight of the blade, but my focus is on the Badhbh. He's sitting cross-legged with his hands resting on his knees, in much the same pose as the first time we met. The surreal light accentuates the deep bags beneath his eyes and gives his whole appearance a sinister edge.

To my surprise, there are cuffs around his wrists and a chain connecting his ankles.

"I see you have been practicing," says the Badhbh, glancing at my sword.

I ignore him. "We've come to find Agatha," I say.

"She's not here," he replies.

"So where is she? I know her disappearance had something to do with you. If you've hurt her . . ." The Badhbh has the ability to infuriate me like no other.

"Do go on," says the Badhbh, remaining as impassive as ever. "If I've hurt her, what exactly will you do?"

"Please," I say. "We haven't got much time."

The Badhbh sighs. "To my knowledge she is still at the palace."

"What palace?"

"The one belonging to King Edmund."

"What? What's she doing there?"

Cray raises a hand in my direction. "Jaime, keep your voice down."

"You took her, didn't you?" I say to the Badhbh, chewing on my anger. "What did you do to her?"

"She was my hostage, yes. I thought if I presented her to King Edmund, I would gain his trust, which would allow me to get close enough to put an end to this war."

I can't get my head around it. Agatha, in the capital, as King Edmund's prisoner. How will we ever rescue her from there?

"I don't believe you ever intended to help. I bet you traded her in exchange for your own protection—that's much more your style."

The Badhbh shrugs. "There may have been an element of that," he says. "But my intentions were not entirely ignoble, despite what you may think. After saving the girl Sigrid . . . " His eyes glaze over as he looks to the ground. "I've spent the majority of my life in solitude, tormented by the demons of my past. But saving that girl reminded me . . ." A slow breath trickles out of his mouth, rattling the back of his throat. "What does it matter? I traveled to the capital thinking I could make a difference, that's all there is to it. As it turns out, King Edmund's death changed nothing."

"Wait, King Edmund is dead?" says Cray.

"He is, but not by my doing. He was poisoned. I don't know who by. It is Konge Grímr who is leading this army now."

"But he's Norvegian; why are they following him?" I ask.

"Why do people follow any leader?" says the Badhbh. "Because he's powerful and strong. And convincing."

I take a step toward him, the sword aimed at his throat. "Whether you went there to help or not, you still gave them Agatha as a prisoner. You're a traitor. I ought to kill you right now."

The Badhbh doesn't even blink. "Perhaps you should, but we both know you won't."

He's right, of course. I lower the sword.

"Jaime, we need to go," says Cray.

The commotion outside has died to a murmur. The soldiers could return at any moment.

"Get up," I say to the Badhbh. "You're coming with us."

"No," says the Badhbh. "I am not."

"We haven't got time for this. I'm trying to rescue you!"

"I do not need rescuing."

"Of course you do. Look at you—you're in chains, for good-ness' sake!"

The Badhbh stares at me. The blade's glare sets his eyes ablaze. "You cannot win this fight," he says. "With these bracelets on, I'm no use to anyone. My actions have chosen my side for me, and my fate is sealed. The only choice I now have is to remain here. Once you have been defeated, my life will be spared."

"You can't honestly believe that!"

Cray grips my arm, firm and insistent. "He's not going to come. We have to go—now—or we're not going to make it out of here."

There are voices outside, approaching the tent. We're too late. The footsteps stop next to the entrance of the tent. I ram my sword back into its scabbard, and darkness descends once again.

The soldiers outside stop talking. What if they saw the light? We wait in silence, none of us daring to breathe.

Nothing happens, but we're now trapped inside the tent.

"Follow me," Cray whispers, close to my ear.

There's a gentle rustle followed by a cautious ripping sound. A thin slice of light creeps through a slit at the back of the tent. From his crouched position, Cray beckons me to follow, then slips out.

Just as I am about to leave, the Badhbh calls to me, his voice quiet yet no less assertive. "Keep the sword strong," he says. "You're going to need it."

I turn back; his whole body is swathed in shadow.

"What do you mean?" I say. I crawl towards him, not wanting the soldiers to overhear us.

"Konge Grímr has a *sgàil*," he says. "The most powerful ever created."

I choke on his words.

"How?" I ask. Then it dawns on me. "You made it for him?"

"I thought once the bracelets were off, maybe I could . . ." He shakes his head.

"Jaime!" Cray's frantic whisper pierces me from the other side of the tent.

"How do I keep it strong?" I ask. "The sword. I've been feeding it my blood and I said the incantation, but it always wants more."

Outside, the soldiers stamp their feet to keep away the cold.

"That is because you did not create the magic within it," the Badhbh says.

"So give me some of yours." I yank the sword back out of its scabbard and hold it before the Badhbh. The red glow smears his face once again. *"Blood magic is stronger when the sacrifice is made by someone else.* You taught me that."

The Badhbh stares at me, his face both ferocious and intense. He peels open his hand.

"This will be the last thing you ever ask of me, Jaime-Iasgair," he says.

The sword quivers, itching for the Badhbh's offering. For my clan, for our future, I grip his wrist and slide the blade across his flesh. He doesn't even flinch as the blood begins to flow.

"Sahcarà om rioht liuf," I say as the sword guzzles the blood with violent greed. The Badhbh watches me, his expression painfully blank.

"Enough," he says, clenching his fist to cut off the supply.

The sword shakes so violently it feels like it's about to explode. I slam it back into its scabbard and plunge us into darkness. In the last flicker of light, the Badhbh's face changes, and his final look is now burned into my eyes — one of loneliness and regret, as if he was asking for forgiveness. But it is not for me to forgive. I have nothing more to say to him.

I crawl through the slit at the back of the tent and I run. The sword at my side pulses with more power than I have ever known.

JAIME

WE SNEAK AWAY FROM THE INGLISH CAMP WITHOUT ANY-
one seeing, and when we reach the edge of the forest, Bras is
already there waiting for us. I tell Cray about Konge Grímr's *sgàil*,
which he takes as one more reason to return to Skye as quickly as
possible.

The moon is high and bright, stained with grubby patches.
After a grueling ride, we stop near a waterfall to stretch our backs
and give Bras a rest. I chew on a couple of dry oatcakes and wash
them down with water from the pool.

"Why does your sword still contain magic?" Cray asks.
"Everyone else's weapons lost their power as soon as the last *sgàil*
was defeated."

"I don't know," I say. Cray lifts his eyebrows. He knows I'm
lying. "Something happened to it during the fight," I admit. "It
came into contact with my blood, and that made it stronger
somehow."

"And it's kept that strength ever since?"

"Well . . ." The waterfall spits at us through the darkness. "I didn't want it to fade so . . . I've been feeding it blood."

"Whose blood? Not your own?"

I give a resigned nod, unable to meet his eyes.

"Jaime, what were you thinking?"

"It was only small amounts. I've barely felt it."

"That's dark blood magic you're meddling with; it could be affecting you in ways you don't even realize. Is it the reason you fainted earlier?"

I shrug.

"Jaime, please, you have to stop. I've heard tales of blood magic. It's like playing with fire—you're going to end up getting burned."

"I don't think it needs any more. The Badhbh gave it some of his own blood in the tent, which made it even stronger."

"Why did he do that?"

"I don't know. Maybe he felt bad for creating the new *sgàil* so soon after we'd defeated the other ones. Even though he refused to help us, I don't think he actually wants us to be harmed."

"He's got a strange way of showing it. Can I see the sword again?"

I hesitate but can't really say no. As I withdraw the sword, the waterfall blazes into life, its droplets caught by the fierce red light. The weapon is thriving because of me and all that I have done for it.

"It looks powerful," says Cray. The crimson glow accentuates the frown on his face.

"It is."

Cray purses his lips. "Have you ever heard the story of the burning swift?"

"No," I reply.

"It's an old tale, one we used to be told as kids. Swifts are incredible birds, you know. They almost never land, just keep on flying forever. They eat, mate, and even sleep in the air. Amazing, when you think about it. It wasn't always that way, though, or so the story goes. Back in a time when the world was new and the air still fizzled with magic, humans and animals lived side by side in perfect harmony. All was well until men discovered they could manipulate magic to do their bidding, and before long they were using it for vengeance and greed. It darkened their souls and corrupted the land."

"You're really getting into this, aren't you?"

"Shush. Just listen. The Gods were distraught and asked their faithful servant, the white swift, to collect the magic and destroy it. The swift left at once and swallowed all the magic it could find. Each mouthful made it stronger and more agile, until it became the fastest of all birds."

Cray looks at me. The reflection of the sword dissects his eyes with two harsh red lines.

"When the humans found out what was happening, they tried to catch the swift with their spears and nets. The swift knew the humans would never give up, and that there was only one way it could rid the world of magic forever. It turned its beak skyward and flew toward the sun: the home of the Gods. Higher and higher it went, but as it did so, the ends of its wings began to singe, for its small body could no longer contain all the magic it had consumed. Eventually, it burst into flames and tumbled out of the sky."

"Bleak," I say.

"I'm not finished yet," says Cray. "The burning swift didn't die, but the fire turned its feathers from pure white to sooty brown. The magic had altered it so much that the Gods no longer recognized it and refused its place by their side. Although the swift's sacrifice took most of the magic from the world, small traces of it lingered, which swifts still chase to this day. And that's why they never stop: because they know if they do, humans will take the magic from them and use it for evil." He rubs his hand over his jaw.

The waterfall beside us continues to gurgle. Overhead, a lone owl swoops out of the clouds, on a silent hunt for prey.

"Why are you telling me this?" I ask.

Cray tilts his head to one side. "I think you already know the answer to that."

I look down at the sword in my hand. Its light burns my eyes.

"I'm doing this for my clan," I say. "To make me strong."

"You already *are* strong, Jaime." He picks up my hand and squeezes it. His eyes are full of concern. "You don't need magic, and you've got nothing to prove. Promise me you won't cut yourself again. Please."

I squeeze his hand back. It's rough and warm.

"I promise," I say, and I mean it.

THE SUN IS HIGH BY THE TIME WE REACH THE ENCLAVE. The Hawks hit the chimes as we approach and signal for the Moths to let us in. Bras charges through the open gate without breaking speed, then comes to a halt inside. Maistreas Eilionoir, Kenrick, and some of the leaders from the other Skye clans march toward us.

"Well?" asks Maistreas Eilionoir. "What news?"

"They're close," I say. I'm so tired, I practically fall off Bras. "There are thousands of them. As many as Sigrid described. More, even. As well as armored horses and these . . . creatures they've got locked up in cages. We couldn't see them properly, but—"

"Jaime, slow down," says Kenrick. I take a moment to catch my breath. "How long until they reach the shore?"

"Depending how fast they travel," says Cray, "it could be as soon as first light tomorrow."

"Tomorrow!" yells a woman from the small crowd that's gathered around us.

Maistreas Eilionoir shoos away her cry. "We knew the attack was imminent. We'll be ready."

"The Badhbh's with them too," I say. "He took Agatha."

"What? Why?" asks Maistreas Eilionoir.

I explain how he kidnapped Agatha and gave her to King Edmund, probably for his own protection.

"What a truly despicable man," says Maistreas Eilionoir with a growl. "Although perhaps, in some ways, she will be safer in the south than here on the battlefield." There's a look in her eyes that I can't quite place.

We also tell everyone about King Edmund's death—which comes as a surprise to them all—and about the sgàil. They make plans to construct large fires in preparation against it, in case the battle wages into the night. Sgàilean can't move through water, so unless someone brings it over in an amulet or something similar, the *sgàil* will be stuck on the mainland and unable to harm us; from the moment the fighting starts, we mustn't let a single person cross that channel.

"With the enemy so close, we have no time to waste," says Kenrick. He starts issuing orders, and the people around him leap into action. His words drift over me like falling leaves.

"Jaime, you should get some rest," says Cray.

"I can help," I say, but my eyelids disagree, fighting to close.

"He's right," says Maistreas Eilionoir. "You've already played your role, providing us with crucial information. Now you both need to conserve your strength for the fight to come. You're going to need it."

I don't have the energy to protest further. As I turn to leave, Maistreas Eilionoir beckons me to one side.

"I wanted you to know there have been far fewer arguments between the clans since that speech you gave," she says. "Hardly any at all, in fact, and no more fights. The leaders of the Skye clans met this morning and discussed things at great length, and we've agreed not to force our values on others, or to punish those who disregard our beliefs. And do you know what I've discovered? It doesn't irk me quite so much as I thought it might."

"Oh . . . Well, I'm glad," I say. There's a lightness inside me, like the world just got a little brighter.

"You have made a real difference, Jaime," she says. "And thank you for teaching this old bird that sometimes even the oldest traditions need to be questioned. In fact, maybe the oldest ones need questioning the most."

I nod in agreement. I don't know what to say, so I don't say anything at all, but I'm beaming both inside and out.

"Now go and get some rest. And don't you dare tell anyone I referred to myself as an *old bird*."

"I promise," I say.

She taps my arm and then turns back to the other leaders, who are deep in conversation over what still needs to be done.

Cray and Bras walk me to my bothan. "Do you think you'll be able to sleep?" Cray asks once we're there.

"I'm so tired I actually might," I say, emphasizing my point with a boulder-size yawn. "I should make the most of it, really—it's probably the last sleep I'll ever have."

"Don't talk like that," says Cray. "If we give up now, there's no point even trying."

I manage a weak nod and place my hand on the bothan door.

"See you later, then," I say.

"See you later."

I pause, sensing he might be about to say something else. Our breaths pour out as clouds of frozen air.

"Jaime . . ." Cray scratches the side of his neck. "This may be the only opportunity I get to say this, so I'm just going to say it. . . ." He nudges a clump of grass with his foot, then raises his head to look at me. "I like you. A lot. I know you're no good at receiving compliments, and I'm even worse at giving them, but . . . well, I've never met anyone like you, and if things were different . . ."

My heart beats faster than it's ever done before. "If things were different, what?" I ask.

He bites his lip and leans in toward me. I meet him halfway

and we kiss, slowly at first and then like the whole world depends on it. It lasts a moment and a lifetime, and I've never felt joy like it. Afterward, we drift apart and it's just Cray and his smile, and how can anything be wrong with that?

"In case it wasn't obvious . . ." I take a breath. "I really like you too."

Cray places his hand on the side of my face. "Good to know," he says. He gives me one last kiss, then mounts Bras and leaves for the Bó Riders' camp.

I watch them go, not taking my eyes off them until they disappear from view.

Sigrid

THE FROST CREPT IN LAST NIGHT AFTER WE SPOTTED THE
army. We couldn't relight the fire in case they saw the smoke,
so it was a miserable evenin of not much nappin. It will of been
worse for the northern women, though, cuz most of them had to
sleep outside. I didn't hear none of them complain, so I'm not
complainin neither.

By the time we woke up, the ground was hard and covered in
ice, and it's been like that ever since. There's too many of us to try
and sneak past the kings' men, so we haven't got no choice but to
follow them, at a distance, all the way back to Skye. Mal-Rakki ses
they'll have spies and scouts lookin ahead and to the sides but not
behind, so that's where we're safest.

The original plan was to lead the northern women back to the
enclave on Skye, but we can't do that no more. We'll have to fight
on the mainland, takin the army by surprise once they reach the
water. Or praps, if the Skye people manage to make them retreat

like they're hopin, we won't need to do no fightin at all. I'm hopin that's what happens, cuz seein the army in daylight really slams hard just how bulkin it is. It takes over the land wherever it goes. The sound of the marchin echoes off the hilltops and shakes the ground.

We spotted Konge Grímr easy. It's hard to miss him with those skap antlers growin outta his kog. He's ridin a bulkin red horse right near the front, surrounded by wreckers and Inglish soldiers. There's a boy ridin with him, and if I squint hard enough through Mal-Rakki's spyglass, I can just about make out the chain what's connectin them. He's got himself a new pair of eyes.

"He's just one man," ses Mal-Rakki, starin at Konge Grímr for the hek thousandth time. "If we can find a way to defeat him, the rest of the army will topple."

"How can you be so sure?" I ask.

"Most soldiers who fight in wars don't want to be doing the things they're doing. They're coerced into it by a false sense of duty or religious fervor. In this case, the majority of them are following a king who isn't even their own. If we can give them a reason to stop, I believe they'll take it."

"Why don't we make some sorta weapon, then, and take him out from a distance while he's not expectin it?"

"It's a good idea," ses Mal-Rakki, "but we don't have the materials we'd need, and Konge Grímr's armor looks pretty impenetrable. Not even one of Sable's darts would pierce it. Not from a distance, anyway . . ."

That's what gives me the thought. The next time Sable comes to speak to us, I ask her for one of her darts—the most potent she has. She gives it to me without even askin what I want it for. I cover the sharp end with a strip of bark and slip it into the side of my boot. If I ever get a sniff of a chance, I'm gunna take out Konge Grímr myself.

🛶

ON OUR SECOND MORNING OF FOLLOWIN THE ARMY, THE snowflicks start comin down thick and fast, turnin the whole world white. The branches of the trees droop under the weight of their latest coverin. I'm wearin all the clothes I brought with me, but I still can't stop from shiverin, like I might turn into ice at any moment, then fall off Eydis and smash into a million pieces.

"The army's stopped," ses Mal-Rakki. I'm in front holdin the reins, so he's got the spyglass. The northern women are some way behind us, hangin back so they don't get spotted while we scout ahead.

"Stopped why?" I say. "They don't never stop durin the day."

He tastes the air. "I think they've arrived at the channel. I can see Skye."

Oh, skap. The battle's about to start.

"It doesn't make any sense, though," ses Mal-Rakki. He's still holdin the spyglass to his gawper.

"What doesn't?"

"They haven't got any boats or ships, so how are they planning on crossing the channel? They can't be thinking of swimming. They'd be easy targets in the water, and with all that armor on, those that did make it across would start the battle exhausted. So what's their plan?"

"What are they doin now?"

"It's hard to make out. They're rolling forward some sort of giant crate."

"Dirty tricks," I say. It sure isn't gunna be nothin good. "Give me the spyglass, and I'll creep closer on foot, see what I can find out." There's a tree-spattered slope what curves around and overlooks the army from above, which looks like a good spot for spyin.

"I'll go," ses Mal-Rakki.

"No, you're too bulkin. It'll be harder for them to see if it's just me."

I jump down off of Eydis's back.

"Did no one ever tell you that you should respect your elders?" ses Mal-Rakki. He's smilin when he ses it, though.

"Plenty of people told me that," I say. "I just don't always choose to listen."

"You're quite something," ses Mal-Rakki, which makes me brim. "Stay alert and don't get too close." He hands me the spyglass and somethin small carved outta wood. "If you get into trouble, blow on this."

I give the wooden thing a sniff—I dunno why; it smells of wood, which I probly could of guessed—then shove it in my pocket.

"I'll circle back to the northerners and explain the situation," Mal-Rakki ses. "We need to finalize our attack strategy. Once you've found out what you can, meet me back here. Agreed?"

I nod, then shoot off in the direction of the army, bein careful to keep myself low and hidden in the trees. I keep brushin against branches what then dump a cowcrap loada snow on my kog. Stupid skittin trees. More than once, I have to bite back the swear words what're ticklin my tongue as the cold slips down my back.

There's enough snow on the ground now that I'm leavin footprints behind, makin it hek obvious where I've been and where I'm headin. I rip down a branch with loadsa twigs attached and use it to try and cover my tracks. It's a deadwaste effort and makes too much noise, so I ditch the branch and forget about it. I creep on my toes instead, so the tracks aren't as clear.

When I get to the top of the ridge, I take out the spyglass and focus on the army. The soldiers are in neat lines, spread along the shoreline, with the ones ridin the horses at the front. They're facin the water and holdin their weapons as if they're about to charge straight over the top of it. What the skit are they plannin? I'm still too far away to learn anythin useful. I gotta get closer, but I promised Mal-Rakki I wouldn't do nothin too risky. . . .

Somethin moves on my right. I stare into the whiteness. Evrythin's still and icy quiet. I turn away, and whatever it is moves again. I crouch down lower, pressin my body into the snow. I still can't see nothin. My breath is comin out smoky. Must be a hare or a beaver or whatever animal they have in this place. It'll be more scared of me, I reckon.

I ignore it and look at the army again. They're all waitin for somethin. But what? I lower the spyglass, and the tree in fronta me makes my heart sickflip. I dunno why, it's just a tree, same as it was a moment ago. Only it's not. There's a shimmer to it that wasn't there before—a quiverin that's not quite right. . . .

I jump up to run, but the imitator is quick. It leaps from the tree, its mouth open, makin a sound in the back of its throat like a skapped mountain cat. Its body is still covered in the rough texture of the tree's bark. I throw myself onto the ground and roll away from its grabbin arms. There's snow in my mouth and my eyes and my hair. I come to a stop and get back onto my feet. I'm spinnin around, checkin all directions. The imitator's gone. Rot them to hell for bein able to disappear so easy.

I reach for the dart in my boot but then change my mind and pick up a hefty stone instead. I raise it above my head and show my teeth and my tongue like a wrecker would, even though I haven't got no ink on my loller yet.

The imitator appears outta nowhere and rushes into my side. I drop the stone and fall to the ground. *Ouuf!* My stogg's throbbin rumbles. I try to pull myself away, diggin my nails into the earth beneath the snow. I'm kickin out at evrythin and nothin and anythin what's there.

I scramble to my feet, but in the same sniff, the imitator has me pressed against the trunk of a tree. It's strong, pinnin my shoulders into the tough bark. My arms hang dead at my sides. Lucky it can't poison me through my clothes. It's almost twice the size of me. Evry time I try to move, it shoves me harder into the tree.

I raise my head, and somethin changes in its eyes. They lose their harsk edge, and its grip on me softens. Next thing I know, it's let go of me completely and it takes a step back. I can see it proply now. Its chest heaves in and out, even though it doesn't look sapped. Its skin is mesmerizin, ripplin through browns and blues like slushy mud and growlin sky. It doesn't have no hair on its head nor no eyelashes neither. Just two bulk, impossibly black eyes. Then I notice its leg.

The bandage isn't there no more and the wound has nearly healed, but I can tell from the shape of the scar that it's the same imitator I sewed up when we first arrived on the mainland. It cocks its head to one side, and its fingers start twitchin, like it can't decide if it wants to kill me or not.

"Hello," I say in the foreign tongue, still not knowin if it can understand me. "Friend, remember?" I point to its leg and mime a sewin action. I know it recognizes me.

It jerks its head the other way like a wary clucker. Sometimes it acts so human, and other times so much like an animal. Its fingers relax, and it turns to leave.

"Wait." I have an idea. It might be hek foolin, but this could be my chance to get close to Konge Grímr. "I need go there," I say, pointin again, this time in the direction of the army. The imitator stares at me. I haven't got no clue what it's thinkin. I peel away from the bark and take half a step toward the imitator. "You help me?"

The imitator snatches out and grabs hold of my sleeve.

"No," I say, tryin to pull away, but it leans its face close to mine until our eyes are almost touchin. Somethin tells me it's askin me to trust it.

I relax my arm, even though my heart's pumpin rivers. The imitator turns away from me and tugs at my sleeve until my hand's on its waist. It then does the same with my other hand so I'm holdin on to its sides, facin its back. It understood me—this is exactly what I wanted!

It steps through the trees and leads me down to the army. Hidin behind the imitator, I can get as close as I like, and no one's gunna see me comin.

Agatha

IT HAS BEEN A LOT OF DAYS SINCE WE LEFT THE BIG building where King Edmund lives which is called the palace. I ride on Gray and we run together a long way with the other wildwolves. Sometimes they stop to eat a cow or a goat or some rabbits they find in the forests. I don't watch when they do that. I ate all the food that I took from the lady in the bothan. I found some damson fruits on a tree and some chickweed and some cobnuts but I am hungry a lot. There were some mushrooms but they might be poison ones that make me sick so I didn't eat those ones.

At night I make a fire except for when there was too much rain and the leaves were soggy. That night was my worst night because it was so cold and I couldn't sleep. Gray is not scared of the fire anymore. She thinks I am very clever to make it and she is right. She likes the hot and sleeps next to the fire and next to me. Some of the other wildwolves come closer too. I don't think they are my friends but at least they don't want to eat me now, because I make them warm and they like it.

Yesterday we crossed the big dip in the ground with the dark grass, which means we are back in Scotia. I am so happy to be here. I have been thinking a lot about how to stop Konge Grímr. It is so hard when his army is so big. The wildwolves can get him, I know they can, but Gray still won't say yes she will help.

We stop by a stream for some water. Gray and the wildwolves lick it fast with their tongues. I go on my knees and try to lick it like they do. It makes my face wet and doesn't go in my mouth. It is not a good way to do drinking when you are a person. I use my hands and scoop the water instead. Aileen taught me how to do that. I have to be quick so it doesn't drip through the holes. I press my fingers tight together but there is always holes.

Sometimes we see places where the grass is flat and dead and there is bones and rubbish and burned patches. It is where the Ingland army was, I think. The wildwolves suck on the bones and crunch them. Gray says the land is ruined in these places and it is sad to see it. I tell her yes, this is what Konge Grímr and his army did and they will keep making the land be ruined because they are bad people. That is another reason she should help me stop them. Gray says stop asking for help and is growly. Wildwolves are so annoying ones.

We have passed lots of lochs this morning. Some of them are small ones and others are bigger. Then we pass a big big one. Its water is black like dark nighttime. I say to Gray to look at it because it is so pretty. She does not like the pretty and she tells me we mustn't go near that one. I ask why not. She says that's the loch where the uilebheist lives. I think it is a joke and I laugh. The uilebheist is not real. I tell Gray she should not be scared of the made-up story. It is only for children. Gray says I am wrong. She has seen the uilebheist with her own eyes and that it is much worse than a person, worse even than the king who locked her in the cage.

Oh. Sometimes animals know more things than people do. That is why it is good to talk to them, to find out the things. If the uilebheist is real . . . I have a thought coming that is maybe a plan. I do not know if it is a good one because it is only the start of it.

How do I make the uilebheist come out of the water? I ask to Gray.

She tells me I do not want it to come out of the water because if it does, it will eat me and I will be dead.

I do not want that. But I do want to speak to it. There must be a way. Gray says only the seals speak to the uilebheist. So there is a way. I can speak to the seals and ask them to talk to the uile-bheist for me. I ask Gray to take me to where the seals are. She says she won't take me there because the seals are on the edge of the big loch and it is too dangerous.

I say please and that it is important.

She stops running then and asks why I want to go there. I tell her because it is my plan and that is all I say. Gray says it is not a good plan and she does not want me to be eaten. That makes me happy because it means she likes me a bit now. I do some thinking and then I say, *If you take me to where the seals are, you can leave me there.* It is a lot of risky to say that one.

Gray thinks and turns her head. She says I am making a bad choice.

Please, I say.

She says okay, she will take me. Good, that is good. I think. But she tells me that whatever happens, she will leave me at the loch and will not take me back to Skye. That is the new deal. I nod my head and agree.

Gray does some barks at the other wildwolves and then we turn a different way, toward the loch. It is a tricky way to get down because of the slopes and the stones that tumble. Gray does lots of huffing on those bits. It is hard to keep having me on her back. I am not very heavy but also maybe I am a bit heavy.

The loch is close now and I can see it. It is big huge like the sea. The only difference is I can see the other side. There are lots of trees there. It is the biggest loch in the whole of Scotia and its name is Loch Lomond. It is where the uilebheist in the stories lives, but also it is a real loch. The beach is lots of tiny stones and water licking them.

Gray stops and says this is where she will leave me. I ask her where the seals are and she points with her head. I still cannot see them. I am good at looking because I am a Hawk but sometimes my eyes don't see that far. She says if she goes any closer the seals will be scared and swim away so she has to leave me here.

I climb off her back. There is wildwolf hair all over my clothes. I brush it off but a lot of it stays on. I don't like it sticky on my fingers. Gray looks at me with her yellow eye and her blue one.

Thank you for bringing me here, I say to her.

She says her promise to me is finished. That is true but I say to her once more to help us stop the army, for my clan and for hers. She doesn't reply when I say that. She turns from me and runs back up the slope where we came. She did not say goodbye and

I didn't say goodbye either. Now she is gone and I am by myself alone.

I do not know if it was a clever plan to come here. If the uilebheist is not in the loch or doesn't speak to me, then I am stuck and I will have to walk all the way to Skye by myself. I hope that's not what happens because I don't know the way. Okay, time to speak to the seals so off I go.

When I am nearer, I can see the seals more better. There are lots of them flopped on a big rock and also some on the smaller rocks that poke out of the water. I walk slowly so I am not a scary one. When I am close enough to do the talking I say hello to them in my head. The talking makes them scared and they go plop plop plop into the water. They make lots of splashing because they are a fat shape like slugs.

Wait, don't go! I say in my head. I run to the big rock where the seals were and climb to the top of it. The rock is wet and there are limpet shells on it. Also there is some green that is slippy-slimy.

I look into the water where the seals went. It is only ripples now and dark. *I am a friend,* I say into the water. I do the arrows fast to make sure all of them hear it. I am good at doing those arrows now. *I want to speak to you seals please.*

One of the seals' heads come out of the water, then another one and more. There is lots of them. I have never seen a seal close before. Their eyes are big and shiny. Water goes drip from their whiskers. They have funny faces and I like them.

I want to speak to the uilebheist, I tell them.

One of them makes a honk noise lots of times. Then the other ones do the same noise. I think they are laughing at me.

It is rude to laugh at people, I say. I stamp my foot because I am cross.

They stop doing the honking. That is better. It is smelly here. I think it is seal poo or the slime.

No one speaks to the uilebheist, says a seal voice in my head. The one that says it swims forward. It is not the biggest one or the smallest one. It is a middle one.

You speak to the uilebheist, I say.

The seal tells me no, they do not speak with the uilebheist. All they do is show it the best places to find food so the uilebheist doesn't eat them instead.

I am having another dangerous plan. I am good at thinking of plans today, but all of them are the dangerous ones.

I am food, I say to the seal. *Bring the uilebheist here so it can eat me.*

The seal is confused. *Why?* it asks me.

If you do it, the uilebheist will be happy and not eat you, I say, and then I say, *Please.* Always remember the manners. They are important for being kind.

The seal's head dips under the water and is gone. The other seals go under the water too. There is no splash noises when they do it. I do not know if they have gone to find the uilebheist or if they are gone away and won't come back. I have to do the waiting to find out.

Clouds go over the sun. They are thick ones. It is cold now like maybe it will be icy and snow. I wrap my cloak around me tighter. My clothes are dirty from all the days not changing them. Also my hair is the worst ever because I didn't wash it. When I am back on Skye I will clean it and stroke it and then it will be pretty again.

The water moves in the middle of the loch. It is only a small bit of a wibble and then it is a lot of wibbles. The rock I am standing on goes shaky. I hold out my arms to keep from falling over. Something is coming out of the water. My eyes go squint to look. It is not a seal. It is bigger than a seal. Much, much bigger. Its head comes out first and it is a huge one. It has a scaly face with all bumps on it and nostrils. Then its neck comes and it is so long it keeps coming more and longer. Two big arms come out of the water next and they are wings. They spread up to the sky the size of trees. Water drips from them like it is raining. The wings flick up and down to shake off all the water.

The animal looks at me with big orange eyes and then opens its mouth and roars.

It is the uilebheist.

JAIME

I WAKE UP WITH A JOLT. IT'S LIGHT OUTSIDE; I SLEPT FOR
the whole afternoon and right through the night. I throw off my
covers, grab the sword from beneath my pillow, and pull on my
boots. In the bed next to mine, Aileen stirs and her eyes blink
open.

"It's morning," she says. Misty sunlight drifts across her face,
making her wild hair shine.

"It is."

"And we haven't been called yet?" She sits up, suddenly wide
awake. We both slept in our clothes, and hers are now thick with
creases.

"Let's find out what's happening."

We hurry to the bothan door and discover that the world has
changed overnight, transformed by a thick blanket of snow. The
ground, the trees, the bothans, are all glistening white, reflecting
the sun with pride. I can't help but smile; I've always loved how
magical the year's first real snow is.

"It must have snowed during the night," I say.

"Whatever gave you that impression?" Aileen stares at me in mock disbelief.

I stick my tongue out at her and then, as if unleashed at the same moment, the two of us race out into the snow. It creaks under our boots, submitting to our weight. I bend down and scoop up big armfuls, throwing them into the air and then watching the powdery clumps fall. Aileen jumps up and grabs a tree branch above me, causing it to drop a load of snow on us. I cry out, somewhere between a laugh and a scream.

"Right, you asked for it," I say. I scramble together a handful of snow and launch it at her. She opens her mouth to protest, and the snowball hits her directly in her face. She squeals and spits, not quite believing the luck of my aim.

She retaliates by launching a snowball of her own. I leap behind the wall of our bothan, and her missile misses. When I lean back around to throw another clump at her, she's nowhere to be seen. I step out, alert, scanning all the places she could possibly be hiding.

"You can't hide forever!" I say.

"I don't intend to," comes a voice from behind me. She grabs my waist and shoves me forward. The two of us topple to the ground. We grapple, alternating between laughing and spluttering as we shove handfuls of snow into each other's mouths and up each other's noses.

Our shouts attract the attention of some of the children, who run to join us. Soon a full-blown snow fight has erupted. Shrieks of glee ring through the enclave as we duck and dodge, leap from trees, and throw handfuls of snow in one another's faces. All thoughts of the army are pushed from our minds as we laugh and tumble with an almost giddy joy.

The sound of a bass pipe brings an abrupt halt to our game.

Everyone freezes. The blast is long and low, sending tremors through the ground. When it stops, the only sound is that of heavy breathing as the twenty or so children try to catch their breath.

"What does that noise mean?" asks Owen, the young messenger boy who always has the messiest hair. He's covered from head to toe in snow.

There's no point hiding the truth. "It means the enemy is approaching the channel," I say.

His eyes bulge wide. A girl nearby lets out a sob.

"Go, now, to the nursery," I tell them. "All of you. You'll be safe there."

Owen scampers and the others follow him, creating dirt tracks in the snow as they sprint toward the nursery. Our play-fighting has trampled the crisp whiteness into sludge, destroying all its former beauty.

The bass pipe sounds again as Lenox strides toward us. The slightest frown appears on his face when he sees us so disheveled, but he decides not to comment.

"Time to leave," he says.

A large group has gathered by the Lower Gate with Maistreas Eilionoir at the front, trying to organize everyone. The Bó Riders are there too, ready to transport as many of us as they can to the channel. Cray seeks me out from within the mass of bulls and makes his way over. My heart leaps, remembering the moment we shared outside my bothan.

"Hi," he says. "You ready for this?"

"In no way whatsoever," I reply.

"Excellent. Care for a ride?"

I climb onto Bras's back and put my arms around Cray's waist, already knowing that when we reach the shore, I won't want to let go. Murdina—Cray's mother—trots over to us on her bull. She doesn't say anything, but when she sees the pair of us, there's a knowing look in her eye and the hint of a smile on her face. I introduce her to Aileen, who she helps onto her bull.

Lenox tries to convince Maistreas Eilionoir to stay in the enclave, but she's not having any of it. "I need to be where my people are," she says. "Now, which one of you strapping young men is going to offer me a ride?"

"It'd be my pleasure," says Finn. He dismounts and lifts Maistreas Eilionoir onto his bull as easily as if she were a made of feathers.

"It must be my lucky day," says Maistreas Eilionoir, admiring Finn's biceps.

Finn smiles and takes his position in front of her. One by one, we break away from the crowd and charge in the direction of the channel.

By the time we arrive, hundreds of allies have already gathered, including Mal-Rakki's rebel warriors, who look fierce and ready to fight. There's no sign of Mal-Rakki himself, though, nor Sigrid; they still haven't returned from Ingland. I suppose we've run out of time for them to help us now.

Despite how many people are spread along the shoreline, it's almost silent. All eyes are on the mainland, on the enormous rolling blur that is creeping ever closer. The echo of the soldiers' marching feet and clanking armor reaches us from across the water. My fingertips start to prickle, and not from the cold. I breathe in the brittle morning air, trying not to choke on it.

I have the sword. The sword is my strength. The sword will protect us.

Lileas's parents, Hector and Edme, beckon me and Cray over to a large catapult. Aileen and Murdina join us. As I dismount, Hector pats me on the back and says, "There may be a lot of them, but they've never encountered Raasay weapons before. We'll need your help loading the boulders, if that's okay? No job is a small job in times of war."

"Of course," I say, my focus still on the army. It's positioned along the Scotian coast, many men deep. For a long time, no one moves. The wind weaves around us without so much as a whimper. My teeth begin to chatter despite the fires that have been lit to combat the cold. The stillness is sharp and menacing.

"What are we waiting for?" Cray mutters under his breath.

"For them to make the first move, I guess."

There's a shift in their ranks as a large object makes its way through the mass of soldiers. It's a giant crate, although not one of the ones I saw when we were on the mainland. This one doesn't have bars, so it's impossible to see what's inside. The soldiers push it onto the water on some sort of raft, accompanied by twenty or so men, who then begin rowing it toward us.

"What's that?" asks Murdina.

"Whatever it is, it doesn't look good," replies Aileen.

The crate bobs closer. As one, the Raasay islanders swivel their weapons until they're all pointing at the raft.

"Hold your fire," Kenrick yells from some way farther along the coast.

"There could be anything in that crate," Conall MacLeod calls back. He's poised by one of the nearby launchers. "We need to sink it while we've got the chance."

The crate is now halfway between us and the mainland. Conall's finger is on the trigger of his launcher, itching to shoot.

"Wait," shouts Kenrick. "Once it's close, we'll be able to take out the individual members of the crew, leaving whatever it is stranded."

"Forget that," says Conall. "It needs destroying now." He puts his eye to the scope, adjusts his aim a fraction, and fires.

We hold a collective breath, wondering if Conall has made the right decision. A giant spiked javelin hurtles toward the crate, which explodes on impact, sending the rowers flying overboard as the whole construct sinks. There's a cheer from many of the allies, but it is short-lived. A low buzzing sound emanates from the obliterated crate, and then a swirl of flying creatures curls out of its remains.

"Uh-oh," says Cray.

"What has he done?" says Murdina.

"Fire your weapons! *Tilg urchair!* Fire your weapons!" shouts Conall.

All at once, I'm surrounded by the ear-splitting cracks of the catapults as rocks and arrows and everything at our disposal is launched at the approaching creatures. I bend over and cover my ears. The ground rumbles with every shot. As the missiles reach the swarm, it spreads and then shrinks again, dodging the attacks with ease.

"Again! Keep firing," Conall shouts.

"No," shouts Maistreas Eilionoir, drawing her sword. "That's exactly what they want us to do. We're wasting ammunition."

The Raasay islanders fire again and again, ignoring her pleas. The creatures are close enough now to make out their individual shapes. They must be the result of another of King Edmund's experimentations. They look like wasps but are the size of eagles, with hooked beaks, clawed feet, and sharp stingers at the end of their curved black-and-yellow bodies. They dive toward us, their collective buzz cacophonous. All around me, I hear the metallic swish of swords being drawn. Without taking my eyes off the writhing mass, I pull out my own sword. Its vibrant glow attracts a few looks, but no one mentions it. Its heat pulses through me.

I have the sword. The sword is my strength. The sword will protect us.

I brace myself for impact.

Murdina makes the first strike, piercing one of the giant wasp creatures out of the air with her spear. In the same motion, she spins the spear around and kills another with its opposite end. The two creatures split open and crash at her feet, oozing thick black liquid.

The whole swarm is upon us now, dipping and diving in a bedlam of wings and bodies and shouting and stings. I hold my sword higher, waiting for it to take over like it did against the *sgàilean*, but—even though I can feel the power coursing through it—it doesn't react. *No, no no. It can't be.* But I already know the truth: against anything but a *sgàil*, it's just an ordinary sword. In my hands, that makes it practically worthless.

I swing the blade around me in wild circles. The creatures' incessant buzzing fills my ears. I somehow land a strike across one of the creatures' backs and then clip the antennae from another, although that does nothing but enrage it. It comes at me with renewed vigor, opening its beak to let out a shrill cry. I stumble backward, swiping at it from the ground. Someone else's sword pierces its side. The creature hardens, its wings frozen in time as it's grabbed by death. My eyes follow the length of the sword and discover it's Maistreas Eilionoir who's come to my rescue. She shakes the beast from her blade and helps me to my feet.

"Keep going," she says. "We're winning."

I nod, and the two of us launch another attack. The whole coastline is a riot of shouting and bodies and the clang of weapons as they slice through their targets. The giant wasp creatures fall to the ground, littering the smashed snow with their corpses.

Once the last one has fallen, a collective cheer rings out. I join in until I see Murdina on the ground, clutching her shoulder. She's sweating all over, and her arm is pulsing red, inflamed to twice its normal size. Cray and Mór are both by her side.

"What happened?" I ask, rushing to join them.

"She was stung," says Cray.

"We need to get her to Finn," says Mór.

Between them, they lift her and start carrying her toward one of the emergency tents that have been erected.

"Can I help?" I call after them.

"We'll be fine," says Cray. "Stay here and stay alert. I'll be back."

Murdina is not the only casualty—plenty more people are limping or holding throbbing wounds. The brittle bodies of the dead creatures crunch and snap beneath their feet.

I turn back toward the mainland. The army doesn't appear to have moved, nor is it displaying signs of another attack. Balgair MacSween climbs on top of one of the launchers and raises his arms.

"The enemy's first attack has been defeated," he bellows. "It is time to show these *cnuimhean* exactly what we are capable of. For our island, for our lives, we fight as one. Fire your weapons— directly into the heart of the enemy. This time, they will not miss. *Tilg urchair!* Fire your weapons!"

On both sides of me, winches are turned, levers are locked, and ropes are pulled taut as the barbarous constructs are reset and reloaded. Then the brutal pounding begins again as the triggers are pressed in close succession, each one sending a shudder through my chest. The Raasay islanders prove they deserve their reputation as the world's greatest weapon makers, as the projectiles soar across the width of the channel; a mesmerizing arc of lethal splinters rains down on our enemy with silent fury. Even from this distance, cries shake the air as deamhain and Inglish soldiers are pierced, pummeled, and burned. Their neat lines break as their ranks are torn into chaos. The thought of all the pain that's being inflicted makes me want to be sick.

"Jaime, we need your help," says Hector, crouching next to a pile of boulders with a couple of other Raasay islanders. I stumble over to them; I forgot I have a role to play in this too. I help them half-roll, half-lift one of the largest boulders toward the catapult. Aileen and Edme pull back the weapon's arm, and then together we heave the load into position. Edme takes aim and fires. The power of the swinging motion is so great it almost knocks me off my feet. No one waits to see where the boulder lands—they've already left to collect the next. I shake my head and turn to help them.

I work with the others, hauling boulder after boulder into the catapult. Despite the cold, sweat drips from my forehead onto the thick mud and slushy snow. The few glimpses I snatch of the opposition show their ranks in disarray, their soldiers injured and fleeing. Our onslaught is working.

"They won't be able to take much more of this," Hector yells above the booming of the catapults. "Soon they'll have no option but to retreat."

I actually think he might be right. I presumed they'd have long-range weapons of their own, but they're not showing any signs of retaliation. Perhaps they thought the attack from the giant wasps would be enough to make us abandon our position. If so, they underestimated us. As confidence grows, some allies start jeering and shouting—fierce cries that match the roar of the weapons.

A short while later, Cray returns and adds his strength to our efforts. Under the strain of the giant rock we're carrying, I ask him about Murdina.

"She'll be all right," he says, but the reply is full of masked concern.

"Hold your fire! Hold your fire!" comes an order from

somewhere along the beach. We abandon the boulder and turn our attention to the enemy line.

An eerie silence descends as something odd happens to the water in front of us. It flattens. That's the only way to describe it. The tide stops, the waves die, and whole channel becomes still. I blink and shake my head.

"What's happening?" asks Aileen.

No one answers her.

Then there's an almighty eruption on the opposite side of the channel, as if the water's been struck by something heavy—but we're no longer firing any weapons. A murky stain appears on the surface of the water. No, not on the surface; it's where the water *used* to be. The channel is splitting in two, revealing the dark, slime-covered earth beneath. Great walls of water burst up with a thunderous boom, flinging spray in all directions.

My mouth hangs open. I forget to breathe. How . . . ?

Within moments, there's a wide path leading all the way from the mainland to us. The enemy raises their weapons high. Then, with a gut-wrenching cry, they pour through the parted waves, straight toward us.

SIGRID

THE IMITATOR LEADS ME ALL THE WAY TO THE BEACH
without no one seein. I step into each of its footprints and keep
my hams on its waist. Its skin is clammy and cold.

As we were walkin down, there were hek clatters from across
the water. It sounded like fightin, and there were some sorta creatures in the air. I couldn't see nothin more than that, though. It's
gone quiet again now; I don't know if that's a good sign or not.

The imitator and I sneak past thousands of Inglish soldiers—
all of them men and lots of them lookin itchy about what's gunna
happen next. The ones at the front have shields—covered in the
scraggin lynx what King Edmund loved so much—and armor what
shines gold and red. The soldiers farther back aren't as winnin; they
haven't got nothin but normal clothes and old-lookin swords, like
there wasn't enough of the nice ones to go around. I take evrythin
in—the number of soldiers, the positionin of their weapons, the
places they look weakest—anythin what could be useful.

At the front of the army, sittin smug on his horse, is Konge Grímr. He's only a few slogs away from me now. I reach into my boot and pull out the dart Sable gave me. All we gotta do is creep a little closer. . . .

With a boom what could shatter mountains, somethin plummets outta the sky and crashes bangsmack into the ranks of soldiers. A boulder, flung from the other side of the channel. Two sniffs later and more rocks, as well as javelins and flamin arrows, are spewin down.

The imitator's body stiffens, then it bolts, leavin me stranded in the open. *Jarg!* I dive behind a rock near the shoreline, hopin it'll be big enough to both hide and protect me. The army are too distracted by the onslaught. It's the Skye people what are doin it, and they're drivin the enemy back. As I'm watchin, I keep my peepers on Konge Grímr, waitin for any chance to get closer.

Hang on. What the skit's happenin now? A grabful of soldiers have started takin off their armor, even though the javelins and rocks are still crashin down around them. That's hek foolin. Looks like they're bein ordered to do it. They look confused, but obey all the same. They walk out into the water until they're up to their knees and then stop. There's about twenty of them, and they're facin away from the mainland so they don't see the wreckers what follow them in, knives raised. One of the soldiers glances back at the last moment and tries to warn the others, but it's too late: the wreckers slice open the soldiers and let their bodies drop. The water turns red as the wreckers splash back to the land.

There's someone else walkin forward now. I recognize him

straightaways, even though he looks even more scraggin than the last time I saw him. It's the Badhbh. Since when was he Konge Grímr's prisoner? A wrecker walks behind him, pointin a sword into his back and holdin a shield above their heads. He makes the Badhbh walk down to the water's edge.

"Do it! Do it now!" Konge Grímr shouts at the Badhbh. He's not on his horse no more, but he has a whole group of wreckers around him, all of them holdin shields above his head. The boy chained to him looks younger than me. He looks scared and all. I grip the dart tighter in my sweaty hand. "Do it quickly, before you're skewered by a falling spike," Konge Grímr shouts. A javelin lands in the ground not two spits from where he's standin, but he doesn't flinch one flicker. "This is your final task," he continues. "Do it, and you shall have your freedom."

The Badhbh slopes into the reddened water, not mindin that his robe is gettin drenched. The wrecker behind him keeps the sword pointed into his back, one eye lookin at the sky, at the weapons what are still rainin down. The Badhbh rolls up the sleeves of his robe, flexes his fingers, then plummets his hands into the channel. His face tightens, like he's battlin with somethin under the waves, or praps battlin with the water itself.

Blood magic.

That must be why they sacrificed those men, but what's the Badhbh plannin on doin with it? There's sweat burstin all over his face now, from his beard to his brow. Whatever he's doin, it's takin all his concentration.

As I watch, the waves seem to slow until they're not movin at all. It's hek creepin, like the whole world's stopped still. Then the water around the Badhbh begins to shake. At first it's just a tremor, but then the tremblin grows and the water nearby gets sucked away, like someone pulled a plug under the channel. The dip spreads, causin a split down the middle of the channel. I knew the Badhbh was powerful, but this is batwhack. Then, all at once, bulkin waves shoot into the air on both sides, revealin the seabed underneath. The ground is jagged and glistenin, littered with spasmin fish. My lips taste of salt from the mist what's filled the air. The water is hek towerin now. The waves crash back in on themselves with a deafenin roar of shattered white and seaweed black. I can't turn my peepers away, nor blink or nothin. How is this possible?

With the water shifted, there's now a path that stretches all the way from here to Skye. Holy godsmite, it's gunna be a skittin massacre.

"Á-dyrð-á-dyrð-á-dyrð!" shouts the wrecker on the leadin horse. It's a bloodsplash cry, callin evryone to battle. I've heard kidlins shout it plenty when they're playin at fightin, but I never thought I'd hear someone say it for real. The wrecker what shouted it thumps his heels into his horse's ribs and starts chargin through the parted waves. The rest of the wreckers go with him, the sound of their horses' hooves crunchin the seafloor as they descend. They're followed by an endless number of Inglish soldiers, all yellin, weapons raised.

Someone opens the giant cages, and a tangle of harsk animals falls out. I haven't never seen nothin like them before. They're gray and hairy like giant wolves, with snappin jaws and sharp teeth, but they move fast on eight skittin legs. They're the most twistgut creatures I've ever seen, like they're not real or they shouldn't exist. They join the brayin horses and the screamin soldiers, runnin full speed toward Skye with only one thought on their minds.

I'm not breathin. My eyes are stuck wide, starin at evrythin I'm seein. The Skye people are about to be hit by one hekmess of a storm.

Agatha

THE BIG ANIMAL MONSTER FLAPS ITS WINGS HARDER AND faster as it rises out of the loch. The air blows into me and nearly makes me fall over. Water drips from all parts of its body like there is a waterfall. The uilebheist is fat and dark gray color like a death-fin, with four flipper legs that have claws on the end. Its long tail goes swish behind it and is pointy. It is the biggest animal monster I have ever seen. Bigger even than a bothan or the biggest rock on the whole of Skye. It opens its mouth and does a roar again. Inside is lots of sharp teeth. Its head is so big. It could eat me in one bite is what I am thinking. My heart is booming fast in my brain. I am not afraid. I am very brave. I told the seals that it could eat me but I was only lying. I do not want it to eat me. Now I have to make sure it doesn't.

I try to talk to it but it is too big and I cannot do it. I need to be calm in my head and think of the arrow, but the booms from my heart are too loud in my ears.

The uilebheist goes higher in the air. Its neck is like a giant eel sliding. It looks at me and turns in the circle. It is thinking how to get me. I will not run away. The uilebheist stops its circle. It is high above my head. It opens its mouth and dives toward me.

I have to speak to it. I close my eyes and push away the thumping. I breathe and breathe again. All I think about is turning the words into an arrow like I have been practicing. It has to be the biggest fastest one ever. I open my eyes. The uilebheist's teeth are pointy jags. I fire the arrow straight into its head.

NO!

The uilebheist's neck whips away from me when I say it, and it flaps its wings hard to stop its body coming down. The wind from its wings is a whoosh on my face. My legs get the wibbly-shakes and I fall over onto my bottom. It is a bang one and a hurt one. I am not eaten by the uilebheist, though. That is the good part.

It crashes onto the beach where the pebbles are. Its long neck twists so it can see me. Then it turns around and clomps toward me, using its flipper claws to move across the pebbles. It walks in a fast and clumpy way. I think maybe it is going to eat me again. I stand up my tallest bravest and I say, *You will not eat me, uilebheist.*

It does not slow down clomping. It is so big. So so big. Huge. The ground is shaking. It reaches the rock where I am and its neck curls around me in a circle. I do not move. Its breath is hot on my face and smells of dead fish.

Hello, I say. I am still brave even though it is very close. *My name is Agatha.*

The uilebheist sniffs me with its big nostrils. Its eyes are bright orange with red bits in them.

WHO. ARE. YOU? it says in my head. It sounds different from other animals like it is far away and echoes.

I am Agatha, I say. I said that already.

It wants to know how I am doing the voice in its head. I say it's because I'm special. We are both special. I am special because I can do talking to animals and it is special because it is the only uilebheist in the whole world.

It is staring with its eyes. The red bits in them do swirls. I move my body a bit and its head follows me. It is all around me so I cannot get off the rock or run away. I don't want to do that anyway.

I need your help, I say. I tell it about Konge Grímr and the army and how they are going to hurt my clan if I don't stop them.

WHY. WOULD. I. HELP. YOU? it asks me. It flaps its wings once and all the trees shake.

I don't know that answer. I didn't think of it when I was doing the plan.

What do you want? I ask it.

MAYBE. TO. EAT. YOU, it says. *IT. HAS. BEEN. A. VERY. LONG. TIME. SINCE. I. HAVE. EATEN. A. PERSON.*

No, thank you, I say. *I don't want you to eat me.*

It tells me I do not look like I have the disease that killed everyone. I say that it is right: I do not have any disease. It opens its mouth. Its tongue is black and thick.

It says if I answer all its questions then it will not eat me . . . yet. It wants to know more about the army I spoke about. It wants to know so many things, like where the army came from and what Konge Grímr looks like and why he is in Ingland. I don't know why it wants to know all those things. My head starts to hurt from so much talking. Doing the arrows makes my head hurt less, but the uilebheist is so big that the hurt is coming back.

When I am finished talking about Konge Grímr, it wants to know more about Ingland and King Edmund and my clan and Skye and everything.

Why do you want to know all of everything? I ask it.

BECAUSE. KNOWLEDGE. IS. POWER, it says.

It tells me it is a thousand seasons old and was once the most powerful creature in the land, because it knew everything about everything. It roamed the Highlands, flying free, but then the disease came and the world changed. I think it means the plague. It couldn't hunt anymore because all the animals were rotten, so it hid in the loch and has been there ever since. It wants to be a part of the world again, so needs to know all of its secrets.

TELL. ME. MORE. OR. I. WILL. EAT. YOU, it says.

Okay. I tell it more about Ingland and King Edmund and the wildwolves and the bothan lady who dropped her potatoes when she was cross. Still it wants to know more.

My head is hurting the worst now and my eyes can't see properly. I cannot say any more.

No, I say. *I will only tell you more if you agree to help me.*

The uilebheist's head comes very close to mine. It breathes lots of air into its nostrils and then snorts at me. It is hot and horrible.

AGREED, it says.

Agreed! That means it will help me! The only bad thing is my head and the hurting. I cannot do more talking but I have to. I squeeze my head with my hand and scrunch my eyes.

NOW. TELL. ME. MORE, it says.

I tell the uilebheist about the Badhbh man and Norveg and the shadow things and about Knútr the nasty deamhan who was Konge Grímr's son. I say so much but always the uilebheist wants to know more more more.

Please no more, it is hurting me, I say.

MORE. MORE.

I say about Lileas who was my friend and the Nice Queen Nathara who died and Jaime and Crayton and Maistreas Eilionoir . . .

MORE. MORE.

About Aileen and Bras and Mór and Duilleag . . .

MORE. MORE.

About the enclave and the Skye people and the weapons and the wall . . .

MORE. MORE.

I have said too much.

All the world is black and my legs disappear.

❧

THERE IS WET ON MY FACE AND POKING. I DO NOT LIKE IT wet. I don't know where I am. I open my eyes.

There are teeth going to eat me! I move away quick. Under my hands are pebbles.

The uilebheist. It was the uilebheist doing the poking with its nose, and the wet is snot on my cheeks. It is very horrible and not nice. I wipe it off with my cloak and do a spit. The giant monster animal is standing over me. Its shadow makes me cold.

The rock I was on is over there. I am not on it anymore. I am on the beach. The uilebheist must have moved me after I went black. My head bangs sore with a very lot of pain and my eyes don't want to see properly. I blink lots of times to make them better. They are still blurs.

The pain is like when I screamed in the heads of all the wildwolves to make them stop attacking the bull people. When I did that, Finn was there to make me feel better. He is not here now. I wish he was. When it happened before, it broke my head and I couldn't speak to Milkwort for a long time. That was a sad one.

Milkwort, can you hear me? I ask him and he tells me yes. My head is not broken and that is good.

I need some water to drink. The loch is close and also far away. I go onto my knees and do crawling to the water. It is slow crawling because everything hurts. I have to go around the uilebheist. It watches me but it does not speak.

When I reach the loch, I splash water on my face to make the hurt feel better and then I drink some. It tastes too much of yuck and mud. I drink some more. Milkwort is thirsty too so I take him out and put him in the shallow part. He does not mind the mud taste or the yuck. After he has finished drinking, he looks up and sees the uilebheist. He does a little squeak and then runs back into my pocket.

YOU. FELL. ASLEEP.

It is the uilebheist's voice in my head that says that. It's wrong. I didn't fall asleep. I went black in my head because of too much talking.

YOU. TOLD. ME. A. LOT, it says. *MAYBE. TOO. MUCH.* It says it knows how to find my clan and that they will soon be dead from the fighting. All it has to do is wait for the battle to be over and then it will have all the food it needs.

NO! I shout. It cannot eat my clan. I will not let it.

It rushes to me then on its claws over the stones. I am not scared. I am angry. I stand up as it comes. My hands are fists. The uilebheist's neck comes down until its head is next to mine.

DO. NOT. SHOUT. IN. MY. HEAD! it says. Its eyes go wide and it shows all of its teeth snapped tight together.

You don't shout in mine! I say. I show all of my teeth too. They are not big ones like the uilebheist's, but they are tight ones and angry.

We stare at each other for a long time. The uilebheist looks away first. Its head turns on its neck and makes a roar sound like thunderstorms. Then it sneezes. The snot makes big ripples in the loch.

I. WILL. NOT. EAT. YOUR. PEOPLE, it says. Oh, that is good. It tells me it never liked eating people anyway. They have too many bones and not enough meat. It does not understand why I want to help other people, though. It does not know what a friend is. The uilebheist has always only been one.

Now that I am awake again, it wants me to tell it even more things.

No, I say. *I told you lots already. Now you have to help me like you promised.*

MAYBE. I. HAVE. CHANGED. MY. MIND, it says.

It is making me cross and I want to hit it. That would not be a good idea because it is bigger than me. The uilebheist says it will help me, but only if I tell it more about the world on the journey. I don't know if I can talk more. My head is so hurting. I have to do it. It is the only way to save my clan and my people.

Okay, I say. *But we have to go now.*

The uilebheist lowers its head until its long neck is all along the beach. Then it tucks in its wings.

CLIMB. ON, it says.

I am still a bit wobbles so I go slowly. The stones on the beach are crinkly with a crunch sound when I walk on them. The uilebheist's body goes in and out with breathing. I step over one of its big claw flippers and put my hand on its side. Its skin is warm and tough and thick. It feels like it is wet but it is not, like the viper snake I held once, which nearly killed me but it didn't.

It is high up to get on the uilebheist's back and I am still thinking if this is a good idea or not. If it flies up in the air then maybe I will fall off. I will hold on very tight so that doesn't happen. But what if I go black inside my head because of more talking? Then I will not be able to hold on. It will be a long way to fall to the ground and afterward I will be dead. I remember that I am brave and I can do it.

I pull myself up. It takes me one, two, three tries to do it. One of the tries I do a kick in the uilebheist's side and it does a grumpy humph. I say sorry to the uilebheist and that it was only a mistake.

Then I am sitting on the uilebheist's back. It is much higher than when I was on Gray and it is lumpy and not comfortable. There are sticking-up parts which go all the way down to its tail. I hold on to them which is the good thing but other ones stick into my tummy.

The uilebheist asks me if I am ready. I tell it that I am. It spreads its wings wide out to the side and flaps them once and then twice. The bones move under my knees and my legs. The uilebheist starts to run along the beach. I am bouncing and bumpy. It flaps its wings fast and then the bumping stops and we are in the air.

I am flying!

The beach and the trees and the loch are a long far way below me. They look small because they are so far. It makes me a little bit sick in my mouth to look at them. I look at the uilebheist's neck instead. I am so high. I am up in the clouds and they are wet on my face.

TELL. ME. MORE. OF. THE. THINGS. YOU. HAVE. SEEN, says the uilebheist.

I don't want to do it but it was the deal. I tell it about Thistle-River who is a deer and a kind one; I tell it about Lady Beatrice who is my mother and I didn't know; and I tell it about Gray the wildwolf who has one yellow eye and one blue one, who is sometimes nice but also growly.

The uilebheist likes all of my talking and beats its wings faster and faster.

The black swooshes in my head like it wants to come and get me again. I hold on tighter to the uilebheist's back. I can do this and I will.

I tell the uilebheist everything I can think of in my brain. The clouds whizz past us as it flies me toward my clan.

JAIME

IT'S IMPOSSIBLE; IT CAN'T BE HAPPENING. WE ALL STAND aghast as thousands of soldiers hurtle toward us along the newly created passage. Many of them are riding warhorses covered in sharp metal spikes. The twisted creatures that were locked up in the cages scurry along at their sides. At first glance, they look like wildwolves, but they're bigger and have multiple legs growing out of their sides—long spindly ones that look hard and brittle, like those of a giant spider crab. Their movement is inelegant, as if they're not quite used to their legs. Their mouths are open, ready to attack. All I can do is watch, my breath caught in my throat.

A few members of the alliance snap into action and fire their weapons. The leading horses topple as the missiles hit, and their riders are flung aside like scythed crops, but there are too many coming through to make a real difference. The hordes that follow trample the fallen ones without the slightest hesitation. The parted water gushes away from them, rising up high. Anyone who stumbles too close is sucked into the water and shot into the air in a blur of twisted limbs. This is the work of blood magic—that's the only explanation—which means it's the Badhbh's doing.

I wonder . . .

"Retreat!" someone shouts, and the call is repeated by others with growing desperation.

Mal-Rakki's rebel warriors storm forward and position themselves in an arrowhead formation, pointing at the approaching army. Even with their leader absent, they work as one and know exactly what to do.

"Return to the enclave!" one of them shouts. "We'll hold them back for as long as we can."

Several Bó Riders mount their bulls and join the deamhan warriors, their spears spinning above their heads. Maistreas Eilionoir pulls out her sword and stands beside them, as do other fighters from both Raasay and the Skye clans.

"Jaime, you need to leave!" says Cray, turning me away from the nightmare vision, which is now more than halfway through the crossing.

"No. I can fight," I say.

"If everyone fights, everyone dies. Give them something to defend. Go. I'll meet you at the enclave." He turns away and starts to sprint along the beach.

"Where are you going?" I shout after him.

"To save my mother," he calls back.

Instead of turning toward the enclave, I run down to the water's edge, a few hundred paces from the parted waves. I've had an idea. I splash in up to my waist and then, taking a deep breath, I pull out my sword. It's warm and strong in my hand. Without really knowing what I'm doing, I slice open the cut on my palm. I promised Cray I wouldn't cut myself again, but this is different. If blood magic caused the water to part, maybe blood magic can close it again.

I let my blood drip into the water and then bury the blade point-down into the waves. The moment it's submerged, the sword twists and shakes, reacting to both my blood and the magic already in the water.

"*Sahcarà om rioht liuf,*" I say, straining with all my might as I will the towers of water to topple.

Nothing happens. Of course it doesn't; the Badhbh is too strong. Every drop of water thrums with his power. I was foolish to think I could rival him.

I change tack, this time focusing on the Badhbh himself rather than the waves. The sword seems to knows exactly where he is and helps me aim.

"*Sahcarà om rioht liuf,*" I say again.

As I say the words, I pour thoughts of Lileas and Nathara and Donal into my command—all of my sadness and despair for their stolen lives. I also think of Agatha, abandoned and alone in the hands of our enemy. A burst of energy shoots from the sword, across the width of the kyle. It's a plea rather than an attack. It's all I can do. I can't tell whether it reaches the Badhbh or not.

"Jaime, what are you doing?" Aileen comes thrashing through the water toward me. "We have to get out of here."

"I'm trying to—I don't know. I was trying to—"

"If we don't leave now, we'll never make it back!"

She's right—the enemy has reached the island and is about to break through our first line of defense. Aileen grabs my arm, and I let her pull me out of the water, glancing back one final time in the direction of the Badhbh. The towers of water still stand, and the pathway remains open. I tried, but it wasn't enough.

Aileen and I pound over the snow, which groans beneath our feet. We soon catch up with the other fleeing allies. They run with heaving breaths, their feet thumping, faces strained with desperation and panic. A succession of clangs and shouts rings out from the battle behind us. The curdled screams make my skin crawl.

On either side of us, people stumble and slip on the ice. We stop to help them where we can, but it costs us time we can't afford. A quick glance is enough to realize the first of the armored horses have made it past the allies on the shoreline. They come storming among us, their riders striking with reckless abandon. My thighs start to throb, but I push through the pain and keep running.

The arrival of the horsemen has created panic, causing people to lose their way and run in the wrong direction. Without breaking pace, I draw my sword and hold it above my head.

"This way!" I yell. "Follow the light!"

Lots of allies notice the blaze and alter their course, but the glow also draws the attention of one of the horsemen. He charges until he's riding parallel to us, so close that flecks of spit from his horse's mouth spray onto my face. The horse's eyes flash, black and wild. I duck and push Aileen down with me to avoid a swipe from the rider's longsword. The horse doesn't break speed, forcing the soldier to gallop off in pursuit of someone else. The world smells of sweat and fear.

Several bulls join the throng as Bó Riders fend off the soldiers as best they can. Many carry additional passengers, including Duilleag, who thunders past us with Mór and Maistreas Eilionoir, the latter looking pale and unstable. I scan the crowd for Cray or Murdina, but there's no sign of either of them.

A bull careens to a halt in front of us. It's Gailleann.

"Climb on," says Finn, scooping up first Aileen and then me. Without another word from Finn, Gailleann sprints the final distance to the enclave. The people ahead of us are already rushing through the Lower Gate to safety, but when we're a few hundred paces away, the gate starts to close.

"They can't do that; they'll lock us out!" says Aileen.

They don't have a choice: the horses are gaining, and if the Moths keep the gate open, the enemy will breach the enclave.

"We're not going to make it," I say.

"We will," says Finn. He makes a clicking sound with his mouth, and Gailleann lurches even faster. The other day Finn bragged that Gailleann was the fastest bull in their tribe, but right now it's not fast enough. The gate inches shut moments before we arrive.

"Open the gate!" yell several clan members from the ground. They pound its surface with desperate fists, but the gate remains closed.

Finn turns Gailleann around to reveal the barrage of horses charging in our direction. Their hooves kick showers of snow high into the air, and the spikes on their armor glint pure menace. We're going to be slaughtered.

Sigrid

EVRYONE IS STARIN AT THE RUSH OF SOLDIERS STOMPIN
their way across to Skye and the magic of the water walls, so no
one notices me creepin out and makin my way nearer to where
the Badhbh is. Even the wrecker with his sword aimed at the
Badhbh's back is lookin the other way. The Badhbh's hands are
still in the water, and his face is strained from the effort of keepin
the waves up.

I cross the beach on feather feet until I'm squattin behind
another rock, then peer over the top and wave my arms to get the
Badhbh's attention. If he's surprised to see me, he doesn't show it.

Stop! I mouth, my eyes pleadin. I do a cuttin action across
my throat, hopin that means the same in his country as it does in
mine. The Badhbh just looks at me with the most harsk face I've
ever seen. I put all my feelins into my stare, tryin to communicate
through one look that he doesn't need to do this, that he's betrayin
evry single one of the islanders.

At that moment, a surge of somethin pulses through the water from the other side of the channel and hits the Badhbh bamsmack in his legs. He steadies himself, his face lookin both surprised and impressed at the same time. He glances toward Skye, and even though he keeps his hands submerged, somethin about him is not that same. I can convince him, I'm sure of it. I've gotta do it quick-spit, though; the first horse riders have already made it across to Skye and plenty more are followin.

I glance at the rest of the army. Evryone's still watchin the water, sept one person who's lookin directly at me. The boy chained to Konge Grímr.

I shake my head and put my finger over my lips. I want him to understand that *I know* what it's like to be chained to that grot-fiend, to be treated like the lowliest piece of filthmuck what's ever soiled his boot. I've been in his position—we're the same, me and him; we gotta look out for each other. But he doesn't know none of that. He tugs on Konge Grímr's elbow and then whispers in his ear. The king's back goes rigid, and he barks orders at his wreck-ers. The boy points to where I'm hidin.

Isn't no way I'm gettin outta this one. If I'm gunna get caught, I might as well make it count. I jump out from behind the rock and start runnin toward the Badhbh. I've still got the poison dart in my hand, but I'm not close enough to throw it. It's not meant for him anyways.

"Stop! Stop! Please!" I'm callin to the Badhbh. "Konge Grímr kill you anyway."

As I run, I stretch out my hand and show the Badhbh my palm—the one with the scar on it. I know he's got a matchin scar on his own hand. He looks down at his, beneath the water.

"You save me!" I yell at him in the foreign tongue. "You not bad person. Please. Save Skye people like you save me."

Hands are on me then, grabbin me and pullin me back. One of them shakes my wrist so hard, I haven't got no choice but to drop the dart. It falls to the ground and gets stomped into the sand. My hopes of stoppin Konge Grímr get stomped away with it.

A soldier tries to cover my mouth, but I'm not havin that. I bite him hard, and he quickly lets go. The Badhbh's eyes are locked on mine. I thrust out my hand to show the scar again, and remember what he said to me in the sickboth, about who I reminded him of. "Your daughter!" I shout, the plea burstin from my lungs. "Think your daughter. She not want this. You not bad person."

I'm bein dragged away now by I-don't-know-how-many skittin sickweasels—hams over my mouth, my arms, my chest—but the Badhbh's expression has changed. He doesn't seem as dead and defeated no more. He looks around at the wrecker what's got the sword pressed into his back and he looks at the lines of men, women, and battle beasts pourin through the channel. I'm only snatchin glimpses now, in between the pullin and the draggin. The Badhbh closes his eyes, breathes in, and then hauls his hands outta the water, raisin them high into the air. Silent drips fall from his arms.

At first, nothin happens. Then the walls of water stop movin, as if frozen in midair. The people draggin me halt to watch. The soldiers in the channel stop too, their eyes wide, all of them holdin their breaths. The water hangs there for a glistenin blink, catchin the sunlight in a perfect moment of peace. Then evrythin shatters as the sea comes crashin down with a thundercrack roar. Spray explodes into the air like the burstin of a volcano, and the land beneath us shakes so hard we nearly fall over. There's half a blink of screamin and yells as bodies are smashed together and swept off their feet, then the calm returns. The water has swallowed evryone from here to Skye.

A fine, salty mist rains down on the mainland. No one ses nothin. All we can do is stare.

The Badhbh lowers his arms and turns to the wrecker behind him. He knows what's gunna happen next. The wrecker grits his teeth and pushes his sword through the Badhbh's body.

As the Badhbh falls into the water, the expression on his face—the last one he'll ever give—almost looks like relief.

JAIME

PEOPLE ARE STILL BANGING ON THE LOWER GATE, DESPERATE
to be let in. I can't tear my eyes away from the armored horses
storming toward us, their legs striking the earth like angry ham-
mers. The riders sit tall, brandishing their weapons—they're going
to be upon us at any moment. Cold sweat leaks down my sides.
From where I'm sitting on Gailleann's back, I point my sword
in the direction of the horses, squeezing the hilt tight. The lead
horseman leers with a sick grin.

There's a noise to my right—a rumble from deep within the
forest. The sound of the horses' hooves is drowned out by a louder
thumping as something bursts out of the trees at great speed.

I can't believe what I'm seeing. It's the deer!

Hundreds of them, from all over the island. One stag leads
them, and although I can't tell them apart, I'm almost certain it's
Thistle-River. This is Agatha's doing; even though she's not here,
it's her who created the bond between us and them. They charge
at the horses, their heads lowered, fearless and determined.

The soldiers are so surprised that they pull back on their reins, giving the deer the advantage of speed. The stags lower their heads and crash into the horsemen with the full might of their antlers. Soldiers topple in a tangled mess of brays, cries, and thuds. The riderless horses bolt, chased into the forest by the deer. The ambush gives the Moths enough time to reopen the gate. The people closest push their way through.

"Get in," says Finn, encouraging us off his bull.

"You need to come too," I say, leaping down. The fallen soldiers have already picked themselves up and are running toward us, spurred on by a new kind of fury.

"I will," says Finn, "but there are still Riders out here. I have to help them first."

I start to protest, but he won't hear a word of it.

"If you're coming in, you need to do it now!" shouts one of the Moths in control of the gate. Aileen grabs my hand and pulls me into the enclave. The gate closes behind us with a resolute thud, leaving Finn on the other side. A couple of heartbeats later, the enemy crashes against the gate, unleashing cries of anger and frustration. Inside, we let out a collective sigh of relief. We're safe—or at least safer than we were.

Lenox bursts through the crowd and starts barking orders. He needs a group to remain at the gate, he says, another to make their way to the Upper Gate, and everyone else up onto the wall. The Bó Riders volunteer to ride to the Upper Gate and speed off as one. I crane my neck to scan their faces, searching for Cray, but he's not there.

"Let's go to the wall," I say to Aileen.

She nods and follows me up the stone steps.

Several Hawks are already there, raining arrows down on the enemy. Our launchers might not fire as far the Raasay islanders', but at this range they're just as deadly.

Now that we're higher up, we have a clear view of the battle-field, and the sight is sickening. Although lots of our allies made it back to the enclave in time, those that didn't . . . A long smear of death and destruction snakes from the Lower Gate to the channel. I can't look at it.

There are still a few pockets of allies fighting the enemy from the ground. Finn and Gailleann are there, skirting around the main bulk of the army. They stampede past several horses toward a small group of Bó Riders who are severely outnumbered. I squint, praying that Cray isn't among them, but I can't make out their faces. Finn raises his spear and flicks it with brutal efficiency, dis-abling several soldiers in a series of stabs and swipes.

More of the enemy approaches, closing in on the bulls from all sides. The Riders redouble their efforts. Their spears twist through the air as if dancing to an unheard beat, but no matter how many of the enemy they take down, more appear. One by one, the Bó Riders fall, until Finn is the only one remaining. He continues to strike with staunch determination, but there are too many sol-diers. His spear shatters against the sharp edge of an ax, and in the same instant, one of the soldiers slides a sword into his torso. His body falls from Gailleann's back. The bull lets out a heartbroken bellow.

I choke back my own scream as Aileen yanks me away. She's been watching too.

"We need to make ourselves useful," she says.

We're going to die today, all of us. That's all I can think. There's no way we can possibly survive.

My chest caves in on itself, crushing my lungs. I fall to my knees and try to catch my breath, but my insides have turned to stone. My body doesn't work anymore.

"Jaime? Jaime?" Aileen's voice is far away.

I shake my head. *No.* I'm stronger than this. I need to be in control right now.

Without looking up, I raise my hand. Aileen grabs hold of it. Her fingers are cold but not as cold as mine. I squeeze her hand with all my strength. My breath returns; I suck it in, wild and fast. My ribs feel brittle, as if inhaling might split them.

I look up at Aileen, at my best friend, someone who's always been there for me. Her eyes glisten, full of kindness.

"The fires," I say, noticing the majority of them have not yet been lit. I clear my throat and say it again. "We'll help by lighting the fires."

With Aileen's support, I pull myself to my feet. This battle isn't over yet. There are two torches beside the nearest hearth. I pass one to Aileen and use the second to light the kindling. As soon as it crackles to life, we pick up a large pot of sand that's resting nearby and set it over the flames. The sand will make a devastating weapon once it's heated, although I try not to think too hard about that. We run around the entire length of the wall, making sure all the fires are lit and all the sand is put to heat.

It was Donal who made these hearths. Even though he's no longer with us, he's going to help us win this fight. That thought spurs me on—I want to make him proud. As we pass, the Hawks and other allies shout their thanks, using the fires to defrost their hands and light their arrows.

By the time we return to our starting point, the enemy has the entire enclave surrounded. There aren't nearly as many of them as we spied at their camp, though; maybe they're holding some troops back, or perhaps the path through the channel closed before they could all cross—from this distance, it's impossible to tell. It's too much to hope that the burst of magic I aimed at the Badhbh was enough to change his mind. Whatever the reason, it'll be easier to prevent this many from entering the enclave. There are a few deamhain in their ranks, but there's no sign of Konge Grímr.

A group of about a hundred soldiers approaches the Lower Gate under the protection of large shields, each one emblazed with a roaring lynx. The Hawks shoot fire arrows at them, but the arrows rebound off the shields and fizzle out the moment they land in the snow.

Once the soldiers are closer, the shields part a little to reveal a large tree trunk. Its nearest end is chiseled to a point and reinforced with strips of metal. One of the soldiers yells a command, and the others rush at the Lower Gate. The tree trunk rams against the gate with great force, sending tremors across the wall.

"Brace the gate!" someone shouts from below.

The ram strikes again. The soldiers carrying the shields keep them tight above their heads.

"The sand. Unleash the sand!" calls one of the Hawks.

The first pots we set to heat are now scorching, so have to be handled with special gloves. Two Hawks nearest the Lower Gate hurl a load over the rampart. The blistering sand penetrates the raised shields in a way the arrows can't, trickling through the gaps in the soldiers' armor. The soldiers cry out in agony, dropping the trunk. The foray also causes their shields to slip, giving the Hawks with bows a chance to penetrate their defenses. At such close distance, the arrows strike fast and fatally.

"Jaime!" Cray comes running up to us. I almost burst with relief at the sight of him. I want to wrap my arms around him—and he falters as if he wants to do the same—but I don't, conscious of everyone around me. "Are you all right?" he asks.

"Fine," I reply. "How's Murdina?"

"She's inside the enclave, but she needs help—her wound's enflamed and she's becoming delirious. I left her at the sickboth with Bras, but there are too many people there and not enough healers."

"I'll go," says Aileen. "I worked there for a bit, so I know my way around."

"Really?" says Cray. "Thank you. Thank you."

"Look after this one, will you?" Aileen says, gesturing to me.

"Always," says Cray.

I squeeze the top of Aileen's arm. "Be careful," I say.

"You too." She gives me an affectionate punch, then bounds down the stone steps two at a time.

A high-pitched whistle draws our attention back to the enemy lines. It's answered by a collective howl. Ò *murt*.

"What the hell are they?" asks Cray.

The twisted wildwolf-like creatures scurry toward the wall on their long spider-crab legs, summoned by the sound of the whistle. They're hideous, like they've been created through torture and pain. As soon as they reach the base of the wall, they begin to climb.

They're fast; the first one makes it to the top before anyone can react. It lashes out with the spikes on the ends of its front legs while snapping its wildwolf jaws. Others join it, and before long, multiple skirmishes break out along the wall.

Fighters lean over and swipe at the creatures' legs, attempting to disable them before they reach the top. Some of the beasts lose their grip and topple, but others make it over the ramparts and wreak havoc on everyone around them. Their barks are scratched and gravelly, as if they're choking at the same time. The cruel sound mixes with the sickening clicks of their scampering legs.

Shouts rise from the Lower Gate; new enemy soldiers have replaced the injured ones and started battering the gate with the tree trunk again.

"We have to stop the soldiers at the gate," I say to Cray. "We need more sand."

He looks confused but follows me to a nearby hearth, which still contains a full pot. I don't have any gloves, so I wrap my cloak around the handle. The pot is heavy, requiring both of us to lift it. We work together, dodging past fighting bodies as we make our way toward the gate.

A grotesque leg curves over the top of the wall and slams onto the stones in front of us. We drop the pot, spilling some of its contents. The leg is covered in hard shell and spiky hairs. Cray whips out a long dagger and chops the leg in two. Another leg appears, its spike almost colliding with the side of Cray's face. I draw my sword and sever it with a gristly hack. The creature's great wildwolf head appears over the top of the wall for the briefest moment before it realizes it can no longer hold on, and it plummets to the ground.

We pick up the pot of sand and keep running until we reach the Hawks above the Lower Gate. They grab the pot from us with a garbled thanks and unleash its contents over the soldiers below. I turn my ears away from the screeches of pain that follow.

"Do you need more?" I ask the Hawk.

Before he can reply, one of the wolf-crab things scales the wall and appears in the gap between us. It licks its meaty lips and lunges at Cray and me. We both stumble backward. I scramble for my sword as it leans in, gooey drool dripping from its jaws.

The high-pitched whistle sounds once again, and the beast swivels its head. It takes one final look at us, then rushes back to wherever it came from. The rest of the creatures do the same, the thick clicking of their legs fading away as they scale back down the wall.

"That was close," says Cray.

"Why did they call them all back?" I ask.

The sound of the retreating creatures is replaced by the roar of a war cry. I look over the wall to find out where it's coming from, but the majority of the army is no longer there. The enemy's shouts grow louder, but they're coming from behind me, from *inside* the enclave.

I turn, not wanting to accept what I already know is true.

Hundreds of Inglish and deamhan warriors are spreading throughout the enclave. The spider-wolf creatures were just a distraction; this is the way they intend to defeat us.

"How . . . ?" mutters Cray, staring pale faced as our enemy rages below.

"Catriona," I say, seeing her at once. She's standing by an old well that looks like it's some sort of secret entrance: hordes of Inglish soldiers are clambering out of it, into the heart of the enclave. She's betrayed us all.

"This is for banishing me!" she shouts to anyone who'll listen, her cry barbaric and hysterical. "I said you would regret it, and now that day has come."

The next deamhan to clamber out of the well has something heavy around his neck: a necklace with a large green stone. With a wicked glint in his eyes, he raises the necklace high and opens the pendant.

"Oh, no," I say, knowing what's coming.

A dark shape slithers down the deamhan's body and spreads out over the trampled snow. It keeps growing until it's ten times the size of a man, with hideous clawed hands and grotesque antlers sprouting out of the top of its head.

It's Konge Grímr's *sgàil*.

SIGRID

"WELL, WELL, WELL . . . WHAT DO WE HAVE HERE?" THE SMILE on Konge Grímr's face is pigsick. I'd forgotten how much I hate him. "I'd almost given up hope of us meeting again, and then you run right across my path. You've been a very naughty little mouse."

I spit at his feet. The two bulkin wreckers what are holdin me squeeze my arms even tighter. Konge Grímr moves his non-eyes in the direction of where I spat, then back to me.

"Let's try to remain civil, shall we?" He smiles again, but it's more of a grimace. Behind me, yells from the soldiers mix with the clankin of their armor as they pull as many survivors outta the water as they can. "I've been wondering . . . whatever happened to Bolverk? I presume the fact he never returned had something to do with you?"

"I'm not tellin you nothin," I say.

He adjusts the harsk antler crown on his kog. "This charming creature is called Sigrid," he ses in the foreign tongue, speakin to the boy what's chained to him. It's a startler he even knows my name—he sure as muck never used it before. "She used to occupy the privileged position you now hold, but she made some poor decisions. Decisions which I'm sure she is now very much regretting."

The boy is starin at me and the ink on my face. I let him stare. I should be fiery at him for givin away my hidin place, but it's not his fault—he was only doin what he'd been told.

"What do you think we should do with her?" Konge Grímr continues. The boy doesn't say nothin. His knees are quakin. "You're right," ses Konge Grímr. "A slow and painful death would befit her gross treachery."

"Rot you to hell!" I shout. If only I still had the dart. Not that I'd be able to do much with these two sickweasels holdin me.

Konge Grímr tuts. "Is that any way to speak to your king?"

"You're not my king. Mal-Rakki is!"

Hearin his brother's name makes the king stiffen. "Mal-Rakki is dead. He has been for many years."

"No, he's not," I say. "He's alive and he's gunna be the new leader of Norveg."

Konge Grímr actually laughs at that, like it's the most hek smirks thing he's ever heard. "Enough of this," he ses. "End her life."

The wrecker next to him—a man with bulkin arms covered by the ink of two curlin adders—pulls out an ax, but hesitates.

"Why do you pause?" Konge Grímr asks him.

"She's just a girl," he ses.

"That *girl* just drowned half our army!" Konge Grímr growls.

"I'll do it," ses one of the other wreckers—a woman with a

ferret inked across her eyes. She's got evil in her snarl. She takes a step toward me and—

"Ow!" ses the man with the adder arms. His face is struck with confusion. He lifts his hand to his neck, to the dart what's stuck there.

"Get down!" the ferret wrecker yells at Konge Grímr. She pulls him to the ground and covers him with her body as darts come whizzin past us from all directions. The women of the north! It's gotta be, although I can't see none of them nowhere. Other wreckers also dive to protect their king. No one thinks about helpin the boy, who stands there moon-eyed as the chain tugs at his arm.

A dart lands in the neck of the wrecker on my left, and two blinks later, one hits the wrecker on my right as well. Both of them fall to the ground, releasin their grip on me. I run in the direction of the hillside, thinkin the trees there might offer me some protection. Inglish soldiers are fallin left, right, and evrywhere—the women must be close, cuz they're managin to find the gaps in the soldiers' armor.

The army starts retreatin, only it doesn't know where to retreat to, so evryone's just runnin batcrazy. I pick my way around their collapsin bodies, headin for the hillside, away from the chaos. I climb higher, not lookin back. It's a hard slog through the snow, and my breaths are comin out fast and loud. A hand reaches out from behind a tree and pulls me to the ground.

I bang my knee, twist away, ready to fight.

"Ow . . . Oh."

"Thought you'd be a bit happier to see me than that," Sable ses.

"I am. Women save me. Thank you."

Sable loads a dart into her blowpipe, leans around the tree, and fires. The dart finds its target, and another soldier collapses.

I quickly tell her evrythin I saw while I was down with the army. Sable nods, then picks up her stick with its hek blades tip and leaves to spread the word among the other women. I lean my back against the tree trunk, hushin my breath. The next time I look around, all of the northern women are runnin toward the army with their sticks held high. Even though the soldiers have better weapons and proper trainin, the ambush with the darts has headwhacked them, allowin the northerners to get the upper hand.

On the other side of the fightin, a rush of black gallops through the masses. Eydis's white mane streams behind her as Mal-Rakki bounds across the fallen bodies. It gives me hek frets, seein her around that many flailin swords, but I'm guessin they're lookin for me. Praps I can help Mal-Rakki get close to Konge Grímr.

I sprint back down the slope, tryin to keep my gawpers on Eydis. I haven't got no weapon. There are plenty strewn around from soldiers what've been struck with darts, but they're all bulkin swords what wouldn't be no good in my hams. A thousand soldiers stare out from where they've fallen, their eyes bright and pained. The venom from the darts has frozen their bodies, but they can still see what's happenin around them. And what they're seein is a hek wreckmess of a bloodsplash. If I'm not careful, I'm gunna be a part of it. I need to get Mal-Rakki's attention.

The whistle. I reach into my pocket and take out the wooden whistle Mal-Rakki gave me. I'm not really expectin it to be heard over the yells and shouts of the battlefield, but when I blow it, the

sound of a cuckoo cry is loud and piercin. I blow three times. Mal-
Rakki looks up and then straightaways turns Eydis toward me. I
shake my head and point to where Konge Grímr and his wreckers
are. He nods and holds up one finger as if tellin me to wait where
I am.

He rides lightnin toward Konge Grímr, drawin his sword.
Thanks to all the clutterflap caused by the northern women, Mal-
Rakki's able to ride right up to him, but the king is still surrounded
by a clump of wreckers. There isn't no way Mal-Rakki's gunna
be able to get past them all. At the last moment, he leaps off of
Eydis and sends her in my direction. He strikes the first wreckers
down easy, but more are on him in a blink. Mal-Rakki's sword arm
moves at an impossible speed. Wreckers are the greatest fighters
in the world, but they can't stop Mal-Rakki; all that trainin in the
ice caves has made him the best there is.

Eydis whinnies and speeds toward me like most hek *ríkka* horse
alive. Once she's close, she slows down a speck so I can swing
myself on. She raises her head and shakes out her mane, feelin as
chirpin as I am that we're together again. I pat her neck as I scan
the fightin. Things have gotten a hek lot worse since the last time
I looked. Now that the confusion caused by the drownin and the
Inglish women has passed, the army are back in their formations,
rememberin their trainin. The northern women are tryin their best
to keep up their momentum, but their sticks are no match for the
soldiers' swords. Evry direction I'm lookin, there's more and more
women fallin. A stabbin feelin wrecks my insides. This isn't what
I wanted when I asked for their help. But what did I think would
happen? This is a war, and war never ends well for anyone.

I remember what Mal-Rakki told me: if the head of the army falls, the rest will topple. Stoppin Konge Grímr is all that matters. Mal-Rakki's still fightin off the king's wreckers, but it looks like he's tirin. I gotta help him.

"Come on, Eydis," I say. The last thing I wanna do is put her in danger, but if we don't stop this fightin soon, there isn't gunna be no hope left for any of us.

Jaime

AS THE *SGÀIL* EMERGES FROM THE DEAMHAN'S PENDANT, daylight fades as if pulled away by a hungry tide. This shouldn't be possible; the *sgàilean* have only ever come out at night before. This *sgàil* is clearly different: bigger, stronger, fewer weaknesses. I suck in a painful breath. The sword rests in the scabbard at my hip. This is the moment it's been waiting for—the reason I've kept it strong—yet something stops me from drawing it.

A group of our allies rushes at the deamhan in an attempt to steal the necklace, but they're too late—the *sgàil* is already loose. It dives among them, tearing and flinging them aside in a series of vicious swipes.

Above the cacophony of clanging swords and pained cries, Catriona continues to screech. "You brought this on yourselves," she says. "All I asked is that you put your trust in me, but you were too weak. I would have led you to greatness!"

Her shrieks catch the attention of the *sgàil*, which glides back through the grass toward her. A look of surprise splashes across her face as the *sgàil* grabs her leg.

"What? No! He promised me you wouldn't—" Her sentence is cut off as the *sgàil* yanks her to her knees, drags her several paces, and then tosses her away. She soars through the air before colliding with the enclave wall. Her broken body plummets to the ground.

I swallow a mouthful of vomit. With a *sgàil* that powerful, we don't stand a chance. Which is why I have to defeat it.

"Cray, you need to go." I say.

"Go where?"

"Anywhere. Away from here. I'm about to do something stupid."

I snatch my sword and raise it high above my head. Its power rushes through my veins, making my whole body feel alive. This is how I protect my clan; I'll die defending them if I have to. The blade's deep crimson glow pulses out around me. The *sgàil* pauses mid-attack and turns to face me. There's no going back now.

"Jaime, no!" says Cray.

"You need to run."

"Give me the sword; I'll do it."

"No. It's my blood that's strengthened it—it has to be me."

The *sgàil* sweeps toward us with an earth-crumbling growl.

"Then let's do this together," says Cray.

"You can't, not without magic. Please. It'll kill you."

"I'm not leaving you."

"Dammit, Cray, get away from here!" I scream. I point the sword at his throat.

He stares at me, his eyes pleading with mine.

"You're the bravest fool I've ever known, Jaime-Iasgair," he says. One last look, and then he leaves, holding his spear high as he races to join the fight below.

"Get down from the wall!" I shout to the remaining people nearby. "Quick, get away from here!"

They follow my instructions, leaving me alone where I stand. The *sgàil* swoops over bothans and around trees, snatching, grabbing, killing as it goes.

It's started to snow again. The flakes drift around me, weightless and at ease. The light from the sword makes them glow a dazzling pink. A couple land on my eyelashes, and I blink them away.

The *sgàil* is now directly beneath me, traveling up the wall to where I am. I turn my sword so its tip is facing down, ready to strike. I breathe through gritted teeth, my body tense. Blood magic pulses through the blade—magic that *I* sustained. The sword is strong and so am I. We can do this. I *will* do this.

The moment the *sgàil* creeps over the edge of the wall, I thrust the sword down, but that's exactly what the *sgàil* is expecting me to do. It shifts to one side, and the blade rebounds off the stone, sending a hard jolt up the length of my arm. The sound of the *sgàil*'s hideous whispering is all around me.

The sword flicks up, almost of its own accord. Sensing its prey, it glides through the air in the direction of the *sgàil*. We work as one, slicing, slashing, jabbing, but the *sgàil* is too fast and shifts away from every strike with impossible speed. I drive the shadow back, swinging again and again, but each attack hits nothing but stone.

I pause to catch my breath, the sword poised vertically in

front of my face. The *sgàil* stops too, waiting, watching. Then it lunges at me, its monstrous claw swiping at my legs. I stumble backward and trip. The moment I hit the ground, an aching cold envelops me, penetrating right to my core. The *sgàil* is on top of me; I can't escape.

The blade is flat against my chest. I try to turn it, but my hands are held firm. An intense burning sears my fingers as the *sgàil* attempts to prize the sword from my grasp. I scrunch my face against the pain, but the *sgàil* is too powerful. My fingers crack open, and the sword flies from my hands. The *sgàil* snatches it up, lifts it high, and then slams it into the top of the wall. The moment it hits, the blade smashes into a hundred pieces and its light fades to nothing.

NO!

The strength the sword gave me immediately disappears. I collapse, exhausted and defenseless.

The *sgàil* slips from my body and lifts its head, displaying Konge Grímr's hellish silhouette. Its body starts to heave, as if it's laughing at me. It's over. Without the sword, I'm nothing. I close my eyes and wait for the *sgàil* to deliver its final strike.

Something flickers from behind my closed eyelids. Fire. It's the one thing *sgàilean* are afraid of. There's fire in the hearths all around the wall. I open my eyes. If I can reach the nearest one, I may at least be able to defend myself.

I scramble toward it, but the *sgàil* anticipates my move and gets there first. It rushes at the flames and sucks them into its body, leaving behind a pathetic tendril of smoke. That shouldn't be possible either—fire is supposed to repel *sgàilean*. Not this one.

The *sgàil* leaves me then and travels in one unstoppable motion around the perimeter of the wall, consuming every fire it passes. I follow its progress, watching its darkness swallow the small dots of light one by one. It moves like a raging boar, wild and uncontrollable.

It's coming back around, its show of power almost complete. I need to get off the wall before it returns. With the blade destroyed, I can no longer defeat it.

Something glints on the ground a few paces from me. A voice in my head screams at me to run, but I have to know.

I approach the glimmer. It's a piece of the smashed blade, which looks like it still retains a flicker of magic. I pick it up but feel none of its former power. Its points are sharp and prick the palm of my hand. Tiny droplets of my blood creep over it, but it doesn't absorb them. It's weak, but weak doesn't mean useless.

The *sgàil* is approaching fast. I conceal the piece of blade behind my back and hold my ground. The magic within the blade may be weak, but I am not. This is me, and I'm going down fighting.

As the *sgàil* turns the final corner, I run straight at it. Blood pounds in my ears. The moment before we collide, the *sgàil* rises to its full, terrifying height, its antlered head piercing the sky. Its edges flicker with black flames from all the fires it consumed. I duck past its taloned hands and launch myself into its torso, swinging the blade fragment around as I do so. I take the *sgàil* by surprise and plunge the sharpest end of the blade into the depths of its body.

For the longest heartbeat, nothing happens. Then wisps of black fire spread out from the point at which the blade hit, scorching my face and singeing my clothes. I stand firm, digging the blade deeper. A shriek rips through the air, louder than the death of a thousand gulls, and then the *sgàil* explodes in an eruption of darkness.

The force flings me high into the air, over the wall. My stomach flips as I fly through the dispersing flickers of black. The ground spins and the sky is scorched. I'm on fire, burning.

The echo of the *sgàil's* screech fades to nothing, and the world turns silent. Above me, the sun breaks through the clouds, and I reach out for it as if it might save me. Then I start to fall.

Sigrid

EYDIS DOESN'T HESITATE ONE SNIFF AT RIDIN BACK
through the battlefield. Mal-Rakki's jaw is clenched tight as he
strikes one way, then another, blockin an attack from a wrecker
behind him, then takin down one that's in front. His face is spat-
tered red.

A yell to my left pulls my attention. The whole battlefield is
filled with yellin, so I don't know why this one shout grabs me, but
it does. There's a northern woman runnin from a wrecker who's
chasin her with his ax raised high, ready for slammin. She's limpin,
so doesn't stand much chance of outrunnin him. The wrecker
doesn't look like Bolverk, but somethin about the way he's pursuin
her reminds me of him. The woman is Sable.

Now what? Who do I help — Mal-Rakki or Sable? If Mal-
Rakki can get to Konge Grímr, this whole madness might end,
but if I don't help Sable, there's no tellin what that wrecker's
gunna do to her. It was me who dragged her into this; I can't
abandon her now.

I whistle and give Eydis the slightest tug on her rein. She responds straightaways, recognizin Sable as soon as she turns her head. We chase after her, splashes of brown sloshin our legs as we tromp. The wrecker is less than a spit from Sable now, and we're still too far away—we're not gunna make it. The wrecker lifts his ax. I can't look.

A dark shape leaps through the air and crashes into the wrecker, knockin him off his feet. The ax flies from his hand. He tries to find it again, but the beast has him pinned. It's a wildwolf—like the one King Edmund made us chase on his hunt—sept this one hasn't got no muzzle over its gobbler. It opens its jaws, and one flittin scream later, the wrecker isn't movin no more.

"Sable," I call.

She was so distracted by the mess, she didn't notice we'd come.

The shout makes the wildwolf turn our way too, its bloody jaws drippin. Its fur is matted gray and its teeth are hek blades. Eydis takes a couple of trots back. I dunno if she can outrun a wildwolf, should it come to that. Sable doesn't move none. The wildwolf pierces me with its eyes, which are diffrunt colors: one yellow, one blue. It looks from me to Sable, then shakes its scraggin kog and dives back into the battle.

Now I'm lookin, there's a whole load of wildwolves all around us. They're leapin and gnashin this way and that, and from the looks of it, they're only attackin the enemy soldiers. They're *helpin* us. I haven't got no time to be wonderin why.

"On," I say to Sable.

She leaps onto Eydis quickspit, and then we're back racin toward Mal-Rakki. The whole way there, I'm prayin to the High

Halls that he can keep fightin just a little longer. He's surrounded by bodies now, still thrashin his way to the king.

As we approach, a couple of wreckers try to smuggle Konge Grímr away. I nudge Eydis in their direction. From behind me, Sable shoots darts at them, and the wreckers collapse onto the ground, leavin Konge Grímr exposed. It gives Mal-Rakki the opportunity he needs. He pushes past the wreckers he's fightin and grabs Konge Grímr from behind, holdin a sword up to his throat. Konge Grímr knows it's over and puts his hands up in surrender.

Eydis skids to a halt. Mal-Rakki peers out from behind Konge Grímr and gives me a speck of a nod.

"Stand back!" ses Mal-Rakki to the remainin wreckers in a voice what's powerful without needin to be loud. "And lay down your weapons."

The wreckers look to one another like they don't know what to do. Konge Grímr's mouth is chewin malice. The boy on the other end of the chain has it pulled tight, wantin to get as far away from Mal-Rakki as possible.

"Are you going to kill me, brother?" Konge Grímr asks.

"Tell your warriors to stand down," Mal-Rakki ses in his ear.

"If I were you, I'd kill me now, while you've got the chance. But then you always were weak."

Mal-Rakki presses the sword tighter against Konge Grímr's neck. "Not weak; principled. But I will do what's necessary. Tell your fighters to put down their weapons. I won't say it again."

Konge Grímr's face slumps a sniff. "Do as he says."

One by one the wreckers drop their axes and swords. Evryone's attention is directed at Mal-Rakki and the king, includin mine. Eydis shuffles on her feet like there's stingers in her hooves.

Konge Grímr lifts his hands to his head.

"What are you doin?" ses Mal-Rakki. "Hands down."

"I'm taking off my crown. Isn't that what you want?"

Mal-Rakki blinks back the sweat what's dribblin into his eyes. "Do it slowly," he ses. "No tricks."

"I'm blind and you have a sword to my throat; what could I possibly be planning?" ses Konge Grímr. He lifts the antler crown off his head real slow. "With the removal of this crown, I relinquish my power as leader of this army and supreme ruler over the Kingdom of Norveg," he ses to evryone around. The tension in the air is so thick you could bite it.

"Throw it on the ground," ses Mal-Rakki.

"A crown is not thrown, brother; it is placed. You'll never get anyone to respect you if you treat sacred objects with such flippancy."

"Throw it on the ground," Mal-Rakki ses again, with more force this time.

Konge Grímr holds the crown out in fronta him as if he's about to drop it. "Remember what I told you," he ses. "If I die, you die."

Mal-Rakki looks confused, as if he's never been told that before, but Konge Grímr isn't talkin to him. He's talkin to the boy on the other end of the chain.

The boy doesn't hesitate. His eyes wide with terror, he runs in a circle around Mal-Rakki and Konge Grímr, wrappin the chain around their legs and pullin it tight.

"Look out!" I shout.

Their legs buckle. Konge Grímr doesn't miss the opportunity. He swings his crown over his shoulder, crackin one of its harsk antlers into Mal-Rakki's face. Mal-Rakki cries out and trips over the chain, the sword falling from his hand. Eydis leaps toward them, and Sable jumps down to help, but the wreckers are too quick. They've already picked up their weapons and are grabbin Eydis's reins. Swords are pointed at me and Sable. I put my hands in the air. There isn't nothin we can do.

The wrecker with the ferret across her face drags Mal-Rakki away, her sword at his throat. Konge Grímr returns the antler crown to his head and then reaches out and puts a heavy hand on the boy's shoulder. The boy's lookin around as wild as a goose. Konge Grímr's smile drips evil.

"I told you that you should have killed me when you had the chance," he ses to Mal-Rakki. A cruel laugh erupts from the pit of his stogg. Mal-Rakki doesn't say nothin in return. "And did I hear Sigrid has joined us as well?"

I keep my yapper shut.

"She's over here," ses one of the wreckers what's holdin Eydis's reins.

"I think you've caused more than enough trouble," Konge Grímr ses to me. "It's time for evryone to see what happens to those who betray me. . . . Pass me a bow and arrow!" Someone hands them to him. By feel, he nocks the arrow and draws back the string. "Point me in her direction, boy," he ses.

"Don't do this," shouts Mal-Rakki, strugglin against the wreckers what are holdin him back.

The Inglish boy moves the bow in Konge Grímr's hams until it's pointin in my direction. The aim is off, though. I dunno whether the boy's done that on purpose or what.

"Seems a little high. . . ." ses Konge Grímr.

"She's on a horse," ses the boy, makin his excuses. It's the first time I've heard him speak. His voice is hek quivers.

Eydis whinnies and shakes her head, not likin how tight the wreckers are holdin her reins.

"Keep still, you dumb horse," ses one of the wreckers, yankin hard on the reins.

Eydis stamps her feet.

"Don't you hurt her," I say.

I shouldn't of spoke. Now Konge Grímr knows exactly where I am. He adjusts the bow until the arrow's pointin at my face.

"Any last words?" he ses, grinnin like the worst grotfiend what's ever lived.

I look at Mal-Rakki, then back to Konge Grímr, raisin my head high.

"Hate is not the answer," I say.

Konge Grímr snarls and pulls the string taut, but before he has the chance to release it, the most hek bulkin creature I ever saw comes swoopin outta the sky. And on its back is Agatha.

Agatha

THERE ARE SO MANY PEOPLE. FROM WHERE I AM IN THE sky they are small like ants. It is all white and brown because there is snow on the ground. The sounds of weapons banging and people shouting comes up to the clouds where we are. We found the army and I am not fallen off dead. My head is pounding the worst ever ever and I mean it. I stopped the black from coming but only just.

The uilebheist turns its wings and we go down to where the fighting people are. My tummy does a funny-flip. I have to hold on tighter so tight. The wind is fast and makes my cheeks wibble.

When we are closer to the people, the uilebheist flies over their heads and does its roar. The fighting people stop to look at it and they look at me riding on its back. They cannot even believe it.

Then I see the wildwolves! They came and helped like I asked them too! I knew Gray was a good one. They howl at me and the uilebheist and the sky. I wave at them a little bit but then I nearly slip off so I don't do the waving anymore.

We fly lower, and now that we are closer, I can see too much of the horrible. There are dead people and broken people and hurt. It is not nice to see and I do not want it in my eyes.

Then I see him. Konge Grímr. His antlers are what make me see him. They stick up in the air above everyone else. They are a stupid thing to wear. He is on the other side of the fighting people near the water and he is holding a bow and arrow. Sigrid is there too on her horse. Konge Grímr is going to shoot her.

That's him, I say to the uilebheist. *The man with the antlers on his head. That is who we have to stop.* I grit my teeth tight because of the talking pain. I hope it is the last thing I have to say.

The uilebheist speeds fast toward Konge Grímr and lands with a big crash on the ground. Snow and mud flies up in the air, which smells like inside boots. There are lots of deamhan bodies on the ground and more deamhain standing up with weapons. Erika the ferret face is one of them. She has her sword at the throat of a deamhan man on his knees. I don't know why she is doing that.

Konge Grímr hears us crash down and moves his bow so the arrow is pointing at us. There are drips of mud on his clothes. He asks the boy on the chain what's happening but the boy cannot speak. His mouth is open and he has big eyes at the uilebheist.

"What is it, boy? Speak to me!" Konge Grímr says.

"It is me, Agatha," I say. "I am here to—stop you."

Konge Grímr moves the bow again to where he hears my voice. "You will never stop me, you pathetic girl. I am a king and you are nothing. You have been nothing since the day you were born. You will always be nothing."

The uilebheist roars once into the air. It swings its neck and knocks off Konge Grímr's crown. Then it opens its big mouth and bites off Konge Grímr's head.

I shudder all through my body. It is because of the surprise. I didn't know the uilebheist was going to do that. It was so quick when it happened. It is a good thing because Konge Grímr was a very bad man but also it is horrible to see it.

"I am not n-nothing," I say.

Konge Grímr's body wobbles on his legs and then falls to the ground in crumples. The Ingland boy screams.

Some of the deamhain run at the uilebheist and try to stab it with their swords, but the uilebheist's skin is too thick. It whips them with its tail and they fly a long way into the air. Other ones come too close and get snapped in its mouth. The rest of the deamhain run away because they do not want to be dead. The only ones left are Erika with the ferret face and the man in front of her.

"Lát frað, ela þu munu anzarr," says a voice. It is Sigrid on the horse. She says it to Erika.

I don't know what it means those words. I think she wants Erika to let go of the deamhan man. Sigrid gets off her horse and picks up a sword from the ground. She points it at Erika. There is another woman pointing a sword at Erika. She has two lines of mud on her face. That is dirty.

"Lát frað," Sigrid says again.

Erika ferret face looks at Sigrid and at the uilebheist and at me. She moves her sword away from the deamhan man's throat and drops it on the ground. Then she walks backward with her hands in the air. When she is farther away, she turns around and she runs.

"Agatha," Sigrid says to me. "It is good you come!" I forgot she speaks our language the funny way. She looks at the uilebheist. "It not bite me?"

"No, it w-won't hurt—you," I say.

She nods and goes to the deamhan man. She says something to him but I do not hear it. I don't know why she is helping that one. Then she looks at me and says, "Friend." She points to the deamhan man when she says it. Okay, so he is a nice one like she is a nice one. It is so confusing when there are some deamhain who are bad ones and also some that are good ones.

The deamhan man stands up and goes to Konge Grímr's crown. He picks it up and walks toward the uilebheist with one of his hands in the air.

"You're Agatha?" he says to me.

"Yes," I say.

"I am Mal-Rakki. You saved my life. A thousand thank-yous."

Actually, it was the uilebheist that saved his life by eating off Konge Grímr's head but I don't tell him that.

"You're w-welcome," I say, because that's manners.

He holds the crown up toward me. One of the antlers is broken where it fell.

"It looks like the word of Konge Grímr's defeat has started to spread, but the army needs proof. Do you think you could fly this crown over the battlefield so everyone can see it?"

"Y-yes," I say. "We can do that."

I tell the uilebheist the plan. Mal-Rakki puts the crown on the ground and the uilebheist picks it up it in its claws. Then the uilebheist does its wings flapping and we go up into the sky.

This time we do not go high. We fly close over the heads of the people. The uilebheist does its roar sound lots of times and I do loud shouting. "Konge Grímr is—d-dead!" I shout. "Stop the f-fighting! I have the crown."

The uilebheist swings its neck down to the fighting people and snaps its teeth close to where they are. It is not going to eat them. It only wants them to be scared. They *are* scared. When they see the broken crown, they stop fighting and throw their weapons on the ground. They know the uilebheist will get them if they don't. The wildwolves are scared of the uilebheist too and run away into the hills. I want to say goodbye to them and thank you for coming. I hope they know that they helped to make the world a better one.

There is cheering from some of the other people on the ground. I don't know who they are but all of them are women. I look at them more closely. They are not my clan and they do not look like the other Skye clans either. Where are all of my people?

I look to where Clann-na-Bruthaich's enclave is on Skye island. It is too far to see properly, but there is smoke. Maybe there is fighting there as well. I have to find out.

I tell the uilebheist to fly to the smoke please. The uilebheist takes me higher into the air and I hold on very tight. My cloak is swooshing behind me and my hair is messy in my face. The cold is in my ears and on my nose.

When we are flying over the water, the uilebheist lets go of Konge Grímr's crown. It falls all the way down. I watch it until it is only a tiny spot. Then it is gone. I think of it sinking under the waves. The crown is gone and so is Konge Grímr. We did it!

The uilebheist and me. Konge Grímr can't hurt anyone anymore.

My happy thinking goes away when I see Clann-na-Bruthaich's enclave. There is people fighting inside it. They do not know that Konge Grímr is dead so they do not know they have to stop.

Then I see the even worse thing. It is the shape of Konge Grímr but it is bigger and black and it rises up from the top of the wall. It is his shadow thing. There is someone on the wall next to it. The person runs at it and jumps. The shadow screams the loudest noise I have ever heard and then explodes in a burst of flames. The explosion throws the person into the air. They are on fire and they are falling. We are closer now and I can see who it is.

Faster, I say to the uilebheist. *Faster.*

JAIME

THE WORLD IS SPINNING FAST. MY EYES CAN'T KEEP UP. Enclave-wall-sky-ground, enclave-wall-sky-ground. Flames lick around my flailing limbs, but nothing can stop the fall.

My heart bursts and my body splits apart. At least that's what it feels like. At first, I think I've hit the ground, but then there's a breeze on my face and I'm *rising*—so fast that the flames on my clothes are sucked away. There's a dark shadow above me, and something tight digs into my stomach.

A deep, repetitive whoosh draws my attention upward, to the underside of an enormous creature with two gigantic wings. What on earth—? I've never seen anything like it. I try to free myself, but its claws hold me tight.

The beast dips, flying down toward the snowy grass outside the enclave. It lands, the impact sending judders through my body. It releases its grip, and I roll away, toward the enclave wall. I'm expecting its mouth to swoop down on me at any moment, but it just stands there. As I peer up, the last thing I expect to see is Agatha, sitting on its back, beaming.

"Hello, J-Jaime," she says. "This is the uilebheist."

I open my mouth to reply, but nothing comes out.

"I have to g-go and save the—other people now," she says.

The uilebheist beats its wings and rises from the ground. A moment later, it's disappeared over the enclave wall.

I shuffle to the wall and lean against it, grateful for how solid it feels. The sounds of the battle seem faint and far away. I should get up, return to the fight, but my legs are weak, like they might not support my body. I sit there, staring at nothing, thinking about everything that just happened: the *sgàil*, the fall, the monster, Agatha.

"Jaime? Jaime? Can you hear me?"

It sounds like Cray, but it can't be.

I turn my head and blink the world back into focus. It *is* Cray. He's kneeling next to me. My clothes are wet and there's snow all around us. How did I get here?

"Jaime, you're alive!"

I scrunch my eyes as pain comes flooding in.

"I'm so cold," I say, and I start to shiver.

Cray pulls me to him and wraps his arms around me.

"I've got you," he says. "You're in shock, but you're going to be all right." He strokes my forehead. I never want him to stop.

"How—?" I say. "How did you know I was here?"

"I saw you fall. You were on fire—it was hard to miss you. And then that creature flew in and snatched you out of the sky. I didn't know what was happening. . . . But you're alive, you're safe, and you did it—you defeated the *sgàil!*"

Yes, I defeated the *sgàil*. Now I can sleep. I close my eyes.

"The sword broke," I say, "but you were right: I don't need it anymore. I'm strong enough without it."

"You are, Jaime. You are."

From somewhere far away, I hear the roar of Agatha's beast and the sound of muffled cheering.

"Did we win?" I ask.

"Yes," Cray replies. "I think we did."

EPILOGUE

JAIME

"ARE YOU SURE THIS IS WHAT YOU WANT?" MAISTREAS Eilionoir asks me.

"Yes," I reply. "I'm sure." So much has happened in the past few days that it's hard to keep up, but this is one decision I'm certain about.

After the battle, I spent a couple of days in a makeshift sick-both, since the main one was already full. My body was bruised and battered, but it didn't take me long to recover. The whole time I was there, Cray didn't leave my side.

There were no celebrations to mark our victory, in respect for the huge number of fallen allies, but a ceremony was organized in their honor. The bodies were loaded onto several barges—Clann-a-Tuath and the other Skye clans lying side by side with Raasay islanders, Bó Riders, bulls, and Norwegians—and then the barges were pushed out to sea and set on fire. We all watched from the shore as the plumes of smoke turned the sky gray.

The next day, we returned to our enclave—a moment I've been dreaming of for months. The Raasay islanders gave it back to us without any opposition, and in return the Skye clans have agreed they can remain on the island and establish an enclave of their own. The leaders have even offered to help them build it. Change is in the air, and the change is good.

It feels odd to be leaving our enclave so soon after returning to it, but this is what I want. I look at Cray, and he smiles.

"Ready?" he says.

"One moment," I reply.

I take Aileen's hand and lead her away from the rest of my clan. Everyone has come to wish me farewell.

"So . . . how much are you going to miss me?" I ask her.

"Not *at all*," she replies. "I can't wait to see the back of you."

"Liar," I say.

I expect her to land a playful punch on my arm or rub her knuckles over my head, but instead she holds on to my fingertips and gives them a squeeze.

"You'll come back and visit, won't you?" she says.

"All the time," I reply. I reach into my cloak pocket and pull out a piece of wood, roughly carved into the shape of a swift. "Here, I made this for you."

Aileen smiles. "It's beautiful," she says. There are tears in her eyes. She takes the swift and presses it to her heart, then pulls me into a tight hug.

Agatha comes bounding toward us and joins in the embrace.

"Easy, Agatha, you'll knock us over!" says Aileen.

"No, I won't," says Agatha.

"Here, I made something for you too," I say. I take out another carving—this one a majestic hawk—and hand it to Agatha.

"Wow!" says Agatha. "This is a g-good hawk, Jaime. A great one. Just like—me!"

"Just like you," I say.

"I'm going to m-miss you, J-Jaime."

"I'm going to miss you too, Aggie. More than you'll ever know. But at least we'll get to see each other at the conclave."

"That's—true, Jaime. We will."

I came up with the idea for the conclave while I was in the sickboth: a monthly council made up of representatives from all the different clans and tribes, with the aim being to support one another and help maintain the peace we've established. So far, everyone's agreed to it. Sigrid's invited Mal-Rakki, and Agatha's going to send a request to Queen Beatrice. Apparently, the two of them met while Agatha was a prisoner at the palace, and now they're friends. Knowing Agatha, that's probably true—it's just the sort of impossible outcome only she could make happen. Agatha and I are both on the council too—it's our future we're planning, after all.

"Is Crayton your b-boyfriend?" Agatha asks me now with a mischievous grin on her face.

My cheeks burn flaming hot. I didn't know people knew. "Um . . . I suppose you could call him that. . . ."

"Wow. It must be nice to—kiss him all the time."

My mouth drops open. I can't believe she just said that!

"Stop teasing him, you terror," says Aileen.

"I'm not a terror, you are!" says Agatha, and she starts laughing at her own joke. Her laugh is so infectious that Aileen and I can't help but join in.

"Come on," says Aileen. "The others are waiting."

Agatha puts her arm around me, and the three of us walk back to Cray, who's now sitting on Bras. Sigrid's horse, Eydis, is standing next to them. I take out a couple of carrots and feed them to her, like I did when Sigrid first arrived and was recovering in the sickboth. Eydis thanks me by rubbing her head into my shoulder. I give her nose a scratch in the way Sigrid taught me she likes, then pull myself onto her saddle with such enthusiasm I nearly fall off the other side.

"Easy," says Cray. "You're going to have to get better at that now that you're a Bó Rider."

His words make my heart soar.

When Cray first asked if I wanted to come and live with him and the Bó Riders, I thought he was joking. No one has ever willingly left our clan before. He'd already asked Murdina and Mór and the other Riders, and they all thought it was a great idea. Once he'd convinced me he was serious, I realized that was exactly what I wanted—to be with him; to be the person I've always known I am.

He reaches across to me and takes my hand. I let my fingers weave into his, unafraid to let the rest of my clan see.

Maistreas Eilionoir approaches and places her own hands on top of ours. The gesture means more to me than she'll ever know.

"Clann-a-Tuath wishes you nothing but happiness," she says to us both. "And you are welcome back here any time."

"Thank you," I say. I give Cray a small nod to let him know I'm ready.

Bras leads the way and Eydis follows. I wave goodbye to my clan as the animals take us through the Southern Gate toward the mainland, to start my new life with the Bó Riders, and with Cray.

Sigrid

THE LAST TIME I WAS ON A BOAT I WAS BEIN DRAGGED away from evrythin I knew and loved, chained to a scragthief king with no hope of ever escapin. This time, I'm surrounded by the beamin faces of Mal-Rakki's rebels, and Mal-Rakki himself is standin next to me.

"How are you doing this morning?" he asks me.

"As chirpin as a pig in guttermuck," I reply. It's the same answer I gave yesterday and the day before that. He'd never heard the expression before, so it always makes him smile. It's somethin Granpa Halvor used to say.

"Look, dolphins." Mal-Rakki points over the side of the boat.

I'd already spotted them. They've been weavin around us in the wake of the boat. Evry now and again, one leaps outta the water, performin a spin in midair before crashin back under the surface.

"They're hek smirks," I say.

I could watch them all day. When they're done in ink, dolphins mean new beginnins. Praps I'll get one inked when I get back. I thought about havin it done over the top of my raven, to cover it up, but I've decided I like that one the way it is. It may not be perfect, but it's part of who I am.

"*Róhh! Róhh! Róhh!*" The repeated call of the rowers bounces over the rushin of the wind. I've asked plenty of times if they want my help—specially cuz there's not as many people on board as there should be—but they tell me they can manage. Despite the hard grind, they always seem happy. How could they not be? We defeated the army, and Konge Grímr is dead—eaten by that whatever-it-was beast. I dunno how to say its name, but it sure was brimmin.

Evrythin's gunna be diffrunt when we get back. Mal-Rakki ses it's gunna take time, but with Konge Grímr dead and the support of the masses, he can turn the country around. He's asked me to help him and all. He said he wants me to be the voice of the people, and that evryone can learn a lot from me, includin him. I was beamin at that. Course I'll help, in any way I can.

The most chirpin thought is that I'm gunna see Granpa Halvor again. Evry time I think it, I get lightnin splashes in my insides. He's not gunna believe for one speck evrythin I've done, specially when I tell him I've been with Mal-Rakki. Soon as we're back, I'm gunna go live with Granpa; I decided that already. Mal-Rakki ses he can help us move to a bigger place or a better one if we want to, but I told him Granpa Halvor's place is perfect as it is. It might be small, but it's all we need. Mal-Rakki smiled when I said that, like I'd understood somethin important about the world.

I'll have to see Mamma again at some point, which isn't gunna be chirps, but I gotta do it. I know what Mal-Rakki said is right, and when I find a way to forgive her, it'll release some of the pain. She needs my help, not my fire, and that's what I'm gunna give her. Maybe my returnin will give her back some of the hope she's been lackin for so long. That's all that I can wish for her.

Sayin goodbye to the Skye people was hard, even though I haven't known them long. Before I left, I took out the plum stone I've been carryin this whole time, and Maistreas Eilionoir helped me plant it in their enclave, in a spot that gets the best sun. Lots of people came to watch, includin Jaime and Agatha.

"In years to come, when we and our future generations eat the fruit from this tree, we will speak your name and remember the great deeds you did for our people," Maistreas Eilionoir said.

Evryone around me shouted my name and cheered. It was one of the most hek brimmin moments of my life.

Then I had to say goodbye to Eydis. That was the hardest part. I was desperate for her to come back with us, but I didn't wanna risk her gettin sick on the journey. Horses aren't made for boats, and there wasn't really no space for her neither. I wrapped my arms around her one last time and told her she was the bravest and most hek *ríkka* horse in the whole world. She replied by rubbin her wet snottin nostrils into my neck like the great slobberin beast she is. She's got a new rider now, and I know they're gunna take the best care of each other.

A bulk wave sends the longboat up into the air and then into a dip, makin my stogg yap. The dolphins go deeper under the water so we can't see them for a couple of blinks, but they soon come back again.

Mal-Rakki breathes in the salty air. "I've been meaning to say: when my brother asked if you had any last words, your reply made me very proud. That hate is not the answer."

I stare out at the ocean, at all its impossible, wild beauty.

"It's the biggest truth I ever learned," I say.

AGATHA

TODAY IS A NICE DAY. THERE IS SUN A LITTLE BIT AND THE sky is a blue one. It is nearly summer now. Summer is my favorite because of the flowers and they smell nice. I pick a pretty yellow flower and feed it to Milkwort. He is on my shoulder and he eats it and says thank you.

I am outside our enclave, walking with Thistle-River. It is the biggest best to be living in our enclave again. I know where everything is and I am never lost. Also it makes me happy in my heart and on my face.

I come to see Thistle-River every week because we are friends. I tell him about the new things that are happening on Skye island and he tells me about the deers. Sometimes we don't talk much. We just walk together and I like that too.

Thistle-River lifts his head. *What's that sound?* he asks.

It is the chimes on the wall. One of the Hawks has hit the Second one time at the bottom. That means people from another clan are approaching our enclave. I know all the chimes because I am a good Hawk. The Second means it is not a danger person, so I don't need to be worried.

"Agatha! Hello, Agatha!" says a shout voice. A boy is running toward us. I know him and his name is Owen. He is the fastest at running so he does lots of the messages.

"Hello, Owen," I say, and I do a wave.

"I have a message for you," he says. His voice is a loud one. "There is someone here to see you. You have to come to the Southern Gate, and Maistreas Eilionoir said no dawdling."

"Okay," I say. I bow my head to Thistle-River and say that I will see him soon.

Stay strong, Sun-Leaf, he says, because that is what he calls me. He does the bowing too.

Owen runs off fast because he is the fastest. I follow him but more slower.

"Agatha!" Owen turns his head and calls. When he sees that I am not running, he comes back to me. "You have to run fast," he says.

"I don't—like running fast," I say. "It makes me all out of p-puffs and sweaty."

"All right," says Owen. "We can walk. I'll walk with you, Agatha."

Owen likes me a lot. He saw me on the uilebheist during the big fight with the Ingland army and he thought I was a really great one. He is right about that. He came up to me afterward and said, "You are the girl who was riding the big monster with the wings. I saw it and it was really good. You are a monster girl."

He asked if he could be my friend. He is only seven but I said,

"Yes, you can be my friend," because I am kind. Also he is a funny one and I like him. He wants to be a Hawk one day like me.

We go into the enclave and walk to the Southern Gate. When we see the gate, there are already lots of people there. I do not know who are the people but there are long poles in the air with big flags tied to them. On the flags are pictures of a big cat the same as there was on the Ingland army soldiers, but no one is fighting or worried. The Moths have opened the gate and the Ingland people are coming in.

There is a big cart made of wood. Actually, it is not a cart because it is taller and has a roof. It is painted nice colors like red and gold and brown. Brown is not a nice color but the other ones are. A door opens on its side and someone steps out.

I cannot even believe it. It is Lady Beatrice! She is here in my enclave! Prin the pig comes out next to her. He sniffs the ground and pokes it with his nose.

"That lady has very nice clothes," says Owen.

"It's L-Lady Beatrice," I say. "She is the—queen of Ingland." I do not say the other part, that she is also my mother. That is the secret part.

"Oh, wow," says Owen. "A queen is a very important lady. Why is she here, Agatha?"

"She has come to s-see us," I say.

Maistreas Eilionoir told me she was hoping to come. I wanted Lady Beatrice to live with us and stay here forever, but Maistreas Eilionoir says that now she's queen that's not possible. She has the most important job of all which is to change all the bad things King Edmund did.

"For as long as she is queen, we are protected," Maistreas Eilionoir told me. "But in order for her to keep that position, her past must remain a secret. No one in Ingland would accept a queen from the Isle of Skye. Not yet, anyway. Perhaps, in time, she will be able to change their minds. . . ."

Queen Beatrice goes to where the elders are waiting. She squeezes Maighstir Lenox's fist first and then does the same to Maistreas Eilionoir.

"Thank you for your warm reception," Queen Beatrice says to Maistreas Eilionoir. "It is lovely to meet you."

They are pretending they do not know each other but they do. Queen Beatrice is Clann-a-Tuath and she has come home.

She sees me and walks to where I am. She squeezes my fist and I let her.

"Nice to see you again, Agatha," she says. "Maybe you could show me around your enclave?" She does a wink that is just for me.

I do my biggest, prettiest smile and hold on to her hand. "Of course, Your Majesty," I say. "Follow me."

A NOTE ON THE LANGUAGES

THE "OLD LANGUAGE" USED BY SOME OF THE CHARAC-
ters from Scotia and Skye is, for the most part, Scottish Gaelic.
Occasionally, I modified words and made alternative choices for
artistic reasons or in order to aid the reader; I take full responsibil-
ity for any errors or inconsistencies.

The language spoken by the Norvegians is a fictional one,
inspired by Old Norse. Much of Sigrid's idiosyncratic slang also
stems from Old Norse.

ACKNOWLEDGMENTS

THIS SERIES HAS BEEN SUCH A HUGE PART OF MY LIFE for so many years that I can't quite believe it's come to an end. But in some ways this is just the beginning, as my characters now go out into the world and find a new home in your imagination. Thank you for sharing this journey with me, and thanks to each and every one of you who has helped spread the word about the Shadow Skye trilogy. To all the booksellers, teachers, librarians, and bloggers who have encouraged children (and adults) to read this series—you are awesome.

Huge thanks to Gráinne Clear for swooping in to join Susan Van Metre on the editorial team for this book. Along with Megan Middleton, the three of you helped shape *The Burning Swift* into the thrilling finale I always hoped it would be.

This book would be nowhere near as good if it wasn't for the following people: Claire Wilson (agent extraordinaire), Lindsay Warren, Betsy Uhrig, Maggie Deslaurier, Matt Seccombe, Martha Dwyer, Emily Quill, Rebecca Oram, Jamie Tan, and John Moore.

I will forever be grateful to Maria Middleton and the Balbusso twins, Anna and Elena, for gifting my trilogy with the most stunning works of art I have ever seen on a series of books. You are so talented, and I am so very lucky.

Thanks for a multitude of different reasons to Sam Coates, Emily Hickman, Frank Cottrell-Boyce, Heather Macleod, Hilary Van Dusen, Amy Sparkes, Matilda Battersby, and Safae El-Ouahabi. To Katrina Bryan for the candle that transported me to Skye, Bethan Fowler for the impressively on-brand mug, and Jade "Prinny J" Chaston for gifting her name to Prin the pig. (You're welcome.) To Fiona Hardingham, Gary Furlong, and Nina Yndis, a massive thanks for bringing my characters to life so spectacularly in the audiobook versions. (Eeeek . . . we won!)

To all the staff and writers I met at Moniack Mhor, where large sections of this book were written, thanks for the hospitality, the roaring fires, and the happy memories.

Henrietta, Luca, Matilda, and Beau: books are one of the greatest gifts this world has to offer; keep practicing your reading and one day (when you're a bit older) you'll be able to read my books too. I can't wait to discuss them with you.

Thanks as always to my amazing family and friends for your support and enthusiasm throughout the series, with a special shout-out to my mum (because she gets excited whenever she gets a mention).

To my Aunty Linda, Uncle Pete, Grandma Joyce, Grampy, and Grandpa—even though you never got the chance to read these books, I know you would have been very proud. You're always in my thoughts.

And finally, the *biggest* and *most important* and *most special* (etc.) thanks of all goes to my husband, Richard. For the multiple rereads and your invaluable feedback, for the crafternoons we spent making Highland bull fridge magnets, and for the 200+ signed posters I made you fold up and put into envelopes . . . but mostly for the love. x

ABOUT THE AUTHOR

JOSEPH ELLIOTT is a British writer and actor known for his work in children's television. His commitment to serving children with special educational needs was instilled at a young age: his mother is a teacher trained in special needs education, and his parents provided respite foster care for children with additional needs. He has worked at a recreational center for children with learning disabilities and as a teaching assistant at Westminster Special Schools. Agatha was inspired by some of the incredible children he has worked with, especially those with Down syndrome. Joseph Elliott lives in London. You can find out more about him on his website, www.joseph-elliott.net, or say hello to him on Twitter @joseph_elliott.